Terra

R.S. O'Neal

The Quest for the Aura series: Book Two

Books in the Quest for the Aura series:

- The Lightworker Trials

- Terra

- Aqua

- Caelus

- Incendium

Note to readers: The Quest for the Aura series is set in beautiful, sunny Australia, and all spelling and grammar is consistent with Australian English.

Terra print edition ISBN: 978-0-9954473-3-2

To the beloved sisters from the same mister
Tory and Nean

To Brigitte, Pam, Zoe and Jack
Without you we would have stopped

And to Kim, a sister from another mister

"Live as one with the Earth" – Kofi E Vygn

"You're not trying hard enough if you don't fall sometimes" – the
Kikkuli Master

"The world needs the rule breakers sometimes, the ones with courage to
venture out and think for themselves" – Ranger Chrysanthe

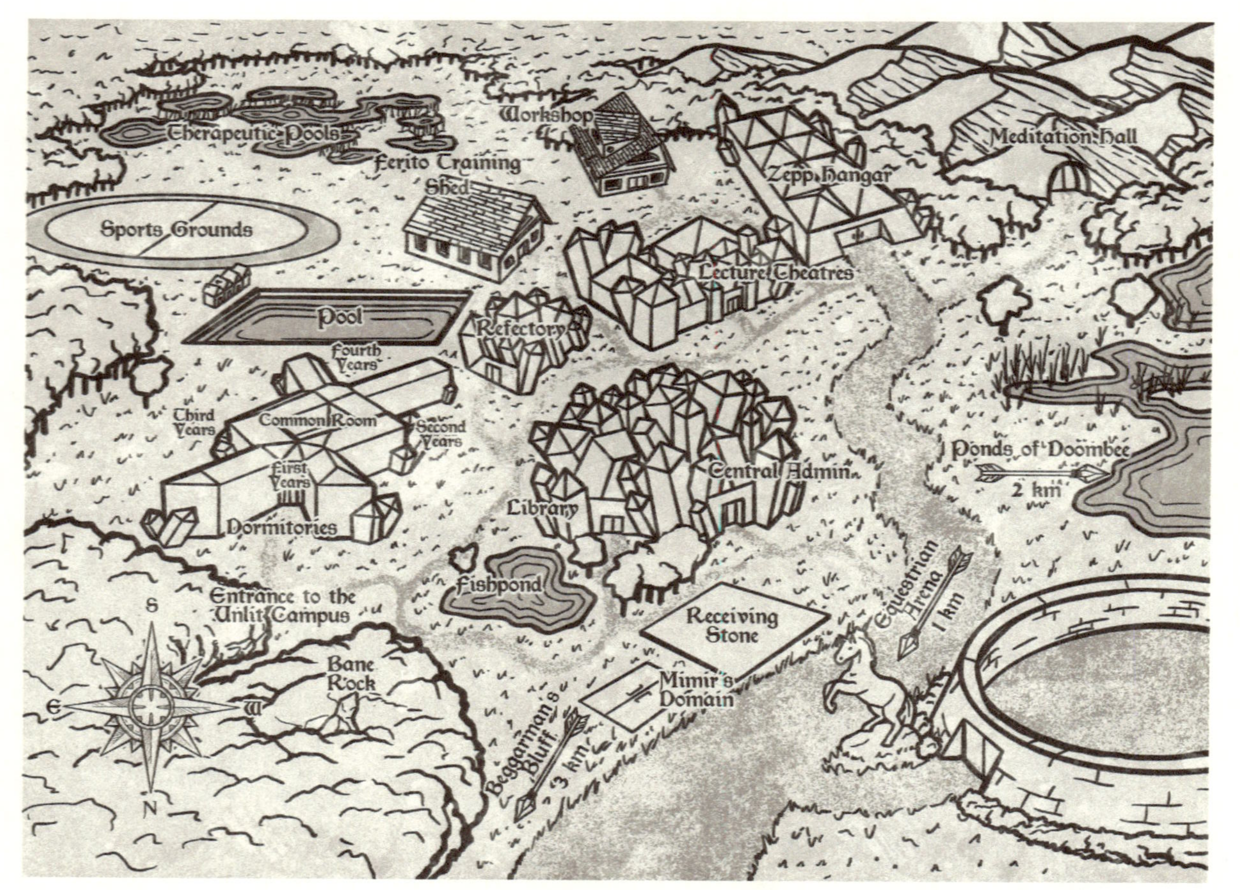

Therapeutic Pools
Workshop
Meditation Hall
Ferito Training Shed
Zepp. Hangar
Sports Grounds
Lecture Theatres
Pool
Refectory
Fourth Years
Third Years
Common Room
Second Years
Central Admin.
Ponds of Doombee
2 km
First Years
Library
Dormitories
Fishpond
Equestrian Arena
1 km
Entrance to the Unlit Campus
Receiving Stone
Bane Rock
Mimir's Domain
Beggarman's Bluff
3 km
S
E
W
N

CHAPTER ONE

EYRE HESITATED ON TOP of the tall cliff, the breeze ruffling her hair. Then, closing her eyes, she stepped off the edge. For a whole minute she hung in the air, wobbling up and down, and then like a huge weight had suddenly been placed in her arms, she plummeted downwards, shrieking.

There was a huge splash as she plunged into the dark water at the bottom of the cliff. It seemed to take a long time for her head to break the surface, but when she did, Beatrice was there, laughing in delight, her long dark braids floating around her.

"Awesome!" Beatrice said, beaming. "That's the best one yet!"

Abby swam over to join them, her blue eyes merry. She trod water in the deep billabong as she regarded Eyre.

"You can stay up there almost as long as me now! Looks like your Viq is getting stronger!"

She was referring to the Lightworker energy force that they all had recently acquired. Eyre's Viq had taken quite a bit longer to appear than her friends', so she wasn't as practised at the Lightworking skills—like levitation—as they were. But Eyre was so relieved to have actually acquired any Light force at all, she didn't mind that she was behind the others in her skills.

She floated in the dark, cool water as she thought back to the tests they had taken, only a few weeks ago but already seeming like a long time had passed. A series of physical and mental challenges had been scheduled for the two hundred students at the Academy of Light's 'Training, Evaluation and Placement'—or TEP—camp, tests that used every bit of the training they had undertaken during ten intense weeks. To Eyre's great joy, she and her friends had all been accepted to start at the Academy as first-year students. Now they were enjoying an idyllic summer in the Blue Mountains, where each of them had a cabin at the campsite called 'Highlight'. The break had been blissful after the time at the Academy, and everyone was tanned and rested. Even Beatrice's pale skin had a golden glow from the sun after their weeks outside exploring the bush and the mountains.

Suddenly, something grabbed Eyre's ankle and she shrieked in shock, instantly terrified. She kicked desperately so whatever it was clutching her ankle let go, and to her annoyance, Nick emerged, cackling with laughter, from under the water.

"That was SO not funny!" she said sharply, whacking him on the shoulder. At the TEP training a bunyip had attacked the students in the lake, nearly killing one of them, and it had been a horrifying experience. Eyre's mind was always going to be imagining creatures lurking in the deep, and her heart was pounding wildly. Nick's smile began to fade and he looked suddenly unsure. Eyre put a cross expression on her face. "You're lucky I didn't use Occido on you! How could you do that?"

Nick looked crestfallen. "Oh, er, sorry..." he began, when Eyre *pushed* with her hand towards him, sending a surge of energy across the top of the water that splashed a wave into his face. Before he could respond, she pulled herself on top of the water, raised her hands and shoved him under the surface with a blast of Viq. She wobbled up and down above the water with a satisfied grin on her face.

"On the other hand," she said as he emerged spluttering, "this is actually quite entertaining!" Nick finally collected his wits and shot out on top of the water, skittering away from Eyre across the surface. Turning around blindingly fast, he fired waves of energy towards her, and she gasped as the water smashed into her.

"Right!" Beatrice said, scrambling up out of the water and hovering above the surface. "I'm in!" Abby also hauled herself out with a gleeful squeal and then it was chaos as a wild water fight began. Even the white cockatoos shot out of the trees surrounding the billabong, startled by the shrieking and walloping boom of Viq energy hitting the water. The billabong rocked as wild waves splashed back and forth across its surface, smashing into them all. Eyre choked as a particularly large wave knocked her feet from under her and she plunged into the water. Struggling out, she blasted a wave of water back at Beatrice, sending her skidding across the surface. Beatrice laughed and sent a roiling ball of water high into the air above Eyre's head.

"Bombs awayyy!" she cried with glee, and the water ball dropped fast, breaking over Eyre's head. She spluttered and Abby screeched with laughter. Then Nick levitated three metres above the surface of the billabong and did a perfect somersault before diving into the dark depths. Eyre scanned the impenetrable water, hands up, ready for him to surface. Suddenly the water started churning and bubbles of all sizes emerged, popping out of the water and floating upwards in a spherical, slow-moving cascade that filled the air, bumping into the girls and drifting off across the clearing. The bubbles turned rainbow colours in the sunlight, and the girls stopped, riveted by the beautiful sight.

"Ohh..." said Abby, captivated. Nick claimed his first victim as she looked upwards. She shrieked as he pulled her down into the billabong. Moments later Beatrice and Eyre followed and they all reappeared on the surface, laughing as they trod water.

"Nick loses due to the use of illegal force!" Eyre cried in a pompous voice, imitating Professor Mandig Vela from the TEP training camp. That time it hadn't been a laughing matter, but today everyone hooted as Eyre continued. "Creating something so beautiful is most unfair!"

Nick yawned, floating in the sunshine. "Well, I'm done," he said. "You ladies are way too tough for me! I'm going to sleep it off." He swam to the edge of the water and lay down to dry off on the broad sandstone rocks that surrounded the billabong.

Abby made a sound of agreement, and swam over and clambered up onto the rocks too, but Beatrice and Eyre stayed in the water, floating on their backs. Eyre sighed blissfully. The cool water was delicious in the hot January sun, and the bright blue sky arced above them. Summer! She thought. The best time of the year.

The thought caused a pang of sadness—normally she would have celebrated Christmas and been at home with her parents, enjoying the school holidays with them. But her parents had been killed by the Gothak, the evil creatures of the Underworld, only a few months ago, and now Eyre's home was her family's log cabin in the Blue Mountains, where her friends' families also had cabins. It had been a terrible time of adjustment for her as she came to terms with this abrupt and shocking change in her life, and the pain was still there, unmoving. It was always going to be hard, but gradually she was getting used to her new reality and she was learning to cope with the waves of grief that could arrive at any time, without warning. She knew it would never go away, but she was dealing with it.

Eyre closed her eyes, feeling her muscles relax. The Buyabarra Billabong was a special place, situated above a ley line and known for its healing qualities. A visit here was a tonic for the body and the mind, and Eyre felt herself drifting off into a reverie. After the exertions of the TEPs—the intense training and the arduous tests—the chance to relax was blissful. Eyre had only known her friends for a few months, but already it felt as if she had known them forever. And like the stalwart friends they were, they had all supported her when she had received her dismal, indistinct Inguz after the TEP exams—possibly the most embarrassing moment in her life.

She looked at the dimly-etched symbol with its dull grey centre on her upper arm, and then at the one on Beatrice's arm, which glistened silver in the sunlight. Beatrice's Inguz was brilliant yellow in the centre, showing that she was part of the Flava Sector, the Sector that people with intellectual gifts belonged to. Abby's Sector was Sappir—a shining cobalt blue, and Nick's Sector was Tyros, a bright purple colour. Sappir was the Sector for people with gifts in the spiritual areas, while Tyros meant Nick had strong physical and spiritual strengths. Eyre's Inguz was flat and uninspiring, faintly outlined in black, and of no Sector colour ever seen before. Even now she winced at the memory of standing in front of the crowd of parents, and the resounding silence that had greeted her Inguz when it was revealed.

Eyre had been put into the 'Hese' Sector, the group of people with general skills—usually for people with no one area stronger than the other, but in her case really because they didn't know where else to put her. Her three friends had been incredibly supportive about it—they didn't care at all that her Inguz was different from theirs, they were just glad she was coming with them. Eyre knew that she was in for a lifetime of quizzical looks with the strange mark on her arm, and she couldn't help the feeling of failure that washed over her every time she looked at it. But she had come to terms with it now, her pragmatic nature deciding that at least she *had* an Inguz, and she had been accepted to the Academy. Not everyone who applied was accepted, so she had decided to be happy with that. Eyre was looking forward to seeing some of the students next year that she had met at the TEPs and she was particularly looking forward to improving her Light skills.

Her musings were interrupted when Beatrice swum over to her, kicking swirls of cool water around her legs.

"We'd better get back, we don't a repeat of that time we left here too late!"

One of their previous visits to the billabong had nearly ended in disaster when they had been stalked by a terrible creature from the Underworld, a Saevus, and it had chased them down the track to the border of their compound. Eyre shuddered as she thought about it. She'd had another encounter with a Saevus at the Academy, and that time she had actually been attacked—she knew what fearsome creatures they were and wasn't keen to ever meet one again. The memory spurred her into action and she splashed over to the side and climbed out onto the sandstone rocks.

"The mere thought of a Saevus is enough for me – I'm off! See you at the compound!" she called, and started clambering up the rocky side of the billabong towards the pathway that led back to the cabins. Then, as the others laughed and struggled to catch up with her, she began running down the track through the bush that led to the compound. The first time she had run down this path, she had been hot, sweaty and very uncomfortable. But her time at the Academy had given her a love for running that she had never experienced before. She was fit now, and it was exhilarating to race down the sandy track that wound through the white-barked eucalypts. The sound of feet behind her let her know that Nick was hard on her heels and he soon passed her—she had improved a lot at the Academy, but she would never be at his level. A natural athlete, he was small but fast.

Beatrice and Abby had obviously decided to join in the race; as Eyre looked back she could see them in hot pursuit and could hear their good-natured grumbling. She laughed out loud, a sudden joy overwhelming her. Life was good.

They arrived, out of breath and puffing, at the compound where their cabins were located.

"I liked you better when you were a sloth like me," Abby complained to Eyre, her fair skin beet red after the run. "I need another swim now!"

"Well I need something to eat!" Beatrice said, as usual. "I'm going to…" Eyre was waiting to hear what culinary delicacy she was going to prepare this time, but Beatrice didn't finish her sentence. Eyre looked at Beatrice and realised she was staring over Eyre's shoulder, her mouth open and her face turning various shades of red. For once Beatrice was speechless, that in itself such an extraordinary occurrence that Eyre swivelled her head to see what Beatrice was looking at.

Everyone stopped as they realised who was walking towards them. Eyre gasped and Nick clenched his fists hard.

"Well, if it isn't the Loser Club," Ben Perrill sneered. Lumbering, huge and jug-eared, he exuded his usual menacing aura.

Abby was the only one who could find her voice. "What are you doing here?" she choked.

"We own the cabin at the end," Ben Perrill said, gleeful, enjoying their discomfort. "We just arrived."

"YOU own the cabin?" Abby said, dumbfounded. "Since when?"

"Since forever," Ben sneered. "My dad had it built when yours did—from the stupid look on your face, I guess you didn't know that." He looked over at Eyre. "Eerie," he said. "Good to see you."

Eyre ground her teeth. "It's pronounced 'Air', and you know it, you jerk."

Ben sneered. "Eerie, Air, Airhead, who cares? Looks like we're going to be neighbours."

Beatrice finally recovered, glowering as she spat back at him, "Well, we'll see about that!"

A noise from Beatrice's cabin made them all look up and Peter and Robyn Edmunsun, Beatrice's parents, came down the front stairs, followed by Beatrice's younger brother Lachie.

Temporarily distracted, Beatrice ran over to them. "You're back!" she cried. Everyone walked over to say hello, as the Edmunsuns had been gone from the compound for a couple of weeks. The Edmunsuns, Whittaker Ray, who was Nick's guardian, and George Wilson, Abby's father were all part of the Echelon, the Lightworking Government of Australia, or E.Au as Eyre now knew it was called, and there had been many meetings over the past few months. The Gothak were crossing the Seam from the Underworld with increasing frequency, killing Lightworkers and sending the hideous Strigis out to cause terrible destruction. The country was in such crisis, the Echelon had been meeting with increasing frequency to try and work out how to deal with the problem.

Eyre felt Ben Perrill's eyes upon her as everyone talked. He gave her the creeps; the dark malevolence that she sensed permanently lurking within him was almost like an uncontrollable beast writhing under his skin. She had seen what happened when he let the monster out, and it was violent and frightening. Nick had permanent scars from his encounters with Ben Perrill; he also knew what Ben was capable of.

"We're staying until tomorrow," Robyn said as she rested her arm on Beatrice's shoulder. "We all thought we should check in with you and have a breather in the mountains."

Eyre could see that Robyn was well aware of the consternation at the appearance of Ben Perrill, but she was ignoring the piercing looks Beatrice was giving her. Just as the conversation faded awkwardly, more people came around the corner; Whittaker Ray, beaming as he looked around at them all, and Mr Wilson, who hugged Abby as she ran over to him. Behind Mr Wilson was a tall man who Eyre had not seen before. He had greying hair and watchful eyes that seemed to move incessantly behind his glasses.

Whittaker Ray nodded to Ben Perrill. "Ben." Then he introduced the man, indicating each person as he spoke. "This is Dr Perrill—Nick, Eyre, Beatrice, and Abby."

Dr Perrill stepped forward to meet them, and Eyre noticed that he had a pronounced limp and walked with an ebony, silver-topped cane. But there was nothing weak about the steel-blue eyes that looked at them all closely.

"Well, it's nice to finally meet some of Ben's friends," he said, as Beatrice choked. "We're going to enjoy spending some time with you."

Abby's face was going so red, Eyre thought she was going to explode. If it wasn't such an abysmal situation she might have burst out laughing, the look on their faces was so comical. Dr Perrill, sensing the vibe, looked around quizzically as the silence grew.

Beatrice finally managed to speak. "We didn't know you owned that cabin. You've never been here before."

Her voice was bordering on discourteous and Robyn Edmunsun stepped in smoothly with a warning glance at her daughter. "Actually, the Perrills were here quite often when you were a baby." Eyre noticed Dr Perrill's eyes flicker before he replied.

"Yes, but then of course we got too busy and never seemed to get back here. But now we're here and hoping to spend some more time."

Ben looked at his father, but didn't move towards him in any show of welcome. "Where's the wife then?" A muscle twitched in Dr Perrill's jaw, but when he spoke his voice was light. "*Sarah* is back in Sydney sorting a few things out, there's a lot to arrange—" he paused and looked around at everyone. "We're selling our house and moving here permanently and it's a big effort to pack everything up. Ben's mother is planning to join us the next time we come."

"*Step*mother," Ben snarled, his eyes furious. As everyone stood uncomfortably he turned and stalked off towards his cabin. Dr Perrill's eyes followed him and he took a deep breath. But when he turned to the group he gave nothing away.

"Well, we're tired after the past few weeks, so I might turn in. We'll look forward to seeing you tomorrow."

Everyone watched them go, a flatness in the air. There was a definite feeling of gloom—the fun of the afternoon had long since dissipated. Eyre felt the pain of losing her family welling up again—in this group she was the outsider, the odd man out, and she hesitated, not knowing what to do as everyone turned to head off to their cabins. As she moved awkwardly on one foot, Beatrice, always perceptive, understood.

"Do you want to come to our place for dinner Eyre?" she said, and Robyn nodded encouragingly. Eyre was grateful for their kindness, but she decided it would be better to be alone while she dealt with the bombshell of Ben Perrill's sudden appearance. Until she'd had a chance to think it through, she didn't want to see anyone, really.

"Let's meet at the Mantle Basin for hot chocolate later?" she suggested, and there was a low murmur as everyone agreed.

Eyre looked at the Perrill's cabin with a strange feeling of disquiet. It was a mixture of fear and uncertainty—why were they here? Now, after all these years? She walked up the stairs, heading for the place that she now called home—at least here she felt safe.

CHAPTER TWO

UNSETTLED, EYRE HEADED FOR the brightly coloured sofa and nestled back into the comfortable cushions, listening to everyone chat to each other as they went to their cabins. She could hear Mr Edmunsun's deep voice underlining the higher voices of Robyn and Beatrice, and Lachie's excited chatter above them all. Eyre suddenly felt very alone.

The last rays of the summer sun flickered through the coloured glass in the windows, sending rainbows dancing across her skin and she traced the patterns with her finger and tried to feel positive. She had only known this place for a couple of months, but already it was home for her, and the custodian of memories of her family. She might have lost her parents, but everywhere there were reminders of her mother and father, and she would be eternally grateful that she had this beautiful cabin to help her adjust to their loss. She looked around at the cosy space—her guitar in the corner, the old piano she'd brought upstairs from the basement, the coloured windows and the glossy carved wood of the cabinets. So special—it was hard to believe it was hers.

Her stomach rumbled as she lay there, but she didn't feel like getting anything to eat. Ben Perrill's arrival had cast a shadow over the compound, and she was filled with disappointment that his presence would perpetually affect the time she spent there. She knew that Nick, Beatrice and Abby would feel the same way, and she hoped desperately that the Perrills wouldn't be there all the time. I might move to Sydney myself, if so, she thought gloomily, feeling like a child who'd had her birthday party cancelled.

Eventually, trying to shake off the blue funk she was in, she decided to go downstairs to the basement and 'visit' her parents. When she had first arrived at the compound, she had discovered her family's Lightkeeper—a crystal box made of precious crystal that held their 'Wisdom'. The Wisdom was a book of knowledge, genealogy and communication that was passed from generation to generation in the Lightworker families, and was normally only received when a Lightworker reached the age of twenty-one. Unless—as in Eyre's case—the parents died, in which case the Lightkeeper was passed to the child upon their death.

Eyre had accessed her Wisdom several times over the past few weeks, but it had only one message in there—the one her parents had originally left for her. It was obvious that the messages were not coming often, but Eyre was happy just to see the same message, to hear her parents' voices and see the lighted hologram of their images. She headed towards the basement, knowing that just opening the book would help her to deal with the uncertainty she was feeling.

She scurried through the blast of cold air from the warding that guarded the door, and headed down the twisting staircase into the dark basement. As she walked, blue pinpoints of light illuminated her way until, at the bottom of the stairs, the whole ceiling was covered in blue glowing lights.

She padded over to her old oak sea chest, which sat in the centre of the basement. It was her most treasured possession, and the guardian for her Lightkeeper, which nestled in a depression at the bottom of the chest. Opening the lid, she carefully pulled out the beautiful little box with the Inguz on the top. Holding it up, she marvelled anew at the craftsmanship of the precious object. It nestled in her hand, surprisingly warm, almost as if it was alive, the lavender-blue colour of the tanzanite crystals glowing in the blue lights. Settling down on the ground, Eyre blew a note with a whistle-like object called a Tone Blow that permanently hung from the chain around her neck. The moment the sound piped through the air, the lid on the Lightkeeper swivelled and released the Wisdom.

There was a soft *swoosh* and the large leather book materialised in front of her on the ground. She stroked the aged leather with the gemstones in it, the cover embellished with designs of vines and strange creatures, feeling again the sense of reverence at this ancient, mystical object that was essentially now her guardian in life. There was a lock on the front of the cover that she unlocked with a key that also hung from her neck chain. Then she lifted the cover with almost a sense of panic, needing desperately to see her parents and wishing they were here to give her some advice.

As she opened the book, bright beams of light speared from it and twined together to form a hologram on the concrete floor in front of her. The image of her mother and father, standing side-by-side and twirling around slowly shone brightly next to the book on the ground. With a surprised sense of joy, Eyre realised that this was a *new* hologram, a *different* image than the one she had been seeing for weeks! She watched in anticipation as the image of her mother lifted her head and spoke.

"Hello, my darling. I wonder how you did at the TEPs? I'm sure you have gone well and we would be proud of you." Eyre lifted her eyebrows, feeling the gloom deepen as she looked at the indistinct Inguz on her arm. Not her finest hour, that was for sure. She wasn't all that certain her parents would be proud of this—it had been quite obvious that no one else thought she should be proud of it. But she ignored the unhappy thought and focused on the hologram as her father began to talk.

"Our next message to you is to help you understand your heritage. It is critical that every Lightworker knows where they come from, as it helps when you set your goals for where you are going. You will learn from the history of your ancestors; it sets a path that illuminates the future of your life. Learn from their experiences and it will help you understand your destiny."

Eyre's mother began to speak again. "Whittaker Ray is the one to ask questions of if you have them; do not talk about any of this with anyone else! Your family may not be here, but their power will hold you safe. May the Aura guide your steps, my love."

"Go Lightly, Eyre," her father said, and the hologram disappeared.

Eyre felt a sense of loss as the light dimmed, as she always did when the hologram disappeared, but was comforted that she knew now whenever she opened the book again, the image would reappear. She turned the page, not expecting to see anything—the pages had been blank every time she'd looked through them previously. But to her surprise, there were two palm prints in the centre of the next page—one obviously her mother's and the other her father's. Grief stabbed her heart yet again as she slowly put her own palm between them, resting her hand on the page, remembering their lives together. Then she jumped as beams of light began to shoot out from the book around her hand and an elaborate hologram appeared in the air in front of her. She took her hand off the page and studied the image that hung before her more closely, and realised it was an intricate genealogical chart that went back hundreds of years. She could see names, photographs and details about people from as far back as the 1500s. The chart was so big it stretched right across the basement, and was almost a metre and a half tall.

Walking around in amazement, she could see that the branches of her family history ran off in many directions, and if she looked at the bottom of the chart, she could see her mother's and father's separate family lines stretching up the hologram, heading off into the various family branches. It was so detailed there were little sections extending right across the room. She ran her finger over one of the images of her ancestors and it enlarged to the size of a portrait, hanging in front of her eyes, with birthdates and details of the person beneath it. Marol Lightward, born 1624, was a big man with a black beard and laughing eyes. Apparently he had been a woodcutter in Ireland, married Elsie Raleigh and had three children: Patrick, Seamus and Bridget. As she peered closely at his picture she jumped in fright when his eyes swivelled towards her.

"Marol Lightward!" he boomed in a heavy Irish accent. "Born in Rath Luirc, in 16 hundred and 24. I like going to the alehouse, killing Gothak and bad jokes..." He kept talking about his life and the place he lived until Eyre realised that he was going to speak for a long, long time. He obviously liked to share! She touched his image again, laughing as his hologram disappeared mid-sentence.

Eyre spent some time looking at the images on the genealogical chart and found it fascinating, all these details of people who had lived so long ago, people who were her relatives. Blacksmiths, soldiers, merchants—she had so many different people in her family tree. As she scrolled through, her eyes suddenly caught on a name from 125 years ago: Dulci Richardson, a small, blonde woman dressed in the clothing of the time and smiling a shy smile. Dulci was a relative on her mother's side, a distant aunt, and Eyre wondered whether she might be a relative of Nick's—Richardson was his surname too. She felt a small glow of happiness: wouldn't it be wonderful if he were a distant cousin? He would be family officially; she already felt like she'd found a new family in him, Beatrice and Abby. As she looked at Dulci's image, she realised there was an unusual symbol next to her name, and when she looked around the chart she realised that some of the other names had the same symbol next to them, including her mother. It looked like two triangles placed one on top of the other, forming a star shape, and she wondered what it meant. One of those questions to ask Whittaker Ray sometime.

She was about to close the book when she looked for herself on the chart. She'd been concentrating so hard on the information above her mother's and father's names, that she hadn't looked at her own name. She studied the chart in confusion, wondering where she was, and as realisation dawned, her eyes grew wide with shock.

As she looked underneath the branches that linked her mother and father—the branches allocated for their offspring, she understood why she'd had trouble locating her name. It wasn't 'Eyre' written beneath the Lightward—Tyson union, her parents' union, it was 'Erin'. *Erin*! Thought

Eyre with a shock of memory. That was the name that Jengles had called her at the Academy last year when Ben Perrill had attacked her. It had confused her at the time, and she'd thought Jengles must have made a mistake, or that she'd misheard him. But now it appeared that Erin might actually be her real name, if the Wisdom was correct. How could that be? Eyre thought in confusion. *Why would I not know my real name? Why would I grow up thinking my name was Eyre—and why would Mum and Dad keep the truth from me?*

And then she had an even bigger shock. She had been so confused, trying to find her name amongst all the information on the chart, that she hadn't noticed there was a second name underneath the Lightward—Tyson union: Eric. Eric? Eyre thought in confusion. *Who's that?* Looking at the chart, the position of the name, next to her on the line with the same birth date, meant that Eric could only be her brother, her *twin* brother. *So where is he?* she thought numbly.

She was so shaken she was gasping, struggling to get her breath and she slammed the Wisdom shut, snuffing out the genealogical hologram. Her mind was churning, unable to think as she tried to make sense of what she had seen.

Ask Whittaker Ray, her mother had said. But ask him what? she thought. *What is the question that will give me answer to all this, and most of all explain why, in all her fifteen years, she had never been told her real name, or that she had a twin brother? Why all the secrets?* She'd reconciled herself to her parents not telling her she was a Lightworker—but now this new mystery?

A strange feeling simmered within her as she left the basement and headed up the stairs, and it took her a while to identify what it was after the roller coaster of emotions she'd had that afternoon.

Rage. It was rage against her parents for keeping yet more secrets from her, for destroying the image of the family she thought she'd had. She felt like she'd never really known them. And clearly they hadn't trusted her to let her in on whatever the hell was going on.

CHAPTER THREE

EYRE MARCHED OUT THE front door and headed towards the fire, where Beatrice, Abby and Nick were sitting gazing into the silvery matrix in the Mantle Basin. As she neared the trio, a stocky red-headed figure rounded the corner and clumped towards her.

"There you are, my beauty," he said, bowing deeply to Eyre, "I'm going to reinforce the Mantle, if you'd like to watch." Beatrice made a huff of annoyance over her shoulder. It was a continual source of irritation to Beatrice that after years of enduring rude remarks and bad temper from the bossy dwarf, he had somehow decided that Eyre was the object of his adoration. Normally Eyre herself was bemused by it—she had no idea why Jengles was so taken with her—although she knew that she definitely preferred it to the insults he dished out to everyone else. But tonight Eyre just stared at him, her eyes narrowed in anger.

"Well, *if* it's actually me you want," she said sharply, "or perhaps it's *Erin* you're after?" At her tone, all three of her friends turned as one to look at her, surprise hanging off their faces.

Jengles took one look at Eyre's furious stance: hands on hips, jutting jaw, and positively *scurried* to the other side of the wood stack. Beatrice was so surprised she fell backwards off the log trying to take it all in.

As Beatrice picked herself up off the ground, Eyre stalked over and sat on the log beside her other two friends, ignoring their curious eyes. Beatrice, Nick and Abby traded glances and waggled eyebrows at each other as Jengles industriously—but quite determinedly staying on the other side of the fire —selected branches to put in the matrix. His head remained down, focused on the task, but occasionally his eyes would flicker across to Eyre and then skitter away again. Beatrice watched in amusement. Whatever was going on, she was enjoying the sight of Jengles looking so chastened.

Silence hung in the air as they watched Jengles weave the branches carefully into the silver matrix that glowed in the large metal dish at the centre of the campsite. Normally Eyre loved to watch Jengles place each branch within the shining depths, and seeing the resultant blaze of light that travelled through the matrix and out the top, to form a shielding mantle of light around the compound. It was a lighthouse of protection, a shining barrier against the beasts of the darkness that could arrive at any moment from the night. But tonight she eyed Jengles up like she was one of those murderous creatures.

Just as the silence started to become really uncomfortable, Whittaker Ray walked in holding a coffee mug. Nick smiled at him in relief.

"How are we going here?" Whittaker Ray asked, taking a sip, and appeared slightly nonplussed at the range of noncommittal grunts that answered him. Looking around, he took in the scene and registered something was going on. Misreading the cause of the silence, he attempted to explain.

"Well, you know, we would have let you know about Ben..." he began, when he was interrupted by a furious, red-haired fiend who jumped up and faced him, causing him to take a step backwards, coffee slopping over the sides of his mug.

Eyre's eyes blazed.

"WHERE IS MY BROTHER?" she shouted, her fists clenched in rage at her side. Whittaker Ray started to reply when a wild dust storm began to swirl at his feet, pulling leaves and debris up in a whirling mass in front of him like a miniature tornado. The dust swirled faster and faster and then suddenly exploded with a loud bang, raining leaves and dirt all over Whittaker Ray. He brushed himself off.

"Eyre..." he began, but Eyre interrupted furiously.

"ERIN!" My name is, apparently, *Erin*!"

Beatrice's mouth was hanging open as she looked from Eyre to Whittaker Ray and back again. Abby and Nick were exchanging glances, no one game to say a word. Beatrice raised her eyebrows at them and indicated Jengles, who could be seen walking rather rapidly away from the Mantle Basin. *What* was going on?

"It is Erin, Eyre, but there's a reason for that. And I think I should talk to you tomorrow and explain a few things. Now is not really the time..."

He broke off as sticks from all over the clearing raised in the air and gathered together, swirling in a turbulent circle above their heads like a logjam in a flooded river. The noise was deafening, a macabre clattering that sounded like bones clacking together. Everyone looked up, speechless, as the wild torrent got thicker and louder as more and more sticks flew up from the ground and joined the whirling morass. Eyre's eyes glowed golden and she seemed lost in a trance as she raised her hands, drawing more branches into the deafening swirl.

A sudden flash of light interrupted the spectacle as Robyn appeared by their sides. She walked up to Eyre and put a hand on her shoulder, speaking quietly.

"Eyre, stop now."

Eyre blinked and looked blankly around. The sticks clattered to the ground, piling up in uneven drifts and everyone ducked as branches rained down around them. Finally there was silence, and all Eyre was aware of was eyes looking at her with shock and confusion.

"I'm sorry," she managed, before she dropped to the ground in a faint. As Robyn and Whittaker Ray rushed to pick her up, Beatrice looked at the pile of wood around the clearing and shrugged.

"Well, at least we won't have to gather wood for the Mantle Basin for a while," she said awkwardly.

CHAPTER FOUR

THE NEXT MORNING EYRE woke as the sun streamed through the stained-glass window in her bedroom. Orbs of colour danced over her bedspread and decorated her carved wooden headboard and she traced the flickering patterns with her fingers. She normally loved waking every morning to this. It was like sleeping in a rainbow.

This morning though, there was no peace to be had in the comfortable bed. Memories of yesterday came crashing in on her—Ben Perrill arriving, here of all places. The worst person of all—he would destroy the lovely sanctuary of Highlight. Finding out she'd had a *brother!* And then, despite her mind trying not to think of it—the memory of the strange torrent of wood flying above their heads. Had she done that? She couldn't remember much about that part of the evening, except for the burning, ferocious rage inside her. What had she done? She felt sick when she remembered the clattering of the sticks above everyone's heads, a threatening, violent cascade that sounded like the march of the dead.

She put her hand over her face and groaned. She would have to go out and face everyone—and apologise. How awkward—and how could she have done that? Her mother had taken her to a counsellor when she was young to learn how to deal with her intense temper, but she hadn't had an attack like that for years. Last year, at a school she had attended briefly, she had let her anger get the better of her at a sports day, which had somehow unleashed a massive surge of energy that had given her unearthly strength. But that event hadn't come close to the violent intensity of the hurricane of sticks yesterday. She still felt weak and shaky this morning—it had taken a lot out of her.

Eventually she got out of bed and dressed, realising that she might as well get out there and start apologising. There was no excuse for her behaviour, whether she was upset or not. These were people she cared about, and she had put them in danger. The realisation caused a dark pull of dread in her stomach. Obviously her Viq energy had gotten way out of control last night, and she felt sick about it.

But when she ventured outside, she found she had a reprieve. Beatrice, Abby and Nick were sitting on the log having breakfast and they looked up and smiled as she joined them. Encouraged, she started to apologise.

"I er, ah... I mean, how can I say it, I uh..."

Beatrice waved her hand at Eyre.

"Sit down, my friend, and don't say another word! Don't worry about it!"

Abby's eyes crinkled. "We've all had meltdowns before—although none quite as spectacular as yours! A wooden cyclone – wow!"

Nick nodded and then chuckled. "And seeing *Jengles* scurry away? That was worth every minute!"

They all dissolved into laughter and Eyre sat on the log, feeling grateful for her kind friends. They passed her a bowl of cereal and she ate in silence for a while, aware of their eyes upon her.

"I guess I'd better go see Whittaker Ray," she said. "Was he really angry?"

"No," Beatrice reassured her. "In fact he just seemed worried about you. But you won't have to face him today—he and Mum and Dad and Abby's dad have gone back to the Echelon until tonight. He said he'd talk to you when he got back."Eyre smiled, grateful to be off the hook, for now at least. And she was relieved that despite their obvious curiosity, no one was asking her about 'Erin', or her brother. They must be wondering what it was all about. But until she spoke with Whittaker Ray, she really didn't want to talk about that at all. She looked around.

"Has Perrill shown his ugly face yet?"

Beatrice shook her head. "Nope. Haven't seen him since yesterday afternoon. I wish he'd seen your stick tornado though. Might make him pull his head in!"

Abby laughed, but Eyre noticed Nick didn't smile. Nick had scars covering his body—he didn't seem to want to go into depth about it really, but she knew that some of them had come from Ben Perrill. Over the years, both Ben and Nick's dad had added to Nick's scar collection, so she wasn't surprised that Nick found little amusement when Ben's name came up. But Nick had taught Ben a lesson last year at the TEPs when his Viq came in, so she doubted Ben would target him again. She shook her head mentally. How could the worst bully she'd ever met suddenly turn up in this wonderful paradise? The stars were laughing at them, obviously.

Sensing the turn of mood, Abby jumped up. "Well, let's not waste the day! What are we going to do today?"

Beatrice looked up at the cloudless sky as she collected their bowls. "The weather's good and we haven't been to the caves yet this summer. Why don't we do that? Nick and Eyre won't have seen them before."

Nick looked thoughtful. "I went to the Jenolan Caves once," he said.

Beatrice nodded. "The famous ones. These ones are closer to us—only Lightworkers know about them. They're called 'The Transit'. It will only take us an hour to walk there. They're definitely worth looking at too. Grab some stuff and let's meet back here when everyone's ready."

Half an hour later Eyre was in the clearing, waiting with Nick and Beatrice for Abby to arrive. Jengles stood across the clearing watching them, but Eyre noticed he didn't come any closer. Just as well! she thought grumpily. She was still irritated that he obviously knew something she didn't, something very personal about her and her family. Would the secrets never end? She determinedly looked away from him, scowling. Beatrice saw her and chuckled.

"You're going to break his heart, you know."

Eyre shot a dark look in Jengles' direction. "So where's Abby?" she said, her eyes mashing Jengles into the ground. Beatrice struggled not to smile.

"She's bringing the lunch, won't be long."

On cue, Abby clattered down the front stairs of her cabin, her blonde hair bouncing. She was hauling a backpack over her shoulder and beaming at them.

"Right, let's go then!" she called. "I've got enough to feed a whole regiment of Mimir!"

Beatrice led the way along a path that headed towards the high sandstone cliffs that formed a semi-circle behind the compound. The rugged face of the cliffs towered above them, sending a cool shadow across the ground and making it hard to discern the structure of the rocks in the distance; they appeared as mottled brushstrokes of varying hues of brown and cream. But as they neared the cliffs, Eyre realised that there were a series of dark crevices along the base of the rough blocks that formed the cliff face. And large boulders were flung around at irregular intervals, great chunks of rock that had been torn by gravity from the façade and hurled down to the ground. The boulders were more than three metres high, Eyre guessed, looking upwards uneasily. She hoped another one didn't join the ranks while she was standing there.

Beatrice led the way through the silent monoliths, weaving around them until she reached one of the darkened apertures in the base of the cliff. Eyre was amazed Beatrice could remember which one it was—there were so many shadowy crevices in the cliff and nothing to distinguish one from the other.

Beatrice stopped and rummaged in her backpack, eventually bringing out four round grey spheres about the size of a small basketball. She tossed one to each of them. Eyre caught hers, realising with surprise that it was malleable, it felt like it was filled with jelly. Abby was obviously familiar with the object, but Eyre saw that Nick was as clueless as Eyre was.

"That's a lux," Beatrice said. "Rub it."

Eyre rubbed her hand over the lux and felt a warmth and a zap like static electricity through her hand. Instantly a soft glow began to emanate from the lux and it started to float upwards, humming gently. Then the glowing sphere stopped, hovering about twenty centimetres above her head. As Eyre took a step the ball of light followed her, like a balloon on a string, taking a bit of time to catch up with her.

"It's bonded to your energy field," Beatrice explained. "It gets pretty dark in here."

She led the way into the dark crevice and Eyre followed, her eyes adjusting to the darkness with the help of the lux. She could see a rocky pathway in front of them, curving out of sight into the blackness. The pathway was only two metres wide, cut through the rock and Eyre was surprised at a queasy sense of claustrophobia stirring within her. Beatrice marched ahead confidently into the gloom, but Eyre had to make herself follow. She really didn't like this much at all, with the solid rock forming a tunnel that wasn't too far above her head. But forcing herself to keep walking, she concentrated on watching the pathway and avoiding rocks as she followed Beatrice deeper through the passage in the mountain. Nick and Abby followed Eyre, and all she could hear was their breathing as they headed farther and farther downwards.

After about an hour of steady walking, Beatrice stopped. Eyre had been concentrating so hard on just plodding behind Beatrice, she almost ran into her.

"We're here!" Beatrice said happily, and walked forwards into a large cavern. Eyre, trailing Beatrice's lux, followed behind her into the large open space, and she had to stop herself from gasping as she looked around.

The walls of the cave were covered in crystals of all sizes and colours, sparkling dimly in the reflected light from their luxes. Big green ones, small blue ones, brown ones, red ones... The crystals were sticking out in huge irregular clusters; multi-coloured formations that were breathtaking.

Eyre turned around slowly in astonishment, all her uncertainty forgotten. No wonder Beatrice and Abby wanted to come back here—it was absolutely magnificent. Nick also stood in awe, looking around him speechlessly until eventually Abby broke the silence.

"Come on, let's eat!" she said, unfolding a blanket on the ground. Beatrice leaned back on a huge ruby-coloured shard of crystal, and began to eat her sandwich.

"It's called the Transit," she said, almost unintelligibly, "because apparently there are tunnels leading from here all through the ranges, and going for hundreds of kilometres. So this is like a transit into the heart of the mountains, and some say it also goes a long way downwards. We're not allowed to go further than this, because people have been known to disappear forever in here, they get lost. You can't just zap out of here unless you know where you are, and your Viq has to be strong in any case. But the Mimir are often here, and they know where they're going."

Eyre sat with her back against a large purple formation and ran her finger over the clusters of crystals that surrounded her.

"So beautiful," she said. They ate in silence, and Eyre felt that was right somehow—it seemed inappropriate to talk in this unique place, as out of place as having a chat during a church sermon. Eventually Abby packed up the leftovers and the blanket and they stood up to leave.

A clatter at the back of the cave in the shadows made them all look over.

"What was that?" Beatrice said sharply. They listened for a moment but no further sound came.

"Maybe it was just a crystal falling," Abby said, pulling on her backpack. "No matter, we're heading back anyway. Let's go." Reluctantly Eyre turned away from the walls—she would have loved to study the crystals more—and followed her friends out of the cave.

They began the walk back up the passageway—much harder work now as the track wound steadily upwards. Eyre found herself breathing heavily and sweating. The trip was definitely worth it, but it was hard work!

She had just come around a sharp bend when something grabbed her from behind and she was slammed against the rock wall as her friends walked on ahead, oblivious.

A hand covered her mouth so she couldn't scream out and her lux bounced off the wall, following her trajectory, casting weird light shapes up and down the rock and across the face of her assailant. Eyre's eyes widened in shock as she saw it was Ben Perrill, and she fought him desperately with a mixture of panic and rage, but she was unable to move against his strength. Her desperate eyes watched as Beatrice, Nick and Abby disappeared out of view.

"Airhead," Ben whispered, the softness of his voice sending a chill through her. Suddenly she was desperately frightened and she struggled to get away from him. Ben pulled her back down the passageway and into a darkened alcove, then reached up and snuffed out her lux. It was instantly pitch black and a horrified dread crawled through Eyre's stomach. She tried to shout out but Ben's massive hand muffled the sound.

Then he took his hand away for a second and she took a great gasp of air.

"You jerk!" she hissed, then started to shout for her friends. But she only managed a quick scream before Ben's hands circled her neck, cutting off her air.

"Bye bye, Airhead," he whispered. Eyre struggled hard, but she was suffering from the lack of oxygen and a strange wonderment filled her mind. Was this how it would finish? Killed by Ben Perrill? As she edged towards the blackness in her mind, she heard a strangulated voice, soft and repetitive echoing the impenetrable dark.

"Help me. Help me. Help me."

What? Who was that? Then, with a shock of understanding, she realised that it was *Ben* muttering the words over and over. She would have laughed if it wasn't so frightening—what help did *he* need? But it was all irrelevant anyway, she felt herself drifting into blackness, and she surrendered to the blossoming vacuum in her head.

Just then she heard Beatrice's voice, far away, calling for her.

"Eyre! Where are you?" The voice echoed around the passageway and reached Eyre's mind just before she slipped into unconsciousness. The sound caused a spark of adrenaline to run through her blood. Her friends! Would they be next? The thought suddenly ignited something in Eyre, and she struggled anew, fear for her friends and rage giving her the strength she didn't have for herself. Her whole body shuddered as a white-hot fury surged through her, and a single word exploded from her mouth.

"No!"

Her body began to burn and a bright light filled the passage, lighting it all the way up and down the tunnel. Then, as she turned her furious eyes towards Ben's contorted face, a wild wind started to swirl through the tunnel. Ben's grip relaxed slightly and he looked behind Eyre, listening to the calls of her friends echoing down the passageway. Eyre stared at his hands and they blew apart, releasing her throat. She breathed in tortured lungfuls of air and put her palm up at Ben, feeling a surge of intense energy blast powerfully outwards. Ben was blown violently back from her, slamming into the rockface. Screaming in rage, he jumped up and lunged for her, but Eyre stood her ground, filled with a burning force she had never felt before, consuming her very being like a furnace. She stepped towards Ben and *threw* energy at him, pinning him against the wall as a wild tornado of wind rushed through the passage, howling in an eerie wail. Ben was struggling, three metres in the air, shouting profanities at her until she let him go, and he fell to the ground, his eyes burning.

Holding her throat she spoke in a whisper that resonated around the walls.

"Get out of here Ben or I will kill you."

Ben staggered to his feet, malice brimming in his eyes.

"This is not over, Airhead," he said, and then looked over his shoulder at the sound of footsteps racing towards them. He stumbled off down the passageway and disappeared into the darkness just as Eyre's friends rounded the corner from above.

All Eyre's strange energy disappeared and she fell to the ground, exhausted, her throat on fire and tears spilling from her eyes. Beatrice slid to the ground beside her.

"Eyre! What happened? Are you okay?"

Eyre wiped her eyes and nodded.

"I'm fine," she whispered. "Let's just get home." Unable to speak more, she relit her lux and waved away their questions as they began to walk back up the passageway, through the bouncing shadows thrown by the light.

Eyre cast quick glances over her shoulder as they walked, feeling that Ben was still skulking in the gloom somewhere, stalking them. Now that the drama was over, she realised she was shaking and feeling quite nauseous. The malevolence within Ben was like a skulking beast and Eyre once again felt intensely confused about his hatred of her. This was combined with the disturbing thought that disliking someone was one thing—trying to kill them was something altogether different. As her head throbbed with these crashing thoughts, Eyre became aware of a strange sound coming softly from the darkness down the passageway behind them. She stopped and turned, already on alert because of her altercation with Ben. Beatrice, Abby and Nick stopped too and they all stared back down the tunnel, ears straining. It was a soft buzzing that eventually became louder—something was moving towards them through the darkness.

"Now what?" Beatrice said softly, and they all clustered together, as if by bunching up they would be safer.

The strange whirring got louder and louder until Eyre's ears were deafened with the noise but still nothing came out of the blackness. Her stomach crawled in fear—the sound was unnerving, and it didn't sound good. Then, when the noise had reached an ear-splitting screech, a black cloud swarmed out of the inky darkness and into the light from their luxes. Instantly they were surrounded by a thick shroud of buzzing creatures that landed on them and crawled all over them. *Flies!* Eyre realised in disgust, trying to brush them off her. But there were so many they were impossible to get rid of—as soon as she flicked them away, more took their place. The cloud of insects was so dense she could hardly see her friends, who were frantically trying to get the flies off themselves as well.

"Run!" choked Beatrice, stumbling forward up the path. Eyre gave up trying to swat the flies away, and staggered along the passageway behind Abby, with Nick close behind her. Hardly able to breathe with the horrible creatures crawling all over her face, in her ears and up her nose, Eyre pushed her way along the path, the terrible buzzing increasing in volume around them until she was unable to hear anything except for the whirring of millions of wings. The luxes had fallen to the ground and rolled down the passageway, taking the light with them and Eyre was trying to find her way in the blackness. Her footsteps got slower as the weight of the winged creatures forced her down to the ground, but then with relief she realised that the smothering blackness was lifting as external light filtered from somewhere up ahead. Crawling on her hands and knees through the swarm she strained to see her friends, but they were hidden by the swirls of flying insects.

"We're nearly there!" Beatrice's voice choked through the wall of flies and Eyre pushed her already exhausted body a bit harder until she burst through the end of the tunnel and out into the sunlight. The flies buzzed away from her and disappeared back into the aperture in a coiling tornado. Eyre's stomach heaved and she vomited violently, throwing up clumps of the black insects onto the ground and causing her already damaged throat to burn with pain. Beatrice and Abby were lying on the ground beside her listening to the deafening drone from the swarm echoing around the cliffs. Unable to move, Eyre watched with anxious eyes until Nick crawled out the opening, covered in clumps of flies, like strange growths protruding from his body. As soon as the light touched it, the swarm swept back into the tunnel and Nick lay face down on the ground, gagging. Eyre rolled onto her back, looking up at the blue sky as she sucked in the sweet fresh air, hearing the unnerving drone of the swarm recede into the depths of the mountain, until once again there was silence.

The four of them lay in the blessed sunlight, just looking at each other.

As always, Beatrice had the last word. "Told you it was fun," she said.

CHAPTER FIVE

THE FOUR OF THEM trudged back wearily to the campsite, not speaking. They were so exhausted from the wild race back up the passageway that they didn't say a word to each other until they were almost at the Mantle Basin. Beatrice turned her filthy face back towards them and gave a short laugh.

"We've got a welcoming committee."

With a shock, Eyre realised that Ben was standing by the Mantle Basin, his habitual sneer plastered across his face. How did he get back so quickly? And it didn't seem that he'd had any problem with the flies—he was lounging quite casually against a pile of wood. Despite her exhaustion, Eyre felt a slight embarrassment as she registered the number of piles of wood that had been neatly stacked by the Mimir around the campsite—no doubt all sourced from the results of her tantrum this morning. The thought fell away as she strode up to Ben, her fists clenched.

"You absolute pig," she spat, her throat throbbing with pain. Ben just laughed.

"Enjoy your walk?" he asked and turned his back on her. A ferocious rage consumed Eyre, burning like acid through her veins. But before she could do anything, a voice came from behind them.

"What's going on?" Whittaker Ray walked out the door of his cabin and down the steps towards them, his eyes concerned. He could read that something serious was brewing and he moved over to the campsite quickly.

"Ben? Eyre?"

Neither of them answered him and Whittaker Ray sighed. "Ben, you should go to your cabin. I've just arrived back and I'm sure your father is on his way too."

Ben sneered and shrugged.

"Suits me. Don't like the company here anyway."

Whittaker Ray watched Ben with troubled eyes as he sauntered off. After a moment he turned back to Beatrice, Abby, Eyre and Nick, taking in their bedraggled forms.

"I need to speak with you, Eyre," he said. "Half an hour?"

Eyre nodded and headed to her cabin, aching for a hot shower. She wanted to cleanse the memory of those horrid crawling flies from her skin, as well as the feeling of Ben Perrill's hands clutched around her neck.

Whittaker Ray passed Eyre a glass of cold water and she took a small sip, feeling the wonderful coolness slide down her tortured throat. She sat back on the worn leather lounge that was in Whittaker Ray's cabin and waited. His intelligent eyes looked at her.

"What happened to your neck?" he asked softly.

Eyre felt tears gather in her eyes at the gentleness in his voice, but she blinked hard.

"Ben Perrill," she whispered, her voice raw. A vein pulsed in Whittaker Ray's temple and he looked out the window. But when he turned back to her his voice was even.

"I need to explain some things," he said and gave a slight smile as Eyre raised an ironic eyebrow. "You've got reason to be annoyed at all the secrets," he continued, "but we had to keep you safe."

Eyre said nothing and waited, her eyes focused on the photograph of Nick's mother that Nick had put on the on the mantlepiece. She wondered if his mother would have told him about Lightworkers. Whittaker Ray was right—she *was* angry, and she was sick of all the mysteries.

"You did have a twin brother, Eric," Whittaker Ray said, and Eyre felt a terrible surge of disappointment at his use of the past tense. *Did have*, not *have*. So obviously she no longer had a twin brother. The thought made her sad and she looked at her hands as Whittaker Ray continued.

"The two of you were the most beautiful babies—fiery red hair, both of you. Your parents adored you—Erin and Eric, or "Er 1" and "Er 2", as they called you. Your mother was always so careful of your fair skin in the Aussie sun, and always had hats on your red heads. When Eric—went—your mother dropped the Er 1 and just called you 'Er' and that eventually became 'Eyre'—it was really just an adaptation of Erin." His eyes grew sorrowful. "I think she couldn't bear to use your real name again once Eric died."

Eyre processed the information, which was such a shock. To have a brother she'd never known about! With sudden understanding she remembered the cupboard doors in the kitchen of her cabin—an 'E' in the centre of each door. She had thought both the 'E's stood for Eyre, but now she realised the letters were for 'Erin' and 'Eric'.

"So what happened to Eric?" she said at last, feeling a strange sense of grief for a brother she had never met, or at least couldn't remember meeting. A cloud crossed Whittaker Ray's face.

"The Gothak attacked the compound, when you were eighteen months old, and Eric was killed," he said. "In the early days, when the cabins had just been built, your family, the Edmunsuns, the Wilsons, the Richardsons and the Perrills would often come here to holiday together. They were all great friends. It was a terrible tragedy when we lost your brother—and the others—and the compound was never the same again."

Trying to get her head around the fact that her parents were friends with the Perrills, the other names Whittaker Ray mentioned finally dawned on Eyre. She looked in surprise at him.

"The Richardsons? You don't mean Nick's family?" Whittaker Ray nodded his head slowly and hesitated.

"Yes, this is actually Nick's cabin. It's not mine."

Eyre gave him a startled look and he continued. "I haven't told Nick yet —we decided to keep it quiet until after the TEPs. I'll tell him tonight, if you could just keep it to yourself until I do."

It was surprising news, but Eyre knew Nick was going to be as happy as she had been at finding out he had a home of his own. Why they would keep that from him was beyond her, but it was a question for another time, as she had so many more important questions for Whittaker Ray at that moment. The most burning one came out of her mouth first.

"Why didn't my parents tell me I was a Lightworker?"

Whittaker Ray gave a regretful smile. "Some Lightworkers are more powerful than others, and those are the ones that the Gothak are targeting and trying to eliminate. Your mother was one, Eyre, and they have been hunting her for decades, trying to kill her and her relations. Your mother felt guilty about Eric—she felt *she* had drawn the Gothak here and caused the three deaths."

Eyre turned surprised eyes towards him. "*Three?*" Whittaker Ray again looked out the window and spoke quietly.

"As well as Eric, Nick's mother also died that day, as did Ben's older brother, who was four at the time. It was a terribly tragedy. The three women were having a picnic with you and the boys when the Gothak attacked, killing the two boys and Nick's mother instantly. They didn't have a chance." His voice drifted off, almost in a reverie, then he turned back to Eyre. "Your mother was very powerful Eyre, as I said, and she managed to fight them off and save you, Ben and Nick. But she never forgave herself for those deaths. After that day, we never saw you back here, and your father and mother would only come very occasionally. Losing Eric broke their hearts, and I think that's why they never told you about the Lightworking community. They wanted to protect you while you were young—you know how often you moved."

Eyre nodded. She had spent her life packing up and moving from one house to another, never settling down or finding any constants. It did make more sense now—her parents were afraid the Gothak would hunt them down. And eventually they did. The familiar pain ran through her as she thought about her mother and father. She swallowed hard, and her throat throbbed.

Whittaker Ray saw Eyre rubbing her neck and he gave her a regretful look.

"The family was never the same and Ben's parents split up a few years later. Ben's father had a terrible time after his wife left, and Ben over the years has become a very angry boy. Dr Perrill remarried about eight years ago and his wife is a lovely woman who cares for Ben, but he has issues. The Academy is trying to help him, but it is very hard when he is so violent and angry. And over the years he has been getting worse." Whittaker Ray stood and looked out the window, his back to Eyre. He sighed heavily.

"Ben's behaviour is unforgivable, and there will be consequences for what he did to you, Eyre. I will talk to Ben's father and we will figure out what punishment he will receive."

Sensing that the talk was over, Eyre stood and walked slowly to the door.

"Thank you Mr Ray," she said. "I have wondered about so many things in the past weeks. It does help to finally know the truth."

Whittaker Ray looked at her for a long moment as if he was about to add something. But "Go Lightly, Eyre," was all he said.

CHAPTER SIX

EYRE LAY AWAKE A long time that night, mulling over the many secrets and revelations she had heard that day. A twin brother! Killed by the Gothak, like her parents. If she didn't already hate the malevolent beings, she would now—burning with a fierce desire for revenge. And then there was Ben's strange mutterings in the cave—had she really heard that? And what did it mean? Or was it just a hallucination from the lack of oxygen? She drifted off to sleep with even more questions than she had started with.

The last two weeks before they headed back to the Academy passed quickly. Ben was not there the morning after the cave incident, and he didn't come back. Eyre wasn't sure what punishment had been meted out to him, but she dearly hoped it involved a cage, a chain and a whip. She did know they wouldn't go easy on him: Jengles had been speechless with fury when he had been told about the incident, and the look on his face guaranteed that Ben would be receiving a lifelong lesson on acceptable behaviour.

In any case, once it was obvious he was not coming back Eyre was able to relax and enjoy the final days of the summer holidays with her friends. They visited the Buyabarra Billabong again, and the surrounding bush but didn't venture near the caves. Whittaker Ray had seemed very worried when they told him what had happened, and he was quite insistent that they keep away from the tunnels. Not that they needed to be told—the memory of those swarms of flies was enough to keep Eyre away for years.

Eyre also spent a lot of time in her cabin—looking at her Lightkeeper and studying the amazing genealogical map, listening to the voices of her parents. And she sat for quite some time in her attic, mesmerised by the beauty of the changing images in the stained-glass window that was set into the wall. Diamond shaped, it stretched from the floor to the ceiling and it was one of Eyre's favourite places.

Nick had been amazed to hear that the cabin he was in was actually his —and Eyre felt happy for him when she saw his quiet delight. She understood how he felt—after years of a gypsy life, both of them suddenly had roots.

And Eyre had told her friends about Eric. They had been lovely, in their usual supportive way. And surprised too—to realise that they had all been friends a long time ago was strangely comforting. Like they were family almost. Eyre wondered if the death of Ben's brother had contributed to his vicious temperament—perhaps on some level he remembered the encounter. And it was possible he blamed Eyre's mother for the loss of his brother, which might explain his hatred of Eyre.

In any case, the weeks passed without further drama and the day came quickly that they were to leave for the Academy. Eyre was packing her bag in her bedroom when Abby wandered in to her cabin. Abby ran her hand over the carvings on the bedhead as she watched Eyre throw in the last few things.

"You don't have much," she said, "you should see my bag!"

"I don't have a designer wardrobe like you!" Eyre laughed. "Of course one must always be smartly dressed for Ferito training!"

Abby snorted at the thought of wearing some of her gorgeous clothes in a martial arts class. Her eyes twinkled and she tousled her blonde hair, which today was sporting blue tips, matching her Sappir Inguz. Eyre was sure that was not just coincidence.

"Well, there are a few cute guys at that school, you might have noticed!" Abby said with a sly smile. Eyre winced, realising she was being teased, but refused to bite.

"Huh, that's all I need!" she replied, her tone indicating the exact opposite.

Abby sat down on the bed. "I wonder if Ben will be there."

Eyre frowned. "I don't know why they are so tolerant of him," she said. "I mean, I *get* that he lost his brother, but a lot of Lightworkers have lost family members and they don't act that way. And Ben probably can't even remember his brother."

Abby looked thoughtful. "You know, Ben wasn't too bad when he was young. Then his mother left and he seemed to change—that's when he really got mean. No excuse though, even if it was difficult for him."

Eyre shrugged, suddenly dismissing the conversation. Already too much time spent talking about that jerk, a waste of brain space. Whatever his problem was, she didn't care—as long as he kept away from her. She zipped up her brightly coloured backpack and slung it over her shoulder. And she picked up her mother's guitar—hers now. That was going to the Academy with her, even though she'd never be able to play it well.

"Are the others ready?" she asked. Abby nodded.

"They're waiting out by the Mantle Basin. Jengles too."

Eyre gave a wry smile. She had forgiven Jengles his secrecy, and he was ridiculously relieved that she was talking to him again.

"Come on then, let's go teleport!"

Abby laughed and they walked out of Eyre's cabin to join the others, who were standing by the Mantle Basin, bags on the ground beside them. Jengles was bustling around with pieces of wood and he bowed as Eyre and Abby walked over.

"I'm going to miss you Jengles," Eyre said, hugging him, and his face turned bright pink, clashing terribly with his orange beard. Flustered, he saluted, forgetting he had a stick of wood in his hand. The stick poked him in the eye and he dropped it, hopping around in pain with his hand over his face.

"Dimmog! Blasted thing!" He looked at the stick on the ground and pointed at it. "You're first in the fire tonight!" he threatened as Beatrice, Abby, Nick and Eyre all spluttered with laughter.

Just then Whittaker Ray arrived with a small suitcase in his hand. It had been agreed that he would take them to the Academy, as he was heading back there too for his position as Dean of Curriculum. The Edmunsuns strolled over with Abby's dad and they all hugged each other goodbye.

"Take care, Eyre, your parents would be proud," Beatrice's mum said as she threw her arms around Eyre. "We'll see you at the end of the semester."

Then Whittaker Ray joined hands with Beatrice, Abby, Eyre and Nick and in a blinding flash of light they disappeared from the campsite.

Eyre opened her eyes, her stomach roiling. Teleporting always made her feel sick and giddy—she wondered if she'd ever get used to it. She took a deep breath and looked around. Her friends were standing beside her, and in the distance she could see the Zepp careering over the plains towards them.

Squinting, she could make out the number on the side of the Zepp: Zepp 1! Eyre recognised the number of the Zepp that Ranger Chrysanthe normally piloted and sure enough, when the Zepp slid to a halt in a cloud of dust, the door opened and the Ranger jumped out. His green hair stuck out in all directions and he clapped his hands with delight when he saw them, the many gold bracelets on his wrists jangling loudly and the irregular green stone on the thong around his neck swung so wildly it hit him in the eye.

"How lovely to see you again—with my one eye!" he exclaimed as he blinked hard. "Dratted thing! Crystals are meant to help with one's wellbeing, not make it worse! Never mind, come on, jump in!" Beetles whirred busily around his head, and, none the worse for wear, his purple eyes were twinkling as he tucked the offending pendant back in his shirt. Eyre took in his bright yellow coat and blue striped pants and felt a surge of delight. How wonderful it was to be back!

They flung their bags into the storage compartment under the bus and climbed aboard. The seats were organised in a circle around the inside of the bus, a metal platform situated in the middle. They all sat down and put their safety harnesses on and the Zepp started to turn around on the track, heading back the way it had come. Eyre put her feet up on the platform in the middle and then jumped with fright as it started to vibrate and rotate. She dropped her feet to the ground and watched in surprise as a bright light began to swirl out from the platform.

"I'm starting the tour guide now," Ranger Chrysanthe called over his shoulder from the driver's seat. "You'll know quite a bit of it, but it's helpful anyway."

The bright light coalesced until the hologram of a woman, about half a metre tall, appeared out of the whirling rays above the metal podium. The hum of the turning platform accompanied the woman's voice as she began to speak.

"Welcome to the Academy of Light!" she said. "We are proud of our school and we are pleased to welcome you to our campus.

"Currently we are travelling across the Plains of Yindi," the hologram continued. "To the left of the Zepp, you will see Beggarman's Bluff, a large cliff which leads down to the Lodge Compound where Orientation and the Training, Evaluation and Placement trials occur."

Eyre was very familiar with the Lodge Compound—she had spent eleven weeks there last year while she competed for a place at the Academy. She craned her neck as they passed the Bluff, the memories of those weeks still very fresh in her mind. As they trundled across the plains the hologram continued talking, describing a large area of swamplands to the distant right called the Ponds of Doombee—beautiful stretching lakes of emerald water, lit by the early morning sun, and surrounded by eucalyptus trees.

They passed the Receiving Stone—the large green square of moldavite where students left and returned for their TACI tests each year. Eyre studied it with interest as they passed. She'd been there once before to welcome students back and was looking forward to the day when it was her turn.

Finally they neared the school itself—towering crystal shards forming the various buildings in the campus. The crystals sparkled blindingly in the sun and sent out flashing rainbow rays that caused prisms of light to dance across the ground. It was quite a sight.

"We are now approaching the Academy of Light grounds. Of course the most notable structure is our Central Administration building, directly in front of you." Eyre recognised the huge building, with its massive bronze doors. The Zepp slowed and Whittaker Ray unbuckled his harness. The hologram twirled silently as he stood up.

"Well, this is my stop. I will see you a bit later—let me know if you have any questions." He disappeared out the doors and Ranger Chrysanthe revved the engine to resume the trip. The hologram started to speak again as they passed behind the Central Administration building.

"The school is very proud of its gardens and infrastructure, and we strive to maintain the highest of standards in our academic, sporting and creative arenas. To your left are the residence halls for our students. For the betterment of Light and energy, the residence halls have been arranged in the shape of an Inguz, with the Common Room central to the dormitories. Students are housed in their year levels."

Eyre craned her neck, greatly interested to see where she would largely live the next few years of her life. Great shards of shining crystal were laid out on the ground, in four rough areas. Trying to work it out, she supposed the Inguz shape would be apparent from above, because it was certainly not visible from the Zepp.

The hologram now indicated to the left. "Finally, our school buildings and sporting grounds lie at the far end of campus. This is where we impart the teachings of Light to our students for a mandatory three years, and an elective Graduate Year. All buildings have been constructed of the finest quartz crystals to ensure the maximum energy exposure, and enable our students to absorb their learnings at the highest level. Wavelength maintenance is carried out daily, and a team of Master Faceters ensure that our crystals maintain their edge at all times."

The Zepp came to a stop and the hologram smiled.

"We welcome you to the Academy of Light and trust that your years here will be productive and successful. If you have any questions, your Dorm Supervisor is there to help you at all times." The light zapped out and the platform stopped turning. Ranger Chrysanthe spoke into the silence.

"Okee Dokee—everyone out and grab your bag! This is where your journey ends—or should I say starts?"

He hustled them out of the Zepp and they headed towards a curved entrance through the glistening shards of crystal that formed the residence halls. Eyre knew from the hologram's talk that the doorway led to the common room, and next to that was the Refectory. A growing straggle of students were walking along the paths that led to the doors and Eyre, Beatrice, Abby and Nick joined the tail end of the group.

Beatrice as usual was talking in sixth gear.

"How different is this to the TEP compound? I reckon we'll need sunglasses to live here!"

Eyre looked around. Indeed, the light reflecting off the faceted surfaces of the buildings was brilliant, and yet it didn't hurt her eyes. The rays seemed to travel through her, almost humming, and it made her feel safe, secure. She hugged herself mentally. How wonderful to be here!

By the time Eyre and her friends had made their way to the common room the Ranger had talked about, there was a group of about two hundred students milling around, chatting, catching up after the long Christmas break. Beatrice, Abby and Nick headed off in different directions to find people they knew and Eyre cased the room, looking for those she'd met last year.

She spotted several people she had known from her time at the TEPs. She was happy to see that Todd, Colton, Vaughn and Robeson were there, talking animatedly to each other. She was glad they had made it in. Some of them she wasn't so happy to see: Pheria, for instance, who looked at her coolly, raised an eyebrow and gave her a small smile. Whatever that meant. The trio of Barbie dolls: Saskia Anderson, Ambrosia Vollick and Iris Goff, who were already flicking their hair and checking out all the males in the room. Georgia Mahoney had also made it to the Academy. She was one of Saskia's friends, but Eyre had seen a nicer side to her last year, and she gave Georgia a small wave.

Eyre looked around and winced when she saw the rabble raisers, who were hanging around the edges: the Curtis twins, Tec Langford and Wyatt Rankins. How they had made it in, she had no idea. But she had no doubt they would cause some trouble this year—it was in their DNA. Eyre turned as she checked out the room, recognising about two thirds of the students there. And then, her heart thumped. Leaning casually against a tall pillar of crystal behind her was someone else she knew. Jax turned his green eyes towards her.

"Eyre." His voice was low, and Eyre felt herself blushing. Furiously she tried to stop it, which just made it worse.

"Good to see you Jax." She was struggling for words when she was saved by a distraction nearby. Someone was wheeling his way through the crowd and people were slapping him on the back and greeting him as he passed. As he got nearer Eyre recognised him: Jensen Ross, the boy who had lost his leg to a Bunyip at the TEP training last year. He sat in a shining wheelchair and he looked toned and brown—obviously he had been working out over the summer. He smiled as he rolled up to Eyre and Jax. Despite being a small boy, he had a glowing presence that seemed to radiate around him. Eyre didn't know what to say, but Jensen spoke first.

"I believe I owe you both some thanks," he said. "I'm glad to be here."

The conversation was easy after that—the three of them talked about their summer holiday and Jensen spoke of his rehabilitation program. He seemed reconciled to his situation; in fact, he seemed unfazed by it, Eyre realised to her surprise. Somehow he had accepted his new reality and once he'd talked about the program, he didn't refer to it again. They chatted for a while until a familiar voice boomed through the hall.

"Right! Here we are then!" Sergeant Tottingham, as solid as a Tibetan ox, stood on the podium at the front of the room and surveyed the mayhem. Some unwise students kept talking; obviously they weren't here last year, Eyre thought. The Sergeant's voice went up about twenty decibels.

"QUIET!" The silence was so resounding you could have heard Abby's earring drop from across the room. Eyre grinned. Now *this* was familiar.

The Sergeant surveyed the room ferociously and then touched a cloudy pink crystal on the table before her and a hologram shot out of it, turning silently in the air before the students. The shining light beams showed a group of buildings in the shape of an Inguz—the layout of the residence halls, Eyre guessed, remembering what the hologram in the Zepp had said. Her thoughts were confirmed when Sergeant Tottingham spoke.

"This is a diagram of our residence halls. Those of you returning will of course already know this, but for the sake of our new enrolments, I will run through the layout. First-years—" many eyes turned towards her "—will live in the northern arms of the Inguz." She indicated the top section of the buildings, and then she ran through the rest of the dormitory layout. Second-years were in the left-hand side, or western arm of the diamond shape, third-years the eastern, or right-hand side, and fourth-years had the bottom, or southern section of the Inguz-shaped buildings. Sergeant Tottingham touched the crystal again and a menu appeared, with a number of selections shining and swinging slightly in the air.

"If any of you new students—or indeed, some of our forgetful continuing students—" there was muffled laughter at this, "need help with finding anything on campus, you can access the information through this crystal, which is here in the Common Room permanently for the use of students. The information is also duplicated on your Felsics. You will find a map of the campus, timetables, school calendars and other helpful details. Please refer to the crystal directory or your Felsics before you come and ask our staff members. We are busy people and while we are very happy to help you, we do not like our time being wasted. Many of you already know that I am not the most patient of people, so I recommend that you try hard to find the information before you come to see me. The Academy of Light not only teaches you academic and Light skills, it also teaches you to think for yourself and be independent. This starts with an attitude of self-sufficiency! Come and see me for any information you require that is not contained within the directory; otherwise you will find yourself acquiring an array of cleaning skills if you waste my time. Bathrooms are a particular favourite of mine."

Eyre watched as a student she did not recognise muttered something in the ear of the boy beside her, causing them both to titter. The girl was obviously a first-year student who hadn't been at the Academy's TEPs last year—Eyre doubted anyone who knew Sergeant Tottingham would have risked such borderline behaviour. Sure enough, the Sergeant's fierce eyes slid sideways, looking for the disturbance, and then she turned her head towards them like a velociraptor locating its prey. The room was suddenly very silent.

The Sergeant's hand twitched and in through the doors a bucket came spinning, mop handle sticking out of it. It rocketed across the common room floor and then stopped so suddenly in front of the offending students that a wave of soapy water slopped out of the bucket, soaking them in a huge splash of frothy bubbles. A wave of laughter swept through the crowd as Sergeant Tottingham looked at the two dripping students.

"Looks like I have my first volunteers. First-year bathrooms will be sparkling this evening, or you both will be continuing every night until you get it right." She touched the pink crystal and the hologram disappeared.

"Right—first-years follow me and Professor Vela; second-years go with Cyton Smith and Matilda Fraser, your hall supervisors—Cyton and Matilda, can you put your hands up please? Thank you. Third-years, you will know Darius Appleby and Lucinda Potts, so please go with them to your dorm, and fourth-years of course will head off with the Ranger.

"Bring your bags with you and pick up your uniforms and boots on your way through the door."

Eyre and her friends followed along as the students split into four groups, following their supervisors in different directions. The first-years headed to the northern part of the building where two wings were set out in a V shape—one wing for girls and one for boys. As the boys split off to follow Mandig Vela to their wing, Nick gave the girls a pathetic look.

"Wish me luck!" he said, raising his eyebrows as Professor Vela strode officiously ahead. "Could be an interesting year."

Eyre winced in sympathy and followed Sergeant Tottingham's large bulk towards the girls' wing. The Sergeant stopped at the curved entrance to the dorm and indicated down the hall, where a number of doors were cut into the sparkling crystal walls.

"Find your room and get settled in," she said. "For first-years, lights are out at 9pm. Dinner is available for those who want it at 6pm in the Refectory—which is next to the Common Room, and breakfast is from 7am. Lunch is at noon. Look up the crystal directory, or ask an older student, and make your way to Lecture Theatre 1A tomorrow morning at 9am. Sleep well." She strode off as if she'd been called to draft a battle plan for the Prime Minister. Eyre supposed the Sergeant would always stride—walking or strolling were probably impossible for her. But she also knew the Sergeant could be kind, despite her gruff exterior, and Eyre was quite happy to have her as the first-year supervisor. She walked into the hallway with Beatrice and Abby and saw that each door had a small blackboard in the centre, with students' names written on them in shining light.

"Wow!" Beatrice said as they wandered along. "We're not numbers any more. We have names!"

"We're obviously *much* more important now," Abby said. "And By the Light, it's am and pm again. 0800, 1400, argh! I was always two hours early or late with that system." Then she stopped and exclaimed in delight. "Hey, look! We're in a room together! I wasn't expecting that. Isn't that great!"

Sure enough—Beatrice Edmunsun, Eyre Lightward and Abby Wilson were listed neatly on the door.

"Maybe Mr Ray spoke with them," Beatrice mused as she opened the door and tossed her bag onto a bed. "I'm so glad we can be together."

The room was roughly triangular, with one bed and a cupboard along each wall and a triangle of desks in the central area. Light glowed softly from the crystal walls and Beatrice walked towards one.

"Isn't it beautiful!" she said and then jumped as she put her palm on the wall. The light in the room turned a bright red. Touching the wall again made the light change to a blinding orange.

"Give me a turn!" Abby said and put her hand on the wall. The light turned a hot pink. "Well, how does that work?" she mused. Eyre put her hand on the wall too and a sea green colour filled the room. They all looked at each other and laughed.

"Obviously our first class tomorrow!" Beatrice grinned. She kept touching the wall as the colours turned through all shades of the rainbow, until finally she gave up, the walls glowing with a deep purple light.

"Best I can do," she said, studying the crystal panels as if they were a calculus problem to be solved.

Eyre started unpacking her gear and had just placed the knee rug made by Carly's mother on her bed when a sudden knock made them look over at the door. Beatrice walked over and pulled it open.

"Can I help you?"

"I'm looking for Eyre Lightward." The frail voice made Eyre leap towards the door. Sure enough, a familiar bent frame was standing in the corridor.

"Mrs Abnett? What are you doing here?" Tears slid involuntarily down her face as she enveloped the old woman in a hug. "Come in!"

The little woman walked into the room as Beatrice and Abby exchanged question marks.

"I work here, Eyre—I'm the school's librarian—and I wanted to welcome you." Eyre was temporarily speechless, then shook her head with in irritation.

"Yet another unknown fact revealed," she said. "You're a Lightworker. All those years..." Mrs Abnett's look was apologetic.

"I didn't want to bump into you without having said hi. I'm so sorry about your parents, Eyre."

As Eyre finally registered the curious looks on Beatrice and Abby's faces, she introduced the old woman.

"Mrs Abnett was my—I guess—babysitter for many years. Whenever Mum and Dad had to go away, Mrs Abnett came to look after me." She looked at Mrs Abnett meditatively. "I guess it would make sense you're a Lightworker."

"Well, if you have any questions—come and see me," Mrs Abnett said.

"That's my problem," Eyre said sharply. "I only get answers if I ask the questions, but I don't know the right questions to ask. I'm constantly broadsided by things I have no idea about."

Mrs Abnett gave a rueful smile at Eyre's tart reply. She obviously knew Eyre well.

"Your parents were trying to protect you, Eyre. Have faith. They knew what they were doing."

After a very long moment the cloud began to lift from Eyre's face, and courtesy won as she hugged the tiny woman again. "Well, I'm glad you're here—that's awesome! But you're not allowed to tell any stories about me!" Beatrice and Abby chuckled and the old woman turned to go. But she stopped just before she left, a twinkle in her eye.

"You control the light with a finger—one colour of the rainbow spectrum per finger, not the thumbs. The little finger on your right hand will change the intensity and turn the light off and on. Two thumbs together for white light. Don't use your palms, it will confuse the crystals." Beatrice looked intrigued and headed over to the wall again to experiment. Eyre sat on her bed, shaking her head.

"By the Light," she said as the colour in the room changed wildly around her, "my old nanny is a Lightworker? Here we go again. More mysteries."

Just then her pillow lifted off the bed and whacked her in the face. Abby stood with her hand raised and a smirk on her face. "Well before all the mysteries start—first things first! Pillow fight!"

Beatrice took her fingertips away from the wall and gave a delighted huff. She turned her palms towards the bed and her pillow rose unsteadily into the air.

"Hmmm," she mused. "Who to choose?" She flicked her wrist and the pillow hurtled sideways, smacking Abby in the ear. It was on! Pillows and bedding flew in all directions, gleeful shrieks rising above the whumping as pillows found their mark. Eyre, completely wrapped in a sheet, shook with laughter as she gave a muffled shout through the bedding.

"Right! That's it! You are about to end up in Lake Altum!" She waved her hands around wildly but a sudden roar from the hallway made her stop in shock.

"WHAT is going on here?" There was instant silence in the room.

Pillows dropped to the ground and sheets ended up in a heap as Light energy disappeared.

Eyre unwrapped her face and jumped to her feet. Her friends, looking as guilty as she did, stood awkwardly facing the door. Sergeant Tottingham strode into the room, taking in the raspberry-coloured walls and the bedding strewn all over the floor.

"Self-discipline is the central attribute of a Lightworker," the Sergeant said tightly, "and I don't see any evidence of it here. Get your rooms organised immediately! This sort of ruckus is not tolerated at the Academy. Dinner is in ten minutes and you had better have sorted this mess out by then or there will be consequences!" She turned on her heel and left, leaving three chastened girls looking at each other. Eyre gave a feeble laugh.

"We know all about the Sergeant's consequences, let's move!"

They made it to dinner with thirty seconds to spare and scurried to a table, aware of the Sergeant's stern gaze on them. The Refectory was a hubbub of activity—all Academy students ate in the large room and there were groups gathering at the tables. Eyre took in the surroundings, marvelling at the difference between this Refectory and the one from the TEP compound last year. The TEP compound in general was spare and functional, and the Refectory had been the same—formica tables in a large rough-hewn building. This Refectory was dazzling—all the walls made of crystal panels like the dormitories, and chunks of shining prisms spanning the ceiling. The tables were a smooth metal—surely not gold? Eyre thought as she sat down. Her friends looked at the tables in surprise too, and Beatrice ran her finger along its surface.

"Wow," she breathed. "That's cool!"

Someone slapped in the chair next to Eyre and put his head in his hands, groaning.

"By the Light," Nick said, oblivious to the gleaming gold surface that reflected his despairing face. "Vela! I knew it was going to be terrible. He's already given one guy detention before the term has even started. A whole year of him as supervisor? Argh. Kill me now."

Eyre was about to tell him about their encounter with Sergeant Tottingham when the behemoth herself walked up to a podium at the front of the room. Facing the students, her brows turned down.

"Silence!" Like pushing a button, all sound stopped. Eyes turned towards her, and the last stragglers hurried to sit down.

"I would like to introduce our Headmaster, Dean Cecil Fraser."

Eyre watched curiously as a solidly-built man ascended the podium, moving lithely for someone of his size. He was balding and wore glasses, but his gaze was astute as he looked out at the students.

"Good evening," the Dean began. "For some of you, it is welcome back to our wonderful school. I trust you have all returned refreshed and rejoicing." A soft laugh ran through the older students in the crowd—this was obviously an in-joke. "For those of you who are new here, it is simply —'welcome'! Welcome to our school, to our learning, our philosophy and to the beginning of your life as a Lightworker." He walked down to one of the tables and rapped his knuckles on it. "Gold," he said, and waved his hands around the room. "Crystals; priceless. They perform a function for Lightworkers: they align the Viq force within us and strengthen our power.

But they are also here to remind you every day of the focus of our life's journey, and of what is truly important. The treasures that other people in the world clamour for, lust after and even kill for, are just minerals dug out of the earth, they are just *things*. What you are here to learn is that the most important essence in life is the Lightness of being: love for each other, for our earth and its creatures, and for beings of other worlds. That is what is important—helping each other through life's journey. We have been gifted with special skills and you are here to learn how to use those skills to achieve Lightness in every area of your life. You are each entrusted with a very powerful force—you must learn to use it wisely."

The Dean walked back up the podium. "I trust that your stay here will be meaningful and enjoyable. We look forward to getting to know you during the coming years. Live with Courage and Light."

Applause filled the Refectory as he descended to a table where the Sergeant, Professor Vela and some staff members Eyre didn't know already sat.

Sergeant Tottingham then stood up and waved for silence. "Just a housekeeping matter," she said, and motioned towards Professor Vela. "Those of you who have been here in past years will be familiar with the tour of the caves that Professor Vela conducts every year in first term. This is a mandatory undertaking to be completed by the end of third year. Any students who are interested in participating this year, please see Professor Vela for details." Eyre noted that from the looks passing between the students, Professor Vela's tour might be somewhat undersubscribed. She herself wouldn't be going, that was for sure. She couldn't imagine anything worse than being in the depths of the earth with Professor Vela for company.

Troll-like creatures, the Jotnar that Eyre had first encountered at the TEP camp, entered carrying plates of food. Eyre watched the black-haired, stumpy creatures as they unsmilingly deposited the plates on the table. Obviously the Christmas break hadn't cheered the Jotnar up at all. The students who had been at the school before started lining up for their meals, and the first-year students followed their lead.

"So who's in your room, Nick?" Abby asked as she ate. "Do you have a triangle room like us?"

"Nope," Nick answered. "Our room is a pentagon. I've got Warrigal, Todd, Rigmar and Zanda which is great. They are all good guys. The powers-that-be seem to have put us with people we know. You should have seen Zanda mucking with those walls! What a laugh. We've got no idea how to work them."

Beatrice laughed. "They're not very helpful, hey. No instruction manual —we had the same problem. Luckily, Eyre's nanny saved us." Nick's eyebrows went up at the mention of the nanny, but Eyre rolled her eyes.

"Tell you another time Nick. But use your fingertips on the wall for each colour, not your palms—you'll figure it out. Two thumbs for white light."

Later, Eyre settled into bed and lay musing as Abby turned off the light. They'd waved Nick off down his hall, laughing as he pretended to be terribly fearful. Although they'd only experienced the joy of Mandig Vela for a few weeks last year, it had been enough to make a permanent—and unfavourable—impression. They might be laughing, Eyre thought, but Professor Vela really was no joke. She was sure he'd been paid off by Ben Perrill to pass information on the TEP exam. And she also wondered if he was the one who had pushed her under the lake, and stuck her feet to the ground when the Armatura were coming. Not to mention being knocked off the Iridis. As she mulled this over darkly, she heard distant rapping on doors and the sound of voices. When the voices came nearer she realised it was second-year students—come to help the first-years work the lighting system. Probably a good idea—it would be hard to go to sleep with coloured light shining through the room.

She thought she might lie awake for a while, so much had gone on that day to think about. But her body had other ideas, and soon she was sound asleep.

CHAPTER SEVEN

AT 9 O'CLOCK THE next morning, Eyre and her friends had made their way to Lecture Theatre 1A, another huge room created from crystal shards. It had a similar seating arrangement to the lecture theatre from the TEPs: semi-circular rows of seats facing a podium with a blackboard behind it. As Eyre looked around the room, she spotted familiar faces. Some welcome, others less so. Colton sat with his friend Luke Jordan slightly down from her. She was glad to see Luke there—she'd done the TEP exams with him and knew he was a decent guy. As if Colton sensed her eyes on him, he turned and smiled, giving her a slight wave. Eyre could see several of the first-year girls already sussing him out: he was certainly a sight, as handsome as a movie star with his blond hair and tanned skin. She continued looking around the room, seeing many new people in the crowd, but also Vicky, another person she had undertaken the TEP exams with, and some of the other students she had gotten to know during the eleven weeks—Advika Bhaduri and Georgia Mahoney. Some people she wasn't as excited to see— Saskia Anderson and Iris Goff had their heads together down the front. And the Curtis brothers Saxon and Slade, fraternal twins so they were alike but not mirror images, lurked up the back with Wyatt Rankins, Tec Langford and of course—Ben Perrill, who hulked like a hyena scenting the wind for something dead. Their eyes met and he gave Eyre a short salute, but unlike Colton's, there was a world of menace in the small gesture. *Our business is not yet finished* it said and Eyre tilted her chin up defiantly. *Bring it on* her own gesture said silently, her eyes burning. He looked away first and yawned, dismissing her, but the rigidity of his body told her something else. She bothered him, in a huge way. Yet again she puzzled darkly over that, but there was no answer for it. Her thoughts were interrupted by a cheery voice that called from over her shoulder.

"Eyre!" She looked around and saw Carly, her roommate from the TEPs, beaming at her from a few rows back. "How was your holiday?" Carly called.

Eyre smiled. "Awesome! Catch you later? Lunch?" Carly gave her a thumbs up and then they both looked forward as Sergeant Tottingham walked into the room, an echo of the first lecture they'd had at the beginning of the TEPs. She waited until all sound ceased in the auditorium.

"You may think your first day of tuition begins today," the Sergeant began. "But your lessons began the moment you arrived on campus. Here is a picture of your residence halls last night."

Sergeant Tottingham touched the crystal on top of the podium and an image streamed onto the wall. A murmur of amusement arose from the auditorium as the students looked at the rainbow of blinding colours that flooded the doors up and down the residence halls. The Sergeant waited a moment and continued with a hint of disapproval in her voice.

"Quite a sight indeed. A small thing, the lighting system. But even this is representative of our teachings and the true essence of being a Lightworker. What was needed to work the lights was subtlety, one finger; not hands, palms and hard whacking of the walls." Several snickers ran around the room and Beatrice herself looked slightly awkward. "Such is the use of Light energy. A little is enough—and learning to finesse your power is the goal of your journey at this school. A small lesson, perhaps, but remember that every time you use your lights in your room."

The Sergeant touched the crystal again and the image disappeared, replaced by a coloured map of the layout of the Academy campus.

"Now please take out your Felsics and follow me as I go through your timetable for the year and help you identify the areas of the campus this applies to." The students pulled out their obsidian tablets and styluses— ready to write in light on the black surface.

Over the next hour, the Sergeant explained the structure of the week— which had elements of the TEP schedule. Meditation, which Eyre now understood was a cornerstone of centring Viq and the essence of Lightworker powers, started at 8am every morning. Ferito, the Lightworking martial art, followed, and then the rest of the day was lectures. Some subjects were core subjects—such as History of Light; others were specialised, depending on which Sector the student had joined.

Finally Sergeant Tottingham turned the hologram off. "That's our schedule for the year," she said. "And we will certainly keep you busy. But this week we are doing things a little differently. Tomorrow morning you will be visiting the Armament Stores which are organised and guarded by the Mimir. In the afternoon you will be sent out to obtain your staff.

Wednesday you will be sourcing your crystal and Thursday you will spend the day assembling your staff. Friday is the day of Lighthorse selection." A murmur went up through the students—obviously others were as curious as Eyre about what this all meant. But the Sergeant wasn't elaborating.

"Every morning this week you are to meet at the moldavite stone near the Central Admin building at 9am. Leave your bags behind, you won't be needing them. Today you have the rest of the day free to familiarise yourself with the campus and get yourself organised. Thank you, you may leave."

She left the auditorium and the students left in groups, talking loudly to each other. Beatrice suggested that they explore the campus and figure out where everything was, which everyone thought was a great idea. They wandered around putting places to the image on the map and finally figured out where the sports grounds were, the Ferito training shed, the meditation hall, the therapeutic pools and swimming pool and the specialist lecture theatres for each Sector. Like the auditorium, most of the structures were larger, grander versions of what Eyre had experienced at the TEP camp.

Eventually they headed in and sat with Carly for lunch, while she entertained them with stories of her life on a farm in Borabinga with her two older brothers. Carly made the whole table laugh as she told them about the cat proudly bringing a live brown snake into her mum's kitchen and the uproar as they tried to get it out. Carly's obvious love for her family as she told her stories made Eyre wistful, but she loved hearing about the pies Carly's mother baked and that Carly's brothers were always trying to steal, of Carly's silent father who only raised his voice when "the ruddy cattle are out again," and Carly's days on horseback herding cattle across the plains. She might be a Lightworker, but her life was so much more 'normal' than Eyre's had ever been. And now Eyre had no family life at all. Her wistful thoughts were interrupted by someone standing by the table and she looked up to see Jax. Her heart leaped and she tried to look nonchalant, but as always a red flush betrayed her.

"Hey Eyre," Jax said. "Some of us are heading to the therapeutic pools this afternoon. Do you want to come?"

Eyre was about to reply when someone else walked up to the table and put her hand lightly on Jax's shoulder. Pheria, sending quite a clear message. *Mine.* Feeling slightly irritated, Eyre shrugged.

"Thanks Jax, but we had plans this afternoon. Another time." Jax looked disappointed and Eyre ignored Beatrice's raised eyebrows.

As Jax and Pheria walked away, Beatrice looked wry. "And those plans would be...?"

Eyre grimaced. "By the Light, I don't know. But it annoys me so much—what is it with Jax? He's got a girlfriend, but somehow I feel—am I wrong—that he's interested? It's really confusing. I don't want to be part of that—Pheria's not-so-subtle messages or Jax's game playing. Agh! Enough of that. Let's go practise some Ferito—I didn't do much over the holidays."

"He's keen, alright," Abby said. Abby would know, Eyre mused—with her pretty face and blonde hair she was not short of admirers. But neither of her friends could help her with the enigma of Jax and she let the subject drop, deciding emphatically that she'd leave Jax well alone.

They headed over to the Ferito Shed and ran through the moves of all the Clasis they had learned at the TEPs. Eyre found she was rusty after the weeks of holiday and she found it frustrating that the positions of Aditus—attack—and Tego—defence—were difficult again. But after an hour of running through the moves of Basic Clasis, Clasis for Single-Blade Weapon, and Clasis for Two-Handed Fighting—or 'Basic', 'Single' and 'Two' as the students called them—she found her balance and style returning. She had practised so much over the eleven weeks of the TEPs that her muscles eventually recovered their memory and she began to move more smoothly. Eyre found her irritation at the encounter with Jax was quite motivating too —she burnt off some of her annoyance by channelling it into the physical practise. By the time they decided to stop, they were all sweating and Beatrice suggested they head to the school's swimming pool to cool off and recover.

They traipsed over to the pool, a large rectangular-shaped structure about 100 metres long, dug into the ground and lined with sparkling crystal. With shouts of joy they leapt into the clear turquoise water and splashed each other. The coolness felt delicious and Eyre stroked along lazily. The interior of the earth could be seen through the crystal sides of the pool and as she studied the wall edge above the waterline, she could see beetles and worms crawling through the soil.

Eyre lazed in the water, her muscles rejoicing after the Ferito session. They were alone for a while, but eventually a large group of students marched down the path and jumped in, turning the pool into a froth of boiling water as they shrieked in glee. Eyre noticed Jax amongst the students and sighed. There was no escape. Zanda stroked over and laughed.

"By the Light, this is so much better! We were at the therapeutic pools, but it was way too hot. This is blissful."

Someone in the group of students put up a net and a wild game of water volleyball ensued, with great hilarity. Eyre watched as Jax slammed the ball over the net, scoring a goal. His tanned, lithe body glistened with droplets and she was annoyed at herself for the attraction she felt. Could she not control herself? Self-discipline, that's what Sergeant Tottingham said made a good Lightworker—Eyre obviously needed to work on that one. She looked away determinedly. Zanda noticed and laughed.

"He was always a star at school too. But not up himself. A good guy."

Beatrice harrumphed. "Not to his girlfriend, though," she said acerbically.

Zanda looked puzzled. "Girlfriend? What news am I missing? Do tell!"

Abby jumped in. "Pheria, he's always with her. She's definitely got him in her clutches."

Zanda laughed. "Yes, she'd like to—she's always been keen on him. But to my knowledge, they're just friends. Their families go way back—they live in the same suburb. We all went to school together, but unless things have changed, they're not 'together' together. Trust Zanda! He knows all the goss."

Eyre looked at him curiously. "But I saw a photograph Pheria had—and I can tell you, that was no friendship. Quite a romantic embrace, actually. It was in her wallet."

Zanda looked completely confused. Then his expression cleared. "Wait—was Pheria wearing a long skirt? White shirt?" When Eyre nodded, he snorted. "Ha! That explains it. The school musical—Westside Story. Jax and Pheria were the leads. That was the promotional shot we used in the program. She carries *that* around with her? Blimey, poor girl. She's got it worse than I thought!"

"Aha!" Beatrice said. "So he's not a toad after all! That puts a new spin on things." Eyre felt two things simultaneously—a bewildered relief that Jax hadn't been playing her, and an irritation at Pheria who most definitely *had*. She was going to have to think about this for a while. They may not be together, she thought, her eyes upon him, but they are definitely close. I'm not sure I need complications.

Beatrice stirred. "Let's head back," she said. "I want to have a shower before dinner." They all walked back down the path together but Eyre barely noticed the beauty of the campus; her thoughts were fixed solely on a boy with mesmerising green eyes.

CHAPTER EIGHT

THE NEXT DAY THEY were walking along the same paths in a large group of students, heading for the Central Administration building. The day had dawned clear and warm and the prospect of finally seeing what lay beneath the intriguing bronze doors in the ground they'd first seen during the TEPs was the topic of most conversations. Fragments of sentences reached Eyre's ears—everyone was chatting excitedly about it. Heading the stream of students she noticed were a number from Rufa Sector—those particularly gifted with defence and physical skills. They were obviously very keen to see what lay in the Armament Stores.

Sergeant Tottingham, staff in hand, and Professor Vela stood at the side of the moldavite square, waiting until all the students arrived. The Sergeant seemed pleased that there were no stragglers—everyone was very motivated to be on time this morning. She thumped her staff loudly for attention and all eyes turned towards her.

"In a moment the brass doors to the Mimir's Domain will open and a representative of the Mimir, Lieutenant Spinel, will arrive to escort us down to the Armament Stores. You must exercise courtesy at all times. The Mimir are a reserved people and do not like overt displays of emotion or being addressed directly. Please follow and observe and keep your silence."

As she finished speaking, there was a loud clanking and the brass doors opened, lying flat against the ground. A red head appeared and a Mimir trudged up the stairs, his craggy face unsmiling as he regarded the crowd. With a sharp gesture he indicated that they should follow him down the steps. But his roving eyes suddenly noticed Eyre, standing at the back of the group. He muttered an inaudible oath and then fell flat to the ground, prostrate. A murmur of surprise ran through the students. Some had seen this happen before at the TEPs, but it was still strange. Eyre herself turned bright red with embarrassment. The Light's sake!

Lieutenant Spinel jumped back to his feet and bowed low to Eyre, sweeping his arm across his body. Then he turned back to the brass doors and walked down into the earth. The students followed silently, some of them casting bewildered looks at Eyre. She gritted her teeth—she wished the Mimir would stop this, it was really excruciating. And she didn't understand it at all. She ignored the curious glances and concentrated on the journey.

And what a journey it was! Brass stairs curved down into the darkness, the only illumination glowing blue crystals similar to the ones in the basement of Eyre's cabin. The walls of earth were hammered smooth, almost glasslike from years of the Mimir's maintenance and they wound deeper and deeper down. The footsteps of the students echoed in the passageway but that was the only sound—no-one spoke until finally the staircase opened out into a large chamber. Around the walls, weapons of all shapes and sizes were lined, secured into metal stands with carved bronze locks. Shorter ones lined the walls and there were more weapons in specially formed holders on the floor. Eyre could see a row of Antaraks, their sparkling crystal blades and titanium/molybdenum edges gleaming in the blue light. There was a line of Kulbedas—the golden dagger that Lightworkers wore in their belts. Flails, looking like miniature sea mines, lined the ground in specially crafted cases, their chains set neatly in a row. As Eyre drew closer, she realised that the weapons were unfinished—some were rough-hewn, obviously needing more work. Others had handles to be added or blades to be sharpened, or the raw metal to be polished. The Lieutenant gestured for them to follow and they headed into another chamber off the first room. It was a huge cavern, with stockpiles of raw elements heaped around in towering piles. Eyre didn't know what all the minerals were, but they were clearly part of the manufacturing process. One of the piles gleamed—and amazed, Eyre realised it was gold dust.

As they walked past the gold stockpile, Saxon evidently couldn't help himself. He pushed his hand into the glittering mound, bringing out a twinkling heap of golden dust, which he gleefully showed to Wyatt Rankins before stuffing it into his pocket. Eyre was horrified—not only at the disrespect of the gesture, but that it was *stealing*. She looked around, unsure of what to do, when Saxon disappeared. *Zap*. Just like that. Sergeant Tottingham strode on ahead, oblivious, and no-one else, other than Wyatt, who looked positively terrified, had even noticed. So Eyre marched on too, looking back at the depression in the pile of gold that was now the only evidence Saxon had ever been there.

The group entered a third room, which was searing hot from a massive furnace burning fiercely at one side. Many Mimir strode around, and with their red hair and ferocious sweating faces, looking almost like they came from the Underworld itself. Large iron clamps held pieces of metal which the Mimir thrust into the furnace, causing the weapons to burn red-gold in the flames. Then they hauled them out and with large hammers, struck the molten metal against an anvil, forcing it into the shape they wanted. Eyre was sweating in the boiling hot room within minutes, sweltering in the clouds of heat and steam, but fascinated with the process. Although it seemed the metal was being shaped with brute force, there was a mastery in the technique the Mimir used, a precision that was evident with each blow.

The Sergeant raised her voice above the roar of the furnace and the striking of the metal. "This is where the armaments for Lightworkers are created. It takes the Mimir months of work to create just one weapon, and they are experts in weapons manufacture. If you pass your first two years here, you will receive an Arms Endowment in third year. Both Lit and Unlit students are bestowed with an Arms Endowment, but the weapons they receive are different. The weapons you receive will have been crafted here by the most expert metalsmiths in the Overworld; a weapon created by the Mimir is priceless. Your Arms Endowment is a gift you receive only once in your life as a Lightworker, and now that you have been here, you will understand what a gift it is. We hope it will motivate you to do your best during your time with us. Follow me back to the central room please."

Glad to get out of the fearsome heat, the students moved back to the chamber where the stockpiles of elements reached to the ceiling. Eyre's eyes turned to the pile of gold dust. The small hole where Saxon's hand had plunged into the pile had disappeared. Now there was *no* trace he'd ever been here. She looked over at Wyatt, who was sweating profusely, and she was sure it was not just because of the heat from the furnace.

Professor Vela cast his eye distastefully across the students. As always, he seemed unhappy being around them.

"The minerals are mined from the earth, and sourced from the Alterworlds. Some of you will have been there when the crystals from Incendium were brought back last year. The Mimir take those elements and craft them using heat and pressure into the arms that Lightworkers use. The final step in the process of creating a weapon of unmatchable strength and power is to use heat of a degree not able to be produced in these rooms."

The Sergeant continued the narrative. "In a chamber, far down below, resides Aowx, the dragon." A gasp rose from the students. None of them had ever heard about a dragon. "Aowx provides the extreme heat that is necessary for the Mimir to finish the weapons. Once a year the weapons are taken down to the chamber of Aowx where he tempers the blades."

The Sergeant looked around the room. "One of our number today saw fit to try and help himself to some of the minerals in this room, a gross display of dishonesty and discourtesy unbefitting a Lightworker. That student is currently visiting Aowx as a learning experience."

So that's where Saxon went, Eyre mused—the Sergeant hadn't missed his actions at all. The Sergeant hesitated as a line of Mimir entered the chamber, sweating and covered with dust, but full of purpose.

"Thank you, my friends," the Sergeant began, but trailed off as the line moved across in front of Eyre. Eyre could almost see the sigh of frustration cross the Sergeant's face as the Mimir kneeled and crossed their chests with their arms, bowing deeply. Then they stood again and without saying a word, headed back into the depths of the furnace chamber. Professor Vela's eyes were venomous as he stared at Eyre, but he stayed silent and the Sergeant also decided to ignore the display, continuing as if nothing had happened.

"Aowx is a private creature and does not like visitors, so we usually do not take students to his chamber. He is most unhappy at intrusions."

At that moment, there was a flash and Saxon reappeared in the middle of the room, terrified and sobbing. He was dripping with sweat and red-faced, and in his hand, he held an object. As he opened his palm, Eyre could see it was a perfectly round ball made of gold—crafted no doubt from the dust Saxon had stuffed in his pocket. The ball was obviously hot, as it had burnt a round circle into his palm. With tears and snot running down his face, Saxon raced over to Lieutenant Spinel and fell to his knees, holding the golden ball out.

"I offer this apology ball to you and humbly ask your forgiveness," he bawled. He was in a terrible state, but Eyre didn't feel much sympathy for him. Obviously it hadn't been fun meeting Aowx, but he'd brought it upon himself. The Mimir took the golden ball from Saxon's outstretched hand and spoke for the first time.

"Your actions are not worthy. Remind yourself of this whenever you look at your hand. One day that hand may hold one of the weapons of the Mimir. I am particularly disappointed you are of the Rufa: the actions of one reflect upon all." He strode off, heading out of the room. The tour was over. Sergeant Tottingham gave Saxon a scathing look and she and Professor Vela followed the scowling Mimir up the stairs. The students, slightly subdued, scrambled to follow them, none of them keen at being left behind with the Mimir.

As they emerged into the sunlight, Eyre squinted, blinded after the long walk upwards in the dim light.

Sergeant Tottingham dismissed everyone. "You have a Sector meeting next. And then after lunch you will be back here at 1pm promptly to source your staff. If you are late you will be left behind." Students scattered in all directions. Many of them headed for the Refectory—the trip had taken a few hours and it was lunchtime. Beatrice, always very concerned about finding her next meal, led Eyre and her friends into the crystal hall and they grabbed a gleaming table. Eyre stroked the surface again. She knew she was supposed to treat it as just a 'thing'—but in reality it was going to take a while getting used to the fact the structure they dropped their trays on was constructed from pure gold.

"'Staff Sourcing' this afternoon," Abby said as they ate their sandwiches. "I'd love a staff," she added as a sudden burst of raucous laughter interrupted her from the next table. "Good for whacking undesirables!" Eyre looked over to see Saxon Curtis displaying his burnt hand to his cronies. Rather than being ashamed of it, he now seemed rather proud of his brand, and was showing it around the table, obviously forgetting that not so long ago he had been crying his eyes out. Ben Perrill slapped him on the back, saying something inaudible that made the table erupt into laughter. Saxon looked over and saw Eyre watching him and had the grace to look slightly embarrassed. But then he looked away again and rejoined the horsing around at the table. It seemed that group hadn't changed over the summer, Eyre mused. She watched as Saxon grabbed Ben's shirt and yanked it hard. The tug pulled the shirt down and to Eyre's surprise, she saw a thick, red scar circling his neck. She hadn't seen that before and she craned to have a better look. Ben saw her looking over and punched Saxon hard in the arm, so hard he fell off the stool. As Saxon scrambled to his feet, looking startled, Ben pulled his collar up and hunched over, all the previous lightheartedness sucked out of the air. He scowled at Eyre as if it were her fault and his table fell into an awkward silence.

Warrigal, Robeson and Zanda interrupted her speculation when they arrived to join Eyre and her friends. Eyre took note that Robeson was careful to sit beside Beatrice. Sure enough, soon their conversation was revolving around the latest advances in fulminology techniques and the virtues of using double-handed methods for creating a corona. Lord Clarembout would be impressed, Eyre thought. Those two were going to be teaching the course by next year. Then her eyes turned to Zanda, who was playing with something that twirled with colours on the table.

"What is that?" she asked him, fascinated by the glowing object. It looked like a ribbon of light.

Zanda looked crafty. "It's something I'm working on for the Sector Fair."

Eyre looked confused and Beatrice stopped the fulminology discourse to explain. "The Academy has a Sector Fair every year in third term. Each Sector comes up with a display to show their unique talents. They'll start to talk about it at your Sector meetings when the date gets closer. Every Sector tries to outdo each other; it's a really fun day." Eyre studied the swirling ribbon that Zanda played with. He had been placed in the Sappir Sector, so he was strong in the arts and creative areas. Eyre was so curious about what Zanda's creation was, but he just laughed, and put it in his pocket. "You'll have to wait for the Fair," he teased.

Eyre had been to her Sector meeting after the trip to the Armament Store. The meetings in future would happen every month and run for an hour, mostly administrative items to discuss anything of concern to Hese students. No doubt *boring*, Eyre thought. But today had just been a brief, introductory meeting. The Fair wasn't mentioned, although the First-Year dance at the end of the year was. The dance was a much-anticipated event in the Academy, intended to congratulate students on making it through their first year. Maybe she'd hear more about the Fair next time.

She went back to eating her sandwiches as the Jotnar scurried in and out, attending to tables and clearing plates, their dark faces as dour as ever. Eyre ate fast; she was keen to find out about "Staff Sourcing".

The others were just as eager to get there, so it wasn't long until they'd all finished. They headed out of the Refectory and over to the moldavite square, or the Receiving Stone as it was officially known. Eyre and her friends waited patiently until Sergeant Tottingham pounded her staff.

"Listen up students! You will be taken for the session this afternoon by Ranger Chrysanthe, who will now explain what is to happen."

The Ranger appeared, dressed in sky-blue leggings and a long, ballooning shirt covered in yellow daisies. On his head was a yellow velvet, large-brimmed hat with a long blue feather stuck in the brim. As he walked through the crowd there were murmurs and soft greetings until the hated voice of Ben Perrill rose just that little bit louder over the buzz.

"The most ridiculous sight on campus, ladies," he said derisively as the Ranger passed. "You will never be disappointed. Dressed completely by the Salvos." *The Salvation Army*, Eyre thought. A secondhand store. Her blood boiled.

If the Ranger heard Ben's comment, he didn't show it and kept moving nonchalantly through the students. But the Sergeant's face suffused with colour and she banged her staff hard with each stride as she stomped through the crowd until she was face-to-face with Ben. Enraged, she could hardly speak and Ben took a step backwards. Even he had never seen Sergeant Tottingham in this state. Silence fell, all eyes upon them.

"The Ranger," Sergeant Tottingham hissed, her teeth clenched, "is the bravest being ever to walk this earth or any other." She took her staff and everyone gasped as she whacked it across the back of Ben's legs, causing him to fall on the ground. Suddenly she found the volume to her voice. "You should crawl across the earth and kiss the Ranger's feet," she shouted, leaning over Ben, who finally realised that perhaps he had crossed some line. Indeed, the Sergeant pointed her staff at him as if she was about to unleash the entire power of Light energy upon him, but then she collected herself. "Get. Up. You will *apologise* or my staff will be happy to teach you the meaning of RESPECT!"

Ben Perrill got to his feet, brushing himself off. "My father will hear of this," he said in a low, menacing tone to the Sergeant. But he strolled up to the Ranger. "Sorry sir, what do I know about clothing?" It wasn't much of an apology, but the Ranger seemed unperturbed.

"Apology accepted, Ben," the Ranger said in such a kind voice that Ben Perrill took a step backwards as if struck. He finally looked ashamed and unsure of himself, and retreated to the back of the crowd.

The Ranger stood at the front of the student body as the Sergeant rejoined him. The faces of the students were uncertain and the Ranger looked sombre.

"Ben Perrill definitely got my sartorial sense wrong," he said to them. "These are not Salvation Army clothes. *These* secondhand clothes are from the Goodwill Centre." The students laughed in relief; the moment had passed. Sergeant Tottingham gave a small grimace that passed as a smile, but her eyes were still burning fiercely, her fingers clenched around her staff. Eyre doubted there would be any more displays of disrespect. She marvelled at the discord that Ben's group had already raised on the first day of schooling and wondered what the year ahead held. But then the Ranger started speaking and her thoughts scattered. 'Staff Sourcing' she thought. This should be good.

"One of the most ubiquitous items you will receive as a Lightworker is your staff. Today you will be moving through the bush and finding a suitable branch to use as a staff. What you are looking for is a length from 1.5 to 2 metres long, a straightness to the limb, no cracks in the branch, but most of all, a piece of wood that *appeals* to you. It should call to you; you will find an attraction to it that will be undeniable. You will know when you find the right one. It may happen in five minutes or it may take three hours. You have this afternoon to find your branch and bring it back here. I will be hovering nearby—" Out of nowhere, the Ranger's black and yellow striped carpet swooped down and settled on the ground next to him. "—so if you need advice or are in trouble, call out. I am only too happy to help you. But it is a process that is intended to be a personal journey, so try to do this on your own. You may travel in pairs as you search, but no more than that."

Beatrice and Abby were obviously going to go together, so Eyre and Nick paired up and as the Ranger rose in the air on his carpet, all the students headed in various directions into the bush.

CHAPTER NINE

LEAVES CRUNCHED UNDERFOOT AS Eyre and Nick headed off in a vaguely southern direction. The sun hammered down and the bush responded, releasing its strong eucalyptus scent into the air. Soon all the other students were out of sight and Eyre and Nick trudged along, heading further into the undergrowth as they studied the ground, looking for a suitable branch.

"It would be nice if we found one quickly," Nick mused, as he studied the undergrowth. "I'd rather be the five-minute student than the three hour one, I think."

Eyre muttered in agreement and seized a leopard-tree branch that looked promising. But it was severely split down the middle, so she left it behind. Nick was dragging along a borderline possibility: not straight but almost—then decided it was too early to take a poor candidate and he dumped it on the side of the track. The trees were getting more dense as the track headed inland, and Eyre felt a strange sensation of being watched. It's probably just the Ranger, she thought, undoubtedly he's up there somewhere, invisible but nearby. But Eyre couldn't shake the uncomfortable feeling and after walking for an hour, neither of them had found an appropriate branch so they decided to sit for a moment and rest. The track had been steadily tracking upwards through the bush and the heat was intense; already Eyre felt exhausted. And the feeling of being watched had increased too—several times she had turned around quickly to see the bushes moving as if something or someone had just ducked away. It was disconcerting and slightly creepy, and, given her horrible experiences with creatures out in the bush, not at all irrational.

"Err, do you get the sense that we're not alone?" she asked Nick, feeling a bit stupid as she uttered the words. Nick was drawing a picture in the sand with a stick and he shrugged.

"Well, we're not, technically," he responded pragmatically. "There's the Ranger, and no doubt other students aren't that far away. But yes, I do feel a bit strange." He looked over his shoulder. "Although I don't feel worried by it." Probably nothing, Eyre thought, just the local wildlife checking them out. And if Nick, who had strong senses spiritually, wasn't worried, perhaps she shouldn't be either. Still, she couldn't help looking over her shoulder, and sure enough, the leaves and branches were rustling despite the lack of wind.

"Come on, let's keep going," she said, standing up. They pushed leaves aside and walked on further and then Nick let out a triumphant cry.

"Aha!" he said. "Come here my beauty!" He wasn't referring to Eyre, but to a 1.75 metre length of blackbutt that lay on the track in front of him. He picked it up with reverence, running his hands down the length of the beautiful wood. Dark in colour and fine-grained, it was straight and undamaged and nestled in his hand like a beloved pet. Nick took a few stances with it: left foot forward, right foot, swinging the branch side to side and finally twirling around and striking forward. "En garde!" he shouted, laughing. "Well here she is," he said in wonderment. "I've found my staff!" Turning to a large blackbutt tree by the side of the track, he bowed. "Thank you for your gift," he said and nearly fell over when the tree responded. "You are welcome, young master. Use it well." The leaves of the tree shuffled and rustled, and all around them a sighing arose as the whole stand of trees shook their leaves together.

"Now it's your turn, Eyre," Nick said, well-pleased to have found his staff. "Let's keep going." But to Eyre's consternation, the rustling of leaves rose, louder and louder, branches creaked and trees swayed as she and Nick walked through the bush. It made her nervous and her stride increased, so that when they saw in the distance a group of students walking towards them, branches in hand, she was quite happy to see them. Beatrice and Abby were there, and Zanda, and they all carried straight, beautiful branches. Since Nick had his too, Eyre and Nick decided to join the group and head back with them—they were almost halfway through the allocated time anyway and it would take them over an hour to get back.

"I'm sure it won't matter, I'll find one on the way back," Eyre said. The others were obviously very happy with their branches, and used them to lean on as they travelled back towards campus. The rustling and the bending carried on around them, the cracking and creaking, and eventually the sound was so loud, everyone stopped and looked at the trees. And then it started.

Branches of all shapes and sizes rained down on to the track in front of Eyre, offerings flung from every tree within sight. Blackbutt, eucalypts, hoop pine, beautiful wood piling up in front of her, asking to be selected. The trees seemed to groan with the effort of throwing out their treasures to Eyre. Zanda, never stuck for words, let out a low whistle.

"The Light's sake, Eyre, put them out of their misery. Choose one!" Eyre was bewildered, but also felt like she didn't want to hurt any of the trees' feelings—they were all offering her the very best pieces of themselves. She bowed low.

"Thank you all for your generosity, I am overwhelmed." Then she picked up many branches, admiring them out loud so that the trees would realise she valued their gifts. It was very hard—any one of them would do, she thought—they were all beautiful. She was about to decide on a strong piece of redwood when a loud whooshing in the air made all the students look up. Across the top of the forest a missile was hurtling through the air, spinning at top speed like a javelin. It made a singing sound as it whirled, and then it speared into the ground at Eyre's feet, sending sand flying up from the track. The long branch was as straight as a piece of iron and brightly coloured in rainbow hues. almost as if pots of paint had been poured along the sides. Eyre gasped in wonder. There was only one tree this could have come from—the Rainbow Eucalyptus she had met in the TEP exam last year! She picked the branch up as the other students gaped in admiration, and she hefted it in her hand. There was no doubt; the decision was made. This branch felt like it was part of her hand, as if it melded with her body, and just the feel of it made her palm thrum with energy. What a gift!

"Thank you, honoured one," she called into the sky, and then, echoing something the tree had said to her last year, she added, "this resonates with me." Her words were answered by a pressure wave of energy that moved through the air like the low notes of a Moog synthesiser. Clearly her thanks had been heard. Eyre wasn't sure what to do with the other branches that piled up in front of her but Abby, a Sappir and the most sensitive one, had an idea.

"Ranger," she called. "If you can hear me, I think the Mimir would love these beautiful branches for their Mantle Basin. Could you transport them to the Mimir?"

There was no response, but the branches suddenly disappeared, to Eyre's relief. Trust kind Abby to figure out a way to handle it. The trees shuffled and sighed with pride, and all the way back the students were accompanied by the creaking and rustling of leaves. It was a like music, tranquil and magical, and by the time Eyre arrived back at campus she felt serene and at peace—like she'd just undertaken a long meditation session. She held her branch in her hand like a rare treasure—which indeed it was—and joined the growing group of students waiting at the Receiving Stone. When the three hours were up, all the students had returned from the bush with a branch in hand. They were all different: a range of lengths, from different trees, with varying colours of wood. But they were all sturdy, straight and beautiful. Sergeant Tottingham took a long look at Eyre's branch but didn't comment. When the Ranger appeared, settling on the ground on his carpet, the Sergeant and Ranger Chrysanthe stood at the front of the tired students.

"Well done to all of you. This is an important event in your lives, and no doubt one you will not forget. Tomorrow you will be searching for the crystals to energise your staff. It will be another long day, so get a good night's sleep after dinner. Your staff may be kept in your room."

Eyre headed back to her room with her friends. Beatrice had found a glowing piece of redwood for her staff, and Abby had the beautiful branch of a speckled leopard tree. They spent the rest of the evening trying to guess what the next day held for them, but of course they really had no way of knowing.

CHAPTER TEN

THERE WAS A HUM of excitement in the air as the students gathered at the Receiving Stone the next morning. Over by the Central Administration building was a line of Zepps, bringing back more memories of the TEPs. Eyre and her friends had left their staffs in their bedroom, and Eyre felt unsettled leaving hers behind—like she had deserted it. Strange that she should feel so bonded to a piece of wood. Beatrice surveyed the crowd.

"Don't look now, but there's a superstar on the way." Her voice was teasing and when Eyre looked up, she saw Jax moving through the crowd towards her. She had to admit that his interest was flattering, but if she was honest, she had to wonder what he saw in her. He could have any girl he wanted, and Eyre noticed that the amber eyes of the girl he didn't want—Pheria—were watching Jax's every move as he stopped in front of Eyre.

"I hear you got a gift from the Rainbow Eucalyptus yesterday," Jax said. "You must have made an impression on it last year." He laughed. "But then you seem to have made an impression on a few of us."

Once again Eyre's stupid face blushed and Abby turned away, trying not to giggle and feeling sympathy for her friend's predicament. Eyre struggled to reply. Why did she find it so hard to talk around Jax? Normally she could have a conversation with anyone.

"You found a branch too?" *Obviously.* By the Light! But Jax's gorgeous green eyes sparkled.

"Mine is Eucalyptus *Paniculata.* Or Grey Ironbark. A wood worthy of a Lightworker's weapon." Then it was his turn to look awkward and to Eyre's surprise—was that a flush she saw creeping up his cheeks?

Jax hurried to explain. "My family has a timber business. So I know the names of all types of wood in Australia, and overseas."

Wow, Eyre thought. And then another thought hit her. Wait, was he part of *Jackson Timber?* That was a huge company.

"That's really cool. I love my staff and I didn't want to leave it behind," she confessed. Jax nodded and started to reply when an oily voice came from behind them.

"If you could stop your gossiping and move aside, I would greatly appreciate it." Mandig Vela was moving through the students and his presence seemed to create a pathway—everyone stepped back as if pushed away by an invisible force. Jax gave Eyre a wry smile.

"Good luck—I guess I'll see you wherever we're heading." He walked back to join his friends, Vaughn Michaelson and Phillip Outray, who Eyre was glad to see had also made it to the Academy this year. She noticed Pheria scowling at her but Eyre tilted her chin. Pheria had deliberately misled her about Jax. Eyre wouldn't interfere with someone's relationship, but Jax had made it clear he was not with Pheria so she could just suck it up.

Beatrice's eyes danced. "*Eucalyptus Paniculata?* Indeed! Methinks someone is trying to impress you!" Abby and Nick chuckled as Eyre thumped Beatrice softly on the shoulder. She looked across and saw Jax looking back at her, and a warm feeling travelled through her. He was the opposite of Mandig Vela—somehow she was invisibly drawn *towards* him by some unseen force.

Professor Vela reached the front of the crowd and silence descended. He didn't even need to clear his throat. Such was the power of meanness, Eyre thought.

"Today we are heading to the Crystal Grotto, where you will select a crystal for your staff. You will be travelling by Zepp, so please board the craft by the Central Administration building and do it quickly and silently."

The Zepps were piloted by graduate students and they took off with varying levels of expertise. Eyre's pilot was quite accomplished and flew the craft competently with only a few bumps and jolts; Eyre could see as the walls disappeared that others were having a wilder flight than hers—their pilots needed a bit more practise. But none of them could compare to the hilarious trips she'd had with Madame Overmantle last year—those had been something else entirely: bucking, heaving, and generally flying around sideways like a deflating balloon. So she was quite happy to have a graduate student transport her to the grotto.

After half an hour they landed in dense bush where a runway had been carved. When the vehicle had stopped, Eyre's pilot handed each of them a shoulder bag made of some kind of canvas. It hung high up under her armpit, slightly uncomfortable but bearable. As the students descended from the Zepps, Professor Vela organised the vehicles to park in rows at the side of the runway. Then the graduate students remained inside and the first-year students followed Professor Vela into the bush. Eyre could hear the shrill sound of cicadas rising and falling in waves as she walked down the sandy track. At times the noise was deafening, precluding any conversation. The background music of summer, she thought—but occasionally with the decibels of a rock show.

Before long they stopped at an entrance carved into the face of a huge rock. Eyre felt a bit uneasy, remembering her experience at the Transit caves back at the cabins. But when she walked through she was relieved to see that a beautiful pool sparkled before her in an open-air chamber. The area was huge and the water was clear and aquamarine, the unruffled surface enabling her to see to the bottom. Clumps of coloured crystals clustered all over the base of the pool—purples, greens, reds, all different sizes and shapes.

"This pool is ten metres deep," Professor Vela intoned. Several students gasped. The water was so clear it appeared quite shallow. Ignoring them he continued. "You are to dive to the bottom and choose a crystal for your staff. Those of you who do not swim particularly well will be happy to know that the sides of the pool are only two metres deep, so you should be able to reach a crystal at that depth. Some crystals lie loose on the ground; others you may harvest from the formations, but if they do not come easily, leave them. They are not yet ready for selection. Place the crystal in the bag you have been given before you swim back up. Do not take more than one crystal, and once you have chosen a crystal and taken it to the surface you are not permitted to go back to exchange it. Take your boots off but leave your Lightworker uniform on—it will dry off soon enough once you are out in the sun. Please arrange yourself in groups of twenty; we will rotate groups in fifteen-minute intervals until everyone has a crystal."

It was so hot in the grotto that Eyre felt her skin yearning to touch the coolness of the water. The first group went in and she watched the students dive down, some of them in the deeper section of the pool and others at the edges. It didn't take long for them to surface with their bags filled— evidently there were lots of crystals on the bottom and it was not a difficult task. Then time was up and the next group to took to the water. The students slipped in with cries of delight and Eyre watched enviously as they swam around in the turquoise water. It looked so cool! The waiting students sat on the edge with their feet in the water, so many of them, they almost completely surrounded the pool. Time passed slowly as more groups went in until finally, by the time she thought she was about to melt into the ground, it was her group's turn, the last to go in. She dove into the beautiful water and her skin shuddered with delight—it was *gorgeous*! For a minute she forgot her 'mission' and just swam around in the delicious coolness. Then she took a deep breath and dived to the bottom. She headed for the largest in a clump of blue crystals, but although she tugged hard, the crystal would not release from the formation. She dragged her hands over the ground trying to find a loose crystal, but it seemed the momentum of the water was washing them out of reach—she couldn't get any of the ones that lay loose on the bottom. She swam back up to the surface and gulped air, readying for her next attempt. Beatrice was jubilant on the surface, holding up a huge emerald crystal.

"Look at this—it's beautiful!" she cried, and swam over to sit on the edge. Abby was there too—she'd dived in the shallower depths and was holding a yellow crystal of some sort. Eyre was not sure what it was, but it was certainly a magnificent stone. Feeling pressure rising, Eyre dove down to the bottom and tried to take one of the crystals again—purple-coloured this time—but it held stubbornly on. Eyre could see feet and legs kicking past her—no doubt the successful students moving back to the surface. She ran out of breath again and swam upwards again, gasping from the effort as she broke the surface. To her embarrassment, she now realised she was the only one left in the pool, still struggling to get her crystal. She knew it was hot out there and the students would be keen to leave, which just added another layer of stress to the pressure she was feeling. Third time lucky, she thought, diving to the deepest part of the pool. Maybe the students have taken all the crystals from the shallower parts of the pool and she would have some success there. Down she dived, almost losing her breath just from the journey down, and she swam around trying to find a loose crystal. It was harder to see here—the light didn't travel as well. But once again it seemed that the crystals were rolling away from her—almost like they didn't want her to pick them. But surely that was a ridiculous notion. Desperate, she seized a shard sticking out of a clump but it would not budge. Her lungs were burning so she kicked her way to the surface, to see the silent groans on the faces of the waiting students. Professor Vela sneered.

"I think the last group can wait with that one student," he said. "The rest of you can follow me and wait in the Zepps to cool off." The crowd jumped up with alacrity—it was boiling hot in the grotto and they desperately wanted to leave—some of them had been sitting there for several hours.

Professor Vela addressed Eyre, a mean smirk on his face. He hadn't forgotten her from the TEPs, and he was enjoying this. "When you have your crystal, your group may return to the Zepps."

As the students disappeared into the bush, Eyre looked around apologetically at her group, who were trying to look supportive, but with their red faces, she knew they were feeling the heat.

"I'm sorry, I'm finding it so hard," she said. "Hopefully I'll get it this time." Her embarrassed gaze fell upon someone who wasn't supposed to be there—Jax. He'd stayed behind, which only made her feel worse. *This time for sure* she thought determinedly as she dove down, down, down... On the bottom she searched around, trying to pick up anything she could lay her hands on. She reached under a formation of a rosy-hued crystal clump and finally grabbed onto something. But with a start of horror, she realised that whatever it was, it was *alive*. She tried to release her grasp, but a set of legs wrapped around her arm, holding her down. Screaming silently in her head, she tried to pull her arm out of the hole, but it wouldn't come. She realised that she was running out of air, and as her lungs started to involuntarily suck for a breath, she pushed hard with her other hand against the crystal formation, trying to force her shoulder back. With a roiling of water, a force seemed to shoot from her palm as the crystal broke off in her hand and she lurched forward. Whatever was in the hole pulled her further in and she realised with a shock that she was drowning. Strength was leaving her limbs and darkness filled her mind.

But then there was a commotion beside her and the water churned. Someone had plunged down from the surface beside her and as black swirls started to cloud her vision, she saw that it was Jax. A knife flashed in his hand as he thrust it time and again into the hole until finally whatever held her arm was severed. Jax gathered her in his arms and kicked for the surface but by then Eyre had succumbed to the darkness that swallowed her.

CHAPTER ELEVEN

EYRE STRUGGLED TO THE surface of a wonderful dream—Jax, holding her head and kissing her passionately. As consciousness returned, she realised with a drugged surprise that indeed, Jax's lips were upon hers; not with passion, but in a desperate attempt to bring her back to life. Beatrice and Abby were kneeling beside her, Abby with her hand over her own mouth in fear. Eyre couldn't move, she was so exhausted, but Beatrice noticed her eyes had opened.

"She's conscious!" she cried. Jax sat up frantically, and placed his arm under Eyre's head.

"Eyre," he said, and the tenderness in his voice, caused a jolt of electricity to run down Eyre's body, despite the ordeal she had been through. "Can you sit up?"

Groggily she sat up, coughing and retching, pain coursing through her lungs. Her wrist was bleeding heavily—what on earth *was* that creature, she wondered. She seemed to have a knack for finding malevolent creatures in the wild. She looked at Jax, and managed to whisper, "You had a knife?" He nodded—showing her a penknife. "I whittle," he admitted, as if it was something embarrassing. "Timber family—we always have a knife." Eyre hugged him wildly, tears coursing down her face.

"Thank you, thank you, thank you," she croaked over and over, not letting go. Part of her mind registered that Jax didn't seem to want to release his embrace either. As they held each other there was a bright flash of light and the unwelcome presence of Professor Vela appeared in the grotto. He was looking uncharacteristically uncertain as he walked towards them.

"Todd ran and got him," Beatrice muttered as she started to wind the strap of her canvas bag around Eyre's wrist. Then, seeing the expression on the Professor's face, she added cynically, "Leaving students behind is probably not in the AOL Recommended Teaching Guide. He is going to look bad bringing a wounded student back—especially since that student might have died." Beatrice grinned, looking positively joyous that Mandig Vela might be in trouble over this.

The Professor peered at Eyre. "Just a flesh wound," he said. "You must have caught your hand in a crevice. I'll send you to first aid of course, but it looks just a minor injury."

Jax stood up, his green eyes flashing. "There was some creature in there, sir. It attacked Eyre."

Professor Vela's face darkened. "There are no... *creatures* in the Crystal Grotto. Students have been coming here for decades. You will speak of that no more or you will be punished for trying to create a panic!" He stalked around the edge of the pool. "The rest of you can go back to the Zepp." When they hesitated, his voice took on a snarl. "*Now!*" The students headed towards the track, casting backwards glances at the scene. Beatrice, Abby, Nick and Jax resolutely stayed and locked eyes with Professor Vela: a challenge. After a moment the Professor looked away and bent down towards Eyre. Her skin crawled as he neared her. She felt like another vile creature had arrived to harm her.

"You were caught in a hole," he whispered in her ear savagely as he made a pretence of examining her wound and her bruised shoulder. "*That* is the official story or you will regret speaking out. Think of the welfare of that boy you seem so fond of." Despite her exhaustion, Eyre jumped in fright. Was he threatening Jax? *What?* She knew Professor Vela was a vile man, but would he be capable of *that?* Her mind was reeling as she took his words in.

Then Professor Vela waved his hands and there was a bright flash of light. When she opened her eyes, she and her friends were in a room she had never seen before, but from the layout she could see it was a medical centre. Professor Vela strode up to the reception desk.

"This student has had an injury to her arm. Please help her with the wound. You other students, head back to your dormitory please." Then Professor Vela disappeared again, no doubt off to herd the Zepps back to campus.

A nurse came out quickly and led Eyre to a bed where she examined her shoulder and her wrist. She tut-tutted over the bruising and the deep wound, and when she heard that Eyre had nearly drowned, she urgently summoned a doctor. While the doctor listened to Eyre's chest and ran a series of tests, the nurse bound up her wound carefully.

"You were lucky," the doctor pronounced, putting his stethoscope away. "Your chest sounds fine and your other injuries should heal in time. You should be more careful in your undertakings." He left before Eyre could protest, and anyway, she thought wearily, what could she say? She couldn't dismiss Professor Vela's threats, and part of her just wanted to forget the whole thing anyway. The medical staff wanted to keep her under observation for the afternoon, so she succumbed to the tiredness invading her body and fell into a deep sleep.

CHAPTER TWELVE

EYRE WAS RELEASED THE next day and she walked slowly along to her room. Beatrice and Abby were there, having just returned from breakfast. Abby threw her arms around her.

"We thought you were dead!"

Beatrice hugged Eyre too. "Are you okay? How do you feel? Professor Vela has told everyone you caught your hand in a crystal formation and cut it when you pulled it out."

Eyre shook her head in disbelief. What a dishonest man—manufacturing a story to cover himself. Yet again she wondered how someone like this could be a Lightworker. She finally decided that there must be shades of good and bad in the Lightworking world, not only black and white, just like in the normal world. In that case, Professor Vela was definitely a dark shade of grey.

Holding out her arm she said, "It's happened again." Beatrice and Abby looked puzzled until Beatrice gasped. "Your wound, it's gone!"

Eye nodded. "The nurse went to change my dressing this morning and lo and behold. Go figure." They looked curiously at Eyre's arm and then Abby made a small noise.

"Oh, before I forget—here. You'll need it for the session today." She pulled something out of the top drawer of her desk and Eyre realised it was a large sparkling pink crystal. At Eyre's blank look, Abby prompted.

"For your staff, it's your crystal."

Eyre didn't move to take it. "But I thought I had to choose my own..." she said.

"You did—it was in your hand when Jax brought you to the surface. I just brought it home for you."

Eyre's memory kicked in—of pushing wildly at the rosy crystal formation in the depths of the pool, desperately struggling to get free of whatever it was that had clamped around her arm. She vaguely recalled a piece breaking free—she must have held on to it during the uproar. She took the brilliantly coloured gem from Abby and looked at it, marvelling at its beauty. One end was a perfect tetrahedron, but the other was uneven and jagged, like a tooth that had been knocked and broken. It was a sizeable crystal—about ten centimetres across and thirty centimetres long—and the pink colour was unlike anything Eyre had seen before; it seemed to glow with a life of its own.

"Thank you Abby, so much," Eyre breathed, holding the special gem in her hand. "I thought I was going to miss out on having a staff."

"Well, we're all going to miss out if we don't hurry," Beatrice suddenly interjected. "It's nearly nine—we'd better move! Quick—grab your branch!"

They scrambled out the door and raced over to the Receiving Stone where Sergeant Tottingham and most of the students were already gathered. They joined Nick and his roommates on the edge of the Stone. Several curious looks were directed Eyre's way from the rest of the students, but no one came over to make conversation. Evidently they all already knew the story of her catching her hand in the 'rock', Eyre thought sourly. She looked around but was disappointed to see that Jax had not arrived yet.

Sergeant Tottingham thumped her staff at 9am precisely.

"Right!" she bellowed. "Today you will be assembling your staff. I hope you all have thought to bring your branch and your crystal this morning." She rolled her eyes and a look like a sigh crossed her face as about ten students took off running towards the dormitories.

"As always," she muttered. "Well, they can catch up. The rest of you are to follow Corporal Cabochon to the workshop, where you will be spending the day working on your staff." Corporal Cabochon turned out to be a very young-looking Mimir, who practically fell over backwards trying to wave and bow to Eyre at the same time. Eyre noticed some of the students looking quite annoyed at this—evidently, they were getting as sick of this behaviour as she was. Gritting her teeth, she had to admit—if she saw this happening to another student, she would also find it irritating.

The students followed the Corporal along the paths that led through the campus buildings. Right down the end was the workshop—perhaps the most spare building of the school. It was a huge shed-like construction at the back of the Zepp hangar, built from concrete and with large, square openings up the top to let air in. Inside there were workbenches that ran from one side of the hangar to the other, equipped with an array of interesting-looking machinery and gadgets. Tools were lined up on the benches, and underneath was a row of cupboards. At one end of the workshop was a roaring furnace, and near it was a bubbling vat containing a mysterious purple liquid with a pungent smell. And finally, in the middle of the room there were benches carrying racks with jars of various powders, lengths of metal, rolls of wire and string, pots with lids screwed on tight and lumps of a clear, brown waxy-looking substance. It was all very intriguing.

Everyone chose a seat along the benches and waited for the Corporal to begin. A bit flustered, he had several attempts at speaking until the Sergeant stepped in.

"The Corporal is a particularly gifted weapons crafter, despite his age. His public speaking, however, is not such a gift, is it, Corporal?" The Corporal flushed and some students tittered until the Sergeant turned a laser gaze upon them. "That was not supposed to be a joke. That was a request for patience, and I expect you to treat the Corporal with the respect he deserves. Probably the best thing to do first is put your branch upon the bench and clamp it in snugly. But don't clamp too hard, and use the rubber squares in the cupboard below so you don't damage the wood. Put them on each side of the wood before you screw in the clamp."

Everyone hurried to comply and it seemed that the Corporal had gotten over his initial fluster; finally he found his voice. He stepped up onto a podium so the students could see him, and began to instruct them on what to do. Just then, Jax slid in the door with a magnificent piece of blackbutt in his hand and a sparkling blue sapphire. Smoothing his hair he tried to look nonchalant as he strolled to the bench at the far back.

"Sleep in, did we, Mr Jackson?" Sergeant Tottingham asked. "The excitement too much for you yesterday?"

Jax shook his head and looked over at Eyre. Her stomach flipped as those green eyes regarded her so calmly. "I was giving a report to Whittaker Ray," he said. "I'm sorry—it took a while." The Sergeant harrumphed and Corporal Cabochon started to speak again.

The first couple of hours were spent planing the branch to form an even straighter shaft, and then sanding it using sequentially smaller-grained sandpaper. After a couple of hours had passed, the staff was smooth and finely sanded, all the last knots and pieces of bark gone. Eyre loved the wood of the rainbow eucalyptus. The colours were so bright and now it had been sanded it was even more beautiful.

"Okay, uh, students," Corporal Cabochon said. "Now we must make the er—*holder*—for your crystal. Could you please take a lump of that brown sap from the central benches?" Along with the other students, Eyre took one of the clear, waxy lumps that were sitting on the bench in the middle of the room. It was slightly sticky and malleable, and she waited for the Corporal to speak.

"Well, er, could you form the Bingi sap—that's from a tree found in Incendium, by the way—into a sort of hollow cylinder shape. The best way to do this is to make a ball, flatten it and then roll it into a cylinder—like this..." With deft hands he demonstrated how to make the required shape, although the students subsequently found it was a lot more difficult than it looked. Eventually Eyre had one that looked acceptable and as the Corporal directed, carefully stuck one end of the crystal deeply into it, and then took it out again—forming a perfect impression of the shape of the crystal. Then she stuck the end of her staff into the other end of the cylinder, once again creating a hole, this one the exact shape of the top of her staff. She had just put the crystal into the cylinder again, checking the fit, when Sergeant Tottingham wandered up. The Sergeant had been moving around the workshop while the students worked, examining their efforts and offering a suggestion now and again. Looking at Eyre's crystal, the Sergeant's eyebrows raised a little. Peering closer she huffed in surprise.

"I hear you had a bit of drama obtaining your crystal," she said to Eyre and Eyre nodded, but didn't say anything. There was no point in contradicting Professor Vela's story. The Sergeant kept examining the rosy stone.

"Well, despite the problems, you've managed to acquire one of the rarest gems in the pool. There's only one formation of pink diamond in there, and it's at the deepest point. It's been a long time since a student obtained one, they don't detach very often."

Eyre's ears coloured. "I—er—well, in actual fact," she confessed, "the crystal broke off when I was trying to get up to the surface. See—" She pulled the crystal out of the Bingi sap, showing the ragged end and the Sergeant looked thoughtful.

"Oh, I do see." She hesitated, then continued slowly. "But how you managed to break a diamond of that structure is quite an enigma—the Grotto Pink is the strongest crystalline structure in the known Overworld, apart from Zha'kara diamonds. Perhaps the mixture of adrenaline and Light energy was enough...?" Her voice had dropped as she mused over this puzzle. "And how a broken crystal will perform... well, we've never had one before to my recollection. Still," she turned the diamond in the air and the deep rosy hue seemed to pulse in the light, "it's rather a magnificent gem. Well done, under the circumstances." She handed the diamond back to Eyre, her face conflicted. Eyre's earlier elation at discovering she actually had a crystal after all subsided a little; from the tone of the Sergeant's voice, a broken crystal didn't sound too promising.

"Should I continue then?" she asked. The Sergeant looked at her.

"Oh yes," she said. "You only get one trip to the Crystal Grotto in your life, and unfortunately you've had yours. This is it, for better or for worse."

The Sergeant continued on and Eyre sat back, deflated. But then she clenched her teeth and continued checking the sap imprints. If 'this was it' then she would do the best she could with her broken crystal.

The Corporal stood on his podium, enthusiastic about the process. Obviously he loved doing this, and his earlier awkwardness had disappeared. "Righto then! Now you must put the cylinder in the metal basket you will find on your bench, and dip it into the setting liquid—that's the purple stuff bubbling over there. You have to dip the basket ten times, and then thrust the basket into the furnace for exactly twenty seconds. The basket will ring when it's time to take it out."

The 'basket' was a long-handled latticed cage, that opened from the middle. It looked a bit like a chip fryer with a timer on a long arm of metal. Grasping the protective wooden handle on the end, Eyre took her cylinder over to the setting liquid and dipped it in ten times, as instructed. Each time she dipped the cylinder a sizzling erupted from the purple liquid and the strange smell intensified. Then, carrying the dripping basket over to the furnace, she held it in the searing flames until the timer bell told her the time was up. All the baskets were then lined up on a centre bench to cool down a little while the Corporal gave them the final directions.

"Now, when the Bingi cylinder is cold, you will find it is very hard. The firing will imbue the sap with incredible strength, yet flexibility, and this will hold your crystal perfectly tight. But while the sap is still cooling, you need to put your crystal into the top of the cylinder, and the shaft of your staff into the bottom of the cylinder. The Bingi cylinder will shrink to fit your crystal and wooden shaft snugly. Then you will secure your staff using the leather straps here, and finally the gold thread. This process requires care and patience, or you will have to start again. Please ask me for help if you are having trouble."

The last hour passed slowly. It was indeed difficult, and fiddly, and Eyre took her time, determined she would not be one of the students who had to start again. Already a couple of them were dismally beginning the process again after dropping the Bingi sap, or being too heavy-handed while trying to insert the crystal and cracking the mould. She realised she had to be gentle with the cooling sap, but move quickly so that she could insert the crystal and the shaft in time. Finally she had the Bingi sap in place and it cooled and tightened around the wood and the crystal. As it cooled it glowed like a golden piece of amber, a toffee-coloured, smooth cradle for the gem it protected. Then she wound the leather strap tightly around the Bingi sap and knotted it. The gold thread was wound on top of the leather evenly so it shone like a golden band around the staff.

"Eventually you may like to add, uh, special items to your staff, like rare feathers or talismans. It is your staff, and yours to finish how you see fit," Corporal Cabochon said. "Finally, please use the Eeb nut oil to oil your staff. Brush it on and buff it off with the cloth under your bench. Eeb nuts are found in Terra and they are frequently used in furniture manufacture because of the high gloss it gives to wood, a barrier that is impenetrable to the elements."

The Eeb nut pots were lined up on the centre bench next to the lumps of Bingi sap. Eyre grabbed a pot of the oil and used the stiff brush the Corporal had talked about to apply the oil the full length of her staff. The clear oil soaked into the woodgrain instantly, giving it a depth and a glow. Then, Eyre buffed it hard with the cloth and the wood, already well polished, took on a high gloss that shone like glass. The rainbow of colours in the wood of her staff was startling, and the pink crystal (*diamond* she thought in wonder) at the top sparkled in the light. What an amazing object, all the more special because she'd created it herself. Broken crystal or not, she loved the staff she had made.

Beatrice stomped the ground with her staff—glossy redwood with the deep green emerald at the top—and grinned; and then Abby twirled hers around like a windmill, the leopard-tree shaft with the yellow crystal (sapphire, as it turned out) looking equally impressive. In fact, all the staffs, each unique and beautiful, were quite spectacular to see, and the Sergeant strode around the room looking, for once, quite pleased.

Corporal Cabochon thanked the students for their participation—and for their patience with his public speaking skills, which made them laugh—and then they all headed back along the paths towards the dorms. Jax caught up with Eyre and her friends and he thrust his staff forwards in an Aditus move.

"I wonder how the staff would work on *staff?*" he said. "One person particularly I have in mind. I'd love to give him a blast of Light energy. Are you okay, Eyre?"

She nodded, feeling a bit embarrassed as she remembered how she had held Jax on the side of the grotto. "Yes, good as new. Thank you. I wouldn't be here if it wasn't for you."

Jax's green eyes deepened but he spoke lightly. "Yeah, well you owe me one. Don't worry, I'll call it in." Eyre's stomach flipped at the way he was looking at her, Jax continued before the moment got awkward. "I spoke to Whittaker Ray about yesterday and he's going to prepare a report. But I don't think anything will come of it—Professor Vela has obviously convinced everyone there's nothing down there. I have to say I'm confused —wouldn't you want to check it out? But hopefully whatever it was is dead. I gave it a good hacking."

"You obviously know how to use a knife," Nick said. "Maybe you can show me sometime?" They walked on ahead, discussing the merits of various blades and knives and Beatrice looked at Eyre. "Well, from the sound of it, that's a favour I would be hoping he calls in soon, if I were you!"

Abby giggled and Eyre joined in, but her eyes were on Jax's back. She had a feeling like falling and although it was not unpleasant, she suddenly felt very vulnerable.

CHAPTER THIRTEEN

THE NEXT DAY EYRE was feeling a lot better as she joined her friends on the Receiving Stone. All her injuries had disappeared, and the residual aches from the struggle underwater had gone. Today was the day of Lighthorse selection, whatever that was, but she was looking forward to it. She thought horses were beautiful creatures. Beatrice and Abby were equally uninformed as to what a Lighthorse was—their parents had never mentioned it. So they hovered around the Receiving Stone with a great deal of anticipation.

The Sergeant strode up at precisely 8.45am and waited until all the students were assembled.

"Today we are heading out to the Academy Equestrian Centre and Stables." Eyre raised an eyebrow and looked at Beatrice. The stables had never been mentioned before, and they certainly hadn't been included on the campus tour they'd had. Sergeant Tottingham registered the quizzical looks shooting around the students and she nodded.

"Lighthorses are amongst our most precious assets, and because of their remarkable power, they are of great significance to people who do not have the best interests of the world at heart. Therefore, the locations of Lighthorse stables are not discussed openly in our community. It would not do to have our horses fall into the wrong hands.

"Every Lightworker has a Lighthorse, which is kept at a stable. Academy students keep their horses here; when you leave you will find a specialist Lightworking stable to permanently house your horse. When called upon, your Lighthorse will appear instantly.

"Lighthorses are bred and guided by specialist members of our Virens Sector, in a secret location. These expert trainers are called Kikkuli Masters and they have taken years to learn the skills of their vocation. Some of you may be interested in following a life path in this area." Eyre noticed Carly's eyes spark at this. All the students were looking interested, actually, and

Eyre had to admit she was anxious to see the horses too and find out what they were like. Sergeant Tottingham looked up as a graduate student from the Virens Sector walked up.

"Right. Follow Lisa please—she is our graduate student in charge of the Academy's stables this year. She will take you to meet the Kikkuli Master."

The students followed Lisa away from the campus grounds and down a hill where they could see the emerald waters of the Ponds of Doombee shining in the sunlight. The mosaic path they followed meandered through the trees until they eventually reached a huge bronze sculpture of a horse rearing on its hind legs. The statue gleamed in the sunlight, towering ten metres above them. Behind the magnificent horse was a set of large bronze doors laid into a five-metre-high sandstone block wall. It was impossible to see behind the wall, but there was a very alarming roaring coming from somewhere within. It sounded like a pride of lions enjoying a smorgasbord, and the hair on Eyre's arms prickled at the unnerving sound. Lisa waved her hands.

"Step back, please and watch the doors. They don't stop once they start opening."

With a metallic groan, the bronze doors started to open outwards and a couple of the students had to move in a hurry to avoid being hit by the great panels of metal. When the doors were finally open, there was a long moment when no-one wanted to move towards that fearsome sound, but then the students slowly walked inside as the doors heaved shut behind them. Obviously keeping things inside, Eyre thought uneasily. But what *things* were they? The ferocious roaring echoed off the sandstone walls and all the students looked around fearfully, as if they might have unexpectedly walked into a colosseum and *they* were on the menu.

But there was nothing to be seen, so after a moment Eyre started to take stock of her surroundings. They were standing in an open sandy circular area, completely surrounded by the high sandstone walls. At one end of the compound, where the awful sound was coming from, was the opening of a building. Eyre hadn't had much to do with horses over her life, but it was obvious this was the entrance to the stables, as she could dimly make out a number of stalls heading into the gloom of the building. Lisa spoke in a bright voice.

"Okay, well, if you head into the stables down the end, the Kikkuli Master will be there and he will take you through the Lighthorse Selection Process." She headed off towards a small shed at the other end of the area, leaving the students looking rather dubiously at one another. Nick shrugged.

"Well, I've never heard a horse make that noise before, but this *is* the Academy after all. Off we go then, into the lions' den!" His tone was dry but Eyre could tell he wasn't completely joking. Was this another test?

Slowly the large group of students moved into the building at the end of the compound. The roars still echoed around them, but there was nothing to be seen and Eyre began to relax. It was strange how she was getting used to the noise and it was becoming rather monotonous really, sort of a background hum—although a rather loud hum.

The stalls in the stables extended a long way down and Eyre couldn't see the end of them. All the stalls were empty, recently cleaned out with clean straw on the floor and fresh clumps of hay in the feeding bin. It was an immaculate set-up, Eyre thought as she looked around—obviously Lisa was good at what she did: this must have taken a while.

As she looked down the hall a figure appeared from the gloom, walking towards them. He was about thirty years old, not overly tall, but with very defined muscles in his arms, the left one sporting a Virens Inguz. His skin was swarthy and his black hair shone in the sunlight. Like most Lightworkers, he carried a staff and he also had a whistle on a thong around his neck.

He stopped in front of the students and surveyed them soundlessly, his gaze serene but perceptive. He reminded Eyre of someone, and she wracked her brain but was annoyed when she couldn't think who it was. Finally the man spoke.

"Welcome. As you will have no doubt realised, I am the Kikkuli Master for the Academy of Light. Thank you for your courage in entering the unknown, with the sounds that you can hear. It reflects well upon you." The Master snapped his fingers and the roaring stopped. Eyre's ears were almost ringing from the sudden silence. So it *was* a test? The Master continued speaking.

"Today is a great day for you and I know you will remember it for the rest of your lives, the day you meet the horse who will form a partnership with you for life. We call it a partnership because you do not own or dominate a Lighthorse; you are equals who must learn to trust and rely on each other."

Ben Perrill called out from the back of the crowd—he'd been one of the last in the door, Eyre had noticed.

"When do we pick our horse?" As always, his voice was tainted by a tinge of disrespect that didn't need to be there. As the Kikkuli Master turned his calm eyes towards Ben, Eyre finally realised who the Master reminded her of: UD₁. He didn't look like UD₁, but his quiet manner and the strong sense of inner calm was very similar to UD1. His eyes were gentle as he looked at the ill-mannered boy.

"Ah," he said. "You have it wrong. It is not you who choose your horse, but the horse who chooses you. The Lighthorse selection process is all about the horse deciding who it is prepared to share its life with. Not a decision that should be left to uneducated students I feel."

There was a small whirlpool of laughter and Ben stepped back, embarrassed. Eyre loved it when he was put in his place, but that gleeful thought was lost in the churning of her mind as she considered the Master's words. The horse would pick the *student*? Wow! I hope mine realises I can't ride, she thought.

Madeleine de Haven spoke up—thinking as usual. "Where are the roaring creatures?" she asked. "That's not the Lighthorses is it?" Several students laughed and the Master's eyes crinkled.

"No, it's just a recording I play daily for the horses." He snapped his fingers and the roaring filled the air, then he clicked them again and the sound ceased. "It's a mixture of sounds from the Saevus, the Nahtaivel and the Menax." Eyre didn't know what a Nahtaivel or a Menax was, but she assumed they were also creatures of the Strigis, like the Saevus. More 'lovely' creatures to learn about sometime, she thought.

"I play the track so that the Lighthorses get used to the sound of it. Then, if they are ever called to battle, they will not be spooked by the cries of those vile creatures. They are highly-strung animals, Lighthorses— extremely courageous but inclined to startle at the unexpected. So we train them over many years to overcome their natural instincts and handle extreme conditions. Desensitizing them to the sounds of the Strigis is just one technique we use in their schooling. And yours, I might add. You will be hearing it a lot over the years too. Over the coming months you will be instructed in many areas of horsemanship—training, riding, caring for a Lighthorse, and the strategies for fighting on a Lighthorse—undesirable but unfortunately necessary skills. But you'll start that education next week— for now we need to introduce you to the horses. Please follow me."

They followed the Master down the very long hall of stables until finally the building opened out to a number of fenced paddocks, thick with green grass. There was fencing extending off into the distance—too far to see, and the dotted forms of animals in the distance—Lighthorses, Eyre supposed. The animals were spaced all over the gently rolling pasture, heads down as they ate the lush grass.

The Kikkuli Master used the whistle around his neck to blast a high-pitched note. The horses in the distance instantly looked up, and from all over the huge paddock a muffled thudding arose as every horse charged towards them. From way in the distance, from every corner, the scattered group of horses clumped together and merged as a fierce, thundering herd. They swept past the gobsmacked students, galloped down the hallway of the stables and stopped in a swirl of dust in the arena surrounded by sandstone walls. Whinnying and snorting filled the air, and the sound of hooves pawing the dust. It was a show of strength and wildness that made Eyre's heart sing.

"They are as excited to meet their partners as you are," the Master explained. "The bond between horse and Lightworker is a force that cannot be broken." The students walked towards the arena and had almost made it out to join the horses when Eyre heard someone speaking behind her in a very annoyed voice.

"Didn't wait for me, did they, dratted nags." She craned her neck, looking between the crowd of students, trying to work out who had spoken, but it wasn't obvious. She got a few curious looks from the people following her, so she stopped looking around and walked out into the arena where the magnificent creatures waited.

The last student had just walked into the arena when another horse came wandering out from behind them. Everyone's eyes were on the shaggy, old brown horse as it clumped lethargically into the arena. It had a strange black patch around his right eye that made it look as if he had been punched in the face and was bruised. Wyatt Rankins was standing near the end of the stables as the horse walked by and he snickered.

"There's yours, Ben!" Suddenly he was sailing through the air as the horse's rear hoof connected with his stomach. Wyatt landed with a strangled gasp at Ben's feet.

"Nope. Don't want any of you," the horse said as it wandered up to the herd.

Eyre laughed and nudged Beatrice. "Well said!"

Beatrice looked at her strangely. "Eh? I didn't say anything."

"No, I meant the horse," Eyre explained. Beatrice looked at Eyre, then sideways at Abby, then snuck closer to Eyre.

"Horses don't talk," she whispered as if revealing a secret, and then erupted in in laughter. "*What* are you talking about, Eyre?"

Abby was laughing also. "No, Beatrice, she said the horse was well bred. And I'd have to agree - any horse that can kick Wyatt Rankins across the arena has definitely been well trained I think!"

Eyre dropped the subject. The others obviously hadn't heard the horse, and she wasn't about to debate the issue. The Kikkuli Master raised his voice over the hubbub.

"Walk among the horses and feel the connection. Get to know them. You will know you've been chosen by your Lighthorse when he or she puts their nose in your hand. Please walk with them down to the pasture once you have been chosen."

Eyre loved walking with the beautiful creatures, their smooth and glossy coats, their defined muscles and proud necks. She stroked quite a few of them, admiring the different colours of their coats and their flowing manes. Selection was happening fairly quickly, and quite a few people were already walking down the alley to the paddocks. But Eyre found it quite distracting to hear a voice constantly whining on throughout the whole process.

"Dumb hacks, stupid children," the sour voice complained. "It's hot in here and I want to go back to the paddock." This time Eyre realised it was the scruffy brown horse with the dirty grey mane, standing in the corner muttering away to himself with his back turned to everyone. She also realised that she was the only one who could hear the old horse, so this time she didn't mention it to anyone.

"Dusty hot place. WHAT am I doing here with these losers?" the horse carried on, and Eyre wondered also. They should have left the poor old fella out in the paddock rather than bring him in here. She carried on walking around as more of the students were chosen by their Lighthorses. Beatrice walked out with a beautiful Palomino horse, and Carly had a huge brown Clydesdale. Eyre saw an Appaloosa put its nose in Abby's hand and the joyous smile that crossed Abby's face when she realised she'd been chosen. As the numbers were dwindling, Eyre was starting to get the same feeling she'd had at the crystal grotto—the stirring of panic that she was going to miss out. But it was worse here, because she couldn't do anything about it-- all she could do was wait—a horse would have to choose her. Jax walked by with a chestnut thoroughbred, the fire-red of its coat shining golden in the light. Despite her disappointment at not having a horse yet, Eyre couldn't help watching him until he was out of sight.

"Blasted Selection Process," grumbled the horse. "I want my dinner and my stall." How appropriate that he has a black eye, Eyre thought, maybe he *has* been punched, with an attitude like that.

Someone moved beside Eyre and stroked the grey horse she was standing next to. She looked up to see the Kikkuli Master looking at her with an understanding smile.

"It's a process that can be a bit hard for the last few people," he said. "But the horses know who is right for them." With a pang, Eyre watched as the grey horse put its nose in Georgia Mahoney's hand. And then, the worst thing of all—Ben Perrill walked past with a big bay horse.

"The poor thing doesn't know what it's in for," she thought sourly, but then panicked as she looked around. Only two horses left and two students. Robeson Paul and Eyre looked at each other and then at the old brown horse with the black eye patch.

"I don't mind, I'll take him," Robeson said, but then the other horse, a chestnut with white socks, wandered up and put his nose in Robeson's hand. With an apologetic look at Eyre, Robeson headed down through the stables. The old horse looked at Eyre with a bad-tempered look in its eye.

"Great. I get the ridiculous looking human with strange hair," he said.

"I do *not* have strange hair," Eyre said, annoyed. The horse rolled its eyes.

"Yes you do, and I don't like you." Eyre was suddenly speechless. Now what?

The Master walked over.

"Ischyros," he admonished. "Choose Eyre. She's the only one left and she needs a mount. You've missed out for so many years, aren't you happy you have a human now?"

"No," Ischyros said, and promptly deposited a pile of steaming processed hay onto the arena. Eyre was horrified.

"Ischyros!" The Master's voice was steely, and the tatty brown horse finally moved towards Eyre, every step conveying its disdain. He put his nose into Eyre's hand and *nipped* her!

"OW!" she shouted. "What a horrible creature you are!"

"So are you," the horse answered, and stalked off away from her down the hallway to the paddock. Eyre looked at the Master.

"Do I have to have that horse?" she asked. "Can't I get another one? He obviously hasn't chosen me—isn't that against the rules or something?" The Master shrugged regretfully.

"For the duration of your school years, unfortunately you and Ischyros will be together. It is possible to get another horse once you leave and," he looked at the receding form of Ischyros, "you may choose to do that. But for now, unfortunately, you two are stuck with each other."

Eyre trudged down the alleyway and out to the paddock where the students were grooming and talking to their new mounts. She could see that Ischyros was halfway across the paddock and heading for a boundary probably somewhere in the United States. Eyre felt very disappointed— she'd been looking forward to getting a horse so much. It didn't help when Ben Perrill turned his malicious eyes towards her.

"Looks like your horse is a good judge of character," he chortled. "Can't wait to get away from you, Airhead!" Eyre couldn't help herself. With a flick of light energy, Ben Perrill had suddenly face-planted into the rear end of his horse. Eyre stomped past, heading for the far boundary, in the opposite direction to Ischyros.

CHAPTER FOURTEEN

THE WEEKEND PASSED QUICKLY in a haze of swimming, catching up with people and getting settled into the new rooms. There was so much to look at on campus, and so much to process about the previous week's activities. Although her Lighthorse had proven to be a dismal failure, Eyre loved her staff passionately, and kept picking it up and looking at it. Beatrice and Abby felt the same way, and their staffs were secured carefully in specially crafted holders that were attached inside a designated arms locker that was part of their cupboard.

Monday morning arrived and there was a flurry of activity as they got dressed and gathered their gear together before heading to meditation. A Tyros graduate student called Jason led them inside to a magnificent crystal hall similar to the one Eyre had experienced at the TEPs—towering shards of crystal and intricate mosaics created from coloured jewels and gold inlay. In the centre was a sparkling water feature that appeared to rise and fall without mechanics and Eyre knew from last year that it was a form of electromagnetic energy that made the water magically hang in the air like that. The hall was glowing and peaceful and—unlike her attitude last year —Eyre was glad to sit and use the time to focus her mind and energy.

The next lesson they were to undertake was Ferito, and Eyre was surprised to see Terrigal Furnace walk to the front of the Training Shed. Terrigal was Rufa, and last year he had been a graduate student who tutored them in fulminology. Eyre thought he should have graduated last year. His first words explained it.

"Hello to all of you, some of whom will know me already. I'm Terrigal Furnace—I was a graduate student at the Academy last year, and this year I have been accepted as a student teacher. I will be taking you for Ferito every morning, and also during the week for other defence skill training such as lightning skills and pounding. I have to tell you that I am passionate about defence skills and I plan to train you hard this year. Sergeant Tottingham will have explained to many of you last year that attack and defence in Ferito—Aditus and Tego—are really *both* about defence. The goal of these skills is to learn and become proficient in methods to defend oneself and overcome an enemy. And if you are successful at that, you will become a valuable contributor to the defence of the Overworld. Repetition is the key to becoming good at defence. It is a survival skill that is based on training your mind and your body to react without thinking.

"So let's get started. Find a spot. We are going to run through your Basic Clasis first, then Single, and finally Two." Eyre found a place near the rear door so some air would flow through and keep her cool—she knew she was going to sweat. She felt a bit unsure starting off, but because she, Beatrice and Abby had already done some practise on their Clasis, she was able to handle the moves relatively well. As Terrigal walked around, correcting students' techniques and making general comments, she concentrated on trying to make her moves smoother as she changed from one position to the next in the Basic Clasis.

After twenty minutes Terrigal held up a wooden stick from a pile at the front of the hall.

"The Palum for Single and Two are up here. Come and get the one for Single and practise that Clasis for the next twenty minutes. Put your hand up if you need help."

Eyre got the long wooden Palum that was the substitute for the Mnae—the strong broadsword that students would be allocated in fourth year once they had mastered the Clasis. She went through the moves continuously, working through the twenty positions. It was hard to remember them all, and hard for her body to do what her mind was telling her. And the wooden Palum—which weighed a lot less than a Mnae—made her arm ache as her muscles strained to keep the stick steady in the position it should be. She was sweating with the effort, but she focused and every time she made a mistake, she just did it again. She had learned at the TEPs that nothing came easily, and she knew it was going to take time and practise to get good at this. And she wanted to get good.

As she ran through the Clasis yet again, she became aware that Terrigal was looking over at her. He walked over to her and watched her run through some movements.

"You were here at the TEPs, weren't you? 88?" Eyre nodded but didn't reply as she continued through the moves.

"Your attitude has improved, that's good." He moved away to look at other students and Eyre supposed that at least it had been a positive comment, although he hadn't mentioned her technique at all. No doubt he was remembering her rather disastrous attempts at lightning skills last year —she hadn't been the most enthusiastic student. It was a bit woeful to realise that was the reason he'd remembered her. More determined than ever, she took two shorter Palum from the pile at the front—the ones that substituted for the crystal Antaraks—and started her moves for Two. It might take her all year, but she was resolved to be remembered for more than being a pain in the butt.

The hour passed quickly and she walked with Beatrice, Nick and Abby to Lecture Theatre 1A for their first History of Light lecture, a core subject for all students. The hall was already crowded as they took a seat and waited for their lecturer to arrive.

When he did appear there was an almost psychic groan from the auditorium. No one would be game enough to actually mutter a sound, but it was a shock to see Professor Vela walking in. I suppose I shouldn't be surprised, Eyre thought—he *had* presented the topic at the TEPs. But he was the head of the Runes and Symbols Department, and she didn't realise this was also his subject. How depressing.

Beatrice and Abby shot her a look that said it all, and Nick put his head in his hands. Poor guy—his hall supervisor as well! But you had to admit that Vela was smart, and judging by his talk last year, passionate about the subject, so Eyre decided she should try to listen and make the most of it. Even though, given his attitude towards her, he would probably fail her for everything, no matter how well she did.

Professor Vela turned to the blackboard and words began to appear in light. *History of Light, HOL.* It was an echo of the lecture he had given last year and already Eyre felt like she wanted to put her head on the desk and snore.

The Professor started with the history of Lightworkers and led into the Tunguska event on June 30, 1908—the event that had destroyed the Aura around the world and which Lightworkers called the Proditio, or the Betrayal. Although it was one of the most—or *the* most—significant events in Lightworker history, Eyre's eyes were starting to droop. She'd never been very keen on great chunks of information being presented in class, and this type of information dump was probably the worst she could endure. But then a buzzing from the back of the auditorium drew her attention and as she craned her neck, she could see a piece of paper being passed along the row. Something was going on, and as Ben Perrill caught her eye with a sneer, she knew that somehow it must involve her.

The growing ruckus finally drew Professor Vela's cold eyes to the students.

"*What* is going on up there? You! What is that in your hand? Bring it down here!"

The offending student, mortified at being the one caught with the paper in his hand descended the steps like he was heading to execution. If only he'd passed that paper more quickly! Professor Vela waited on the podium with an outstretched hand, and the student handed over the paper—which Eyre now could see was a piece of newspaper—to him.

"Go back to your place," Professor Vela said in an acid tone as briefly looked at the piece of paper then back up at the student. The student practically scampered off the stage. He got to live another day!

"Who is the instigator of this?" the Professor said, scanning the back row. Unsurprisingly, after a hesitation, Ben Perrill stood up.

"I am, sir. We're in History of Light and that article is an item of history that affects Lightworkers."

"How could *this* possibly affect Lightworkers?" Professor Vela said, holding the newspaper cutting up. "It looks to me like a story on a sports event." Eyre's heart clenched as she looked at photo on the front of the newspaper. She recognized it instantly—there she was on the front page, holding a trophy with the sports mistress from one of her previous schools, Eaton High. Eyre had somehow managed to throw a shotput that day—not three metres like she normally did, but the whole length of the sports field. A particularly mean girl had sparked her temper—and that was *it*. The poor shotput was the recipient of all her anger and it went a long, long way. Eyre's family had moved the next day—apparently for yet another job her parents had been called to, so she never went back to that school, to her immense sadness at the time. She hadn't understood about Lightworkers, or Viq, or light energy then, so she hadn't realised why she managed to throw the shotput so far. But she did now, and she also realised that her parents had obviously decided to get away from the attention her impossible throw would cause. She understood all this now, but not why Ben Perrill would choose to bring it to everyone's attention in such a dramatic manner. If anything, it only made her look good, in a strange way, with that incredible throw.

Confused, she waited for Ben Perrill to reply.

"Lightworkers are not supposed to use their Light powers in the Entis world. Eyre used Light force to throw that shotput and it was never reported." A low murmuring came from the gathered group of students and many eyes turned towards Eyre. As well as the apparent transgression of using Light energy, there was the fact that Lightworkers weren't supposed to have any Viq until they had elevated, and Eyre had demonstrated some inexplicable skills before she elevated that could only be attributed to Viq. So undoubtedly some of the students were talking about that too. Some who didn't know her would be asking who she was. And some who didn't know Ben Perrill were craning to look at him, amazed that a student would be so bold. Professor Vela, who hated interruptions of any sort, was turning a violent shade of purple, so incensed at the disruption that he was unable to speak. He opened his mouth, but Ben Perrill got in before him, looking at Eyre venomously.

"It wasn't reported, but my father told me the Gothak tracked your family down because of that newspaper report, Airhead, showing truly what an airhead you are. They found you even though your parents tried to hide again. *You* caused the death of your parents, just because you wanted to show off."

The voices in the auditorium rose even louder, but Eyre's ears were ringing with a muffled white noise. Beatrice's arms were around her, but she couldn't move or speak. Dimly she heard Professor Vela shouting in rage for Ben to sit down, and for everyone to BE SILENT! Finally the auditorium was indeed silent, all the students sitting uncomfortably, eyes shooting over at Eyre. Ben sat down, having accomplished what he wanted. It seemed he was a genius at creating an uproar.

Professor Vela crumpled the paper into a ball and stalked across the stage, throwing it into a rubbish bin.

"Perrill, you are on cafeteria duty for a week. It seems you have a lot to learn about courtesy in lectures. As for that article, it is hardly worthy of my time or any Lightworker's time. And certainly not worthy of a report of any kind. I am not stupid, Ben, and I won't be used like this for one of your vindictive schemes. Any behaviour like this again and you will be banned from my class, which of course will result in a failure for the year and you'll be out of the Academy, no matter who your father is." Ben Perrill beamed. He didn't care about any of that. He was just brilliantly happy at having delivered such a devastating sucker punch to Eyre.

Professor Vela, still huffing, turned back to the blackboard and began to write a series of names on the board: St Illuminado, Sir Lonegan Burnish, and then a long list of people that Eyre hadn't heard of. Beginning with a dateline of major events in Lightworking history, Professor Vela set out to bore the class into a coma. But Eyre heard none of it. She felt like she'd been beaten around the head with a cricket bat, the pain was so intense. It had taken many months for her to find an equilibrium after her parents died; the trauma of their deaths and subsequently finding out about the Lightworking world had been a terrible shock that had been painful and difficult to deal with. But she had managed to come to terms with it, and was living with the reality of her parents not being here any more.

But now… to find out that they were dead because of *her*? That *she'd* drawn the Gothak to her home? It was more than she could bear. She felt like she couldn't breathe, the shock was so great. She couldn't hear anything; she just sat like a stone as the Professor droned on and on. When the lecture finally finished she jumped out of her chair and ran out of the building, heading for the trees. Her friends called after her, but she ran fast, wanting only to get away from there.

Eventually she stopped when she was sure no one would follow. Last year she had gone AWOL into the bush for hours and had nearly been killed. She wasn't that stupid now, but she did need to be alone. She felt physically sick and her head was ringing as thoughts clanged around inside. All this time she'd been blaming her parents for their secrecy, and hating the fact that they were dead. And yet, it was *her* lack of secrecy that had brought the terrible situation on her family. Clearly, they had made the right call—she couldn't be trusted with the information, and it had been *her* who had killed them! Destroyed their family. And then had the temerity to whinge about it for months. What an idiot. Ben Perrill was right. She was an airhead, naïve and stupid, and she would pay for it for the rest of her life.

She sat behind a large sandstone boulder for hours. The bush made her feel safe and hidden; she couldn't bear to face anyone just yet. The whole first-year student body now knew of her shame, of her stupidity and what she'd done. She knew she was missing lectures, but she didn't care, no matter what the consequences. There was no way she could go back there right now. Even the thought of standing up seemed impossible so she sat on the sandy ground in the shade of the boulder, a large lump of blackness in her stomach as the sun rose above and then started its journey down the other side. She brooded with her back against the rock until finally the healing qualities of the natural surroundings started to break through her sadness and self-disgust. The scent of the eucalyptus leaves was soothing, and the calls of the magpies made her feel less alone, and the breeze blowing through the bush was gentle and peaceful. As the hours passed, slowly the dark pall began to lift.

She had just decided that she had better head back—the last thing she needed was a repeat of the drama of last year when she had been attacked by the Saevus—when she heard footsteps approaching, so quietly she barely registered someone was nearby. She slid further into the shadow of the boulder and kept silent. She wasn't sure who would be out here, but they probably shouldn't be here either.

Someone walked into view about ten metres away, checking behind him as he went and after a moment Eyre felt relief. Warrigal! He'd told her he liked to walk through the bush—he called it his country—and he was obviously out doing that, needing some peace of his own. She was about to call out to him when something strange started to happen. As she watched in shock, Warrigal's body shape began to morph and change, his legs shortened and he fell to his hands and knees, writhing in pain as his muscles clenched and turned. Eyre watched in astonishment, her mouth hanging open as within a few minutes Warrigal was gone and a dingo stood in his place. A large, healthy animal, it sniffed the air and then bounded off into the bush.

Eyre finally expelled the air she had been holding in her lungs and leapt to her feet. The shock of seeing Warrigal's transformation had suddenly restored all her energy—how amazing was he? That was incredible! She looked around but he was gone, so she picked up her bag and brushed herself off. It was time to go back and face the drama. Strangely, her time in the bush had somehow restored her equilibrium. It was her fault her parents were dead. That was indisputable, and she was going to have to live with that knowledge for the rest of her life. But during the course of the afternoon, she'd had time to think about the past. It was evident that her temper was a trigger for her strange non-Viq power, and it made sense now why her mother had taken her to so many self-control and anger management classes over the years—obviously Eyre had shown signs of it before. But her parents had chosen to keep the real reason for the classes from her—and maybe if she'd known about the Lightworking world, she would have been a bit more careful and restrained. Whatever the case, it couldn't be changed now, and she had to just get on and live with it. There was no point wondering about what might have happened—it was way too late now.

She headed back along the track as the shadows lengthened across the ground. Although she'd been well out of sight, she hadn't actually ventured far into the bush—she'd well and truly learned her lesson last year. So it didn't take long until she was back on campus and heading for the dorm room. In a way, Warrigal had done her a favour—the distraction of his amazing transformation was keeping thoughts of Ben Perrill's revelation at bay. But she wasn't going to go to any more classes today, or dinner for that matter. She thought she might go and play with the lighting system in her room for a while.

But when she got there, Abby, Nick and Beatrice were waiting for her. Relief crossed their faces as she entered the room and Beatrice enveloped her in a hug.

"That pig Ben Perrill, he is a *monster!*" she cried. Abby nodded seriously.

"We're going to feed him to the Zyx."

"How about we give him to Ischyros?" Nick said. "That would be worst of all!" At his comment they all dissolved into laughter and sat on the beds.

"We thought you'd done an overnight trek into the Blue Mountains again," Beatrice said. "We were getting ready to battle a Saevus." Eyre noticed their staffs were lined up against the wall and felt overwhelmed as she realised Beatrice was actually serious about that.

"We were just coming to look for you," Abby added. "It was starting to get a bit late."

"We thought you'd be okay, but god Eyre, what would we do without you?" Nick said. "We're a team! Don't worry about that hyena Perrill, he's just trying to get to you. Anyone with any sense would understand it wasn't your fault about your parents."

"You didn't know about Lightworking, and anyway, you shouldn't have been able to do it, even if you did know! So it's definitely not your fault." Abby added in a convoluted sentence. Eyre looked at them and felt better than she had all day. Somehow, despite the awful few months she had endured, she had ended up with the most wonderful friends.

"I just needed some time alone, I'm sorry to run off—again," she said slowly. "I promise I won't make a habit of it. It was just such a shock. It helped to get away for a bit, I didn't want to face all those people." She didn't mention about seeing Warrigal out there, or what had happened. For some reason, she felt that was a violation of his privacy in some way. Beatrice nodded.

"Well, I've been thinking, we should have a code word for each other— when we need to meet in secret for something really important. Then we go to a place we know about but no one else does. Only for emergencies, but then we don't have to explain. Just do it."

Nick nodded. "Great idea! It needs to be nearby but hidden."

Eyre looked at them. "Well, my spot was as good as any—I'll show you where it is."

Beatrice concentrated. "Hmm... what to call ourselves? An acronym maybe from our names? ENAB? Nope. BEAN, haha, not particularly auspicious. BANE! That's it! Perfect. Because we're going to be the bane of Ben Perrill's existence from now on—any way we can bring him down."

Abby laughed and clapped her hands. "So clever Beatrice! BANE! I love it. And it's secret. Our special group—we'll always be here for each other, no matter what."

They all high-fived, sealing the pact. Then Beatrice looked solemn.

"I'm there for you always, Eyre," she said. "But I'm not going to skip a meal for you. Come on, let's go. You can face the paparazzi with us at your side!"

CHAPTER FIFTEEN

AS IT TURNED OUT, it hadn't mattered that Eyre had missed classes the previous day. She got the notes from Beatrice for Lord Clarembout's lecture on fulminology, and for Madame Overmantle's class on cognitive energies, both of which were required courses for first-year students. Nick had given her lecture notes for alchemy, an elective that he had in common with Eyre that had been held in 1B after lunch. The classes were so large, no staff had even realised she had been missing for the rest of the day. There had also been a visit to the stables, one of the daily requirements of the weekly schedule, but Eyre was quite happy to have missed that. She was sure, Ischyros would have felt the same way. So there were no repercussions from her absence the previous afternoon. Many of the students had looked at her curiously, but in actual fact, whether or not she had used Lightworking energy a year ago was of little gossip value to them. Ben's main aim had been to hurt Eyre publicly by making her realise it was her fault the Gothak had tracked her family down; her fault her parents were dead. He'd achieved that, but Eyre wasn't going to give him the satisfaction of realising how devastated she was by the knowledge. So she'd ignored him in the cafeteria when she'd passed by him, and felt a twinge of satisfaction when she saw the disappointment in his face at her lack of reaction. She was learning. Self-control was a powerful force.

After meditation and Ferito, Eyre headed with her friends to 1A amongst a buzz of excitement. Today the guest lecturer from Terra was being introduced to the students. He or she would be here for the year, instructing them about Terra and helping them to learn the skills they would need to pass their TACI exam at the end of the year. The race of beings from Terra was called the Nemoris and like all the other students, Eyre was really curious about them.

Sergeant Tottingham stood at the front of the auditorium and waited as students took their places. Then she moved to the podium and touched the crystal, causing an image of a very green, hilly place to stream up onto the screen.

"Today you will meet our guest lecturer of the Nemoris, Kofi E Vygn." She wrote the name of the Nemoris on the blackboard. "You will call him 'sir' or 'E Kofi', as the surname of the Nemoris is, unlike English, the first word of the name. E is a word that shows he is male in Nemoris, and when addressing him you say "E Kofi", which is a respectful way of saying "Mr Kofi". You will learn more about the language if you specialize in that area, but if Kofi was female, you would refer to her as O Kofi. In any case, that is a discussion for another class. So 'Sir' or 'E Kofi' is what you need to remember today. Okay..." The Sergeant was about to continue when a high, breezy voice could be heard offstage.

"This way, this way..." A second later, a force of nature burst onto the stage, followed by a creature Eyre could only assume was E Kofi. But her eyes didn't know who to look at first: the large woman at the front, or the unusual Nemoris.

"Thank you Sergeant, you may go now," the woman twinkled, dismissing the Sergeant with a wave of her bright pink nails. The Sergeant hovered for a moment, looking like she'd swallowed a puffer fish, but as the buxom, blonde-haired woman held her hand towards the door, the Sergeant uncharacteristically gave in. Fascinated, Eyre watched as the normally strong-minded Sergeant yielded to a woman who looked like the fairy floss cart at a fair. Completely dressed in pink, tall and voluptuous with a creamy complexion and large cornflower blue eyes, the woman's aura completely filled the auditorium with—well, the only image Eyre could come up with was pink swirls and flowers. Even the strange creature who had arrived with her seemed overawed by the woman's presence, as he hung way back by the blackboard when she moved to the podium, advancing in a regal way as if she was anticipating applause.

"Good morning students," she said and looked around brightly. "I am Jemima Periwinkle, the new Ambassador for Alterworld Relations, and I will also be teaching Lightworking Genealogy at the Academy. It is very nice to meet you all, and I'm sure I'll get to know you all—and all of your ancestors..." She tittered but when no one laughed with her—most of them were just trying to keep up with the whirlwind of her dialogue—she swept on, unfazed, "... over the coming years. May I introduce to you Kofi E Vygn, and I see the Sergeant has already very kindly written his name on the board. I will leave you now and I know you will enjoy this class."

Finally the attention was off the spectacular woman as she swept out of the room and the Nemoris quietly stepped forward. He was the same size as a human man, but covered in shiny scales of varying green hues. His feet were long, with talons, and when he lifted his hand in a greeting, Eyre could see it had talons also. He had large black eyes that took up a third of his face, and a very small mouth. When he spoke Eyre could see that his teeth were small and pointed. His voice was dry and raspy, as if he desperately needed a drink of water and he had a strange inflection to his way of speaking, making it obvious that English was not his native language.

"Greetings students," he said. "I am pleased to make your acquaintance, and I am looking forward to spending the year with you. My time at your school will be a learning experience for me also—I have not spent a lot of time in Entis and I will be taking my experiences back with me to share with my people. Your Sergeant has asked me to express to you her wishes that these experiences are positive ones."

The students laughed and E Kofi's eyes twinkled. "We have a lot to learn together, but the most important thing I will be teaching you is the prohemium for travelling to Terra. If you do not learn that, you will be unable to pursue your TACI test at the end of the year. So we will be spending a lot of time on that."

Advika Bhaduri put her hand up.

"Excuse me, Sir, but could you tell me what a prohemium is? I haven't heard of that before."

Eyre was glad Advika had asked the question—she had no idea what a prohemium was either.

E Kofi walked to the front of the stage. "Your name?" he asked.

"Advika, sir."

"Well, Advika, I commend you on your question. Admitting you don't know something is admirable. And asking the right questions is a gift. This is good.

"So what is a prohemium? It is the way that we transit between all worlds in the Overworld. To open a Seam, you must perform a movement known as a prohemium, and there is a different one for moving back and forwards between each of the Alterworlds and Entis. I will be teaching you the Terra prohemium and I must prepare you for the fact that it is not easy to perform a prohemium. It is going to take you many months to master the technique. Observe."

E Kofi put his hands up and wove them together and outwards again, then made a sudden downwards movement. In front of him on the stage, a bright light that Eyre recognized as the Seam appeared. It was about three metres high and one centimetre wide, a thin strip of blinding white light. E Kofi slipped into the light and disappeared, then the light snuffed out. A few seconds later the light appeared again onstage and E Kofi walked out from behind it. With a movement of his hands, the light was extinguished.

"I have just been home and back," he said. "My wife would like me to fix the fences."

The students erupted into laughter and E Kofi smiled. "I have two children at home as well. We have families as you do, and a very similar community arrangement to Entis."

He walked to the board and started to write a list, explaining as he wrote.

"I can't tell you everything about Terra this year, but here are the areas we will need to learn about in order for you to pass your TACI test. One, as we have just discussed—the prohemium. Two, what my beautiful world Terra looks like. Three, dangers and safety issues of the area, and four, locating the gazae from Terra. The gazae—or for those of you who haven't heard the term before—treasure—from Terra are pollen grains from the rare Lux plant. The lux orbs float when released, and they are used by Lightworkers for creating light—they are a very treasured item in your world."

Eyre, Beatrice, Abby and Nick looked at each other. So that's where the luxes came from. Eyre hadn't really thought about it—when Beatrice had given her the lux at the cave, to Eyre it was just another wonder of the Lightworking world she was trying to get used to. E Kofi touched the crystal on stage and the image of a brightly-coloured dragonfly appeared, mostly blue, but with arrow-shaped flashes of pink streaking its carapace. The dragonfly, which was called a Zhuzhu Flutter, had six transparent green wings and four fluffy antennae rising from its head, with bulbous iridescent eyes. It was being ridden by a muscular Nemoris and a large bundle of something wrapped tightly hung below the dragonfly, swinging out backwards as they flew through the sky. E Kofi smiled.

"That is an image of my brother, who is conveying food to our community. We use the Zhuzhu Flutter for transport—we ride them through the sky to get from one place to another as the place we live is densely forested with steep mountains. It is very hard to walk through. And Zhuzhus are very useful for carrying large things we are unable to move ourselves. They are intelligent creatures, and they are an important part of our society."

E Kofi touched the crystal and a video started to play on the screen. It showed thick foliage and dark green trees in an extremely mountainous area. It was hard to make out individual plants, but the country was unfamiliar and shadowed by deep crevasses in the hills. Then the screen switched to a stretching red desert with strangely-shaped rocks scattered across it. A tall bird-like creature strode across the terrain, uttering sporadic sharp cries. Then the bird dashed off-screen as out of nowhere, sticks flew violently through the air. Beatrice nudged Eyre as they watched the turbulent display —sticks and rocks flying in all directions.

"You must have been there," she whispered as Eyre gave a slightly awkward grin.

The whirlwind of rocks and sticks stopped suddenly and fell to the ground, and the screen changed to another picture. This one was of a clear blue grotto where huge brilliantly coloured flowers of all shapes and sizes rose from the water, their petals large enough for a man to stand on. From time to time a red flower that looked like a giant chrysanthemum released orbs that floated upwards gently. Small birds flittered around as a pale blue mist wove its way through the flowers.

"These are the Lux plants," E Kofi explained. "Impossible to get to unless you are on a Zhuzhu."

For fifteen minutes E Kofi displayed an array of photos from Terra—all unique and fascinating. There were many of its people and also of the structures they inhabited—thatch-like houses on very tall stilts to bring them to the very top of the forest canopy. He didn't show them any images of the dangers he'd mentioned—possibly saving those for another day. It was very evident that he loved his world passionately; pride was in his voice as he spoke.

"I am looking forward to taking you on your journey to Terra. I know you will enjoy it greatly. But first we must prepare! Let us start with the movements of the prohemium. Observe."

Slowly E Kofi ran through the sequence of hand gestures that would create the Seam to Terra. They were simple and yet mystifying—they looked straightforward, but there was obviously some unnoticeable technique that made the difference between success and failure, because despite practising carefully for half an hour, not one student had managed to generate anything like a beam of light. E Kofi was encouraging.

"Do not expect to successfully perform the prohemium yet—in fact, it will take you several weeks to even get the sequence smooth enough to generate the necessary energy. Once the sequence of hand gestures is flawless, then you must concentrate on perfecting the hand gestures themselves. Nothing will happen until the hands have created the exact positions to open the Seam. You must practise on your own; we do not have enough time in our allocated lectures for you to master the prohemium. I have here something for all of you to wear."

He produced a box from behind the podium and started to pass around containers holding objects that sparkled in a rainbow of colours. When the container reached Eyre she saw that it was a metal rectangular clip inlaid with crystals of many different colours. She looked at it curiously as E Kofi explained.

"You clip this on your belt permanently from now on. Should you have success with your prohemium and the Seam opens, that clip is a locator for us to find you, if you end up somewhere you shouldn't be. You don't always end up in the place you were expecting! If you are wearing the clip, we can bring you back immediately. Saves you a long walk," he added, and the students laughed. E Kofi bowed and picked up the box.

"Our time is up, students. I shall leave you with a blessing from Terra: *Live as one with the earth*. I will see you next week."

CHAPTER SIXTEEN

EYRE PACKED UP HER gear and joined Beatrice, Nick and Abby as they headed to their next class: Lighthorsemanship. It was typically held before lunch so that the horses' bellies weren't too full; after the hour of training, the horses were put out to pasture for the rest of the day and then returned to their stalls at night.

Eyre walked with her friends towards the stables feeling a decided lack of enthusiasm. Her friends knew where their horses were, as they'd been to the stables yesterday. But she had no idea where Ischyros was. Probably still walking, after their last encounter, she thought gloomily. She wasn't feeling good about this class, and the thought of dealing with that scruffy, cranky creature for the next four years was definitely uninspiring. She watched wistfully as other students greeted their horses, and the joyful interaction between them. Whinnies from waiting horses filled the air, and then the clatter of hooves as students brought the animals out from the stalls and down the alleyway into the training arena. Still walking down the long alley, Eyre looked left and right, trying to find Ischyros. The Kikkuli Master was waiting for her as she reached the end. Ischyros wasn't anywhere in the stalls and Eyre looked at him, a question on her face.

"He's over there," the Master said, "he doesn't get on well with the other horses and he has his own stall."

"Great," thought Eyre grumpily as she trudged towards a small barn at the back of the stable complex. "An antisocial horse. Why didn't he pick Ben Perrill? Would have been a perfect match I would imagine."

Finally she got to the barn and opened the doors. Ischyros was down the end, his back to her. Sighing, she walked up to him, preparing to lead him out to the arena. But before she could speak he had planted both feet squarely in her stomach and kicked her across the stable, where she landed flat on her back. And it hurt! Furious, she jumped to her feet, wiping god-knows-what from the back of her uniform.

"*What* is wrong with you?" she shouted. "We have to get out to the arena and get training!" Ischyros turned his head to her.

"I don't have to do anything," he said, and yawned. That did it! Eyre stomped up to him and grabbed his scruffy grey mane, hauling on him.

"You... are... *coming*!" she yelled, her face bright red. Ischyros turned back to his hay and began munching as if she wasn't there.

"Not today," he mumbled with his mouth full. Eyre stood in utter disbelief, filthy, hurting and furious. But what could she do if he wouldn't co-operate? She spun on her heel and headed for the door.

"Fine by me," she spat at him. "I'm not sure what use you'd be anyway." She slammed the door on her way out and started walking up the alleyway, steam coming out her ears. A few last students were organising their horses and one of them stepped in front of Eyre as she approached. Looking up, she realised it was not by accident he had waited until last. He was waiting for her.

Warrigal stroked his glossy brown horse gently. It was a strongly built animal with a dark mane and it nudged his face with its nose. Eyre felt pensive as she saw the bond they already had.

"Bunu, it means Evening Star. She's an Australian Stock Horse," Warrigal said. "One of the most hardy breeds of all, and known for its brilliance in working cattle. We'll make a good team."

Eyre smiled. She knew they would. Warrigal seemed to have such an understanding of his horse already. There was an awkward silence for a moment as both of them stroked Bunu's shining coat. Finally Eyre spoke first, putting the words to what was on both their minds.

"I saw you, Warrigal, the other day in the bush. I thought it was awesome." Warrigal looked at her, his brown eyes serene.

"I knew you were there once I turned," he said. "I scented you were in the area, but I wasn't sure if you'd seen me."

"What are you? A sort of werewolf?" Warrigal's eyes crinkled and he smiled.

"No, my gift is therianthropy, or 'shape-shifting'—I can become any creature. Some of my people have this ability, and it was passed on to me. I hold a great responsibility for secrecy, and I guess I stuffed that up the other day."

Eyre shook her head. "Not your fault, Warrigal. It was the drama queen hiding behind the rock who blew your cover. But I won't say anything, I promise."

"Thank you, Eyre," Warrigal said, and they started to walk towards the arena. A sudden thought struck Eyre and she looked at Warrigal as realisation dawned. "It was you!" she cried. "Last year with the Saevus! *You* brought the dingoes to save me?"

Warrigal looked at her for a moment and then nodded. "I'd been walking in my country and I heard you." He looked at her apologetically. "You weren't exactly strolling quietly—more like a bulldozer crashing off track, actually." Eyre laughed aloud and he continued. "I scented the Saevus and called to my dingo brothers to help. The Saevus is a threat to them also, so many came to fight. They are a ferocious breed when they protect their own."

Eyre walked on in silence. How lucky she had been. She stroked Warrigal's shining horse thoughtfully. "I owe you my life Warrigal. Your secret is safe with me."

They walked out into the arena where many horses were prancing around, excited at being together and with their person. The Kikkuli Master was in the centre, a long stick with a whip attached in his hand. The horses and students were milling around until he raised his voice.

"Right, we will continue our lessons from yesterday. As I said, we base our teachings on the need to properly warm horses up, to have their muscles ready for training first. Then we use a combination of techniques to help your horse learn to adapt to having a rider on his or her back. We do not break horses. We do not hit horses. This whip is never used to touch the horse; it is a communication tool. We ask them to perform a task for us, and we hope that we have created, over time, a strong enough bond that they will acquiesce to our request. It takes a long time to gain the trust of a Lighthorse, and an even longer time to perfect your teamsmanship with them. They are intelligent creatures with a long history of bonding with Lightworkers. The desire is there: it is your job to nurture and develop that connection.

Not in my case, Eyre thought sourly. I've had a connection all right, right in the solar plexus. She wasn't sure how to develop *that* connection, but as she rubbed her sore midriff, she knew she sure as hell wasn't interested in any attachment, teamsmanship or bonding today. She hovered at the back of the crowd, trying to learn by watching the other students. Lighthorsemanship, it appeared, didn't involve any form of bridle or saddle, stirrups or any of the other riding gear she was familiar with. It was bareback riding, using the mane and legs to guide the horse, and balance to stay on its back. The horses were patient, and the students walked around the arena for the hour, trying to get used to staying on by using the legs.

There were quite a few students doing well at it—Carly for one, and they were the ones who had obviously ridden before. But even so, the lack of a saddle was proving a challenge for all but the most experienced riders, and despite the restraint of the horses, several people landed in the dust as they circled the ring.

"That's fine, that's fine," the Kikkuli Master encouraged. "We all fall off. You're not trying hard enough if you don't fall sometimes. Keep practising. Round you go. Use your knees, use your hands—but gently! The horses will respond to the slightest of touch. You don't need to yank or pull hard."

For a second Eyre felt guilty as she recalled hauling on Ischyros's mane when she tried to get him out of the barn. But then she set her jaw. He had, after all, just kicked her into the never-never, so what did he expect?

After the hour lesson the horses were brushed and washed and given a bucket of water with molasses in it. Then the students let them go and they galloped down the alleyway out into the open pastures. It was a wonderful and joyful sight.

It was a morning of conflicting experiences for Eyre, but perhaps one of the strangest ones was when she turned and saw Ben Perrill with his horse, just before he let it go. Most of the lesson he had been slouched atop his horse as if he wanted to be anywhere but there, trying to look cool, no doubt. But just before he let his magnificent bay go, Ben reached his hand and gently ran it down the middle of his horse's face, and the horse nuzzled Ben's shoulder. Eyre nearly fell over in shock, doubting her eyes for a moment. But then the moment was over and Ben's horse took off to join the thundering herd down the alleyway. Hot and frustrated by the morning, she realised it really bothered her seeing that interchange. Even *Ben Perrill* had a horse that liked him. There must be something seriously wrong with her.

CHAPTER SEVENTEEN

EYRE, BEATRICE, NICK AND Abby sat at a table in the Refectory and soon Rigmar and Zanda joined them, and then after a while, Robeson and Luke Jordan appeared also. The air was abuzz as they all talked about the lecture with E Kofi and the Lighthorse training—it had been a busy morning. Eyre ate silently, feeling a dismal failure. No one mentioned that she alone had not been riding; they were being kind to her and stayed away from any mention of Ischyros, which made it more awkward somehow. She was trying to figure out how to raise the subject when Warrigal turned up with his tray and sat down, shooting a look at Eyre.

"Heard your horse took a vacation today?" Eyre smiled in relief that finally *someone* had mentioned it and opened her mouth to make some sort of excuse. But then she burst out laughing.

"He can't *stand* me! He literally kicked me out of his stable! I think I'm going to have to be a foot soldier—because I don't think I'm ever going to get that horse to do anything."

Everyone laughed and the awkwardness passed as they all talked about riding techniques and the various attributes of their horses. And everyone was intrigued about Terra, discussing the places and the creatures they had seen. Nick was very happy because one of the electives he could take was 'Fireweaving', something he was very interested in: lighting the Mantle was central to the safety of Lightworkers and a very difficult subject. No doubt, Eyre thought a bit sadly, physical safety was something he valued greatly, after his years growing up. But then her musing and their conversation was interrupted as a high voice cut across the noise in the Refectory.

"Well, hello, *Cecil*," the coy voice said, and Eyre looked up to see Jemima Periwinkle flouncing across the room in a voluminous floral dress that outlined every curve. She shoved a chair between Sergeant Tottingham and E Kofi, manoeuvring the chair so it faced Dean Fraser across the table. Eyre choked back a laugh at the look on Sergeant Tottingham's face. The Dean muttered politely, turning red, and half stood in welcome, knocking his glass of water right into the Sergeant's lap. Jemima twittered and sat her voluptuous frame down with a puff of fabric next to the Sergeant. E Kofi half-passed his napkin to the Sergeant but got one of his talons hooked on the tablecloth, dragging it sideways and sending everything on it flying. With speed worthy of any Lightworker, Whittaker Ray scraped his chair back fast, just dodging the airborne china before three of the staff's dinners ended up on the ground with a loud clattering and smashing of crockery. The Sergeant, her face turning as red as ripe cherries, threw her napkin on the table, and stood up.

"By the Light, Jemima, it's always the same!" she said tightly, and stalked out of the room, which by now was completely silent.

All the students looked at each other and the staff fussed around trying to sort the mess out, when thank goodness, a tribe of Jotnar bustled out and began to bring things to order. In a few minutes the dishes and splattered food had been cleaned up and everyone had a meal again. The staff started chatting amongst themselves and the hum of students' conversation filled the room again. But Eyre kept looking at the Sergeant's empty chair. For some reason, she felt sorry for the Sergeant—it was such an uncustomary loss of control.

Zanda was curious too. "Looks like the Sergeant and Ms Periwinkle know each other?" he said with his mouth full, looking over at Jemima, who was talking vivaciously, her cornflower blue eyes directed at Dean Fraser. He looked decidedly uncomfortable, but was rallying to the cause, maintaining the conversation without knocking any plates off the table.

"I must investigate! A task for Zanda!"

Eyre laughed. "You should start a gossip column, Zanda, except I think I'd feature too often in it. My dress sense, for one," she indicated the wide green stain down her back and the table roared with laughter.

"Not a bad idea," Zanda said thoughtfully. "I might just do that."

"Aargh," Beatrice muttered, "you've created a monster!"

"Well, here's my first tidbit, approaching now," Zanda said, his eyes alight with amusement.

Jax walked over, raising his eyebrows at their laughter.

"I normally don't cause that much hilarity," he said. "Although my riding skills might. I think you've got the right idea, Eyre: staying on the ground is not so silly."

So he'd noticed, Eyre thought dismally. But was nice enough to conceal it in a joke.

She opened her mouth to make a light-hearted reply when a strange wailing seared through the air. For the second time that lunchtime, Dean Fraser leapt to his feet, but this was something far more serious, as all the staff had jumped up with him. Whittaker Ray dashed out the door and Professor Vela raced to the front of the room.

"Students!" he shouted above the noise. "You are to return to your rooms *immediately*! And stay there!" As the awful siren filled their ears, students started to get up.

"MOVE!" Professor Vela ordered, his voice betraying an apprehension Eyre had never heard before, and a tone that made the students suddenly move, *fast*. With sudden panic, students raced across the hall and away from the Refectory, as the siren intensified, and the dull sound of thuds and booms could be heard in the distance.

"What is going on?" Beatrice cried as they dashed towards the dormitory wings. "They never mentioned anything about a siren. What does it mean?"

"I don't know," Abby huffed, "but I'm getting to the room as quick as I can!" Nick and the boys separated off at the turn to the boys' dormitory and the girls careered down their hallway, the shriek of the siren deafening in their ears.

Finally they made it to their room and slammed the door. Then they crept to the window fearfully. Because now, not only could they hear sirens and explosions, but there was the spine-chilling sound of screeches and roars, sounds that Eyre knew could only be made by the Strigis. Strigis in the middle of the day? *Outside the school*? What was happening?

Then Sergeant Tottingham's voice boomed through the hall.

"Girls, open your door so you can hear me, but stay in your rooms." As the doors opened slowly, she stood in the middle of the hall and called out to the frightened faces in the doorways.

"We have a breach. The Gothak are on the perimeter of the school, and they have released the Strigis. But do not worry. The Lightworking forces were straight onto it and the powers of Darkness are already being forced back to the Underworld. Runic protections guard this school against attack and they are impenetrable. There is a lot of noise and drama, but the battle is under control. The wards are holding and the Mantle is keeping the Strigis out. The Mimir have safeguarded the boundaries and soon you will be safe to come out again. While it sounds severe, all is well. The Gothak have tried this occasionally in the past but they will not get through. Hold tight while our forces drive them back through the Seam to the black hole where they belong. You are in your rooms as a precaution only, but you must stay there until the sound of the siren ceases. I will be back soon. Shut your doors. Stay inside."

Doors slammed up and down the corridor and Eyre mused that she didn't need to be told twice to stay inside. No one with any sense would venture out into that uproar.

Distantly she could see fires and explosions on the boundary of the school, and swirls of dark forms in the sky that she knew must be the Zyx. Beams of light cut through the haze and smoke of the battle, and a rhythmic stomping and chanting could be heard: the sound of the Mimir in full battle mode. Jags of lightning, no doubt from the Mimir's feet, or the fulminology from Lightworkers, streaked upwards in the distance, and the spine-chilling screams of creatures dying filled the air. Eyre hoped they were the Strigis, and not the Lightworkers. The thud of feet marching echoed off the crystal walls of the school, and the sound of galloping horses, underlined by the deep, melodic chanting and the thump of staffs on the ground. Eyre could see rows of troops outlined in the shadowy haze, and the huge figures of creatures not of this earth rearing up amongst them. But the sounds were diminishing, and the troops far outnumbered the strange shapes that she knew were the Strigis, until eventually, to their great relief, the siren suddenly stopped. There were no more shapes of malevolent creatures to be seen, just lines of troops moving back and forwards along the perimeter, clearing the debris. Fires were still burning but it was obvious that the Gothak had been driven back. It had been frightening though, and Eyre wondered how long they would stay there. Although Sergeant Tottingham had told them not to be concerned, her face had held another message. This was not normal, and she was worried. Eyre turned away from the window.

"Well, looks like the good guys won. What should we do?"

They all looked at each other.

"How about a game of cards?" Beatrice suggested.

CHAPTER EIGHTEEN

THE NEXT MORNING A strange smell hung in the air throughout the campus—a mixture of smoke and sulphur that was slightly nauseating. In the distance the trees at the perimeter of the Mantle were blackened and burnt, and heaped up around them were piles of something—bodies, Eyre supposed. The Sergeant had been in after the turmoil the previous afternoon to announce that classes were cancelled until the following day, and that the Jotnar would bring them supper in their rooms. It had been unsettling and strange, especially as darkness fell with the sight of fires still burning along the perimeter.

But getting back into the usual routine the next morning helped—apart from the distant signs of battle, all was the same on campus. The Mantle had protected the school from any effects of the fighting and the students ate breakfast and went to meditation and Ferito as usual. As Eyre practised her Clasis—with more focus than ever this morning—she couldn't help wondering why the Gothak had attacked the school. Of all places in the world—or Overworld—to choose.

Apparently that was the question on the minds of people far more important than her as well, for as she walked out of the Training Shed with her friends, she noticed the bloated shapes of Zepps circling down to land in front of the Central Administration building. Flashes of light announced that Lightworkers were arriving by teleportation, and even old-fashioned means of transport were being used as cars pulled up to park on the landing pad normally reserved for Zepps. In fact, as Eyre, Beatrice, Abby and Nick watched, a whole stream of people and unrecognizable creatures were filing into the Central Administration building.

"Not exactly discussing the curriculum, are they," Beatrice said, her eyes on the crowd.

Eyre could see some creatures that looked like E Kofi, and there were several Armatura too, which brought back a flood of memories from the TEPs. She must remember not to laugh at them. She hardly felt like laughing though, as the immense number of attendees at whatever meeting was being held showed how serious the attack was being taken. As they walked nearer, Abby exclaimed.

"By St Illuminado! There's your parents, Beatrice, and my dad!"

"Whoa... and Rigmar's dad—he's the Chairman of the Echelon! Something important *must* be going on. This is Inter-World level stuff." Beatrice looked gobsmacked.

Eyre nodded, watching as the familiar coloured robes of President Zircon, head of the Mimir, entered the bronze doors of the Admin building behind Chairman Essendon. Something important indeed. She wished she could be a fly on the wall.

She hadn't realised she had spoken the thought aloud until Abby looked at her thoughtfully.

"Well why not? What's to stop us? No one said we couldn't go in! I want to know what's going on."

Beatrice nodded slowly. "Me too, I'm keen! So how do we do it?"

Eyre looked around. "Well, I don't have my Nemoris costume in the cupboard, so we might have to come up with another idea."

Nick was thinking. "Eyre, Jax told me something about your TEPs, how you masked to hide him and you from the Armatura. Can you do all of us? I can't do it, but if you can, perhaps we could sneak in that way and then hide somewhere."

Eyre was dubious. Under the conditions of the TEPs she had felt her life was under threat, and it had given her an immense energy to create the mask that hid her and Jax. She had managed to mask another time, but that was also when she felt in great danger—in the auditorium when Professor Vela was conducting some underhand business with Ben Perrill, something she still hadn't gotten to the bottom of—yet. But bringing up a mask at command? She hadn't attempted it since the TEPs and it would require an awful amount of energy to mask four people. She screwed her face up.

"Well, I'm happy to give it a try, but I do seem to have rather irregular success at using Light energy. Sometimes it's brilliant, other times it's dismal. There doesn't seem to be a happy medium for me. But I guess the worst that can happen is we're thrown out."

"I'm happy to risk it," Abby said. "Dad won't be too mad."

"Count me in too," Beatrice said.

"Then it's decided. Come on," Nick said, heading for the corridor. "We'll have to hurry or the doors will close."

They walked casually across campus, chatting to one another as if nothing was amiss.

"Ditching classes already," Abby said. "What appalling students we are."

Eyre chuckled. Personally, she was ecstatic at missing History of Light. The thought of enduring that class all year was a woeful one. She watched as two more delegates entered the building.

"Well, here's the plan. Let's hide behind a Zepp until someone else arrives. Then I'll try to get the mask going, and we'll hurry in to the building behind them while the doors are open."

"We're going to need a bit of luck," Beatrice predicted, rolling her eyes.

They wandered along the path in the general direction of the lecture theatres, but when they got near the Central Administration buildings, they ducked quickly from trees to statues to slip against the side of the of the sandstone wall unseen. There was a hubbub of activity at the front doors and Eyre could hear Dean Fraser and Whittaker Ray welcoming everyone and directing them to the boardroom on the first floor. Beatrice lifted her eyebrows and gave a thumbs up. A bit of the luck she'd mentioned had just come their way. Now at least they knew where they were going.

They eased their way around the rear of the Zepps and the cars that had filled the landing pad. No one noticed them—all attention was focused on the important guests that were arriving. A group of strange bald-headed men with blue skin materialised at the entrance of the building and were ushered through by Whittaker Ray. They wore flowing purple robes and did not acknowledge Whittaker Ray, as if they were far too important to greet him.

"Now or never guys. Get close," Eyre whispered, and began to concentrate hard on creating a mask. Her life was not in danger this time, but she had managed the feat twice before and understood the process. And her Viq was undoubtedly stronger than the last two times she had accomplished the mask. So in spite of her misgivings, she was hopeful she might manage it. But despite her efforts, the disappointed faces of her friends showed that nothing was happening so she put her hands to her temples and focused *harder*. But still the mask did not appear; her friends were all still visible. She was about to shrug her shoulders and apologise when she heard the pompous tones of Mandig Vela's voice close by, coming from behind the Zepps. Eyre's heart jumped in fright. Why was *he* here? Someone else must be taking his class today—what a disaster it would be to get caught by him in this compromising position! The extra spurt of adrenaline must have given her Viq a prod, because suddenly the four of them disappeared. Gasping with surprise, she reached for their hands and, huddling close together, they moved awkwardly towards the front of the Admin building, like an uncoordinated eight-legged creature.

"This way, this way, Sir Rayburn," Professor Vela intoned importantly as he helped a regal-looking old man wearing a top hat from Zepp 4. The two of them walked to the bronze doors and Professor Vela swept through, ignoring Dean Fraser and Whittaker Ray as he led the old man to the elevator. The chagrin Dean Fraser and Whittaker Ray felt at Professor Vela's discourtesy must have distracted them, because they didn't notice the surge of energy as four students moved by them under a mask. Eyre was sweating with the force of concentration, clenching her jaw as she struggled to maintain the intense energy.

"Hurry up guys, I'm losing it," she whispered through gritted teeth as they reached the staircase. Fortunately more guests arrived at the front of the building, distracting the Dean and Whittaker Ray, and Eyre and her friends were able to make it to the top of the stairs without being detected. A crowd of people and creatures milled around in front of them, waiting to be ushered into the boardroom, so the invisible four slid by them and up the next set of stairs.

Footsteps clattered at the bottom of the staircase, so Nick pulled open the first door he could and they all piled inside, closing the door softly behind them. It was dark inside, but Eyre could tell by the smell, and the objects that stuck into her, that it was a cleaning cupboard. The handle of a mop stuck uncomfortably in her back and they were cramped together, but they were safely hidden. With a gasp of relief, Eyre let go of the energy and the mask dissolved. She had a massive headache and felt completely drained, but exhilarated at the same time. She'd done it! They were in!

Nick spoke softly. "Let's wait here until everyone has gone in. Then we can try to find a place to listen once the doors are shut."

So they waited amongst the brooms and buckets and cleaning supplies while the sounds of footsteps walked and clattered and thudded on the floor below from the very diverse array of creatures. Muted voices from the various delegates drifted up to them, but Eyre couldn't hear what they were saying. There were an enormous number of participants in this affair, that was for certain. Finally they heard Dean Fraser and Whittaker Ray talking from halfway up the stairs, and they scarcely dared to breathe.

"That's everyone," Dean Fraser said, "except Ranger Chrysanthe, and I'm not altogether sure he will turn up."

"Indeed," Whittaker Ray said. "Well, I will reserve him a seat by me in case he does show. I hope he decides to join us."

There was a shuffle of footsteps heading downstairs, the sound of the boardroom doors closing and then silence outside. Nick leaned his ear against the door. After a moment he looked back and whispered, "I think we're safe. Let's see if we can find a good spot."

Gingerly he eased the door open a wedge to peer out and then stopped, a horrified look on his face. Slumping, he opened the door wide.

"Out you come," Ranger Chrysanthe said, his face inscrutable. Beatrice rolled her eyes. Evidently their luck had run out. Eyre was incredibly disheartened—just when it looked like they may have made it! The Ranger surveyed the crestfallen group before him.

"As always, there are the rule-breakers, the risk-takers, the curious and the independent of thought," he said. "Not necessarily attributes of a good Lightworker. How did you get up here?"

"Er... I masked, sir." Eyre was miserable. She hated disappointing the Ranger as much as anything. The Ranger's eyebrows rose, but he said nothing for a moment. Abby jumped in.

"Yes but it was all of us who made the plan," she said. "We're all responsible."

"Hmm," the Ranger said. "And you are here because...? I'm assuming you're not here to mop the floors."

Beatrice replied, a rueful look on her face. "We just wanted to know what was going on. We were going to eavesdrop," she finished, looking anything but contrite.

The Ranger tapped his fingers together and made a decision. "Well then, you'll need a good place to hear properly. I know just the spot." When they stood rooted in surprise he turned and gestured to them, his purple eyes twinkling. "Hurry up, someone could be along at any moment!"

Needing no further encouragement, the four of them jumped forward, hurrying to keep up with him. Eyre's mind spun with inner glee as she scurried along, still trying to process the fact that they hadn't been tossed out on their rear ends.

The Ranger led them around the corner, walking quietly and quickly. Halfway along the corridor was a door which led, as they saw when he unlocked it, to a small viewing balcony encased with glass.

"It's one-way," he said. "We use it for students usually when we have guest lecturers we would like the students to hear, but when we don't want the lecturers to be disturbed by them. Often it's for visitors from the Alterworlds, who don't take kindly to disruptions from students who don't understand their customs—it can cause a bit of a ruckus sometimes if students are unintentionally discourteous." Remembering the Armatura's reaction to laughter, Eyre understood perfectly. The Ranger continued.

"You can hear very well up here and no one will see you, but stay quiet all the same in case anyone is passing by the door here. Once the meeting is over, you must find your own way out—and for reasons of protocol, you will understand that I can never admit to being a part of this if you are caught. Now I must go down to join the revelry."

As he turned to go Nick spoke. "Sir—why...?" He didn't need to say more; they all knew he was asking why the Ranger had helped them. A shadow scudded across the Ranger's face. But he answered in a light tone.

"The world needs the rule breakers sometimes, the ones with courage to venture out and think for themselves. I hope you will prove yourselves worthy of my faith in you."

After a moment he was gone and Nick locked the door behind him. Then they all crowded to the glass, to look at the delegation in the boardroom below.

CHAPTER NINETEEN

ALTHOUGH THEY KNEW THE gathering would be unusual, none of them were prepared for the fascinating sight in the boardroom below them. Slabs of thick quartz crystal ran from one side of the room to the other, forming benches for the delegates to sit at. There were ten lines of the crystal benches down the room that enabled about two hundred people to sit there. At the front of the room was a semi-circular table made of green and pink fluorite crystal, where Dean Fraser and Whittaker Ray sat facing the delegates. Alongside Whittaker Ray was an empty chair, and a further eight chairs were occupied by a man Eyre didn't know, Madame Overmantle, a Nemoris and a massive Armaturan, as well as two strange types of creatures Eyre hadn't seen before, and Lord Clarembout and UD1. With a tilt of his head UD1 looked up at the viewing room, and they all ducked for cover, despite the Ranger's comments that they couldn't be seen. You never knew with UD1.

Throughout the crowd there were other familiar faces—Beatrice and Abby's parents, obviously, and staff members including the excruciating Jemima Periwinkle, who fluttered her fingers at Dean Fraser. E Kofi sat quietly at the back with a group of Nemoris and several members of the Mimir were there, including Jengles and President Zircon. Sergeant Tottingham sat alongside them, her staff in her hand. Five Armaturan warriors sat fiercely at the front of the room, saying nothing, but their posture implying they were readying for attack. Interestingly, the purple-robed men with blue skin that Eyre had seen entering the building earlier were sitting at a table alone, at the side of the room. They also did not speak, but occasionally turned their heads to observe the crowd, no expression on their faces. There was a quiet hum in the air as others chatted politely to their neighbours, but there was also a sense of waiting to get on with it. Clearly everyone in the audience was as keen for the meeting to start as Eyre and her friends were. Whittaker Ray looked at his watch, then made a wry face at Dean Fraser, and the Dean rose.

"The Determinant Dozen..." He was interrupted as the door to the boardroom burst open, causing several of the audience members to jump up in alarm. Ranger Chrysanthe dashed in, jangling bracelets and his green hair flying and hesitated as he looked around the room. Whittaker Ray smiled and indicated the seat beside him and the Ranger hurried past the front row of delegates, knocking off the top hat of Sir Rayburn in the process. He picked up the hat and put it back on the rather affronted looking old man's head backwards, then continued the mayhem as he approached the fluorite table.

"So sorry, so sorry, was mulching my garden and the time got away from me," he apologized as he tripped up the stairs and stumbled over to sit by Whittaker Ray. Eyre laughed as she looked at the faces of the Armatura. It seemed the Ranger was fortunate they had not made a shish kebab of him as he careered past: they had automatically gone into attack mode at the intrusion and every one of them had raised their spears ready for slaughtering something.

The hubbub died down and Eyre noticed that not all the attendees were horrified by the melee the Ranger had caused. UD1 for one had an amused smile on his face and Madame Overmantle patted the Ranger's shoulder as he went past. And through the audience a few faces had indulgent smiles like you would afford a naughty but endearing toddler. But then she caught the faces of the purple-robed men who sat on their own, and was surprised to see that their until-now impassive faces were filled with a distaste that was almost palpable. Evidently they weren't a fan of unseemly behaviour, she thought.

Finally the Ranger had settled himself and the Dean turned back to the audience.

"Welcome Leo," he said. "We are glad you could join us." Eyre and her friends looked at each other. *Leo?* They hadn't heard that before. But then they were drawn back to the Dean as he began to talk to the delegates.

"I am Cecil Fraser, the Speaker for this four-year term. The Determinant Dozen have asked me to welcome the representatives of the Overworld who are here today, and to thank you for coming. For those of you who are not familiar with our Dozen for this four-year term, may I introduce you. President Balthazar sends his apologies today—this meeting has been called at short notice and he has been detained in Egypt. However, the rest of the Dozen are here. Whittaker Ray from the Academy. Leo Chrysanthe you have just met..." a soft flurry of chuckles ran through the crowd. "As many of you know, the Ranger is not one of the Dozen, but remains a permanent Honorary Guest at our meetings."

The four students watching from above looked at each other and their eyebrows moved upwards at the same time. Beatrice shrugged. Another mystery. As they turned back, Dean Fraser continued.

"Beside Ranger Chrysanthe is David Essendon, Chairman of the Echelon. Madame Overmantle, you will all of course know from previous years.

"Our representative from Terra for this term is Chaga O Ton, and beside her is Field Marshal Xenolith, of the Armatura." Then the Dean indicated one of the creatures Eyre hadn't seen before. Tall and slim, it was encased in an all-over tight-fitting garment like a wetsuit that didn't hide the fact that the creature had flippers on the end of its feet, and extremely long hands with elongated fingers. Its face was humanoid, but covered in iridescent scales, and it had long blue hair. Eyre thought it was quite a stunning creature.

"Aqua has sent Princess Nacre to speak for the Pinnae and Kyori will speak for the Caelites and Clementis of Caelus." Kyori was a small creature with wings covered in purple and white feathers and edged with gold. It had a green beak and large eyes that watched everyone carefully.

"Sir Philius Clarembout, Lord Clarembout, is also known to you for his work in Overworld defence, as is UD1. And finally, our Secretary, Quillpro, an Aquarian." Both Sir Philius and UD1 nodded as their names were called, but Eyre was too fascinated by Quillpro to look anywhere else. Quillpro was a human-sized, green-ringed octopus with very big eyes that wore glasses. In each of its twelve arms it held a pen, all of which were currently writing across a very large piece of paper, in very neat script. In fact, 'very' seemed the perfect adjective to describe the industrious mollusc. Everything about it was an extreme. After introducing the final member of the Dozen, the Dean walked to the front of the room.

"We have called this meeting as the Determinant Dozen, the Light Bearers for the Overworld this year, have agreed unanimously we must discuss the great increase in activity of the Gothak, not only the most recent event at the Academy, but around the entire Overworld. Many of us have experienced similar events, and it must be obvious to all of us that Rhabdor is planning something of dire significance to our continuing existence."

Once again the friends looked at each other. Rhabdor? Another puzzle. Who was that? Eyre had experienced Kaar at first hand, and she had thought he was the head of the Gothak. It appeared there was another of the terrible creatures that the Dozen—as she now knew the front panel was called—considered more important. And who seemed to be the Gothak's leader. Already she was learning a lot.

Dean Fraser stepped back to his seat. "I would now invite Madame Cheska Overmantle to speak."

Madame Overmantle stood up and walked forward. "As many of you will know, over the past few years my visions have increased and become more intense in regard to the future of the Overworld. I have previously shared with you the warnings I have received of a fearsome Darkness that is about to descend upon us all. Recently Whittaker Ray has been undercover at the Sunshine Coast, as I had received a vision that something of huge import was to occur in that area. We are still to decipher the meaning of that message, but we do feel it was connected to recent events. More worrying is the fact that somehow the Gothak have obtained the message from one of the visions I shared with the Determinant Dozen five years ago." Her voice changed and she seemed to turn inwardly. In a soft whisper she uttered the words and they appeared in light on the blackboard behind her:

The Darkness can only be ended when the Aura is restored by one of the two Triangles. Then her eyes fluttered and she looked out at the audience, her lined face deeply concerned.

"The Gothak are targeting our Aether," she said. "So there has been a leak. And it is of the most utmost importance that the Aether are protected, or the Overworld will cease to exist." She returned to her seat as voices started to mutter amongst the delegates.

A representative from Aqua, a creature resembling Princess Nacre, stood up from the middle of the audience.

"Do you have any information on where the leak may have come from?" he asked in a strangely bubbling voice.

"No, we don't," Lord Clarembout answered. "But we are working on it." The tone of his voice suggested that the person responsible would be fortunate if he didn't find them.

"Why was the school attacked?" Sir Rayburn asked. "It seems an unlikely target out of all the possible places in the world."

"We have three Aethers at the school," Whittaker Ray replied. "Whose identities are concealed, for obvious reasons. Over the course of the last five years, eighty percent of the Aethers in the Lightworking population have been eliminated. You will remember that tragically the Lightwards, who were members of our Lightworking Echelon, died last year. Alia Lightward was an Aether, as you know, and it appears that she was targeted specifically. It is a sad day indeed that we must examine our internal structure for darkness, instead of concentrating on the Darkness from the

Underworld. The school was not the only area targeted last night. Several Aethers from all over the world were attacked, and I am desolate to say, some did not survive."

A low murmuring filled the boardroom as the attendees turned to each other, obviously shocked. Eyre's friends turned to look at her and Abby put her arm around Eyre. Eyre's head was spinning at this information, and she thought of the genealogy chart she had seen back at the cabin—and the star formed from two triangles that had appeared at the side of some of the names dotted through the chart. So that's what the symbol meant—an Aether, supposed to be a secret known only by a few. She didn't know what being an Aether meant, but obviously the Gothak wanted them gone. And someone from the Lightworkers had given out information that had resulted in her parents dying because her mother was an Aether. Her stomach clenched in rage as a dark hatred bloomed for that unknown person. Lord Clarembout was not the only one who would be trying to identify the treacherous person. She was flooded with fury and a determination to bring her parents some justice.

Dean Fraser stood by Whittaker Ray.

"So our purpose here today is to ask you to be vigilant. Dr Botolfe—" he indicated the Doctor where she sat at the end of the row, "—has kindly agreed to take any comments, suggestions and particularly information about events that have been happening in your own world, so that we can get an accurate record of the movements of the Gothak, and their frequency. Please contact her should you have any information at all. And we ask you to be aware and cautious of the communications we pass to you—they can be a weapon in the hands of the wrong people.

"O Chaga, would you start with your report?" The Nemoris sitting beside Madame Overmantle stood up and walked to the front of the stage. Over the next hour, representatives of all the worlds spoke of their commitment to the cause, and described tragic and awful events that had occurred in recent times in their own world. It was a terrible list of sad losses, and it was indisputable as time went on, that the Gothak were rising; that the Darkness was strengthening.

Finally Dean Fraser stood and thanked the delegation for their time.

"We will be sending regular updates and communication to you as information comes to hand. Please look within your own communities for any sign of treachery—we must find the source of this betrayal. Go Lightly, my friends, we are one."

As the auditorium started to fill with the sounds of people standing and talking, Nick ran and unlocked the door of the viewing room.

"Time to go! Quickly, let's get out of here before we're seen!"

Eyre, Beatrice and Abby didn't need any further prompting—they were out and down the two sets of stairs in a flash. They raced out the front doors of the Central Administration building just as the first delegates walked from the boardroom.

Finally making it to the pathway that ran between the buildings, they slowed to a casual walk.

"Time for lunch," Beatrice said, as usual.

CHAPTER TWENTY

AFTER LUNCH EYRE TOOK her friends to the spot in the bush where she had hidden behind the boulder earlier that week. They all agreed it was a great place for their new 'BANE' meetings, and they wanted to talk about what they'd seen at the conference that morning.

"What about *Leo*?" Eyre said. "I thought his name was Ranger!"

"Me too," said Abby. "And I've never heard of an Aether! Maybe one of us is an Aether—I wonder how you can tell if you're one?"

"Mm, well what I think we should do," Beatrice said, "is take a question each and find out the answer. But surreptitiously—be careful how you ask the question, we can't let anyone know we were there at the meeting."

"Ok," Nick said. "Who wants to take what?"

"Well I'll take the Aether question, since my Mum was an Aether," Eyre said. "I've seen the genealogy chart of my family, and it's got the two triangle symbol besides her name, so I suppose that's what it means after what Whittaker Ray said. If Mum was an Aether I've got a good excuse to raise the topic. I'll go see Whittaker Ray."

"I'll find out about Leo—not that it's a particularly important piece of information. But I'd like to know." Abby said. "I'll try to find something about it at the Central Admin building—there's bound to be a school prospectus, or a staff directory in there."

"I'll research Rhabdor," Nick said, after a pause. "My dad is an Ex, so I've got a reason to look into the dark side of Lightworking. Maybe the Library will have something on it." His mouth turned down as he said it; he clearly felt ashamed, despite his friends reassuring him many times in the past it was not his fault that his father had been excommunicated from the Lightworking community.

"Okay, so that leaves me... what will I find out?" Beatrice mused.

"What about those blue guys in the purple robes?" Eyre suggested. "No one referred to them at all, and they never said a word. I'd like to know who they are."

Beatrice's eyes lit up. "Great idea! I was wondering about them too. A good one for me to track down. So let's go do our research and call a BANE meeting when we've all had some success?"

In agreement, they all headed back to campus and off to their various elective classes. This afternoon, Eyre had Lightworking Genealogy with Jemima Periwinkle, apparently a subject that was important for Hese students to know. Members of the Hese Sector were often involved in management, leadership and administration, so Eyre could see how the subject might be relevant—it might be of some importance to understand the lineage of its people. However, a class with the pink and white Ms Periwinkle was not something she was looking forward to. Sighing, she looked for a seat in Lecture Theatre 1C, a smaller auditorium as there were fewer people involved in the class. Fortunately she knew some of the students there: Todd, Vicky and Georgia had been put in Hese Sector. Rigmar was Hese too, so Eyre went to sit with him.

Ms Periwinkle eventually breezed in with a face full of makeup and her blonde hair coiled in a long plait around the top of her head. In a sparkling voice she asked them to open their books and then began an interminable discourse on the various lineages of families with 'ray' or 'sun' or 'light' in their surnames, which apparently gave an indication of the age of the family line, and where they may have originated. Todd was clearly as enthused about the topic as Eyre, because he was snoring on top of his desk within ten minutes. The excitement of the night before, coupled with the anaesthetizing discussion on genealogy had proven too much for him. The hour went by excruciatingly slowly until thankfully Jemima Periwinkle finished, assigning them homework on tracing the student's own lineage back three generations, with an explanation of which country their surname originated from. How on earth, Eyre thought as she picked up her Felsic, were they going to fill a whole *year* with this subject? It seemed the most superficial of topics.

The next subject she had was Psionics: Levitation, Telekinesis and Pyrokinesis, a subject all the other Sectors took, so Eyre walked over to the larger 1A lecture theatre and found Beatrice and Robeson already in there.

"Abby's at Music and Communication," Beatrice said. "And I think Nick's at Astral Travel. But Rufa, Flava and Virens are in here too. We have a lecturer called Oorlock."

She giggled. "Arant, Sappir and Tyros take Levitation and Telekinesis with *Dr Botolfe* apparently, on Thursday afternoons." Eyre was so relieved it wasn't Dr Botolfe taking this class, with her cold, scimitar eyes and her heart of stone. Not least of all because Dr Botolfe regarded Eyre as a prideful show-off and a liar. Eyre could do without that this year; she'd had enough of it at the TEPs. Looking around, Eyre realised that although she'd dodged Dr Botolfe, unfortunately she would share the class with Ben Perrill and the Curtis twins and that awful Tec Langford. She would have to choose her seating carefully.

Moments later Oorlock walked in—a serious, middle-aged man who certainly didn't look as exotic as his name. He got right to business, drawing on the board in light as he went through the physics and the energy derivation of levitation and telekinesis. Once again Eyre felt her mind drifting off—evidently Wednesday afternoons were going to be the low-point of the week, it was so *boring*. But the afternoon was saved when Oorlock told them to pack up their bags and head to the Training Shed to practise the physical skills of psionics. It didn't take long for the auditorium to clear—it seemed that the other students had been as thrilled with the lecture as she was. Except for Beatrice, whose eyes sparkled.

"Wasn't that fascinating?" she said in an awe-struck voice. "The physics of Lightworking skills—just incredible. I can't wait for the next lecture!" Speechless, Eyre just smiled but rolled her eyes mentally. Only a superbrain like Beatrice could find a subject like that interesting.

They all walked along the path to the Training Shed and found Terrigal waiting for them.

"Find a place, hurry up," he called to everyone. "We don't have a lot of time, so make it count. You know what to do; this hour is for practise. Get on with it and let me know if you need help."

Eyre found a spot and started to practise her levitation. She wobbled up to the top of the ceiling, quite pleased that she seemed to be getting stronger at it, although she still definitely looked like a beginner. Someone beside her swore and plunged down onto the padded mat, landing on his back. It was Luke Jordan and surprised, Eyre looked over to see what might have broken his concentration. Luke was Rufa, and normally good at the physical side of things. The reason became clear when Saskia Anderson turned and tittered at him from the ceiling. She'd just performed three cartwheels in the air, and obviously Luke had been rather impressed. Terrigal, however, was not.

"Poor concentration there, student," he chastised Luke. "Not going to save your life when you need it."

Red-faced, Luke picked himself up and levitated again, moving easily up to the roof. Once up there, he 'picked' a medicine ball up with his mind and threw it into a hoop on the wall. Saskia definitely looked enthralled, and Terrigal was satisfied, moving on to the next sweating student. Clearly he'd been trained by Sergeant Tottingham; he had a similar teaching method—no patience for incompetence.

Once she'd practised her levitation for a while, Eyre decided to work on her telekinesis. Sitting on the mat, she focused hard on a hoop on the ground, trying to move it. After a while, she managed to lift it slightly off the ground and then it fell back again. Encouraged, she focused harder and the hoop slowly rose in the air until it rested on its end. She was aiming to just hold it there for a while, when she became aware of a familiar voice from across the room. She turned to see Ben Perrill and the Curtis twins taunting Rigmar, who was red-faced and puffing as he tried to levitate higher than a few metres. A heavy boy, it was evidently going to be harder for him, despite the fact he had strong Viq.

"Tub of lard," Slade hooted. "Ever seen anything wobble that much?"

"Had his head in the trough too often over Christmas," Ben said, "you're going to need a crane to get up there, Essendon."

Sweating and trying to ignore them, Rigmar inched his way up a bit further, but his muscles gave out and he crashed to the floor. Not much practise over the holidays, Eyre supposed, feeling sorry for him. She knew Rigmar could look after himself though, he'd been one of the first to Elevate last year and he was smart. So she waited to see what would happen. It didn't take long.

With a flick of his wrist he snapped his fingers first at Ben and then at Slade. They looked at him strangely, then began to screech as flames shot from their boots, sending an evil-smelling black smoke into the air. In a second they had pulled their boots off and were sitting on the ground rubbing their feet hard as their boots smouldered beside them.

"You'll pay for that Essendon," Ben Perrill snarled, but Terrigal got there first. "You!" he said sharply to Rigmar. "What do you think you're doing?" Rigmar said nothing and Terrigal's face darkened.

"The use of Light force against one another in anything but practise is forbidden. You are banned for the rest of the afternoon, and I had better not see anything like it again! Out!"

Rigmar left, scowling as Ben's sniggers followed him. Sending her hoop rolling against the wall, Eyre jumped up and ran to join Rigmar. She didn't care if she missed the rest of the lesson—there wasn't much time left anyway.

"Ben's a jerk, Rig, don't worry about him. He's causing so much trouble already I doubt he'll make it through the year. Sooner or later they've got to chuck him out."

Rigmar smiled eventually as they walked along the path. "I know, but it's hard to ignore him, he's just got a way of pushing the right buttons—or perhaps I should say, the wrong ones." After a few steps he added, "he's also annoyed that my father is the Chairman of the Echelon. His dad—Dr Perrill, who's Head of Aura Research, ran for the position last year and didn't get it. Dr Perrill didn't mind apparently, but Ben does. Every opportunity he gets he has a go at me."

"I've met Dr Perrill," Eyre said, causing Rigmar to raise his eyebrows. "Briefly only, but he seemed pretty decent. I wonder why Ben is such a pig, it doesn't make sense really."

"Genetics, genealogy—perhaps we could ask Jemima Periwinkle?" Both of them burst out laughing and headed to the Common Room. Soon they were immersed in a game of Crystallography—a game where you had to match the crystal structures by putting stones into holders. If you got the sequence right, it would generate an electrical current and eventually the goal was to have your stone spinning in the air on its own. It involved octahedron-shaped dice and cards and was quite complex, so by the time Rigmar eventually won, the afternoon had passed.

"Thanks Eyre," he said as the left. "That helped."

Eyre wandered back to the dormitory as the last heat of the day started to leave the campus grounds. Summer was nearing an end and the welcome coolness was beginning earlier in the afternoon. As she neared the dormitory, she could hear an awful high-pitched sound emanating from her room. Sensitized by a year of strange events, she approached cautiously lest it be some unknown creature waiting to seize her when she walked in the door.

It was no malign creature lying in wait, but all the same, she was truly amazed. Abby was standing in the middle of the room in front of a small wooden box, moving her hands around wildly in the air. And as she did so, a weird synthetic sound was emitted with each movement. At Eyre's questioning gaze, Abby stopped and exclaimed in excitement.

"It's called a theremin and I'm learning it for music! Isn't it beautiful?" Eyre wasn't sure how to respond—the sounds she'd heard hadn't actually been all that tuneful; to be honest, about as pleasant as listening to someone playing the violin for the first time. A lot of screeching and zinging. But she didn't want to ruin Abby's enthusiasm.

"Wow, that's awesome," Eyre said, "but you're not holding an instrument. Where is it?"

"Here," said Abby, indicating the box in front of her. Looking more closely, Eyre could see a metal loop and an antenna attached to it. "My left hand changes the pitch via the antenna, and my right hand changes the volume using the loop. It's awesome! Like playing music from the air!"

Eyre was actually impressed—it was like magic and she was sure the sounds would become more harmonic with practise. Unfortunately, sharing the room with someone learning to play the shrieking instrument might be a bit of a challenge. But she was happy for Abby's sake—she was positively glowing with excitement.

Beatrice arrived soon after and was also given a demonstration, much to Eyre's amusement. Beatrice's eyes were as round as saucers and Eyre couldn't even look at her, lest she crack up with laughter. Sometimes less honesty was the best policy with friends.

CHAPTER TWENTY-ONE

"HOLD IT OUT STRAIGHT, then concentrate with your mind on the crystal at the end," ordered Sergeant Tottingham. "You'll feel an energy start to run down your arm and through your staff. It takes years of practise, obviously, to become accomplished at using your staff, but within a couple of weeks you should be able to produce a beam from the end of it. After that you will start learning the different ways to use your staff—you will use it to find your way in this life, whether it's for defence, for illuminating your path, or for healing. Some of you may wish to undertake post-graduate studies on learning to use your crystal to focus your third sight—a gift that takes years to develop. It is a magical tool, and you will come to rely upon it in a great way."

Eyre and her friends were in the Training Shed with the rest of the first-year students. They were starting later today. The whole school had been to the Lifting of the Halo ceremony that morning for the third-year students who had finished last year, and also for the graduate students who had completed their studies last year. The ceremony had been happy but also emotional for the students—the culmination of the intense years of study and the end of their time at the Academy. Most of the students had their parents there and the ceremony was held in the school's auditorium, where all formal occasions were organised. Dean Fraser and all the staff dressed in their formal robes, and the Dean removed the Halo from each of the graduating students as they came up onto the stage and handed it to them. It had been a busy morning, finishing when the students threw their Halo into the Ponds of Doombee like a Frisbee. It was symbolic of throwing away childish props and moving on to maturity, and there was a lot of laughter and back slapping amongst the graduating students, especially when someone did a bad throw.

Now the four of them were at Staff Forces, a part of Physical Training and a compulsory subject for all students. Eyre thought her staff was beautiful, but it wasn't working at all, despite the fact they had been trying in this class for three weeks. Similar dejected looks from around the room lifted her spirits a little—no one else was managing any energy either. There was a whole forest of glowing wooden shafts topped with sparkling crystals, but not one of them had managed to create the current Sergeant Tottingham was describing. The sound of thumping wood on the floor filled the training shed, and faces were crunched up in concentration.

After half an hour of this, the Sergeant sighed.

"Not yet then. Take a break," she said. "We'll try again in a moment. But I want you to sit on the floor during the break and concentrate on that energy travelling from your staff. If you can see it in your mind, you can produce it from your staff."

Despite the concentration, by the end of the training session still not one student had managed to generate any energy from their staff, and the students left the Training Shed looking disappointed, particularly the Rufa students, who were supposed to be good at the physical arts. Still, Eyre mused, looking at Ben Perrill and his mates, there's a large mental component to it also, and some of them are decidedly lacking in that area.

"Practising outside of class will help," Sergeant Tottingham called to them as they walked away from the shed. "Schedule some time daily into your week."

Despite the fact she knew it wasn't supposed to be easy, Eyre felt a bit dismal that she hadn't managed to energise her staff—raising the right kind of force was so difficult. But it was nothing compared to the class that came next—her least favourite, and that included Ms Periwinkle's boring Genealogy lectures. Lighthorsemanship. The most frustrating, horrible lesson of the week. The only thing Eyre was learning from it was the hardness of the ground and the taste of dust in her mouth—Ischyros could not stand her and was definitely not letting her anywhere near him. Over the past three weeks she had been kicked, bitten and dumped on the ground countless times. One day Ischyros had not even been in the stall and Eyre had spotted him munching on clover in the far corner of the paddock. She'd spent the whole hour chasing him around the grass, trying to get close to him.

Gloomily she trudged over to the stables with her friends. Unlike Eyre, they were looking forward to the class. Many of them had made great progress with their horses and enjoyed the time outdoors hugely, a fact that made Eyre's own lack of success even more grating. The Kikkuli Master waited for the students patiently as they entered the riding complex and headed off to find their horses. Taking a deep breath, Eyre trudged through the stables, heading for Ischyros's shed. Pitying looks accompanied her: the students had been audience to her supreme failure as an equestrienne, and the spectacular lack of progress she'd had with her bad-tempered mount.

To her relief, Ischyros was actually in his stall, so at least she didn't have to go and find him in the field today. He was head down in the trough, back to her, ignoring her as she entered. She sidled around the shed walls towards him, knowing well enough to steer clear of his feet. He looked at her briefly, then went back to his hay. Eyre sighed.

"I don't know why you dislike me so much," she said. "Did I do something to offend you?"

With his mouth full, Ischyros answered, not looking at her.

"Your very existence offends me."

Eyre sighed. "Well I have to try and learn to ride..." she said, opening the stall door. To her surprise, the mangy old horse stood still for once and let her lead him outside.

"Good boy," she said, as she pulled on his mane, preparing to swing her leg up and over his back. But Ischyros had other ideas. She had barely got her foot over his neck when he let out a huge whoop and took off down the centre of the stables.

"Yippee kay ay!" he hollered, his feet clattering as Eyre bounced along, one leg half over his back and the other hanging down the other side.

Eyre screeched loudly, scrabbling desperately at his mane. As he launched himself out into the training arena, she finally managed to pull herself upright on his back. Clinging to his mane with hands like claws, her fear suddenly gave way to a blossoming anger.

"STOP!" she shouted. "Stop stop stop you *stupid* beast!" Shrieks of laughter followed her around the ring as she jounced along at 100 kilometres per hour, hanging on as the horse swerved back and forth. This only served to increase her rage until suddenly swirls of dirt began to fly up around her in small cyclones, rising up to the sky in dusty spirals. Eventually the whole arena was engulfed by a blinding dust storm that howled maniacally as the students covered their eyes from the gritty cloud. Then Ischyros rose in the air, his legs still pumping but unable to go anywhere.

"LET ME OFF!" Eyre screamed at him through the dust and finally Ischyros stopped galloping, his legs dangling down uselessly.

"Put me down, you dumb human," he said crossly, and Eyre let her mental grip go a little. The force of her Viq dropped and the wild swirls of dirt subsided. With a thump Ischyros landed on the dirt, the awkward movement tossing Eyre flying into the ring. She landed hard on her rear end on the ground and cussed out loud.

"That's it!" she shouted. "I'm done. I do not need a stupid horse." Jumping to her feet she strode past the filthy, dust covered students, her jaw set. But as she reached the entrance gates, the Kikkuli Master walked out to meet her.

"If a challenge was easy, it would not be a challenge," he said, his eyes kind. "Lightworkers must have a horse, and that is yours." Eyre stopped, frustration bringing tears to her eyes. "That is not a horse. That is one of the Strigis," she said, and started off down the pathway.

"You cannot run every time you have a problem," the Kikkuli Master said in a soft voice. "That is not the way to develop strength."

Eyre slackened her pace at his gentle tone. If he'd shouted at her, she would have kept going. But his soft words stopped her like a light hand on her shoulder as she realised that he was right. She *did* have a habit of running off when she got upset. Last year at the TEPs; more recently when Ben Perrill had brought the newspaper cutting to class... She charged away from anything that made her feel bad, and she realised with a clench of her stomach that it wasn't very admirable. Not really something to be proud of. Slowly she turned, her head down.

"Nobody else is having this trouble," she said softly. "What am I doing wrong?" The Kikkuli Master looked understanding as she raised her eyes to his.

"Patience," he said. "Like the most precious of crystals, sometimes a thing of great beauty and value is created only after much time and much pressure."

Raising a grubby hand, Eyre rubbed her forehead and sighed.

"You are wise, Kikkuli Master. Although I can't see much beauty coming out of this relationship," she said. "But I'll try." Looking over to the arena she could see many students watching them and she raised her chin and took a breath. "Even if he tosses me off for four years, I'll stick with it."

The Kikkuli Master nodded in approval as Eyre walked slowly back to the arena, dusting herself off. Ischyros was still there—something to be grateful for, I guess, Eyre thought despondently as she led him back down the stable building towards the other side, curious looks following her all the way. She could hear Ben Perrill hooting after her.

"Giving up, Airhead?" he cackled, and she could hear the derisive laughter of his cronies as they revelled in her embarrassment. But she ignored it and walked on, grabbing a grooming bag as she reached the end of the stable block. Instead of heading back to Ischyros's stall, she led him out into the paddock.

"I think we both need a bit of fresh air," she said to Ischyros when she reached the fence, and patted him tentatively on the neck. Bringing out a wide toothed comb from the bag, she began to comb his mane slowly, getting the tangles out. His eyes followed her, old and red, inflamed by the dust, but he didn't play up. Gently Eyre teased the knots out of his straggly mane, steering clear of his back feet, with their rough, cracked hooves, as she walked around him. It took a while, but finally the comb ran freely through the long hair. Then she got a currycomb out and began to brush his coat with the plastic brush, freeing the dirt and dust that was caked in stiffly. She could hear the other students cantering around the arena, and their shouts of enjoyment as the Kikkuli Master called out instructions. But she ignored the sounds and concentrated on swirling the currycomb around with gentle strokes.

"It seems to me we've gotten off on the wrong foot," she said, encouraged a little by Ischyros's silence. At least he wasn't insulting her for once. "And I don't expect you to like me. But perhaps, since whether we like it or not we have a long association ahead of us, we could agree to put up with each other." She stopped and looked Ischyros in his bleary old eye. "What do you say?"

Ischyros leant down and took a mouthful of grass. "Horses can't talk," he said. Sighing, Eyre looked at him for a moment, then pulled out a soft haired brush from the bag. She carried on grooming him until Ischyros's tatty old coat looked cleaner. He didn't exactly shine, but the mud and dust were gone. The old horse didn't say anything else for the whole time she worked, and eventually she led him back to his stall. He said nothing as she left, but he didn't kick her either, so she felt that maybe she had made some progress. Anything less than a brawl at this point was looking up.

She headed for the arena and found her friends waiting for her. Everyone was covered with dust from her earlier display of rage and they all looked at her with slightly worried expressions. Fair enough, Eyre thought, feeling guilty. I guess no one ever knows when I'm going to blow a gasket. But Beatrice just clapped her on the shoulder as they headed back to campus.

"Glad there weren't any sticks in the arena," was all she said.

CHAPTER TWENTY-TWO

EYRE SAT UP LATE that night, looking out the window as her roommates slept. Her mind was churning with so many things. The Gothak attacking, the revelations at the meeting they'd spied on, Ischyros and his difficult behaviour, even Warrigal and his startling talents. Her lack of skill in any direction—useless at controlling the staff, hopeless at riding, and the gnawing shame of her uncontrollable temper. Her mind was roiling with the worry of it all, and once again she just felt like running away. Only a few months ago she had known nothing about any of this—and her parents had been alive. Now there was this strange new world that she didn't understand, dangers that threatened the *earth*, and mysteries that she couldn't fathom. It all made her head ache. But as she looked up at the sparkling stars, a certainty took hold of her. She was going to participate in this fight, and do whatever she could to drive the Gothak back to their hell-hole forever. And she knew that this meant that for once she was going to have to run towards the thing that stressed her, not away from it.

So, the next morning, she rose just after dawn and quietly took her staff out of the locker. She also took her backpack with a set of spare clothing in it—given the way things were proceeding, she was resigned to the fact she may need it, as it looked as if she might be spending some time grovelling in the dust.

Breathing lungfuls of the fresh, cool air, she set off running through the trees towards the stables, holding her staff out in front of her like a spear. She was gasping by the time she arrived—she'd lost some of her cardio fitness over the Christmas break, and her body was protesting. But she felt happy to be back charging along the track, realising that she'd missed it.

The stables were empty apart from the horses who pricked their ears at her—no one was around and Eyre moved silently through the complex, her footsteps muffled by the dust. She grabbed a shallow basin from the storage cupboard and put a few items in it, and then headed to Ischyros's stall, dumping her backpack by the gate. He tossed his head crankily as she walked in.

"What the...? It's the middle of the night, you idiot. You're not taking me anywhere," he said, and turned his back to her. Eyre raised her eyebrows as she leant her staff against the wall.

"I don't want to take you anywhere," she said. "I'm here to do your feet." She produced a file and some hoof dressing and picked up one of Ischyros's back feet. Eyre acted confident, but part of her was expecting to be ejected through the door and across campus by that foot. But Ischyros held off, and she slowly started to rasp at his hoof.

"I don't really know what I'm doing," she said. "But I figure I can smooth these out a bit. Bear with me." Over the next half hour, she filed away at Ischyros's feet, getting rid of the sharp edges and smoothing the areas that were riven by cracks. It was hard work with his horny, dry feet, and she didn't do a perfect job, but eventually the uneven edges smoothed out. Then she rubbed the hoof dressing in, polishing his feet with the oil until they shone.

"Amateur," Ischyros said, shuffling his feet as she fumbled around. But she noticed he kept glancing at them. Finally she finished and straightened her aching back. Immediately a suspicious glare came back into Ischyros's eye and his ears went back. Knowing this preceded a nip, Eyre grabbed the bucket and her staff and hurried for the door.

"I'll be back tomorrow," she said, dodging his teeth and gritting her own.

Heading out to the paddock, Eyre stood in the middle and raised her staff —aiming at a fence post. But no matter how she concentrated, or where she pointed it, she couldn't generate one bit of energy through the crystal. She practised for a while, getting nowhere, and then decided it was time to head back. Not today, but maybe tomorrow, she decided... however long it took.

Her legs were shaking as she stopped after the run back through the bush, and she bent over, breathing deeply to catch her breath. As she straightened a familiar form emerged from the depths of the foliage.

"Hard run?" Warrigal said, taking in her sweaty form.

"Yeah, it's a struggle. Have you been out all night?"

Warrigal stretched his arms.

"Yes, I've been asked to keep an eye on things since the Gothak attacked. I like it, and I know the country around here really well."

"Did you see anything?"

Warrigal frowned as he looked deep into the bush, his brown eyes sombre. "No," he said slowly. "But the signs are there. Things are not the way they should be.

Eyre left him on the edge of campus and headed towards the dormitory, deep in thought. Things were changing, and if Warrigal was worried, she knew it was serious.

CHAPTER TWENTY-THREE

EYRE WALKED WITH ISCHYROS through a series of paddocks, entering the gates and latching them after her. Over the past weeks he had allowed her to lead him, so she'd made the most of it by releasing him into the far paddock every morning. She didn't for a second believe he put up with the extra walking time because he liked her presence—she knew he tolerated her leading him around because the grass was greener and thicker in the far paddock, and he wanted to get to the best grass on the grounds. They arrived and she opened the gate. It had taken a while to get there this morning, because he kept stopping and hauling his head down to grab a mouthful of the delicious cocksfoot grass. It was bad equestrian manners to eat while being led, but he was so strong and had such canny timing, he would snatch the mouthfuls despite her trying to keep his head up. It was annoying, but given his general irritating behaviour, just one more thing to deal with. Eyre had given up thinking he would ever be trainable. Or that he would even like her. Leaning on the gate, she waved her hand at him.

"Off you go—enjoy the grass!"

But Ischyros just stood there, looking at her, making none of the usual acerbic comments he normally would. Eyre was surprised, but slightly hopeful. Was he beginning to soften? She leaned her staff against the fence and took a slow step towards Ischyros. When he didn't move away, she leant against his side, smoothing her arms up and over his neck. To her amazement he said nothing and she rubbed further up his back. Then, when he still stood there, she grabbed his mane tightly, but gently. There was no reaction, so Eyre took a breath and swung her leg up and over the back of the old horse, hauling herself up, expecting to be launched into the stratosphere. But to her joy, he stood calmly, with no sign of irritation at all. Encouraged, she touched the side of his neck softly as she'd seen the Kikkuli Master instruct the other students to do, asking their mount to walk forward. And Ischyros did! Right to the centre of the paddock, and Eyre could barely contain her excitement. After months of rude comments from the recalcitrant creature, she was finally getting somewhere! It was so lovely being seated up on his back, and she enjoyed the feeling of moving over the ground, uneven gait or not. Ischyros stopped in the middle of the paddock and Eyre took in the glow of the early morning. The best time of the day, she sighed. The moment was slightly marred when Ischyros deposited a steaming pile onto the ground, but given the amount of grass he'd gobbled on the way to the paddock, she wasn't surprised. A sound from behind her made her turn to look. Someone was here?

But then, with a hunching of his hindquarters and a huge kick of his back legs, Ischyros bucked Eyre off, high into the air. With amazing accuracy, she landed on her back, hard, in the middle of the sizeable pile of horse poo Ischyros had just decorated the paddock with. Hurting and winded badly, she gasped for air as someone cantered up and jumped off his horse.

"Geez, are you okay?" Despite the agony, Eyre flushed in embarrassment as Jax's concerned face hovered over her. He helped her to sit up as glops of excrement dropped from her back onto the lush, green grass. Eyre could hear Ischyros braying in hilarity from the side of the paddock and she knew with absolute certainty that he had done this on purpose, that he had seen Jax coming and had set her up spectacularly. Ischyros walked over to Jax and nuzzled his back, his eyes on Eyre. A demon horse! she thought, but today she was hurting so much, and was so disappointed after weeks of trying, that her usual temper deserted her. She was horrified to find tears in her eyes, and she wiped her face to hide them as she struggled to get her breath back. Jax rubbed Ischyros's nose and Ischyros bent his head so Jax could scratch under his forelock.

"He's certainly badly behaved," Jax said. "But he's kind of cute." Cute? Eyre thought. *Cute*? The last word in the entire Oxford dictionary she would apply to Ischyros.

"Yeah," she said noncommittally, and was annoyed to hear Ischyros guffaw. Eyre clenched her jaw. She would *not* cry.

"He really nailed you, didn't he!"

"I'm okay, I'll just head back," Eyre said, moving awkwardly, and went to stand up, despite the screech of agony from her bruised back. But Jax's eyes focused on Eyre's neck and he leaned towards her as she sat on the ground.

"That's a neat necklace," he said, holding the silver chain with the charms on it. "Can I have a look?"

"Well, I'd hand it to you," Eyre replied after a moment, "but I haven't been able to take it off. It was my mother's."

"Well, that's understandable," Jax said. "It must be difficult for you. I wouldn't take it off either."

"No," Eyre said slowly. "I mean I *can't* take it off, even if I wanted to—my necklace won't come off any more. Seems I have no choice. Not that I want to take it off anyway." She didn't mention that it would come off when it was near her Lightkeeper; that would lead into too many questions that she didn't want to answer.

"That's strange," Jax said, looking more closely, and Eyre suddenly realised that he hadn't been interested in her necklace at all; he'd just been trying to take her mind off the fall. But now he was intrigued.

"That's a Tone Blow," he said slowly, examining the small whistle. "Wow." Eyre was also thinking 'wow', but that was completely due to the proximity of Jax's face to hers. The necklace wasn't long, so to look at it closely he had to be rather close to her also. She felt her flush deepen.

"Yes, it's for my Wisdom. The key also. I got my Wisdom—you know..."

Jax frowned slightly as he picked up the key and turned it over. "Yeah, well my cousin turned twenty-one last year and he got his Wisdom too, but —" he looked at Eyre apologetically, "—just because of his age. He didn't get a Tone Blow or a key with it though. I'm sure it just opens." Then he shook his head and laughed, dropping the key. "You must have some awful skeletons in your family closet."

Eyre smiled. "No doubt." Hesitating, she opened the locket. "This is my Mum and Dad."

Jax's eyes were kind as he looked at the photograph. "It must be very hard." Eyre appreciated that he didn't try to say that it would get easier. She knew by now it didn't get easier, but you did learn to live with it. And then she realised that Jax's tactic had worked: she had completely forgotten about the fall, and her distress at being duped yet again by that horrible horse had passed. The horrible horse in question had now moved to the side of the fence, his back to them as he ripped up mouthfuls of grass and worked on stripping the paddock bare of the high mountain cocksfoot.

"Can you stand up?" Jax asked, and he helped Eyre to her feet. Despite feeling incredibly stupid, she loved the feeling of his hands on her bare arms and she shivered.

"The fall has shaken you," Jax said, completely misreading her reaction. "Come over and meet Firestorm."

Eyre followed him over to his horse, the beautiful chestnut with flashes of red in its coat. The horse was huge and magnificent, and also very friendly. He nudged Eyre and let her stroke him, and the knot in her stomach started to dissolve. Animals normally liked her, and she adored them, which made Ischyros's behaviour even more difficult to take.

"Come on," Jax said. "Ride with me. Firestorm can handle it. You can feel what it's like to have a decent ride. Do you think you're up to it?"

Eyre heard Ischyros snort through a mouthful of grass and gave a rueful smile.

"I'm okay. Sure. But let me just go grab a change of shirt. It'll just take me a couple of minutes." Eyre's feelings were so wounded that she stalked by Ischyros, completely ignoring him. Her back ached terribly, but far worse was the hurt in her heart. The old nag was so mean!

But then the thought of having a proper ride took over and she flew down the hill to the stables and found her backpack with the change of clothes in it.

A short time later she was back—feeling a bit better after she'd rid herself of her reeking clothing. Jax swung gracefully up onto Firestorm's back, and then helped to pull Eyre up behind him. She put her arms around Jax's waist as he touched Firestorm's neck and the horse started to walk around the paddock. After a couple of circuits, Jax nudged him into a canter. The movement was unusual for Eyre—she'd never ridden before, but it had a gentle rocking feeling and she knew she wouldn't fall off. Jax and Firestorm obviously had a wonderful bond. Despite her enjoyment of the ride, she felt wistful as she looked over at Ischyros, still with his back to them. Wouldn't it be nice to have a connection like they had?

Suddenly the pace picked up as Firestorm tensed his muscles and changed to a gallop. This was a different movement again, but Eyre wasn't so sure about it—they were going so *fast*. She wasn't sure she liked it—the country was blurring around her and she held on desperately to Jax, her head against his back.

"Um—do you think—" she began, but Jax hollered with delight.

"He's never galloped for me before! Isn't this brilliant?"

Eyre wasn't so sure she wanted to end her life at this early age, but she swallowed and tried to enjoy the ride. She certainly enjoyed the feeling of her arms around Jax and decided she would risk her life for that. Then Jax gave a surprised gasp. Firestorm had stopped galloping around the perimeter of the paddock and was charging across it – straight for the fence! Eyre could see Jax pulling on Firestorm's mane, trying to slow him down, but he wouldn't stop. If anything, Jax pulling his head up only seemed to spur the horse on as he raced faster across the field. Eyre shut her eyes as they were almost upon the fence. At least she would die happy.

But when they got to the wire, she could feel Firestorm's massive hindquarters bunch beneath her, and she opened her eyes when Jax let out a loud whoop. The ground disappeared below them as they rose above the fence, sailed easily across and landed with hardly a lurch on the other side. Just hitting his stride, Firestorm galloped fast down the green hill, so fast Eyre felt like she was flying. There was no hesitation in his gait, it was smooth and uninterrupted, almost like a car hitting top gear.

Eyre held on tight as Firestorm flew around the large paddock, down one side and up the other until he reached the fence again. They were going so fast the tears whipped from her eyes, and she laughed in exhilaration. This was absolutely *unreal*! When the massive horse eventually got back to the top of the paddock, with a huge kick of his powerful legs, he jumped the uphill obstacle and landed on the other side without a stumble. Finally slowing down, he started to canter, and then walk the last half of the paddock, barely sweating at all. He turned his head slightly to look at them, and Eyre swore he had a look in his eye almost as if he was saying "*Well, how about that?*"

Jax helped Eyre jump down to the ground. They looked at each other, grinning in delight, but saying nothing. What words could describe that?

As Jax looked at Eyre, his green eyes changed.

"Never a dull moment with you, Eyre..." he said softly, and putting his hands on her shoulders, he pulled her towards him. Eyre exhaled, unable to take her eyes from his. Her whole body fired with electricity.

But the moment was interrupted by slow clapping from the fence line. Startled, Eyre looked towards Ischyros, but realised the sound was coming from the opposite direction. Then, as Jax dropped his arms and looked over his shoulder, to Eyre's huge annoyance she saw Pheria leaning against the fence, her dark hair shining in the sun. Pheria detached herself from the fence-line and ambled over to them casually, but her eyes were narrow as she looked at Eyre.

"Was having a morning walk and caught the spectacle," Pheria said as she rubbed Firestorm's nose. Morning walk indeed, Eyre snorted to herself. More like a morning *stalk*, she thought fiercely as Pheria moved closer to Jax. Firestorm responded to Pheria's touch and Eyre felt strangely betrayed.

"He's never done that before," Jax said wonderingly as he looked back at the fence they'd cleared, turning away from Eyre to talk to Pheria. Eyre was irritated intensely, especially when she heard Ischyros snickering from the fence line, but she also was filled with a sense of awe about the experience.

"It was amazing," she said, stroking Firestorm's burnished coat.

"No wonder Lighthorses are so special." Jax brushed his hand down Firestorm's neck and in the sunlight he looked like a prince, the essence of what a Light warrior should be. His bond with his horse was complete now; it was a tangible force. As Firestorm rested his head on Jax's shoulder, there was an aura of strength and goodness about Jax, and for a second Eyre felt sorry for Pheria. Years of wanting to be with him without reciprocation—no wonder she was sour. But Pheria's next words diminished Eyre's sympathy somewhat.

"When they trust you enough, they'll gallop," Pheria said. "The Kikkuli Master did mention that in my group." She looked at Eyre, who had missed many of the classes. "I guess you wouldn't know, of course."

Eyre ground her teeth at the obvious reference to her spectacular ineptitude with Ischyros, but kept her face impassive.

"No," she said lightly. "But I do know an ass when I see one." A certainty came to her at that moment, despite the grass stained on her boots and her aching bones, and Pheria's mean little smile. Eyre looked over at Ischyros, enjoying Pheria's silence as she tried to figure out if Eyre was referring to her or her horse.

"I'll keep trying though." Ischyros's ears pricked but he moved further away, the only sound the munching of the grass he was stuffing into his mouth.

"I'll see you both later then, thanks Jax." Jax looked disappointed as Eyre headed off to pick up her staff from the fence, and he raised a hand.

"See you in class, Eyre." She could feel two pairs of eyes following her the whole way as she headed back through the paddocks. Although she was annoyed with Pheria for turning up, another happy thought had registered as she trekked back towards the arena. Pheria was only there because she'd followed Jax—so why was *he* there? The only answer—that he'd been looking for Eyre—made the whole morning seem worthwhile, and despite her aching body, a smile lit up her face.

CHAPTER TWENTY-FOUR

EYRE DASHED INTO LECTURE Theatre 2 and took a seat next to Beatrice, Abby and Nick just as Madame Overmantle arrived to start their weekly Psionics lecture. Beatrice raised her eyebrows at Eyre's dishevelled appearance. She'd changed her clothes but her windblown hair was quite a sight.

"Ischyros taken you on a good ride again?"

Eyre laughed and pulled her books out, but for some reason didn't enlighten Beatrice about what had happened that morning. She just wanted to savour the memory for a while.

Madame Overmantle beamed out at the class.

"Well, here we are—only a few weeks to the end of your first semester, and I have to commend you on your concentration and your effort these past months. Today I'd like you to turn to your neighbour and to practise communicating telepathically. I know some of you have been making great progress with this; well done to those people. For others, it will take a bit longer for you to master, maybe even years. But telepathy is a skill that will be crucial in your life as a Lightworker so you must work hard at it. Today our theme is flowers. You have twenty minutes to practise sending and receiving images from each other and then we will have a discussion on your progress."

Nick and Abby started to concentrate with each other and Beatrice looked at Eyre and laughed. Neither of them had been particularly successful with their telepathy. Eyre'd had mixed days—sometimes feeling the telepathy current strongly, on other days, unable to receive or send any messages at all. Beatrice had struggled with it in general. Her intellectual brain found it hard to grasp the technique of communicating in the ether, unlike Abby, who had proven to be brilliant at it. Both Eyre and Beatrice had listened at length to Abby as she tried to explain to them how to let go and *feel* the messages in the air, but they hadn't made much progress.

Then Eyre snickered as she received an image in her mind: a woman tipping the contents of a blue and white bag into a baking bowl. Beatrice and her excruciating puns!

"Not that sort of flour, my friend!" she laughed.

Beatrice grinned widely as she realised that *finally* she had managed to send a message!

Eyre shut her eyes, focusing on a field of brightly-coloured yellow daisies. She tried to *chuck* the image across to Beatrice, but there was no response.

"I get it!" Beatrice said loudly. "Roses, all different colours—pinks, reds, peach-coloured—how beautiful, Eyre!"

"You fraud!" Eyre opened her eyes. "Completely wrong. Communication channels are obviously closed today!"

Beatrice broke into giggles and Eyre was about to try again when she felt a sharp pain across her brow. She rubbed her forehead as the pain intensified, then gasped as a sudden image crashed into her mind. A black, slavering beast charged at her through burning flames, teeth gnashing. She struggled to drive the vision from her mind, but it had a fearsome grip and she fell to the ground, writhing as a ferocious pain pounded her head. Dimly she could hear shrieks and cries from other students in the hall, and she was aware of others falling to the floor as she had. From the vastness of her brain a grating, deep voice started to whisper.

"Eyre will die. Eyre will die." The voice increased in volume until it was shouting in her head, and Eyre shut her eyes with the pain of it. Then over the top of it came another voice, calmer but with an overtone of sharpness.

"Whittaker," it called insistently. "Whittaker! The mali is strengthening!" Through her pain Eyre recognized Madame Overmantle's soft voice. What was a mali?, she thought as she moaned in agony. Maybe it meant a migraine, because that was what this felt like, but worse than any headache she'd ever had. Just when she thought her head was going to explode from the pressure, a blinding white light filled her mind and the image was suddenly gone, cleared out by the flash of light. When she opened her eyes she realised she was face down under her desk next to her friends, and that most of the students in the hall were also on the floor, groaning in pain.

Slowly Eyre pulled herself back into her chair. She rubbed her forehead and blinked at the lights—her eyes seemed overly sensitive after the awful event. Looking down to the lecture platform she saw Madame Overmantle anxiously looking out at the students as they dragged themselves back into their seats. Whittaker Ray was standing beside Madame Overmantle, focusing intently on something over Eyre's shoulder at the back of the room. She turned to see what he was staring at and part of her was not surprised to see it was Ben Perrill who engaged his attention. Ben was lounging back in his chair as if he was sitting in a recliner by the pool. But the stare he returned to Whittaker Ray was anything but casual. Ben seemed to brim with rage and a searing red energy as he locked eyes with the older man.

There was a long moment and then finally Ben looked away, yawning. Eyre turned back to Whittaker Ray who clenched his jaw, looking, to Eyre's surprise, like he was about to go absolutely nuclear. This was such a surprising notion that she forgot the pain in her head as she waited to see what would happen. But after a long moment Whittaker Ray's famous equanimity won the battle and he turned away from Ben, addressing the class with a tight voice.

"Is everyone okay? Please head to the Infirmary if you are experiencing any problems." A couple of students stood up shakily and made their way down the stairs. The pain in Eyre's head was gone, but she felt sick and weak. The worst thing was the worry about what she had heard. What was *that*? "Eyre will die?" Did *Ben Perrill* put those images in her head? She wouldn't have thought he was capable of it—he could barely string sentences together, let alone communicate telepathically. But he was definitely mean enough to do it, and he certainly hated her enough.

She put her hand down, feeling that she would recover eventually. But the questions went on in her mind. Turning to Beatrice, she voiced one of them.

"Did you see a Saevus?"

Beatrice's face was white and she leant her elbows on the desk as she rubbed her temples.

"By the Light, yes, and that *voice*, how creepy." But then she raised her chin, eyes flashing. "You will *not* die, if I have anything to do with it! I'll chop a Saevus up for shish kebabs before I allow that to happen!"

Eyre gave a short laugh and regretted it as pain throbbed through her head.

Madame Overmantle surveyed the class with concerned eyes and then rapped on the podium for attention. Several people covered their ears and groaned. Whittaker Ray waited for silence and then spoke.

"I think we will finish here, students. What has happened is a stray thought has ricocheted through the class, increasing in energy as it moved from mind to mind. It is a rare event and potentially dangerous; I am relieved that it seems no serious damage has been done. You will feel sick and headachy tonight, as if you have the flu, so I will release you from further classes this afternoon. Please see the nurse at sick bay if you start to feel worse."

The students packed up and left the lecture theatre very quietly. Any noise seemed to reverberate through Eyre's skull, so she knew why the other students were making as little sound as possible. Beatrice groaned as she reached the bottom of the auditorium.

"Ordinarily I'd be ecstatic about a day off, but I think all I want to do is have a nap!"

"What's a mali?" Eyre asked. She knew she'd heard the term before, but she couldn't remember what it meant. Beatrice looked at her strangely.

"Where did you hear that?"

"I heard Madame Overmantle in my head—she said 'the mali had strengthened'. Didn't you hear that?"

Beatrice shook her head thoughtfully. "No, I didn't. A mali is a demon. I wonder what Madame Overmantle meant by that."

Eyre remembered suddenly that Jengles had used the term about Ben Perrill last year. A more appropriate word could not be found for that dark soul, she thought. But she couldn't see how the mali fit in with Whittaker Ray's explanation of what had happened to the class.

Beatrice gave up trying to figure out the workings of Madame Overmantle's mind and shrugged. "Another mystery for our BANE group to sort out I guess. Speaking of which," she rubbed her forehead. "I have some news to report on my investigations, and I know Nick does too. Perhaps we should take advantage of the afternoon off and meet at the rock?"

Nick and Abby murmured in agreement and Eyre nodded slowly. She hadn't got any information to share, but she was keen to hear what the others had found out. And sitting in the bush might be just the thing to cure her sore head. "Let's meet after lunch," she suggested and her friends nodded.

They left the auditorium amongst a very subdued class of students. The question of whether other people had received the same ricocheting thought as they had was answered when Eyre noticed several of them looking at her curiously. Not all of them were friendly gazes—no doubt some of them were sick of the upheaval that seemed to constantly surround her, and no doubt some of them were also blaming her for their sore heads. Sighing, she trudged along behind her friends, wishing that the drama would stop; she was heartily sick of it too.

CHAPTER TWENTY-FIVE

EYRE WANDERED ALONG THE path towards the boulder, munching on an apple as she contemplated the upcoming BANE meeting. Her task had been to talk to Whittaker Ray about Aethers, but the opportunity to meet with him hadn't really presented itself. She had been so busy with Ischyros, and settling in to her coursework, that she hadn't found the time to organise to talk with him yet.

Her head still throbbed from the morning's commotion, but she was focusing instead on thoughts of Jax. How divine it had been to sit on Firestorm behind him, her arms around his waist. Something about it had seemed so... *right*. And exhilarating! Flying down the hill on the fiery red horse had been one of the most wonderful experiences of her life. And she had to admit, the experience had been wonderful not only because of the horse.

Fallen eucalyptus leaves covered the path through the bush, and Eyre crunched along until she reached the distinctive granite boulder which had been designated for their BANE meetings. Beatrice and Abby were already there, and Eyre sat down with them until Nick appeared, sprinting down the track with a thick black book under his arm. He plonked down beside them, barely sweating from the run.

"Do we do a secret handshake, or sing a song or something?" he asked, his mouth twitching. Beatrice punched his arm lightly.

"Come on, no jocularity! This is serious stuff! Why don't you start—*what* is that intriguing-looking book under your arm?"

Nick brought it out and laid on the ground. It made a dull thump as the weight of it hit the dust.

"This, my friends, is the textbook for our course next year on the Strigis. Apparently we're very good students for wanting to get a head start on our studies!" He laughed. "Mrs Abnett is *most* impressed with us!"

It was a black leather-bound book with worn gold lettering on the front. Curious, Eyre flipped through some pages as Abby and Beatrice looked over her shoulder. There were so many pages, it was impossible to go through them all, but she skipped through a few diagrams and illustrations. The book was a masterpiece of illustration, and Eyre was fascinated as she looked at intricate drawings of Saevus and other types of Strigis—some she knew, such as the Zyx, and others she hadn't seen before. The most common were the Characs, grotesque creatures about a metre and a half tall, with grey, scaly skin, large ears and wide-set small eyes, who had a round mouth filled with sharp teeth. Characs ran beside the Gothak in battle, and sunk their teeth into their victims like a shark, taking huge circular bites out of the flesh. A horrible scorpion-like creature was apparently called a Tuus. Three metres tall, it was black and had huge serrated claws, and a massive stinger on its tail. The Menax that the Kikkuli Master had mentioned was there too. It looked like a giant, horned lizard with sharp, shark-like teeth. As well as the Nahtaivel, a huge, spiked flying creature with jaws like a crocodile and three rows of teeth. And there was a picture of the Interfector Hornet —a huge wasp-like creature that the Gothak rode. It was a dull black colour, with a massive stinger on its tail, and it was the most dangerous foe of Lighthorses.

Beatrice examined the book with joy. She liked nothing more than getting a head-start on future studies. "Did Mrs Abnett say anything about Rhabdor?"

Nick shrugged. "Well, apparently he's the boss I guess, the head of the serpent. But there are no pictures of him in there—I checked. And Mrs Abnett wasn't really keen to elaborate." After a few more minutes of flipping through the fascinating book, Beatrice reluctantly shut the cover.

"Me next," she said. "I've also got news! My job was finding out about those unfriendly-looking blue dudes dressed in purple we saw at the Echelon meeting. Mrs Abnett helped me research that too—she must be wondering at this sudden surge of interest in Lightworker history!

"Turns out they are not Lightworkers, or from Terra, or from Aqua, Caelus or Incendium!"

"The Underworld then?" Nick said dryly. Beatrice smiled.

"No, they're from our universe—out in the vastness of space somewhere. They're called the Thantos Nex, or the Illuminators—and they observe the Overworld only to document historical events. Apparently they never become involved in what's happening, they only watch and record."

"Weird," said Eyre. "That must be hard. Actually, I don't think I like that idea all that much. Imagine seeing the Gothak attack Lightworkers and not helping, even though you could? To be honest, I'm not impressed."

Abby and Nick murmured in agreement, but Beatrice looked thoughtful and played Devil's advocate.

"I suppose if they don't intervene, then they record history as it happens, without subjective opinions. I guess in a way it's helpful to have someone write an account of what's happened."

Eyre looked unconvinced. "I didn't like the look of them at the meeting, and I like them less now I know that. When evil is involved, you *have* to step up or you become a participant just by doing nothing. Their self-justification is only an excuse."

"Cold," Nick agreed. "Not really admirable."

"Well," continued Beatrice, "apparently they are beings of great power, capable of extraordinary feats. But they choose to not use their force, believing it sets an example for all."

"I think I'd be more impressed if they *did* use their powers," Abby said matter-of-factly and the others laughed.

"Well, they obviously take themselves very seriously," Nick said. "See how they looked at the Ranger? They weren't at all pleased with his lack of decorum."

They all muttered in agreement and then Eyre spoke. "Well, I haven't managed to see Whittaker Ray yet, so there's nothing from me. How about you, Abby?"

"Yep! I didn't lurk around the library but I did get some information from Sherry at Central Admin about the mysterious 'Leo' Chrysanthe. His name is listed with the other staff by the Central Admin office window. Leo is actually his first name—so there's no great revelation there. But hey, this is interesting—Ranger is a rank of the *highest honour* bestowed by the Lightworkers to one who has performed a deed of critical significance to the Lightworking community. Sherry said there has only been a handful of other Rangers in Lightworking history. Imagine that! Ranger Chrysanthe? Hard to believe."

Eyre had to agree with Abby's wondering tone. Although she had no doubt the Ranger was a clever man, with many special skills, he hardly had the look or the demeanour of one who had provided a critical service to the Lightworker community. He looked more like a particularly talented clown than a legend of Lightworking history. Abby's brows knitted.

"Of course, that just raised another question, more curious than the first. But no matter who I asked, no one could tell me what the Ranger had done to earn the title. Obviously we will have to work harder to find that out!"

They settled back against the boulder, contemplating all this new information. Eyre felt a bit frustrated. Some questions had been answered, but now there were more to investigate—Ranger Chrysanthe's good deed being just one of them. Where the Thantos Nex live, what their powers were; then there was a whole truckload of facts she wanted to know about the Gothak. Still, it was a start, and she liked sitting at the rock in their secret group. Time had passed swiftly while they'd been there, a brisk wind had risen, tinged with bitter cold—autumn was nearly over and soon winter would be here. Eyre enjoyed the feeling of the chilly breeze whipping across her face and she realised that thankfully, sometime while they'd been sitting there, her headache had gone, and her sore muscles from the cartwheel off Ischyros had also settled down.

Abby was the first to stir, standing up and brushing herself off. "Well, we'd better get going. Don't want to be out here in the dark."

"Indeed!" Beatrice said as they all stood with her. "We might have an early start to our Gothak education."

"Race you back, Eyre," Nick said, and they took off along the path, leaves flying up in a crackling tornado as they went.

CHAPTER TWENTY-SIX

EYRE KEPT UP HER early morning routine and found that as the semester went on, she had started to enjoy again the feeling of running in the cool air. Her fitness definitely improved, but unfortunately, her relationship with Ischyros didn't. She was able to lead him out to the paddock—but only because of his desire to get to the swaying green grass. After the one time he'd let her get on him, she'd tried to lean across his back a few times, but he always moved away with a toss of his cranky old head. Eyre had decided that he was probably just too old—he hadn't been handled enough when he was young, and now he wasn't going to let anyone get close to him —physically or figuratively. And that day he'd let her climb onto his back had only been for an ulterior motive—he was setting her up to look stupid with Jax. Still, she persevered with the routine, and kept him brushed and clean, and eventually his coat began to gleam from the constant grooming and the vitamins she added to his feed. His hooves improved gradually too until all the cracks were gone and the edges were smooth. He still moved with an odd gait though—that wasn't going to change, and when Eyre asked the Kikkuli Master about it, he explained that it was probably due to arthritis, given Ischyros's age. Eyre wondered why they would give a Lightworker such an old horse—it didn't seem fair to either of them really. But there weren't any more horses, so she supposed it was either him or she wouldn't have a horse. She didn't want to say that she would prefer not to have one, so she carried on heading out to the stables every morning. If nothing else, getting outside early in the fresh air was worth the effort.

She'd also been working hard on the Hese stand for the Sector Fair over the past weeks. It would take them many months to complete the top-secret display, but Whittaker Ray, the head of their Sector, was well-pleased with their progress.

As she walked back towards campus, she felt a happy anticipation. Today the first-years were going on an excursion to Lightning Ridge to watch the National Ferito titles, an annual tradition at the school for first-year students. The Lightness Cup race in June and the National Ferito titles were the two biggest annual events in the Lightworkers' calendar.

The students were staying a night and viewing two days of intense competition from the best Ferito competitors in the country. The winners of the national competition would then be eligible to compete in the international competition, which was held every four years in October, in a different location each time, and the honour to host the event was hotly contested. This year was the year for the international competition, to be held in Norway this time. As Eyre ate breakfast with her friends, the Refectory was filled with a hubbub of excited voices.

Beatrice's eyes sparkled. "Apparently we once had someone from the Academy *win* the Nationals. And do you know who that was?" All eyes turned towards her. "*UDi!*" she said gleefully, happy to have a bit of gossip to pass on.

"Really?" Nick said. "The Unlit can compete too?"

"Apparently," Beatrice said. "It's a contest of skill and focus, so having Viq doesn't always mean you're going to win. Although obviously, it must help. Sergeant Tottingham told me we've had another Unlit student from the Academy compete one year, and we've also had three elevated students who've made the Nationals. All of those were from Rufa. Their names are on a board on the wall of the Central Admin building."

Eyre was impressed. "Imagine being good enough to win the title without having Viq! UDi must be amazing. Who would think it?"

"I can't even do Ferito *with* Viq," Abby said, taking another bite. "There's something very scary about that man."

"Well, I have a bit of info too," said Robeson, who was sitting next to Beatrice as he seemed to do quite often nowadays. "Lightning Ridge got its name from a farmer, his dog and two hundred sheep who were struck by lightning and killed. The book I got from the library said it was the Gothak though. Apparently the farmer saw a Saevus attacking his flock and the Gothak wiped them all out so that word wouldn't get around in Entis. But legends of that black creature are around in Entis anyway, although most people think it's just a myth."

"Always full of interesting information, aren't you," Rigmar said, his head on the table and pretending to snore. Robeson pushed him good-naturedly.

They were interrupted as the Sergeant walked to the front of the room.

"Okay, first-years! The Zepps will leave at 9.30 sharp, so you have fifteen minutes to be at the Central Admin launch pad. Don't forget your overnight bag, but leave your staff, you won't be needing it. We will not wait for anyone who is late, so I suggest you hurry."

Like a multi-cellular organism, the students leapt up together, dumping trays at the window for the Jotnar to whisk away. Breaking into groups the students left the Refectory at top speed—this was one excursion no one wanted to miss. Within the required time frame all the students had arrived at the departure pad for the Zepps, and they stood in line as staff ushered them on board.

Eyre sat in her seat next to Abby, and felt her annoying face flush as she noticed Jax sitting a few seats down from them. He leaned forward and winked at Eyre, to Abby's delight. She grinned and elbowed Eyre.

"He doesn't give up, does he?"

"I'm not sure why," Eyre confessed. "He could probably be with anyone. Pheria's definitely keen."

Abby snorted. "I guess he knows who he's interested in," she said. "Shows good taste, if you ask me."

The subject was dropped as the Zepp took to the air and the walls became transparent. The students fell quiet as the Zepp climbed skywards. They still weren't used to the unique mode of travel, and most of them were staring outwards as birds and clouds whizzed by the now-transparent walls of the vehicle.

It took half an hour to get to Lightning Ridge, nine Zepps flying roughly together over the craggy Blue Mountains until the terrain changed into a green patchwork of farmland, and then to the stretching red plains and desert that surrounded Lightning Ridge. The town was situated on the top border of New South Wales, a dry and dusty area that was often the hottest place in the state in summer. The Ranger—who was their pilot—told them during the flight that the Ferito competition was scheduled there to add an element of difficulty to the contest—the idea being that Ferito was often needed in conditions that weren't ideal, or comfortable. He said that sometimes the international titles were held in arctic areas, or in areas of extreme conditions, such as Gruissan in France, one of the windiest places in the world. As Eyre descended from the Zepp and a wave of heat hit her, she decided that the organisers definitely had achieved the degree of difficulty they were after. Despite Autumn being near, the heat was like a heavy blanket, searing across her shoulders and blazing through her lungs with each breath. She was glad she was only a spectator—just walking in this was hard enough. The local miners must be tough to dig the famous black opals from the sun-baked earth, she thought. And she also mentally applauded the farmers who somehow sustained a living in this unforgiving country.

Ahead of her was a huge structure about a hundred metres high; the walls formed from skilfully placed blocks of ironstone boulders. It was circular like a sporting arena, with entranceways along the sides. Sergeant Tottingham lifted her hand for quiet and the students looked at her.

"This is the stadium for the Ferito Titles, built a few years back after a local man offered his spectacular skills as a rocklayer." As she noticed a few students yawning and glancing away, her voice became sharp. "Please do listen to the information we give you, as there will be an assignment to complete about the excursion upon your return." A groan went up and Zanda winced. He'd obviously hoped this excursion was entertainment only. The Sergeant registered the reactions, but continued without comment. "We will put your bags below in your rooms—I'm sure you'll be glad to follow me out of this scorching heat."

The students followed the Sergeant down into the cool earth where a series of rooms had been cut deep under the ground. Eyre, Beatrice and Abby were rooming together and they dumped their bags in the chiselled-out, rock-walled rooms. Eyre sighed in relief at the drop in temperature—the rooms were much cooler than above ground. The Sergeant's booming voice echoed down the hall.

"You have an hour to look around, and then we will all meet in the foyer to go over to the stadium. Don't be late or you will miss out."

Eyre sighed. "Do we really have to go back up?" she said, lying on the bed. "It's so much nicer down here!"

Beatrice harrumphed and knocked Eyre's feet to the floor. "Come on! We're only here once. It's just sweat!"

Eyre steeled herself as she followed her enthusiastic friend back up to the surface. Abby followed behind, and along the way they knocked on Nick's door to get him to come too.

The heat seemed to rise in waves from the sidewalk, but it hadn't deterred the tourists. The town was filled with people here for the Ferito competition and the crowd spilled off the pathways onto the road. Eyre was relieved when the ever-vigilant shopper Beatrice pulled her friends through the door into a blissfully air-conditioned shop. Beatrice proceeded to stalk around with scimitar eyes as if the latest bargain might elude her if she didn't focus hard enough. Eyre sighed and tried to be patient. Shopping was definitely not her strong suit. Abby had just picked up a pair of black opal earrings when Nick, who had been lounging against the wall, equally bored, suddenly made a choking sound. He raced to the shop window and looked out at the hordes of people passing with a desperation that made Eyre spring to the window beside him.

"What is it?" she said. "What are you looking at?"

Nick didn't reply, just continued his intense search of the crowds, and then he dashed out the front door of the shop. Looking a little annoyed at having to leave all the bargains behind, Beatrice shrugged in a resigned way and headed out the door too. Eyre followed her and Abby put the opal earrings down reluctantly.

"Wait a minute!" she called as she scrambled to catch up with them. "I'm coming!" It was impossible to keep up with Nick though; he dashed through the crowd as if it was a mild Spring day instead of the searing furnace that it was. Gasping, Eyre struggled along, trying to see where he was going in the increasing crowds of people. Eventually she levitated up and spotted him turning right down a street not far ahead.

"That way! Don't lose him Beatrice!" Beatrice, her face bright red and shimmering with sweat, gave an extremely annoyed snort. "I'm not losing him," she said in a chagrined tone, "because I intend to catch him and beat the whatsit out of him for doing this! *What* is he up to?"

Abby, puffing along behind and completely out of breath, could only shake her head in an exasperated way as the three of them ran as fast as they could to the side street Eyre had seen Nick turn into. They expected he would be a long way ahead, but they found him stopped in the middle of the road, just as hot, sweaty and grubby from the flying dirt as they were. He was looking down the lane away from them, his shoulders slumped.

Beatrice marched up to him, infuriated. "We only had an hour to look around," she said, her hands on her hips, "and you've just wasted half of it. What were you doing?"

Nick turned his eyes slowly away from the empty road ahead and sighed.

"I'm sorry," he said. "It's just I thought I saw Dad here." He clenched his jaw and looked away. "Mustn't have been him though, because he saw me. He ran off, so I guess it was someone else."

Beatrice and Abby exchanged looks and Eyre felt a sorrow for Nick well up within her. She didn't know his dad, but from what she'd heard, he wasn't a good guy at all. It wouldn't be a surprise if he'd hidden from Nick. Obviously he didn't want anything to do with him, as he hadn't bothered to get in touch at all in the two years since he'd left.

Beatrice's face softened. "No, I'm sure it couldn't have been him, Nick. What would he be doing up here?"

Nick rubbed his eyes, spreading the red dust even further across his sweaty face, and he wouldn't look at the girls.

"I might head back," he said in a low voice. "I think I'll take it easy until we have to meet back in the foyer."

"Okay, see you then," Eyre said awkwardly, pity causing her voice to wobble. They watched him go and then headed back towards the shops.

"What a terrible man," Beatrice said through gritted teeth. "I would like to give him a piece of my mind!"

Eyre laughed at the thought of Beatrice giving Nick's dad a thorough heads-up on his personal qualities.

"Well, keep your eyes peeled," Abby said grimly. "I'm sure it *was* him; Exes apparently like to lurk in mining towns. The tunnels take them closer to the Gothak, and Exes love the darkness. If we do spot him, you go get him, Beatrice!"

As it was, they didn't see any sign of Nick's dad, if he was there, and after browsing a bit longer through the shops it was soon time to meet the Academy students back at the hotel. Beatrice and Abby shoved their purchases in their bedroom and then they all sprinted up the corridor to be in time for the rendezvous.

Nick was already waiting in the foyer, but he didn't comment on the event earlier, and Eyre decided it was better to leave it alone. His face was white and strained and she could understand how he must feel. Imagine spotting your long-lost father, even if he was a jerk, only to have him *run away* from you? Nick had to be feeling rather ordinary after that.

The Sergeant walked into the foyer and thumped her staff to silence the chattering students.

"Right then, follow me. And remember that we are on display as a school here, I want your best behaviour at all times!"

Eyre, Beatrice, Nick and Abby followed a line of students back up to the surface and along a pathway to the stadium. Studying the huge structure, she decided that it looked exactly like something out of a medieval festival from years gone by.

Eyre and the other first-year students followed a huge crowd of Lightworkers into the stadium, where the tiered seats filled rapidly. A buzz of excitement filled the air and many people had banners and placards to support their favourite competitors. There were families there with young ones' wrists tied to balloons, and vendors selling bright ribbons, hats with logos and mock staffs in the colours of the competitors. Eyre sat next to Beatrice, who had bought a hat saying *"Ferito is Neato"* and Abby waved a rainbow-coloured staff with satin ribbons on the top that she'd chosen from a cart full of competition merchandise.

"I can't decide who I want to win—so I got this one. It's a staff for all the competitors!" she confessed.

Eyre laughed and looked around, enjoying the spectacle. Sergeant Tottingham had told them that the stadium held 30,000 seats, and from what she could see, it was going to be a full house today.

The students passed along cups of bubbly, chilled red cider—the traditional drink of the Ferito competition—and buckets of popcorn peas. Peas were a major crop in the area, and readily available—so the organisers roasted and salted them and piled them in large cardboard buckets, sold by vendors who walked up and down the stadium. Eyre stuffed a handful of peas into her mouth and decided they were delicious—crunchy and salty.

As she munched she studied the arena below.

It was a huge open space that held ten roped-off areas like boxing rings, each of them numbered. Beside each ring stood a Rufa Lightworker with a strange horn hung around their neck. Their hands were clasped behind their backs and none of them moved, eyes directed straight forward.

Soon the internal doors to the stadium flung open and a parade of contestants dressed in competition gear of all colours walked into the arena. A thunder arose from the crowd and spectators jumped to their feet, waving banners and cheering. The competitors sat on rows of benches at one end of the stadium, shuffling along as more arrived. By the time the seats were filled, there were about a hundred participants sitting there. A short man wearing a marshal's vest walked out to a central podium and spoke into the microphone, keeping it brief.

"Welcome to the 283rd National Ferito competition!" he called, as the sound of cheers filled the stadium. "We give honour to all of those who have come to compete!"

The Rufa Lightworkers in the arena raised the horns around their necks and blew hard. A strange sound filled the air, and the cheers from the spectators grew louder. A circle of flames fired up from the ground and surrounded the arena. And then the boxing rings filled with competitors as the first rounds began. The competitors had chosen stage names for the competition, some of them imaginative like Colossus, or Tiger Lily, others just used their first names, opting for less colourful titles.

Over the next few hours Eyre and her friends watched the Ferito heats— intense bouts of 20-minute fighting in three sections: Basic Ferito, Single-Blade weapon using the Mnae and Two-Handed fighting using Antaraks. The results from the three bouts were averaged for each competitor and placed on a leaderboard. By the end of the first hour, a Western Australian man and a woman from Tasmania were battling for first place. By the end of the second hour, new leaders had emerged, and the fight for the top spot intensified as the afternoon passed, with several changes of top scorers and upsets when there were unexpected outcomes in the bouts.

Eyre found it exhilarating to watch. This Ferito was nothing like the Ferito they did at school. It was fast, physical and extremely tactical—sometimes a physically unassuming person was a great competitor because of the strategy they employed. Fast reflexes and quick thinking played a huge part in how successful the contestants were. And luck—usually bad—also influenced the outcome—some unfortunates had weapons fail them, or a glint of sunlight on a blade blinding them at a crucial moment, and they left the arena very despondently. There were a handful of Unlit competitors—the only ones not using Viq in the bouts. Most of the competitors were levitating, spinning in the air, and picking up dropped weapons with telekinesis, but the few Unlit competitors were using their fighting skills alone. The rules stated that as long as contestants stayed within the ropes of the ring, any Lightworking force was valid, and the fights were intense and furious as the entrants fought for supremacy. The afternoon finished with the top ten finalists from the hundred competitors listed on the leaderboard: six men and four women; Queensland and Western Australia had two finalists each and the rest of the four states had one finalist each. And the Northern Territory also had a strong contender for the title, as well as the ACT.

The top finalist was a huge, muscular man from Tasmania—who seemed as tall and as strong as the trees the state was famous for. Appropriately enough, the name he had chosen as his ringside moniker—Regnans—came from one of the eucalypts that produced the hardwood called Tasmanian Oak.

The marshal appeared again to call a close to the day. "A round of applause for our top finalist please—Regnans, take the stage." A roar from the spectators filled the air and Regnans strode around the podium, waving a hand the size of a dinner plate. Imagine facing him across the ring! Even Gegenees might take a breath, Eyre thought.

The marshal continued. "Tomorrow the finals will be contested—another exhilarating day of Ferito! Thank you to all the contestants who participated in the heats, and good luck to all our finalists!"

Eyre and her friends trudged with the crowd out of the stadium and headed back to their hotel. It was still very hot despite being late in the afternoon, and Eyre wiped her sweaty brow as the afternoon heat attacked her from above and below, hammering down from the hot sun and reflecting off the steaming earth. At least they had been under cover in the stadium. She wondered how the competitors managed in the intense conditions out in the open—they must have amazing stamina. It seemed that to compete in the Nationals not only did entrants have to be masters of Ferito, they had to have supreme endurance as well. Eyre was keen to see the finals tomorrow, but at the moment her main thought was how she could cool down.

"I'm melting!" she said, fanning her face desperately with her Ferito program. Abby was red-faced and gasping by her side, sweat running down her face, her throat too dry to produce words. Beatrice coughed in the dust and wiped her forehead.

"This is too much! I'm going to see the Sergeant and find out where we can go to cool off!"

The only positive note of the afternoon was that Nick seemed to have gotten over the shock of seeing someone he thought was his father. The distraction of the Ferito competition, and his own pragmatic nature, had helped him to deal with the disappointment. Typically, he'd swallowed the pain and was moving on. His stoic face gave nothing away, and at the moment, he just seemed as uncomfortable and hot as everyone else.

Eventually, it was thanks to Beatrice's perseverance that half an hour later the first-years had climbed aboard the Zepps again and were dropped off at the Darling River near Walgutt. It was a calm, muddy waterway, but no one cared as they jumped off the low banks into the cool water.

"You're a genius Beatrice," Abby announced as the cool water swirled around her overheated body.

"I've been told that before," Beatrice said modestly, and Nick flipped water at her.

Eyre had been slowly floating around the water, enjoying the blissful coolness on her skin, when suddenly a large snake slid across her stomach, its head turning back towards her. Eyre's memory recalled the Napiat Serpent in the Strigis textbook, a water-dwelling, vicious creature whose bite was deadly within ten seconds, and she was so shocked she shrieked and levitated five metres into the air.

Instantly someone had swum across and grabbed the snake, flinging it onto the bank in one smooth movement. As it slid into the bushes, Eyre came back down to the river, a horrible embarrassment colouring her face as she watched the slithering creature go.

"Agh, er, my bad... just a keelback... god, sorry for being a drama queen."

Jax looked at her calmly. "Easy mistake to make," he said. "Snakes are dangerous."

"I thought it was a Napiat Serpent," Eyre said. "Stupid really, as if one would be up here."

Jax's green eyes were intent on hers. "I don't know what a Napiat Serpent is, Eyre," he said, "But you're smart to be careful," he said. "We all need to survive, and fast reactions are good. Don't feel stupid, you moved quicker than anyone I've ever seen." Despite feeling awkward, Eyre felt a warmth move through her. He was trying to help her with her embarrassment, but she also knew he meant what he said, and part of her felt proud at his praise.

"Thanks, Jax," she said.

Eyre and Jax headed for the bank and lay in the sun as it beat down on them. Eyre's skin was tingling, and she knew it was from more than the adrenaline—what *was* the effect he had on her? Jax leaned on his elbow and looked at her calmly.

"I hear we're heading to the Ridge Convention Centre tonight. We're dining with a few other schools from Queensland."

"News to me," Eyre said. "But it sounds interesting. Good idea I suppose to mass cater for everyone."

"Shall I save you a seat?"

Eyre felt herself flushing, especially as she was well aware of the looks her friends were casting her way.

"Sure, that'd be great," she responded, studiously avoiding Beatrice's eye.

Thankfully Sergeant Tottingham strode up at that moment and thudded her staff on the ground.

"The Zepps are ready—climb aboard and make it snappy!"

"See you later, Eyre," Jax said softly and Eyre nodded. *Fine by me* she thought with an inner delight.

CHAPTER TWENTY-SEVEN

EYRE, BEATRICE, NICK AND Abby walked down the road towards the Ridge Convention Centre. It was cooler now, the sun having gone down about a half hour before, and the slight breeze tingled on Eyre's now sunburnt skin. Her hair hung free, soft and shining after the dip in the river and the cool shower she'd had afterwards. She was looking forward to the evening—not exactly a date, really, but since their ride on Firestorm she definitely felt there was something between her and Jax and it was time to find out what that was. At least she hadn't had to agonise about what to wear—strict instructions from the Sergeant were that the dress code was school uniform only, and to make sure it was neat and tidy.

"You are representing our school," the Sergeant had announced, with a stern look in her eye. "You are to remember that your actions reflect upon the Academy and behave accordingly."

The road was filled with students wandering along, not all of them from the Academy of Light. Each school had their own uniform—different colours and styles, but all designed so they were easy to move in. All the students were eyeing each other up, and a loud chatter filled the air as they walked into the convention centre.

Inside was a buffet-style setup with Jotnar bustling around, carrying dishes and setting up the tables. The room was huge, designed to hold about eight hundred people, but the chairs started to fill very quickly as the students filed in. Eyre and her friends sat at a table against the wall and she scanned the crowd for Jax. What if he'd forgotten the invitation, or worse, changed his mind? But her fears were allayed when she spotted him in the middle of the room, waving at her. She hesitated, looking at her friends. Beatrice laughed.

"Go on then! If you don't go, I will!"

Eyre made her way across the room through the crowd of students. She'd almost reached Jax's table when someone grabbed her arm. Turning, she saw a familiar face grinning at her.

"Eyre!" Doc said, and gave her a hug. "How are you?" Eyre felt completely enveloped—he was a huge bear of a boy. She struggled out, laughing.

"Great now—so good to see you Doc! Your school is here?"

Doc indicated a group of students in dark blue uniforms sitting at a few tables. "Yes, I got in to the Brisbane Academy of Light."

"How's it going? You like it?"

"Yeah, actually—the school is great, and the Unlit is pretty good too." Doc beamed at her, then changed the subject. "Weren't the heats great today!"

"Yeah, but not the *heat*," Eyre laughed. "How do they fight in that?"

Doc shook his head, a look of awe on his face. "No idea, but it's awesome isn't it? I'm looking forward to the finals tomorrow."

"Me too. I guess I'll see you there!" Eyre said, and they slapped hands and went their separate ways.

Eyre finally arrived at Jax's table and she stood awkwardly for a second, feeling like everyone was looking at her. But Jax saved the moment when he jumped to his feet and with an elaborate bow, pulled her chair out for her.

"Your table, madame," he said with a flourish. Eyre sat down with relief.

Luke and Saskia were sitting at the table already, deep in conversation, close to each other. They were clearly an item now. They seemed oblivious to everyone else and Eyre felt a tinge of envy. Imagine feeling so at ease with someone! Two people walked up and sat at the table and as Eyre looked up she realised to her dismay that of course, it *would* be Pheria, chattering away to Georgia. Pheria tossed her head and laughed, but Eyre could see her eyes sizing Eyre up: what are *you* doing here, her look seemed to say. Eyre did feel a little out of place, but Jax leaned over to her.

"I always take my dates somewhere special," he whispered, and Eyre laughed. Pure joy bubbled through her—he'd called her his *date*! A line formed between Pheria's brows as she watched their interaction.

"Not enough seats at your friends' table?" she asked Eyre coolly.

"I invited Eyre," Jax said, smiling, "She has a way of livening things up." Everyone laughed and Pheria's look darkened, but she spoke lightly.

"Yes our rustic cousins do have their endearing ways, I guess."

Eyre was annoyed at the backhanded compliment, and couldn't help herself—she had to retaliate.

"I heard you and Jax used to perform in musicals together, Pheria," she said in an interested tone. "In fact, I think I saw a photo of you once." She was referring to the photograph Pheria had shown her when Pheria had implied that she and Jax were going out together, and Pheria knew it. A blush started in her cheeks.

Jax smiled. "Really? Yeah, we did lots of shows together, how interesting you've seen the press. Superstars of the high school musical we were!"

Pheria's blush reached full throttle at Jax's self-deprecating manner and she turned her back on Eyre, starting a very energetic conversation with Georgia, filled with lots of light giggles and effusive hand gestures. It didn't fool Eyre. With a small sense of satisfaction she knew that she had landed a blow, and she didn't mind a bit.

Everyone went to get their meal and over dinner Eyre talked with Jax, enjoying his sense of humour and his sparkling eyes. He was like a magnet—everyone was drawn to him; his entertaining manner and his innate kindness made him the centre of attention at the tables nearby. Several of them had turned their chairs to join in the conversation: laughing and firing repartee back. Jensen was there in his wheelchair, sitting with Zoe, Nia and Colton and they teased each other as the banter became more hilarious. Soon Beatrice, Abby and Nick had come over to join them, and there was a definite party atmosphere in the air.

Halfway through dessert a hand touched Eyre's shoulder and she turned with a smile, half expecting it to be Doc again. But a stranger in a crimson school uniform stood there—a blond, muscular boy with a carefully styled and gelled hairstyle. As soon as she looked at him, Eyre's defences went on alert. She'd seen enough of his type.

"Thought I'd wander over and see the freak," the boy started.

"Carrison—meet Eyre. I guess that's who you're talking about?" Pheria said with a mean smile. Eyre was temporarily stuck for words. *Freak*? Why?

Jax wasn't so slow though. "Carrison, impeccable manners as always, I see. I thought only Queensland schools were eating here tonight."

Carrison Hamlen turned unfriendly eyes to Jax. "There are only a few of us from Sydney so they lumped us in with you. Not many of us wanted to come—the nationals are pretty lame really. Most of us will go to the internationals later this year in Norway, that's a much better show."

"Well, don't let us keep you," Jax said tightly. "Probably time for you to get going."

"I heard there was a girl who had a strange Inguz," Carrison said, studying the indistinct mark on Eyre's arm. She felt herself colouring and had to restrain herself from covering it up. Carrison stuck a finger out and rubbed at her Inguz. "It is weird. How did you get into the Academy with a mark like that?"

"That's enough, Carrison," Jax said in a low voice. He stood up and eyeballed the other boy. "You're being rude."

Carrison smiled slowly. "Why don't you stop me, Jackson?" Jax pushed his chair back and silence descended in the immediate vicinity. Eyre jumped up and touched Jax's arm.

"Don't worry about it, Jax," she said, "it really doesn't matter."

"Oh yes it does," Jax said softly. "Yes it does."

"Well, I want a better look at that!" Carrison said and reached for Eyre's arm. He never got there. Jax knocked his hand out of the way and stood between Eyre and Carrison, his eyes burning. That was of course what Carrison was after—it was obvious he was spoiling for a fight. He swung at Jax, who ducked and punched back at Carrison, hard. Jax's swing connected with a loud thump, and Carrison's head snapped back. He shouted in fury and swung at Jax, hitting him on the shoulder. As Jax staggered, three boys dressed in crimson charged across the room at them.

"Get him!" shouted one, reaching for Jax. Jax shoved him out of the way, and went to turn when one of the other boys rushed him from behind. But before the boy could connect with Jax, help came from an unexpected quarter when Jensen rolled in and knocked the boy's feet from under him. The boy spun past Jax, flipped over Jensen and crashed to the floor. Eyre grinned as she studied the furious-faced, spluttering figure on the floor, thinking she shouldn't be surprised that Jensen had charged in first. Jensen was Rufa, with a fiery warrior's temperament. Jensen's action seemed to stop the inertia in the Academy of Light students, because all at once, everyone jumped up. Chairs fell over backwards and fists clenched as white-clad and crimson-clad students looked at each other.

Rigmar set it off. Calmly picking up his bread roll, he launched it with pristine accuracy at a crimson-dressed boy's face. It smacked him full on, leaving a smear of butter as it fell to the ground. Unable to believe what had happened, the boy turned to look at Rigmar, wiping the butter from his face and quivering from the insult. When Rigmar laughed out loud the boy launched at him with a roar of rage.

"What ho, my friends," Rigmar shouted in glee, firing potatoes at the charging boy. "Incoming!"

Pandemonium reigned as food flew through the air and students jumped on tables. What had started as two boys having an altercation escalated into everyone in the convention hall—all the schools—throwing punches or food at each other. The Academy students were as gung-ho as any of them—even Colton was in amongst it all, covered in spilled pumpkin soup and grappling on the floor with a large boy in a blue uniform. The air was thick with culinary missiles, and shouts and curses and uproarious laughter filled the hall as some evidently found their mark.

Eyre ducked as a boiled egg whizzed by her ear, but when she stood up, someone's fist connected with her eye, setting off an explosion of dancing lights. She sat down heavily, which also hurt, and then the familiar burn began inside her. Leaping to her feet she stomped through the crowd, searching for the blond-haired boy. She finally found him, still fighting fiercely with Jax, but by now they had worked their way to the other side of the hall. She shoved her way through grappling students and tapped Carrison on the shoulder. When he turned, his breath heaving, she stood in front of him, burning with fury.

"This is for you, *freak*," she hissed, and shoved her palm hard at his nose. The blast of Viq flattened his face and he stumbled back a step. Screeching in pain and rage he lurched towards her, but Jax stepped in and grabbed his arm. Swinging hard, he launched Carrison across the floor, collecting several chairs as he skidded along on his back.

The noise in the hall had reached an ear-splitting level when suddenly a high-pitched whistle rent the air. It was so loud it brought several students to their knees, covering their ears.

By the time the sound had stopped and the students got to their feet, five pairs of fierce eyes stared at them, the Sergeant's most ferocious of all. Staff members from all five schools surveyed the less-than-impressive sight. The bedraggled students—uniforms ripped, covered in food, hair like haystacks—tried to smooth themselves over as they stood under the unrelenting glare. A loud plop! as a piece of sponge cake fell from Zanda's shirt onto the floor made the Sergeant grit her teeth and move forward, her considerable muscles bunching under her shirt as she pointed a finger at the silent mob.

"I think we can all agree that this is behaviour unbefitting a Lightworker," she said in a voice that barely concealed her rage. "You are all to clean up this abysmal mess you have made and when it is IMMACULATE, you are to head back to your respective accommodations. No one will eat tonight, this is absolutely disgraceful!"

The subdued students started to walk around picking up chairs and dishes, making, squelching sounds as they waded through the spilled food and drink. When one hapless fellow slipped over and fell flat on his face, Eyre thought the Sergeant was going to use Occido on him there and then. The Jotnar emerged and handed out buckets, mops and cloths, and the shamefaced students began the mammoth task of cleaning up the disaster area. It took them a long time, and then they left in groups, talking softly to each other. They all knew they were in big trouble.

CHAPTER TWENTY-EIGHT

BACK AT THE ROOMS, Eyre, Nick and Beatrice looked at each other. Eyre was worried. She had never seen the Sergeant in such a state, and she knew there would be repercussions. A knock came at their door and when it opened, Jax stood in the hallway, a kaleidoscope of food decorating his body. Eyre waved him in and he stood in the room looking at everyone. Nick had a Pro Hart masterpiece of pasta all over his uniform; Beatrice's spectacles were cracked and bent, and Abby's hair looked like a cockatoo had been in residence there for a very long time. Eyre herself had a very tender eye where the fist had connected with her face, and she knew it was going to be black in a few days. And her uniform was splotched with crimson where a bowl of beetroot had connected with her midriff. Jax surveyed them all.

"Well, I really know how to show a girl a good time," he said. There was a long silence, and then Abby let out a snort of laughter. That set Beatrice off, and then they were all hooting hysterically, as much from the release of tension as the way they looked. Eventually, hiccupping with laughter, and wiping the tears from her face, Eyre shook her head.

"I don't know what's going to happen after this, but you know, it was almost worth it! It was pretty funny."

"Well," Jax said. "I know what's going to happen to me—that's why I'm here, I wanted to say goodbye. I've been suspended for the rest of the semester and I'm to go home immediately." A shadow crossed his face. "I will not be popular with my family."

"That is so unfair," Eyre said hotly, "we were all involved. I'm so sorry you've been blamed for it—and I guess it was all my fault."

"Not your fault," Jax said. "I've known Carrison Hamlen for years and he's always been a jerk. He wanted to get at me one way or another, and you were just convenient."

Everyone made noises of commiseration, and then Jax looked awkward. "Well, I guess I'll see you when I get back, Eyre." He walked over and gave her a brief hug, which after a moment she returned, her face scarlet and now matching her shirt very nicely. Then Jax left, leaving everyone smirking at Eyre. She sighed, knowing she was in for a roasting. But fortunately she was saved by a booming voice out in the hallway.

"First-years, I want you out here, now!" the Sergeant hollered.

Doors opened slowly and students filed out into the corridor, huddling against the walls as they tried to fit in the narrow walkway. The Sergeant's eyes were like knives as she watched them come out but she didn't say a word. Eyre thought that was worse, actually, like waiting for the guillotine to drop, and she exchanged a worried look with Beatrice. They were in for a blasting. Finally the last door closed and the Sergeant looked up and down the corridor at the students in their food-splotched clothing.

"I couldn't be more disappointed in you," she said, her face a mask. "Pack your things and board the Zepps. We are heading back to the Academy." Then she walked past all the students and out of the building.

There was a moment when no one moved—they'd been expecting a lengthy lecture and this was most surprising. But then, knowing that being late was definitely not an option tonight, there was a mad scramble as everyone rushed into their rooms and started throwing stuff into bags. Eyre moved just as fast as everyone else, but she was feeling terrible. The Sergeant's lack of emotion was a worse punishment than anything—she was obviously so unhappy she couldn't even speak to them. Sighing, Eyre threw her bag over her shoulder and headed out with the rest of the students. And apart from the trouble they were in, it was so disappointing to miss the Ferito finals tomorrow.

It was a very silent trip back to school. Abby turned the lights off in their room and Eyre lay on her back, staring at the ceiling for quite some time. She wondered what was going to happen to them tomorrow.

The next morning a special meeting was called in Lecture Theatre 1 for all first-year students. No one spoke as they filed in and took their seats. Eyre looked around for Jax, but of course he wasn't there. She was sorry that he'd taken the brunt of the blame for the event—really it hadn't been his fault at all. And she wasn't surprised when Mandig Vela walked to the front of the lecture theatre, with his usual sneer on his face.

"I see you have made something of a name for yourselves," he began, surveying the hall. "Not exactly the reputation this school is after and a disappointment to us all. You are fortunate we didn't send the lot of you home."

He paused and gave a slight smile. He's enjoying this, Eyre thought.

"You will report for detention every day after classes until the end of the semester." A quiet groan travelled around the room. Normally the time after class before dinner was a chance to relax, socialize, swim or just chill out in the common room.

"Silence!" the Professor shouted. "In addition, you are all banned from watching the International Ferito Competition later this year." The Professor seemed to relish the look of dismay that travelled around the room —the students were devastated, as it was such an anticipated event in the Lightworking world. The Professor strode across the room, pointing his finger at the silent class.

"If it were up to me there would be more serious repercussions, so count yourselves lucky that this is *all* that is happening after such atrocious behaviour," he yelled. "You will practise your Staff Forces for an hour and your prohemium for an hour every afternoon until the semester finishes. No exceptions. This student group has proven so lacking in ability in those two areas it is probably something you should be doing anyway. You may leave now and go to your usual classes."

There was a collective sigh and Eyre knew she'd received it telepathically —no one would be game to make a noise out loud. She sighed too. What a pain! She would be counting down to the end of semester, there would be no time for fun in the next couple of weeks.

Students packed up their gear and some headed out of the lecture hall. Beatrice and Eyre stayed, as their next lecture was Psionics, but Abby and Nick had Music and Astral Travel, so they left with the crowd. When Oorlock came in he gave a slight smile as he took in the dejected faces around the classroom.

"Not the most impressive conduct, by all accounts," he said. "But one event does not define you. I myself believe there is value in a fall—how you pick yourself up is what matters most of all, more important than the fall itself. So you should concentrate on handling that in a manner worthy of a Lightworker and take the lesson from what occurred.

"If you are to progress with the Staff Forces and the prohemium, you must train your mind to *focus*, which is also the essence of psionics. So let us work on that focus today and hope that it will have a positive effect on your extra training schedule."

Working on focus, Eyre discovered, was sitting in your chair and concentrating hard enough to give yourself a grade 4 migraine. Last year at the training camp she had made relatively quick progress once her Viq came in. But this year everything had seemed a struggle. Nothing was easy, and her level of Lightworking skill had been decidedly unimpressive. She sighed and tried to stop her mind wandering. An exclamation from Oorlock made everyone look up. He clapped his hands delightedly.

"Oh well done!" Someone down the front—Madeleine, Eyre discovered to no surprise as she peered down the rows—had managed to lift their Felsic in the air and was turning it slowly on an angle, like the latest product on display in an electronics showroom. It was a bit like student 10 had achieved at the TEPs last year, but Madeleine had managed to make it move much more smoothly, in a 3D rotational display, as well as moving it vertically. Madeleine's brow furrowed in concentration as she lifted her hand. The Felsic moved up and down as it rotated 360 degrees, then gently descended to the desk. Oorlock clapped his hands.

"Excellent! Progress at last—I knew you could do it. Let us keep practising." After Madeleine, a few others managed to move objects around in front of them, although none of them as spectacular as Madeleine's effort. But Oorlock was happy, walking from desk to desk and encouraging the students. Then a hoot from the back made Eyre swivel around.

"Put me down!" Zanda said crossly as he spun upside down in the air.

Oorlock marched up the aisle. "Who is doing that? Put that student down!"

No one responded, but whoever it was took Oorlock at his word because with a screech Zanda made a sudden descent, flipping in the air and slamming into the seat. It obviously hurt, because he groaned and rubbed his side where the arm of the chair had jammed into his ribs. Eyre didn't have to look far to figure out who had done it: Ben Perrill's derisive sneer made it obvious who was responsible. But part of her was surprised. Ben was good at Ferito and the physical skills of Lightworking, but it seemed his psychic skills were also improving. Even Madeleine's effort with the Felsic faded in comparison—it took a huge amount of force to lift a person like that.

Oorlock was obviously equally bamboozled by the display, and his eyes roamed the class, looking for the culprit. Not knowing the students as Eyre did, he wasn't able to figure it out, and given that Ben wasn't exactly standing up to take credit for his actions, after a moment Oorlock walked back down to the front of the class, a frown creasing his brow. He studied the class from the podium.

"I have to hope that you all know that *that* was an unacceptable use of Light force, and I'm disappointed that the person responsible has not seen fit to own up to it, which is probably worse than the action itself in my opinion. However, given that the perpetrator is lacking in moral courage, we will continue, and if any further transgressions of this nature occur, please be warned that I will be involving the school in the matter."

The class continued as Oorlock tried to help students gain control of their mental powers. But after Ben Perrill's display no one else could manage any Viq other than moving objects a small distance. Even the positive Oorlock looked a little jaded as he waved them out of class.

"Never mind, never mind," he said. "Next time you'll get it. Try and do some practise outside of class; that will undoubtedly help."

The students were subdued as they left the auditorium—everyone was feeling bad. Eyre and Beatrice picked up their staffs from their room and then headed to the Training Shed for the first of their detention activities: Staff Forces. Abby and Nick met them on the way over and Eyre groaned silently when she saw Sergeant Tottingham waiting for them with a steely glint in her eye and a very grim face. The Sergeant surveyed the group for a minute before she spoke.

"Only a couple of weeks 'til the end of semester, and I have to say that I will be glad for the break. This year has been one of the most unimpressive I have ever seen on a number of levels, and it's not for the lack of talent. I don't know what is going on with you all, but unfortunately I have to keep trying to turn you into a Lightworking force. So ready your staffs and we will get started. After this, Kofi E Vygn has very kindly agreed to take your extra prohemium practise for the next two weeks. I do hope E Kofi does not report back to Terra what a dismal lot of students you are."

Eyre and the other students shuffled their feet. Having the Sergeant angry with them was bad enough, but even worse than that was that every word she said was true: they *were* an unaccomplished lot in general, with only a few students standing out and making progress. At least she wasn't alone, Eyre thought gloomily. It would be so much worse if it were only her that was failing so badly. Nick shot her a look: he didn't like it either. Eyre sighed. She was just going to have to work harder.

CHAPTER TWENTY-NINE

EYRE LED ISCHYROS BACK to his stall as the cool mist of early morning hung across the fields. Snow had fallen the previous week, early for the season, and the remnants were still showing at the sides of the fences. Her breath came out in small puffs as she closed the stall door behind her and turned to Ischyros, who as usual was ignoring her.

Today was the last day of the semester and she was looking forward to getting back to her cabin and relaxing for a couple of weeks. Since the Ferito tournament the weeks had flown by in a blur of lectures and training, but the days had been rather subdued. It was obvious that the food fight had been a huge transgression, and a gross embarrassment to the school—unheard of, really—and a pall had hung over the classes since then. The end of semester had wound down with a decidedly flat vibe and a break would be good to blow the memory of the disastrous event out of everyone's minds. And despite the extra sessions with Staff Forces and the prohemium, there hadn't been a lot of improvement in those skills—from anyone. It seemed that there was an unmoveable block holding back the whole year, and the sense of failure hung over most of the student body.

As Eyre brushed Ischyros down, she reflected that she hadn't made a lot of progress with him either. Apart from letting her lead him around and groom him, he wasn't having a bar of her. No riding at all, and it wasn't even within the realms of possibility that she might experience the elusive gallop everyone was after which would prove their Lighthorse had bonded with them. But Abby, Nick and Beatrice were all progressing well with their riding and they really enjoyed the class.

Finally Eyre finished grooming Ischyros and put the brushes in the basket. With the snow on the ground, Ischyros was quite happy to stay in his stall, the cocksfoot grass being well below reach now that Winter had arrived. Eyre gave him some chaff in a bucket and then sprinted back to campus thinking philosophically to herself that if she was going to have the honour of being the only foot soldier in the Lightworking force, it was probably just as well she was keeping her running up.

As she arrived back at the dorm there was a bustle of activity as students packed their bags and parents arrived to take them home. Beatrice had organised her bag the night before, so she was waiting for Abby, who was stuffing things in to her backpack as if she was going away for two months.

"Really, Abby," Beatrice was saying as Eyre walked in. "You probably won't need your shorts. It's wintertime, girl—leave them behind! And we're only away two weeks—you've got stuff at home."

Eyre wiped the sweat off her face and laughed at the sight of Abby's bulging bag. "You'd better work on your telekinesis skills. Carrying *that* around is going to be a pain!"

Abby hoisted her bag on her shoulder. "You never know what you're going to need," she said piously, and flounced out the door.

Beatrice and Eyre laughed. Beatrice picked up her bag as Eyre started to grab things out of her cupboard. "I'll get going too—Dad's meeting us in half an hour so I'll hang around the Admin building. See you over there."

It didn't take Eyre long and before long she'd joined Abby, Beatrice and Nick who were talking to Ranger Chrysanthe in front of the carved doors to the Admin building. The Ranger's strange purple eyes crinkled.

"Not the most auspicious semester, I've been hearing."

Eyre looked down at the ground. "Well, that would be an understatement," she said. "I'm wondering if I'm actually going to have to repeat this year—the prohemium seems way beyond me."

"And I can't get any force from my staff," Nick said gloomily. "I'd be better off using it to whack someone."

Beatrice's mouth turned down. "I knew it would be hard, but I did feel I might be doing better than this."

"Evidently our year is going down in history as the most unaccomplished first-year students ever," Abby added.

The Ranger smiled. "Well, perhaps a break will do you all good. Becoming a Lightworker takes a great amount of time; don't expect to be able to do it all at once."

There was a collective sigh, and then a flash of light flared as Peter Edmunsun appeared in front of them.

"Ready to go?" he asked.

"Yes!" they responded as one.

CHAPTER THIRTY

EYRE STRETCHED OUT ON her bed luxuriously. It was so nice to be home, and more to the point, so nice to have somewhere to *call* home. She loved her little cabin, with its bright colours, but most of all its memories of her family. She was really enjoying the break and had spent the first week walking in the bush and keeping up her running. Snow had fallen again and it was starting to heap up now—earlier in the season it had melted away but now the drifts were mounting, piling up around the eucalypts. Eyre and her friends had still swum at the mystical Buyabarra Billabong though—surprisingly the water was warm in winter and all the more enticing because of the crisp air outside. Lachie was spending the holidays with a friend, and Beatrice and Abby's parents, and Whittaker Ray were at the Echelon, so they'd had a lot of time to relax and recover from the busyness of the semester at the Academy.

Today Beatrice had suggested they venture back to the Transit. Eyre was definitely not keen after their last visit, but she understood the sense in it—to face her fear despite her misgivings. Something had gone terribly awry last time, but this time Jengles was coming with them to make sure they had no problems. Eyre had to admit she felt a lot happier knowing he would be there.

They were meeting mid-morning, so Eyre decided to take her morning cup of tea upstairs to look at the glass window again, as she often did in the morning. She wandered up the winding staircase and sat on the old couch as the sun streamed through the stained glass. The changing of the images still fascinated her, and it was a trip through history to see each image as it depicted events of bygone times. Jolin the Second was a genius, and she felt so privileged to watch his beautiful art transition from scene to scene. Two people in a canoe drifting down an idyllic river. Images from all four Alterworlds, and her favourites: the set of panels that showed breathtaking

Australian scenes. She finished her tea and wandered down to the kitchen, trying to decide how to fill the time before they headed out to the caves.

Since she'd been back to the cabin she'd been down to the basement a few times, although nothing new had been revealed to her from the Lightkeeper. But Eyre liked spending time down there—just seeing the images of her parents was comforting.

So she decided to spend the last bit of time that morning going through the Wisdom and listening to the holograms again, and she thought she might study the genealogy chart—there was so much information in there.

But to her surprise, when she opened the Lightkeeper, the holograms of her parents had a new message for her.

"We have information for Whittaker Ray," her father said. "We had planned to tell him ourselves, but obviously we were not in time."

The hologram of Eyre's mother spun slowly in a circle as she spoke. "Tell Whittaker Ray this, word for word, and do not repeat it to anyone else. It is your burden to keep this message to yourself, as we also had to. No one but him can be trusted; sadly, the Dark forces are working within the Lightworkers themselves. The fact that we are no longer with you is testament to that fact."

"Tell him," Eyre's father continued, that the Sea Crone has told us: "*The Isars can be seen by the Aether during the Leonid.*"

"The Isars can be seen by the Aether during the Leonid," Eyre repeated to herself, trying to memorise the message accurately. It meant nothing to her—although she'd heard of Aethers at the Determinant Dozen meeting. But obviously Whittaker Ray would know what the message meant. It had a feeling of huge importance, and responsibility, which was unsettling. But she also felt uncomfortable that she could not mention it to anyone else— not the Edmunsuns? Surely they were trustworthy? As she sat on the cold floor, mulling it over, clarity suddenly came to her. Perhaps the reason she should keep the message to herself was also for the safety of others—the fewer people that knew the meaning of this critical message, the better. That realisation gave her relief, and a desire to do exactly as her parents asked. She would never do anything to put her friends at risk.

However, Whittaker Ray would not be at the campsite until tomorrow night. So, although she had memorized the message, she would be unable to deliver it until he arrived. Holding the glowing Lightkeeper Eyre suddenly realised she would be late to meet her friends, so she put the crystal box back in the oak chest, deciding the genealogy could wait for another day.

Beatrice, Abby and Nick were waiting by the Mantle when she came out of her cabin, shrugging a bag over her shoulder. "Jengles will be here shortly," Beatrice said as she tightened her own backpack straps.

"I'm hoping for a less dramatic trip this time," Nick said. "Fly soup isn't my most favourite meal."

Abby laughed. "Well, even without the attacking flies, I'm not so keen on caves. It wasn't helped by our last trip there, I can assure you!"

"Well I do agree with you," Eyre said. "I don't like confined spaces. Or heights, for that matter which wasn't helped greatly when I got knocked off the Iridis last year. I guess I'm generally a coward!" During the TEPs last year, a sudden force had shoved Eyre off the huge rainbow, but she was saved by the Ranger who had used therianthropy to change into a pelican. She had mentioned the Ranger's ability to her friends over Christmas, but hadn't bothered to say anything about her fall off the Iridis, thinking everyone had gone through the same experience.

Three pairs of eyes turned towards her.

"You got knocked off the Iridis?" Abby gasped, her eyes round. "How did you survive?"

Eyre hesitated, confused by their surprise. "Well, didn't you?"

"No," Beatrice said, aghast. "And I would have died from fright if I did. I'm sure students aren't meant to leave the Iridis. I should think there'd be a few pointed letters to the school administration if they lost any students."

Eyre frowned. "Well, the Ranger saved me—I told you at Christmas that he could shapeshift. He turned up as a pelican and flew me back to the Iridis."

Nick shook his head. "I'm sure no one else said that had happened. I wonder what went on with you?"

Eyre thought hard and then Professor Vela's enraged face flashed into her mind. He had been so angry when he realised she'd been hiding in the auditorium—could it have been him? Surely not. Surely even he would hesitate at trying to kill a student? But she said nothing to her friends, the recent words of her parents echoing in her ears. If it was true that there was danger within the Lightworkers, they didn't need to know this.

She shrugged her shoulders. "Ah, you know me. Just bad luck I guess. A passing cyclone or something? And anyway, the Ranger was there, so no drama. I just thought it was part of the test."

Beatrice rolled her eyes. "I guess. Glad that one missed me though."

A noise from across the clearing distracted them and when they turned they realised it was Jengles, huffing and puffing in importance as he clomped across towards them, a sack of luxes under his arm.

"Just as well you're ready. I didn't want to be kept waiting for you!" he said grumpily, oblivious to the fact that he was the last one there. He kept walking, and when no one moved, he turned around to them. "Well, come on then! Don't be taking all day! Except you, flower," he said to Eyre. "You can take your time."

Beatrice burst out laughing, causing Jengles to scowl all the more darkly. But he kept stomping on ahead.

"Petal," whispered Beatrice to Eyre.

"Blossom," Abby added.

"Rosebud," Nick sang as he pirouetted ahead of her.

Eyre shook her head and snorted as she followed along behind them.

Jengles stomped on, oblivious to the performance going on behind him. "That mali has been given something to think about after he attacked you last time," he said, his voice dark. "The first mark of the Mimir. I doubt he'll try again, but I'd rather come with you today to make sure." Beatrice looked at Eyre and raised her eyebrows in a question, but didn't say anything as they followed Jengles towards the dark opening in the mountain.

As she walked along Eyre thought about what Jengles had said. She figured he had been talking about Ben Perrill, but what was 'the first mark of the Mimir'? Then with a shock she remembered the scar around Ben's neck she had seen after the trip to the arms depot and huffed in surprise. Had *Jengles* done that? Was *that* the mark? It had looked the result of an awful injury, almost like a terrible burn and it must have been painful. Still, Eyre mused, some days *she* would like to do that to Ben herself. She made a mental note to find out more about the first mark of the Mimir – another enigma for BANE to work out!

They wound their way through the craggy rocks at the base of the cliffs until they found the entrance to the Transit. Jengles passed them each a lux and they rubbed it to light it up. The glowing orbs floated slowly up above their heads and they stepped into the dark passageway of the Transit.

For a second Eyre felt panic hammer against her ribcage, but then she took a deep breath and swallowed her anxiety. The dread she was feeling was a result of Ben Perrill's actions, not the caves themselves, and she forced herself to remember the beautiful cavern at the end of the dark tunnels. They were safe with Jengles, she was sure of that, and she needed to get over this fear.

CHAPTER THIRTY-ONE

EYRE FOLLOWED JENGLES AND her friends through the dark passages, the luxes casting weird moving shadows as they walked onwards. As before, it was about an hour before they came out of the narrow passageway and into the crystal–filled cavern. Eyre's heart sang as she looked around her at the magnificence of the great space, and she felt so glad she had come back. The sparkling rainbow of crystals of all types and shapes was quite something to behold. She walked around the silent cavern, touching crystals and trying to identify what they were. All different types, all together—it was not the usual way of the earth. Some other force had created this glowing arena. She was studying a particularly large sapphire crystal when she heard Jengles exclaim, and the tone in his voice made her turn, fast.

"Dimmog!" Jengles swore. "By the Aura, what has happened here?"

Walking over, Eyre could see that one entire side of the cavern's crystals had been smashed and crushed. Bits were lying all over the ground, and entire formations had been flattened, as if something very large had crashed against it.

"I don't like this," Jengles said softly, looking around at the darkness in the many branches of tunnels leading from the cavern. "This be blasphemous, cursed. We need to head back *now*, I must meet with President Zircon as soon as possible."

The softness in his voice was unlike anything Eyre had heard from him before, and it was all the more frightening than if he had screamed out loud. Jengles waved them towards the passage they had come down.

"Don't be afraid, I can sense that nothing is here now. But we must get back. This be not a safe place."

Beatrice led the way back through the tunnels, with Abby and Eyre following. Nick was behind Eyre and Jengles kept at the rear. Eyre could hear him stopping occasionally and turning around, and the fear she had been trying to suppress came firing its way back up again. If there was nothing to be afraid of, then why was Jengles turning around all the time? Her legs were moving as fast as they could as they travelled back uphill, her mind struggling with the impulse to run, run, *run*! Too many terrifying events lately had made her instantly ready for flight—horrifying creatures and situations with the very real possibility of death had changed her natural reactions forever. She would never hear a strange sound again without instantly getting ready to flee. But apart from the fast pace of walking, and the disturbing echo of their rapid footsteps, nothing happened on the journey back and eventually they emerged out of the tunnels into the light. Eyre was so glad to see the sunlight, though she still felt she had to race away from the caves.

Jengles bowed deeply. "I must be going. I am sorry we didna stay long. I will contact Whittaker Ray." And then a circular lid of soil opened not far from him, and he disappeared inside it.

Eyre looked at her friends and they started walking back, quickly, to the cabins.

CHAPTER THIRTY-TWO

THE NEXT MORNING EYRE woke with a dark feeling in her stomach. It took her a few seconds to remember what had happened the day before, and when she did, she sat up to look out the window. Part of her wanted to check that all was well outside, although she knew they were safe under the Mantle. There was a stillness outside, no wind at all, but a bleak, grey cloud sheared across the sky. The weather was changing; Winter was about to strike.

Dressing quickly in warm clothes, she headed outside, her eyes automatically searching the perimeter. She was becoming a real Lightworker she realised. She would never look at the world the same way again.

Beatrice came down the stairs of her cabin in her track pants and a padded jacket, holding a mug of tea.

"Want one?" she asked. Eyre shook her head but headed over and sat next to her on the step.

"Whittaker Ray came back last night," Beatrice said, and Eyre felt the dread rising.

"Must be bad then," she said, her eyes focusing on the trees.

"I don't know what has been in those tunnels, but Jengles didn't like it. So yep, probably bad," Beatrice replied, smiling ruefully.

"I wish things would just go along quietly for once," Eyre said, rubbing her forehead. "It just seems we get through one thing and then another happens... I feel worried and fearful all the time."

"The Gothak are rising," Beatrice said softly. "It will get worse." She turned to Eyre and hugged her. "If it's any consolation, I feel the same way. It's been a while since things were normal around here."

Eyre sighed. "Well I guess Whittaker Ray will be disappearing again soon, but I really want to talk to him before he goes. So if you see him before me, could you mention that?"

As Beatrice raised an eyebrow, Eyre continued smoothly. "Well, I'd like to get my part of the BANE information sorted—you all have found out about your questions and I haven't found out about Aethers yet. I'd also like to find out what 'the first mark of the Mimir' means. I'd better get on to it – Whittaker Ray will probably be gone soon and who knows when I'll be able to speak to him again?"

Beatrice took a sip and nodded. "Yeah, I guess so. Once he's with the Echelon they'll be tied up for quite some time I suppose. Mum and Dad were meant to come back tonight too, but they're staying longer. Drama afoot, yet again." She looked at Eyre and gave a crooked smile. "You're not the only one whose parents keep secrets from them, you know. It seems to be an Echelon characteristic."

Eyre felt a sliver of guilt at the secrets she was keeping from her friend, but knew it was for Beatrice's good. Eyre was beginning to understand now why her parents kept things from her, and why Beatrice's parents might be doing the same. Sometimes things were complicated.

Abby emerged at that point from her cabin in her pyjamas, rubbing her eyes. But when she felt the frigid air she shrieked and scampered back inside. A few minutes later she was back, dressed in warmer gear and Beatrice laughed.

"Not in your shorts then, my friend?"

Abby whacked her on the arm and looked around, stretching. "Well, I wonder what we're in for today? Never a dull moment is there?"

The door to Nick's cabin opened and he walked towards them. No sleepy face or rubbing eyes for him. His ever-watchful eyes had taken in his surroundings at a glance, Eyre noticed. It was like he could sum up a situation in a second, a good survival skill she supposed.

"Whittaker Ray came back last night," he said as he joined them.

"I know," Beatrice yawned. "I couldn't sleep and I saw the flash when he got here. How is he? Did he say anything about Jengles?"

Nick looked wry. "Well, he didn't say much, but he did look worried. Nothing has been in that cavern for centuries, is all he told me. But I guess the speed he's returned says most of all."

Whittaker Ray appeared and walked over to the group huddled on Beatrice's doorstep. A line between his eyebrows was the only sign that he was troubled.

"Jengles sent a message about what you saw yesterday. It is of concern to us, and I am going to examine the area this morning, and then I must return to the Echelon. Jengles said the crystals were broken in the cave?"

"Yes," said Beatrice, "like something huge had smashed against the wall. It was disturbing."

"And sad," Eyre added softly as Whittaker Ray nodded.

"The Transit is hallowed ground for the Lightworkers. I shan't lie to you —this is indeed serious, so you mustn't go back again until we find out what is going on."

Abby gave an ironic laugh. "Well, no problem there—you'd have to drag me back there with a bulldozer!"

Whittaker Ray turned to go and Eyre cleared her throat. "Uh, Mr Ray?"

He looked at her and she continued. "Could I uh have a word with you?" He hesitated for a moment, and then realising that she meant *alone*, raised surprised eyebrows and recovered.

"Oh well of course, I was just about to have a cup of tea before I left. Why don't you come and talk to me while I do that? Nick, Beatrice and Abby could you grab some branches for the Mantle, we seem to be getting a little low and it is probably important to keep the stack well maintained."

Nick and Abby jumped up, but Beatrice followed more slowly, and Eyre could see her mind ticking over as she eyed Eyre thoughtfully. There was no need for secrecy with the questions Eyre had wanted to ask Whittaker Ray, so why had she asked to see him alone? Eyre knew she was going to have to cover that one when she saw Beatrice next.

As Whittaker Ray made his tea he waited for Eyre to talk. She wasn't sure how to begin, so she asked the easy question first.

"I was wondering what 'the first mark of the Mimir' might mean. Jengles mentioned it and I was hoping you could explain."

Whittaker Ray paused a moment, his bushy eyebrows working up and down as he considered her question.

"The Mimir are the guardians of Light," he eventually began. "And receiving a mark from them is a most dire warning, given under only the most extreme circumstances. I presume you are referring to Ben Perrill?" Eyre nodded and he continued. "Yes, well Ben did receive a mark after your first trip to the Transit. The Mimir take the safety of Lightworkers very seriously, and especially in your case, Eyre. Jengles has disciplined Ben because of his behaviour in the tunnels. The Mimir have a burning lariat that is used to mark the recipient and warn them against behaviour that is considered most extreme, but not quite bad enough to warrant action by the Lightworker Governance of Laws and Regulations. It's a mark taken most seriously by the Mimir. Three marks and the Lightworker is sent underground to be judged by the Mimir. Sometimes those people are sent on to the Governance, sometimes they are put to work down below in the mines. Or excommunicated. It has happened rarely in the history of Lightworkers. Usually one warning is enough."

As Eyre thought back to the mark around Ben's neck she could understand why one warning would be enough. A burning lariat? Blimey. She shook her head slightly and then hesitantly began to state the main reason she had wanted to talk to Whittaker Ray.

"My Lightkeeper gave me a message for you from my parents."

Whittaker Ray dropped his teaspoon and turned from the kitchen sink, a shocked expression on his face.

"A message? By the Light, what was it?"

"The Isars can be seen by the Aether during the Leonid," Eyre recited, careful to get the words exactly right.

Whittaker Ray frowned and concentrated, repeating the words softly to himself. Then to Eyre's shock, a sudden light of comprehension dawned and he clapped his hands.

"The key! The key to it all. By the Aura, I *knew* they could do it!"

He looked at Eyre with a stunned expression. "You have no idea what this means to the Lightworking community Eyre. Your parents have sourced information of critical, unimaginable value."

"They told me to only tell you," Eyre said hesitantly.

'Well, I will have to inform the Echelon, and indeed the Determinant Dozen, but it is important that no one knows where this information came from. So yes, do not ever reveal that you are the source."

Eyre was unsure about this. Her parents said to tell *no one*. But she was sure that Whittaker Ray knew what he was doing. And someone was going to have to figure out what to do with that information.

Eyre thought back to the meeting on campus where she'd seen the Determinant Dozen from the hidden room above the boardroom, and where she'd heard about Aethers. Eyre looked hesitant. "I've heard about Aethers, and I know my mother was one. But I don't know what an Aether can do, and I don't understand what the rest of it means."

Whittaker Ray hesitated as he looked at her hopeful face and then appeared to make a decision. "Normally I would not discuss this information with anyone other than the Echelon. But I feel I owe it to your parents to let you know what it means.

"An ancient prophesy from the Tomsk Prorok of Russia foretold that November is a critical time of year for Lightworkers, but not why. Aethers are Lightworkers with a stronger Light force within them than normal Lightworkers. They are capable of great feats, such as healing, and astral travel, and have been part of our most significant historical events.

"After Madame Overmantle had a premonition, I was searching for information at the Sunshine Coast, and I have to say that I thought Nick might be the reason for the premonition, and that he might possibly be an Aether. Aethers do not get an Inguz, and are often hidden within the ranks of the Unlit. Nick has Aethers in his genealogy and I took him as my Ward to protect him." His face wrinkled in distaste. "Not least of all from his father. But of course, I was wrong." Eyre took this all in.

"Could I be an Aether?" she asked. "I have healing abilities." Whittaker Ray's eyes were kind as he looked at her hopeful face.

"I'm sorry, Eyre, but an Aether is never born to an Aether. The gift always skips at least one generation. So your children might be born an Aether, but you cannot be one. That is why in addition to trying to kill Aethers, the Gothak are targeting their children, to ensure that no more are born."

Eyre was disappointed, but not entirely surprised. She was hardly showing any signs that might indicate super Lightworking powers—in fact she was struggling to find any powers at all most days. But it did explain why the Gothak had seemed to be focused on her.

"Well then, what is an Isar? And the Leonid?" she asked. Whittaker Ray nodded.

"When the Aura was destroyed, four parts of it were condensed into bars of light called an Isar. These four bars were blasted into each of the Alterworlds—Terra, Aqua, Caelus and Incendium. It is said that when the bars are reunited, the Aura will reform. We have spent decades searching the Alterworlds for the Isars, but with no success. No one can find them. We thought November might be significant because of the Tomsk Prorok's prediction, but we still had no success."

His eyes became intense as he looked at Eyre. "That is what your parents were searching for, Eyre, the key to finding the Isars. They told me they had information of huge significance, but they died before we met up. This is what they wanted me to know, and I thought the information was gone forever. They were clever people, your parents—and prepared. Thank the Light that they stored that message. *Now* we can make a difference."

Eyre was still frowning. "But what's the Leonid?" she asked.

"The Leonid is a meteor shower that comes every November," Whittaker Ray explained. "So, *you* have linked the two prophesies—the one from the Tomsk Prorok about November being significant, and the one from Madame Overmantle, who foresaw that Aethers were critical to reinstating the Aura. From what you've revealed, obviously the Isars are only visible *during that time*, and only to Aethers. That is the piece of information we needed! We've sent so many Lightworkers—and indeed members of the Alterworlds themselves—off searching for the Isars and now we know why they were unsuccessful. This is news of such importance". He stopped and a look of joy crossed his face as he mused to himself. "So *only* the Aether, and *only* at a specific time, can see them." He shook his head in wonderment and put his cup on the bench. "Thank you, Eyre, I must now go and check the Transit, but it is all the more important that I get back to the Echelon. The message about the Isars will become known by the Echelon, the Determinant Dozen and the Aethers, but no one except you and I will know where the information has come from. Alia and Rufus may have further messages for me, and it is crucial that the source is kept confidential."

Uncharacteristically, he hugged Eyre hard, causing her face to flush red. And then there was a flash of light as he disappeared. Eyre sat for a moment, composing her story before she went out to join her friends. But a huge joy flared within her—her parents' lives had not been sacrificed in vain, and she could see now why they had travelled so often and for so long. And she understood their secrecy as well. Any residual hurt at being left out of their lives had disappeared with this conversation—she now knew how important their work had been. And the fact that it was not for nothing filled her with a huge happiness.

She realised that she also had learnt a life lesson this morning. Sometimes all you had to go on was faith, and she saw now that she hadn't had faith in her parents, had jumped to conclusions which had ultimately only hurt herself. She didn't have all the facts, and she should have *known* that her parents would have reasons for concealing the truth from her. Faith was a strange concept, holding on to an invisible force, a belief, when all else seemed lost, when all evidence pointed otherwise. But she understood it now—it was a lesson she would not forget.

She walked back out to her friends feeling like a huge weight had lifted from her shoulders.

"Well, I know about Aethers now," she said. "I'll help you gather sticks while I explain." At Beatrice's questioning look, she added, "I wanted to talk about Mum and Dad on my own, I hope you don't mind."

Kind Beatrice nodded; that was enough for her. "Of course," she said. "Come on, fill us in on Aethers then!"

CHAPTER THIRTY-THREE

THE REST OF THE break passed quickly. Beatrice's and Abby's parents and Whittaker Ray didn't come back, so the friends passed the last few days playing board games and walking in the bush. Eyre was realising that it was not uncommon for children of Lightworkers to be left to look after themselves for significant periods of time—she'd always felt it was just *her* life that was like that.

Every morning Eyre went for a run with Nick, and afterwards she practised Ferito with her friends for hours. Shouts of "Tollo!" filled the air as they practised the movements of Basic, One and Two every day. They were improving hugely, despite their lack of progress in other Lightworking areas. Aditus and Tego, and the three Clasis were getting easier and more fluid each time they practised. Eyre found she didn't need to think about what she was doing so much; it was becoming more and more instinctive as the continual repetition of the movements started to make a difference. The trip to the Transit had started it. They all wanted to increase their skills: the idea that they might actually need to use Ferito in a real situation was a great motivational force.

But they didn't work at any other Academy skills. They hadn't brought their staffs with them, so they didn't practise Staff Forces and no one wanted to end up somewhere they shouldn't, so the prohemium was out too. They, Eyre thought dryly, were pleasures to reserve for next semester.

When the time came to return to the Academy, Robyn Edmunsun took them back, apologizing for being away the whole break.

"We don't always desert our children for quite so long," she said. "I did know we'd be busy this break, which is why we sent Lachie to Dylan's place. But then there were developments of huge importance so we couldn't get back." Her face lit up as she said this, and only Eyre understood why.

They arrived back on campus and headed back to their dormitories, touching the walls to flood their rooms with coloured light. The first thing each of them did was get their staff out to admire it again. Although they hadn't been all that effective with them yet, they still loved the beautiful objects. And then Beatrice and Abby raced off to say hello to their Lighthorses. Eyre decided to do Ischyros a favour and wait a day, so she was alone in the room when a strange event began to happen. Flashes of light were exploding like fireworks near the Central Administration building and crowds of Lightworkers were appearing; a most unusual sight. Eyre could see them milling around in the distance, chatting as more and more people arrived. Something was up! And she needed her friends to come and help her find out. So, summoning all the telepathic powers she had, she forced her mind to send out a message as loud as she could: Bane, Bane, Bane she repeated over and over as she raced out to wait at the sandstone rock behind the dormitories.

She had no idea whether her telepathy had worked or not until Nick arrived at top speed, skidding to the ground beside her. He stole a look back down the track from behind the rock.

"Perrill was watching me, I took off in such a rush. But I think I lost him. Good telepathy, by the way—you nearly blasted my head apart!"

Ten minutes later Beatrice and Abby had joined them after sprinting across from the stables, and Eyre felt a glow of accomplishment that her telepathy had been so successful. Nice for a change to be doing it *right*.

"Well I saw all the people by the building," Beatrice said. "So I guess that's what this is about?"

"Yes—something's going on," Eyre replied. "We need to know. Let's go find that room the Ranger showed us."

So they snuck across campus and hid behind the Zepps again as the Lightworkers began to enter the Admin building. Focusing as hard as she could, Eyre got her friends to huddle together and she was elated that she managed to get a mask going fairly quickly. Obviously she was getting better at it.

"It's not going to last long," she whispered. "So move fast up those stairs!"

They waited until a fairly large group of people entered the building and followed behind them closely. Then they raced up two sets of stairs as silently as they could and collapsed on the floor in front of the door to the viewing room. Eyre exhaled loudly as the mask dropped and her friends shimmered back into sight. Her head was thumping—it took so much energy to manage the mask. But she was elated they had done it again, and now they could find out what was going on.

Nick pulled on the door and to their surprise, it opened. The Ranger had used keys to get in last time, so Eyre wasn't sure why it was unlocked. But it became clear when they looked out the viewing window: the Ranger was there looking up at them and Eyre was sure he winked at them. He wasn't supposed to be able to see them, but somehow he knew they were there. And for some reason he was helping them to find out what was going on—he must have unlocked the door for them.

"Assumed we'd be here," Beatrice laughed as she looked down at him. "And here we are!"

They locked the door behind them and settled in to watch what was happening. The members of the Echelon were there, and Whittaker Ray stood beside the podium, waiting. When the final Lightworkers came in, Sergeant Tottingham closed the door and Whittaker Ray began to speak.

"Thank you all for coming. Many of you have travelled from great distances and we appreciate you coming at such short notice. It is momentous news and we all realise how critical the coming months will be." He touched the podium and a photograph of a meteor shower with a list of dates beside it flashed onscreen.

"These are of course the dates for the Leonid Meteor Shower this year. Other schools' TACI exams will be taking place at the same time, so you will be seeing many Lightworking students in the Alterworlds while you are there."

With a start, Eyre realised what he was talking about, and that all the Lightworkers in the auditorium must be Aethers. And then she started to panic—her desire to be nosy was now going to reveal the secret of the Isars to her friends. She felt terrible at letting Whittaker Ray down when he'd asked for her discretion. But she was consoled by the fact that the Ranger knew there were there; if he was okay with them watching, and in fact had assisted them to get in, then perhaps it was okay for her friends to know the message too. In any case, it was too late now—there they were, and all she could do was sit as Whittaker Ray went on.

"Our tactic is to send as many of you as we can to each Alterworld during the next Leonid, in the hope that you will locate and bring back the four Isars that will reinstate the Aura. With that in mind, we will divide you into four groups and send you as soon as the Leonid begins."

Eyre finally noticed that none of the Lightworkers in the auditorium had an Inguz on their arms. Physically they were all different; there was no defining any characteristic that they had in common. Some of them wore sleeves, so it wasn't even apparent that they had no Inguz. Yet this group of people contained some of the most powerful Lightworkers in the world.

"I can see their auras," Abby said. "They're *silver.* Wow. What does *that* mean?"

Eyre stared hard but couldn't see anything at all above the Lightworkers heads. She'd seen Colton's aura once—white, which indicated he was a pure soul. Now that she knew him better, she would have known that without seeing his aura. And that day she'd had a clarity that had enabled her to see the auras of several students. But it seemed that Lightworking energy wasn't a constant thing; it came and went, and since then she hadn't had much ability seeing auras. She certainly couldn't see anything today.

Beatrice's brow was furrowed, trying to catch up. "I'm more confused by what all *this* means," she said. "Obviously we're looking for something in the Alterworlds that will reinstate the Aura."

"Isars," Nick said. "There're four of them." He looked at Eyre, and suddenly she knew that Whittaker Ray had shared the information with him. She felt better now about bringing everyone here: obviously Whittaker Ray expected them to find out eventually anyway.

Whittaker Ray continued.

"I will be compiling lists indicating which Alterworld you will be sent to; please let me know if you have any particular experience in any of them that might be helpful to our cause. And I will be sending geographical and other information to you about the Alterworld you will be searching. Each group will have a guide from the Alterworld they are visiting to help them make their way.

"We have no way of knowing how long this search may take, despite the information we now hold. It may take years for us to find each of the Isars, but the important thing is that we now have hope, and a way forward.

"If anyone has anything to say, please speak up. Otherwise, contact me later with any questions or information you may need."

There was a buzz as the audience started moving and packing up and Eyre raced for the door.

"Time to go, let's be quick! And lock the door behind you—don't want the Ranger to get nailed for this!"

Forgoing the mask, they raced down the stairs and out of the building before the auditorium doors opened.

"So now we know," Beatrice said. "That is so amazing! The *Aether* can see the Isars, wow! That is huge news!"

Nick stared down at the crowd below. "Well the TACIs sure are going to be interesting this year," he said drily.

CHAPTER THIRTY-FOUR

IT DIDN'T TAKE LONG to get back into the routine of classes; in fact, Eyre reflected dismally, it felt as if they hadn't even been gone. Ischyros was his usual sunny self (*not!*), but she persevered through the embarrassing horsemanship lessons, and she continued to walk him and groom him every morning. She realised they would never have a close bond, but she understood somehow that he had had a tough life. Sometimes creatures never got over that—just as some people didn't. So she worked extra hard on his grooming each week. Over the course of the year he had metamorphosed from a bedraggled, shaggy and muddy old nag into an obviously old horse who was clean and healthy. Shiny hooves, brushed glossy coat, and untangled grey mane. He still looked odd with the black patch around his eye, but no one could ever say he wasn't wonderfully looked after.

The fields were covered in snow now, so Eyre didn't take Ischyros out for his morning walk. She spent the time in the stall grooming him and keeping his straw clean. As Eyre ran back to campus through the snow, she felt a slight poignancy as she realised she wasn't even angry at the old horse any more, she just felt sad about it. She wished she could have a bond like some of the other students were developing with their horses, but obviously it was not meant to be and she would have to accept it.

She went to her meditation class and then headed to the Training Shed for Ferito. Since their sessions at the cabins, Eyre and her three friends had improved immensely, causing even the impassive Terrigal Furnace to nod in approval.

"Obviously been working on it," he said as he watched Eyre and Nick go through their moves. "Practise is the key, good for you. More than that, your attitude is improving, 88." Eyre smiled at the reference to her TEP number and felt happy as she battled Nick. It was nice to be doing something well for a change.

After Ferito, 'Terra' class was scheduled with Kofi E Vygn. Eyre felt rather gloomy at the prospect of more ineffectual hand waving, but she did like E Kofi, who was an intriguing creature. So she hurried to avoid being late, racing up to her seat and joining Beatrice, Abby and Nick, who were already there.

But it seemed that hand waving was out for the day, because when E Kofi walked in he was deep in conversation with none other than the very floral Jemima Periwinkle. As usual, she was dressed head to toe in pastel shades—mainly mint tones this time, and her blonde coiffed hair was piled up in a complicated bun at the back and nailed in place with a huge white flower. Eyre assumed Ms Periwinkle was performing her Ambassadorial duties rather than her Genealogy ones, and this was confirmed when the teacher began to speak in her breathy, girlish voice.

"Today, class, E Kofi will have you for two sessions. Later this morning you will be practising your prohemium in the Training Shed, but for now, you need to move on and learn about the dangers of Terra. You must listen carefully, because this is one of your most important lectures this year. Some of the things you will encounter at Terra are not things you would know to be wary of. Concentrate and take notes!"

She left with a flipping wave of her hand, leaving Eyre wishing that she would perform the elusive prohemium and disappear somewhere through a Seam. Something about that woman really irritated her. E Kofi waited a moment until the teacher had gone and gave a wry smile.

"Ms Periwinkle is correct," he said. "Many of the dangers you will encounter on Terra are not obvious, and will be unfamiliar to you, which makes them all the more dangerous. Here on earth, if you see a brown snake, you avoid it at all costs. But on Terra, something that looks really cute or interesting might kill you. So you have to be aware of potential hazards. In general, the areas of danger fall into three categories."

He turned to the blackboard at the rear of the auditorium and wrote with his talon to produce words in light:

1. Creatures

2. Environment

3. The unexpected

Over the next hour he described some of the toxic and dangerous creatures they may encounter in Terra: insects that stung, plants that were poisonous, and strange creatures they'd never seen before that could kill you in seconds. One of the most dangerous things was a coiling vine that would stretch down from the foliage and pluck unfortunate creatures up into the canopy where the vine consumed them. A carnivorous plant! Charming, Eyre thought. Fortunately, the information was on the students' Felsics, so Eyre could follow what E Kofi was saying without too much difficulty. Remembering it all was going to be another thing though!

Then E Kofi ran through the potential dangers of the environment in Terra. Apparently there were great stretching deserts of sand that could at any moment be inundated by a wall of roiling water. Large sailing rocks sped across these deserts and had to be avoided or risk being crushed beneath them. Sudden winds and howling rain could rise at any time, and the risk of earthquakes was high.

"Terra is one of the more recent Alterworlds," E Kofi explained, "and therefore the terrain is still in the stages of settling. But your greatest challenge will be to make your way through our thick forests. Ninety per cent of our world is covered in dense forest. You will need a Zhuzhu to navigate through this, so I hope your riding skills are progressing well."

Eyre rolled her eyes and put her head on the desk as her friends laughed at her. She couldn't even get on Ischyros's back, so this was definitely going to be a challenge.

E Kofi finished talking about the environment and pointed to the third section on his list.

"But the greatest hazard will be the *unexpected* when you go to Terra, as is probably the case with all the Alterworlds. No matter how well I try to prepare you for what you may encounter over there, there is always something that happens that is not anticipated. So, you will have to think on your feet, and deal with it. And to do this, your Lightworking skills must be as good as you can make them. I encourage you to practise hard at your physical and mental skills, as these will be invaluable to you when you get over to our world. You will have a Terra guide with you when you go, but essentially you will have to complete the TACI challenge with your own skills. Are there any questions?" When silence echoed through the hall, E Kofi waved a taloned hand. "Well, thank you for your attention and I'll see you later this morning to practise your prohemium."

CHAPTER THIRTY-FIVE

EYRE AND HER FRIENDS headed over to the Refectory for morning tea. Quite a few students were already there, and several of the staff members were sitting at the staff table, including the flamboyant Jemima Periwinkle.

As Eyre walked in, she was drawn to a laughing group of students at the side of the Refectory, and one person in particular. Jax! He was back, and she hadn't seen him in the month since they'd returned. Trying not to skip over, she walked to his table and beamed at him.

"Hi Jax," she said. "How was your break?" But her smile faltered at the cool look in his eyes as he looked up at her.

"Yeah, great, Eyre," he said, his tone dismissive. "Good to see you." Then he turned back to talking to Georgia. Eyre had never felt so completely dismissed and humiliated in her life. Pheria in particular was enjoying this, leaning back in her chair and studying Eyre with a very satisfied smirk. Eyre stood there for a moment, unable to respond at all, her surprise was so great. Then she turned away awkwardly and headed over to where her friends were sitting. Beatrice had her back to Jax's table, but Abby had caught the display and patted Eyre's hand as she sat down. She took in Eyre's flushed face and narrowed her cornflower eyes at the group who were still laughing at something Jax had said.

"Don't know what's going on there, Eyre," she said, her gaze sending mental Antaraks cartwheeling towards the group, "but he's not worth your time."

Eyre was finally able to speak. "Well, of course, we weren't exactly *a thing*," she said lamely, so hurt and mortified it was hard to get any words out. "It's not as if we were great friends either really. I just thought..." But her words trailed off and then she put her chin up, her face burning. "Oh never mind what I thought. I was wrong I guess. Stupid."

Zanda saved the moment by arriving just then and Eyre was grateful for the distraction. She had sat next to Beatrice, so was spared having to look at Jax and his table of admirers, but the occasional burst of laughter from behind her made her mouth tighten.

Zanda leant over. "I have *gossip*!" he said gleefully, as he stuffed his mouth full of pizza. As the Refectory filled, and more staff joined the crowd, his eyes danced over towards the staff table.

"Two of our esteemed lecturers are *related*! Guess who?" Eyre looked over at them.

"Okay, Oorlock and Dr Botolfe," she said drily and her friends exploded in laughter.

"Well I reckon it's Madame Overmantle and the Ranger," Beatrice suggested, causing more laughter.

"E Kofi and the Sergeant!" Nick hooted, getting more ridiculous.

"No," Abby giggled, with tears running down her face, "*Jemima Periwinkle* and the Sergeant!"

Zanda made a congratulatory movement and pointed at Abby. "Give that girl a gold star, she's got it right! Your telepathic talents have no doubt given you the advantage in this competition."

The roiling laughter stopped suddenly as many eyes looked disbelievingly at Zanda.

"Really?" Beatrice chortled, taking in the Sergeant's "*Walk Lightly and carry a big stick*" khaki sweatshirt and oversized trackpants, and Jemima's mint floral frock with its matching shoes. "You're kidding!"

"Nope," Zanda said smugly. "They're sisters. I found out from a friend in Sydney at the school where she used to teach Genealogy. Apparently she was "let go" under mysterious circumstances."

Rigmar looked over his shoulder. "Still, our gain," he said, deadpan, which caused another eruption of hilarity.

Eyre studied the two teachers, her eyes round. Really, a more unalike pair could hardly be found. She would almost have been less surprised if she'd found out that Ischyros was related to someone—Mandig Vela perhaps. Obviously the sisters weren't close—they were sitting at opposite ends of the table. Jemima was twittering something in an uncomfortable-looking Oorlock's ear while the Sergeant glowered at the other end of the table, shovelling food in her mouth. Eyre shook her head. Families were complicated sometimes.

Whittaker Ray walked to the front of the Refectory. "Attention, please students," he said loudly. As the noise in the hall died down, he waited patiently. "Just a reminder that the Sector Fair will be held at the end of

August. Please see your Sector Leaders for details of the roster and duties that you must undertake."

Whittaker Ray sat back at the staff table, and Eyre finished her meal quickly. Abby gave her a sympathetic smile as Eyre took her plates to the Jotnar—she understood that Eyre was escaping to avoid any further discussion about Jax.

As Eyre headed for her room, a deep pain stabbed through her. What was up with him? She'd thought that he liked her, and if she'd misread him, then surely at least as a friend? Perhaps he was upset because he'd been sent home after the Ferito tournament, and she guessed in a way she *had* started it. But he'd seemed okay with that before he left.

She unlatched her staff out of its holder in her cupboard. Staff Forces was next; that was all she needed. But remembering the look on the Sergeant's face, she thought it would probably be wise to get there on time, so she headed at a run to the Training Shed.

Sergeant Tottingham was waiting at the front in her voluminous tracksuit, her tall staff in hand. Obviously she had left the Refectory early too—no stomach for her sister's carry-on, Eyre guessed. The Sergeant stood sternly at the front of the Shed as the students arrived, carrying their staffs. Beatrice and Abby scurried in the door and slid in beside Eyre.

"You should have walked with us!" Beatrice whispered, but was silenced from further talk by the slight movement of the Sergeant's eyes towards her.

Finally when all the students had arrived the Sergeant cleared her throat. Here we go, Eyre thought, the least memorable first-year class in the history of the Academy is about to get a sermon, again. But the Sergeant's words when she spoke were so unexpected, they were like a blast of Viq around the room.

"I owe you all an apology," the Sergeant said, and a surprised murmur whispered through the shed. Students looked at each other. "I was hard on you at the end of last semester, and critical about your lack of progress with Staff Forces. It is true that you all have found it more difficult, it seems, than previous years at the Academy." There was a shuffling of feet and downwards looks at this.

"You haven't done much better since you've returned. But I've realised, after meditation, and bidding the Light, that this is also on *me*. I am your instructor and at the end of the day, it's my responsibility. It is hard to focus when you feel stressed, and my classes were hardly the most relaxing that the Academy has." A couple of brave souls tittered at this. The Sergeant's eyes travelled around the class. "So let's carry on with this semester on a better note, and start anew."

She looked around, but no one moved or met her eye, so she continued.

"The only weapons you are permitted on the TACI exams in first year are a Kulbeda and your staff. So you will need to be proficient at using your staff in order to make your way through Terra. I know you can do better than you have. Watch again as I produce energy from my staff."

The Sergeant proceeded to talk them through the technique of sending energy through the body, to the wood and up out the crystal at the top.

"It's like you are one with your staff," she instructed. "*You* chose your branch, you found your crystal and it was you who connected this wondrous object. You already *have* a bond with it. Use your mind to focus and reveal what your staff can do."

It seemed that the Sergeant's words had an effect on the class, because there was a determination in the practise session that hadn't been there all year. There was total silence as students grasped their staffs, their eyes narrowing with the effort of concentration. Surprisingly, Beatrice, who wasn't great at the physical forces, suddenly produced a really strong beam from her staff. The emerald at the top shone a brilliant green as light streamed from it and blasted a hole in the target at the side of the Training Shed. The Sergeant was so surprised she forgot her herself for a moment and clapped her hands.

"Edmunsun! Well done! Now *that* is what we're after, students!" Beatrice herself was looking at the staff as if it was the first time she'd seen it. Then a look of delight dawned on her face.

"That. Is. So. Cool!" she said, and promptly blasted another beam across the shed. Her efforts seemed to galvanise other students, because within half an hour another dozen had managed to produce light beams of varying strengths from their staffs. The Sergeant strode around, a look of astonishment on her face. She ran her hand through her short hair and shook her head.

"I don't know what's going on, but keep doing it—this is what we've been waiting for. Focus, send that energy from your body, through the staff to the crystal."

Kofi E Vygn arrived at the shed, and watched as light beams shot across and hit the targets. He watched in silence until the practise finished and the Sergeant, looking well pleased, had left the shed. He smiled at the class, showing his sharp teeth.

"It is good to see progress being made and I can feel the difference here. The inevitable result of focusing properly—I feel many of you have been unconvinced this could actually ever happen. It also is the result of group energy—the force of Light travelling through each of you. Somehow you have learnt from each other.

"This is also possible with the prohemium, and I am hoping to see progress from these extra training sessions. It is my hope that all of you will be eligible to take your TACI test at the end of the year, but of course, that can't happen if you cannot perform your prohemium. Watch again as I show you the hand movements..."

Buoyed by the success of the previous session, the students watched silently as E Kofi demonstrated the gestures again that would open the Seam to Terra. He went through them very slowly so the students could see what he was doing, occasionally pointing out the difference between the angle of the palm, or the direction of the fingers. Even a slight error would render the prohemium ineffectual—or worse, send the person off in the wrong direction.

Rigmar was standing in front of Eyre and suddenly a vertical line of bright light appeared in front of him and he disappeared into it. Eyre gasped in surprise.

E Kofi walked over to the Seam and touched his fingertips together. Instantly Rigmar reappeared, gasping and soaking wet.

"It is encouraging that you managed to travel," E Kofi said kindly. "But the middle of the Ponds of Doombee is not the destination we're after."

The class erupted in laughter and Rigmar grinned. All of a sudden, the mood changed. It was as if everyone suddenly realised that they were capable of doing this, and instead of waving their hands around in frustration, they began to work in pairs with a purpose. By the end of class two more people —Robeson and Georgia—had managed to disappear somewhere and were brought back by E Kofi. Neither had ended up in the right place, but just the fact that they had gone somewhere gave the rest of the class hope. Eyre was encouraged—she'd felt a buzzing in her palms that had not been there before, and she felt she was getting the hang of it.

When the session finally finished the students walked out chattering to each other. What had started out hopelessly had morphed into something else—the desire to succeed. Eyre noticed that E Kofi smiled as they left; a wise creature, that one, she thought. "Live as one with the Earth!" he called, and several voices echoed his call. A great mantra indeed, Eyre thought.

CHAPTER THIRTY-SIX

EYRE WANDERED BACK TO her room after her excruciating Genealogy lesson. Really, she felt she could learn more from her Wisdom than the hour-long lecture, but of course, most people didn't receive their Wisdoms until later. It was helping her understand the structure of the charts, and how Sector skills were passed through generations, so she supposed it wasn't a complete waste of time.

She could hear a haunting sound coming down the hall from her room and when she entered she saw why: Abby was playing a coiled woodwind instrument of some kind and the tone was breathy and poignant. Eyre sat on her bed and waited until she'd finished.

"What is that?" she asked Abby. "It's beautiful." Abby held up the instrument, the mottled wood polished and shining. "It's called a tortilis, it's from Caelus. I've taken it as my second instrument." Eyre looked at the unusual object and was relieved. It sounded a lot better than the theremin, which hadn't gotten much easier on the ear as the months had gone on. Abby pointed to the cupboard. "Why don't you play with me?"

Eyre retrieved her guitar from her cupboard and began to improvise with Abby, following the harmonies as Abby played the melody. Eyre had practised the guitar—although not seriously like Abby worked on her instruments, more for relaxation really—over the year and was slowly improving, and the sound of her picking complemented the mellow tones of the instrument.

They had just finished when a hesitant knock came at the door. Eyre opened it, and was surprised to see Colton there. Colton looked at Eyre and a blush crept up his cheeks. "I er—" he began, and stopped.

Abby, not needing her psychic powers to understand this moment, put her tortilis down and shot a meaningful look at Eyre. "Back in a minute," she said lightly as she walked out down the hall. Eyre was a bit lost for words.

"So... how are you doing Colton?"

"Good, you know—there's a lot to learn isn't there."

"More for some of us, I'm finding," Eyre laughed awkwardly and Colton finally got to the point.

"You know, the first-year dance is in a week and I was wondering if you'd like to go with me?" One of the most anticipated events in a student's school life was the first-year dance, which was intended as a way of students getting to know each other and to feel part of the Academy.

Eyre was so surprised she nearly sat down. *Colton*? He'd given no indication he was interested in her, and really, she thought of him as just a friend. He was so good looking she would have thought there'd be a horde of girls he could have chosen. Colton saw her hesitation and put his hands up.

"Just friends, Eyre, I thought it would be nice to go with you, no strings." Eyre felt sorry she'd been so obvious and smiled—when she thought about it, she realised she thought it was a great idea, actually. It would be a lot more fun going with him than wandering around trying to avoid looking at Jax.

"Well, sure—love to!" she replied. "Thanks for asking."

Colton's face lit up and he smiled. "Okay, well then, see you in History of Light."

He headed off down the hall and Eyre sighed as she saw Abby sneak a peek from the corridor where she'd been hiding. Eyre waved her out, expecting a roasting, but Abby just laughed.

"This is so perfect!" she said triumphantly. "That will show Jax!"

The dance had been a major topic since they'd arrived back at school—it was traditional to hold a social event for First-Years at the beginning of the second semester, a 'Winter Wonderland' they called it and every year it had a different theme. The ball was intended as an antidote to the months of hard studying, but Eyre had noticed that in some ways it added far more stress to the lives of the students. Who was going with whom, what to wear, what the dance would be like—all the intrigue and drama in conversations that bored her to tears. But she had to admit that she was looking forward to it—it would be good to do something other than practise in the Training Shed and attend lectures all day.

She was about to put her guitar away but hesitated. She hadn't been out to visit Ischyros today, and on an impulse she slung it across her back as she jogged across to his stall. It was hard going, running through the snow, but at least enough people had travelled along the track to pack the path down a bit.

Ischyros was in his stall, nose deep in the bag and munching on some oats Lisa had filled it with. The Kikkuli Master had finally given Eyre a break and she was no longer required at riding lessons. It was clear that Ischyros was never going to let her on his back unless he intended to fire her off again through the roof, so she was given some latitude about the class. As long as she visited Ischyros and kept him groomed, she was considered to be passing. Eyre had to admit that it felt like a big fail to her, but after all the months of trying, she knew that she was never going to be able to ride this horse.

Eyre leaned her guitar against the wall as she groomed Ischyros, brushing his coat until it shone, then oiling and rasping his feet. He ignored her while she did it, but at least now he didn't kick her at Mach speed out of the stall. After she finished she picked up the guitar.

"I have a treat for you, Ischyros," she said, and began to play. She didn't know many songs, but she played "Desperado", an old song by the Eagles. The lyrics seemed to fit and she sang in her pure voice as she played. Surprisingly, she wasn't interrupted, half expecting the old horse to tell her to shut up or something equally polite. She finished the song and played the last haunting chords and looked over at him. To her shock and surprise, tears were running down the face of the old horse; he was weeping.

But as she flung her guitar down and raced over to him he sent her flying against the wall with a whack from his head.

"Get out!" he shouted. "GET OUT!"

Winded, unable to get a breath and in incredible pain, Eyre staggered to her feet and picked up her guitar.

"Okay," she finally said. "Okay, I'm leaving."

She walked out of the stall slowly and latched the door. Then, as she turned, still trying to suck air into her aching chest, she groaned. Ben Perrill stood in front of her.

"Singing to Ischyros, the wishy-washy Pissy Hoss?" he taunted. "You know, I think that horse dislikes you even more than I do," he added, taking in the stains all over her uniform.

Eyre shouldered past him, her eyes blazing, but he grabbed the strap of her guitar as she passed.

"Wait on, I didn't say you could go anywhere."

Eyre wrenched her arm out of the guitar to get away from him, and faced him furiously as he stepped in front of her.

"What is with you, Perrill?" she shouted. "Get out of my way. And give me my guitar back!"

"Sure," Ben answered, tossing it to the ground. Then he took a step forward and stood on the neck of the instrument, snapping it in half. "Oops, sorry."

Eyre shrieked and fell to her knees, trying to drag the guitar from under his foot.

"No," she sobbed. "You absolute jerk! *Why* would you do that?" And then the rage started to build within her, searing up from the bottom of her feet until it seemed to blast out the top of her head. She stood up and fired a beam of light at Ben Perrill that would have killed him had it connected. But he was quick, and had improved a lot this year, and he put up a shield so swiftly that the beam was deflected, burning a hole through the roof of the shed. His face dark with hatred, he sneered at her and stomped his foot on the ground, causing a pound so powerful she flipped completely over in the air. But she was fit now, and her running had paid off, so she landed on one knee and launched herself upwards, levitating above Ben as she fired bolts of lightning down at him. He levitated quickly and there were loud booms as the jagged energy blasted the ground where he had been standing. The noise echoed through the building, causing the structure to shake.

Suddenly a wave of sickening energy flooded through Eyre and she fell to the ground, paralysed. Ben Perrill landed hard beside her and they looked into each other's eyes, hatred like a force between them. But neither could move at all. The supple boots of the Kikkuli Master appeared beside Eyre.

"*What* is going on here?" he said softly. "Can I really believe what I am seeing?" He surveyed the scene, taking in the black craters in the ground and the flames licking at the hole in the Shed roof. "You know this is immediate grounds for expulsion, for both of you."

He flicked his wrist and suddenly Eyre could move again. She stood up groggily, but her eyes were flaming. Dirt smeared her face where it had adhered to her tears, and she picked up the broken guitar as if it was a living creature that had died.

"Fine by me," she said softly. "I've had enough."

She walked away, leaving the Kikkuli Master with Ben and headed to the dormitory to pack her bags.

CHAPTER THIRTY-SEVEN

EYRE WALKED INTO HER room with the broken guitar and saw Beatrice and Abby waiting anxiously for her. They took in her dirt-covered clothes and tear-streaked face and then Abby wailed as she saw the guitar.

"Did Ischyros do this?"

Tears streamed down Eyre's face and she shook her head. "Ben Perrill," she said. "And I think I'm expelled. I just wish I'd managed to kill him before they kicked me out."

She sat on the bed and sobbed as her friends comforted her. Beatrice patted her back.

"Everyone on campus heard the ruckus from the stables. We thought the Gothak were here again."

A soft knock came at the door and when the door opened, Eyre was not surprised to see the Sergeant standing there.

"A walk, Eyre?" she said. Eyre rubbed her eyes and followed the Sergeant's huge bulk down the hall. Eyre knew the use of Occido was forbidden, and that this was an unforgiveable offence in the Lightworking world, let alone at the school. So she knew what the Sergeant was going to say. But she knew she'd do it again, given a chance. Ben Perrill was an evil, black-hearted monster and from now on she was going to fight him as hard as she could, whatever it took to survive. She lifted her chin, ready for her punishment. Bring it on.

The Sergeant didn't say anything for a while as they walked one of the snowy pathways through the eucalypts. Finally they stopped at a bench by the side of the track, a place where students often liked to sit for a break.

"A bad morning then," the Sergeant started, and Eyre nodded.

"Ben Perrill is a problem," the Sergeant continued and Eyre's mouth clenched. She couldn't say anything to that and there was a long silence.

"You're not being expelled, Eyre," the Sergeant said finally. "And neither is Ben. We know what happened, and understand your reaction, although there is no excuse for using such force. You threw the first lethal energy, so technically you are at fault.

"However, there are extenuating circumstances and you will both be allowed to stay."

Eyre's furious face caused the Sergeant's expression to soften. "I know it's hard to understand, Eyre, but you must have faith that we are working on it." Softly, almost to herself, she added, "Ben has been to the Buyabarra, and it didn't work. We are struggling to solve the problem."

Eyre was about to respond angrily when the word the Sergeant had used silenced her. Faith. It wasn't so long ago that she'd had a lesson in faith, and believing in people, despite how things looked. She was still so enraged she felt that she could send bolts of lightning out of her eyes, but she held her tongue. Faith. This was a good test of the lesson she thought she'd learned. Finally she swallowed and spoke.

"I know I was out of line. Thank you for not expelling me, I do want to stay." The Sergeant nodded and looked outwards.

"You are a strong girl, Eyre. Your parents would be proud." The Sergeant stood to go, but just then, a strange whirring filled the air. From out of the bushes came a swarm of butterflies—of all sizes, shapes and colour, their wings beating as they fluttered around Eyre, creating a rainbow swirl. Despite her bleakness, she was amazed at the sight, and the Sergeant was just as bemused, judging by the expression on her face. "What the...?" the Sergeant muttered, turning around to take in the huge mass. "In Winter? By the Light, some of the things that are happening in the world at the moment..." She shook her head and helped Eyre get up. Eyre moved slowly; apart from her violent battle with Ben, Ischyros's head had bruised her ribs quite badly.

"Take the afternoon off, Eyre," the Sergeant said. "You and your friends are free to go to the Therapeutic Pools. It will do you good."

The Sergeant strode off towards the Administration building and Eyre went the other direction to the dormitory. Along the way the cloud of butterflies dissipated, circling up to the clouds, until there were none left. Taking a last look upwards, Eyre headed to her room and found her friends waiting there.

"Are you going home?" Abby cried.

"I wish you'd dispatched the jerk," Beatrice said fiercely. "Someone has to!"

Eyre frowned. "The Sergeant said Ben had been to the Buyabarra, and it didn't work. I wonder what she meant?"

But then she was interrupted by a knock at the door as Nick arrived, his face concerned.

"Are you okay? The whole school's heard about it."

Eyre nodded. "Yeah. I'm alright. Just sad." She indicated her guitar. "But I'm not expelled; for some reason they're letting me stay." She sighed deeply and rubbed her face. "The Sergeant said we could go to the Therapeutic Pools this afternoon. Do you want to come?"

No answer was needed for that and within a few minutes they were all heading over to the rainbow-coloured pools. Eyre slipped into a large violet-coloured one and shut her eyes, letting the heat and vibrations soothe her sore muscles. She was glad that she was allowed to stay at the Academy, but a depression hung over her. Ischyros's reaction to her playing, how he'd hit her so hard with his head, and then the awful fight with Ben had impacted greatly on her. And then there was Jax, behaving so strangely. She felt tired and worn out and even the pools couldn't fix that this afternoon.

Finally they went back to their rooms and Eyre found that her guitar had disappeared. Broken or not, she still wanted it, but even though her friends searched for it everywhere, it had disappeared. It was the final straw for Eyre and a terrible grief arose within her; the day had been so intense. But then she closed her eyes and felt the warmth from the pools still within her muscles, and thought of the butterflies, and even the kindness of the Sergeant and a sudden certainty rose within her. Ben Perrill could try as hard as he wanted to crush her, but he would never succeed. And he would never make her cry again, *never.*

CHAPTER THIRTY-EIGHT

EYRE WOKE THE NEXT morning feeling sore and tired, but her spirits had lifted a little. She knew she'd be feeling a lot worse if she'd had to leave the Academy, so she headed over to Meditation and Ferito practise to get the soreness and stiffness out of her body. Something about the fight with Ben Perrill had changed her focus; it was as if she finally understood the forces that she was going to come face to face with some day. The fact that she'd encountered it within a Lightworker made no difference: she was going to train as hard as she could from now on, hard enough that even Rufa would be happy to have her. The next time she fought a violent battle like that, she was going to win it.

After the recent successes in Staff Forces and the prohemium practise, the school had changed the daily schedule so that the whole morning was spent in the shed: first Ferito, then Staff Forces, then prohemium practise with E Kofi. The training was paying off and several students had managed to use their staff and to generate a Seam. Rigmar had actually made it to Terra and back without assistance, and several others had made it one way. Each day was making a significant difference and today Eyre was going to make it happen for her.

The Sergeant strode in to the Shed and thumped her staff for attention. There was no need for instructions though; the students had done this often enough now and they got started, holding their staffs out in front of them.

Eyre did too, and this time, instead of focusing hard at it, she concentrated and let the energy *flow* through her, more like stroking the branch than beating at it. A sudden spark in the pink diamond at the top made her realise that she was on the right track, and she tried again, keeping a steady but gentle flow of energy running from her mind. Suddenly she felt the energy flow into the staff, and at that moment she increased the intensity, like a pulse, so that it finally blasted out the top of the diamond crystal in a brilliant beam. The light fired sideways across the room and hit a target 90 degrees from the one she was aiming at.

"Well done!" the Sergeant encouraged. "Next time, try for the target in front of you."

Eyre now understood how to generate the beam, and once she'd done it, it was relatively easy to keep producing them. But try as she could, they would not hit the target in front of her. They went in all directions, left, right, even striking the roof at one stage.

The Sergeant came over and studied her staff. "Your crystal was broken, I recall," she stated and Eyre nodded. The Sergeant contemplated this. "Well, it could account for the inaccuracy of your staff, and unfortunately, there is not much we can do about that. But well done on the beams, that is great progress. Keep at it."

Eyre spent the hour firing beams in all directions and getting curious looks from her fellow students, most of whom were now able to generate a decent beam *and* get it to travel generally in the desired direction.

She became aware of someone walking up beside her and smiled as she saw it was Colton. Colton's staff shone black like ebony, and a glowing ruby was the crystal on top. He aimed at the target across the wall and hit it dead-centre. Eyre felt a bit ridiculous as her next beam hit a target behind them, but Colton laughed.

"Good tactics, Eyre," he said. "Keep 'em guessing!"

They practised hard together, much as they had during the TEPs last year. Colton was a good person to train with, because he was calm and focused, and always happy to help. Eyre was trying hard to get some direction in her beams, but unfortunately it was always a surprise which way the beam decided to go. But she was happy that she had at last managed to create Light energy from her staff.

A lot of people had been watching her unpredictable efforts, and Rigmar in particular had been calling across making rude comments, which was entertaining. "A perfect ten for the degree of difficulty in that one, Lightward!" he intoned after she'd fired a beam straight out the skylight. But she was aware of an intense gaze and saw Jax watching her from across the room. As she looked over, he turned his back and aimed in the other direction so he didn't have to look at her. *What* on earth? She thought in confusion. She didn't get it at all. And then she saw the other pair of eyes upon her and she raised her staff and pointed it at him. Ben Perrill looked like he might duck but then recovered and hooted at her.

"Give it a go, Lightward. You're more likely to blow yourself up." Eyre lifted her hand suddenly and had the satisfaction of seeing him sprawl backwards, avoiding a blast that never came. He knew how accurate she was with her hands. Getting back onto his feet, he spoke loudly to the room.

"Well, I think if Lightward is going to continue using her staff like this, we should all be wearing fulminology safety gear, and staying behind the shields for protection." Several people laughed and Eyre gritted her teeth.

Deciding that she'd had enough of the drama, Eyre told Colton she was taking a break and wandered out of the Training Shed for some fresh air. A large red kangaroo was sitting under one of the gum trees by the side of the Shed and she stood and watched it for a while.

"Are you doing alright?" it asked her, and she nearly fell over.

"Fine, thanks, and you?" she answered. What does one say to a kangaroo?

But then the kangaroo morphed and changed and suddenly Ranger Chrysanthe stood in front of her. She smiled as he stretched and twisted, loosening his muscles.

"It's fun hopping around, but very hard on the back!" he said.

Eyre laughed. "Well, you're lucky you weren't blasted by one of my staff beams—they were heading in all directions, including out the door. I'm not doing very well with aiming the thing."

The Ranger nodded. "It's like a gun with the sights off. You'll have to work harder to focus the beam and keep it on track, and make allowances for the amount it's out of alignment. Adjust the angle you're holding it. You'll get there, you'll just have to practise. On the bright side, no one else will be able to use your staff with any accuracy—it will be quite unique."

Eyre smiled. "You always make people feel good Ranger Chrysanthe, thank you. Am I allowed to ask you a question?"

The Ranger looked solemn and shook his head. "I will never, ever reveal the source of my hair dye to you," he said as his green hair flopped around. Eyre laughed merrily and the Ranger looked delighted.

"No, I wanted to ask you why you left the viewing room unlocked the other day—it was you, wasn't it?"

The Ranger paused a moment and then his purple eyes were uncharacteristically serious. "These are dangerous, dark times Eyre, and the force of the Lightworkers does not just come from the adult population. I have faith in you and your friends, and I believe it is important that you are aware of what is going on. Others would not agree with me though, so it is best that we do not speak of this again. The *walls* have *ears*," he whispered dramatically at the end.

Eyre smiled and then saw Ben Perrill looking out at her. Her smile disappeared. The Ranger wasn't joking; she would have to be careful.

Just then E Kofi walked in the front entrance of the Shed and stood chatting to the Sergeant.

"Prohemium practise is next," she said. "I'd better go back in. Hopefully I don't end up in Sydney Harbour."

She stood beside Colton again, determined to get her prohemium right. Colton had managed to create a Seam a couple of times, although he hadn't gone where he was supposed to. So they worked together, trying to copy E Kofi and adjust hand positions to get the prohemium right. Colton had hold of Eyre's palm and was turning it over, saying "I think it needs to be a bit more at this angle," when someone walked up. Concentrating hard on her hand position, it took Eyre a moment to register that it was Jax. His dark hair caught the light and his green eyes looked at her uncertainly as anger rose within her. But she hid it beneath a smile.

"Hi Jax," she said. "How's your prohemium going?"

He shrugged. "I've been to Terra, but not been back yet. E Kofi had to retrieve me." Resisting the impulse to suggest he go there and stay there, Eyre was nonchalant.

"Well, keep trying. Colton and I have almost got it, so we'd better get back to practising." She turned her back on him and it felt *good*! She had no idea what game he was playing, no interest in what he'd been going to say, and he could take a hike. Colton looked from one to the other and then put his hands into the prohemium position as Eyre copied him. Jax hesitated but left after a moment. Message received.

Eyre's annoyance at Jax seemed to help her concentration, because the buzzing between her palms that she'd felt on previous practise sessions started, but this time it burned like fire and suddenly a blinding Seam streaked down before her. She was pulled into it as if by a magnetic force and when she shook her head she found she was in the middle of a hot plain somewhere. But she'd barely had time to register any details before she was whisked back to the shed.

"Well done," E Kofi said. "You created a Seam and went to Kenya! Congratulations." Despite ending up in the wrong place, Eyre knew he meant it, and it felt great to have gone *somewhere*.

"What is happening when you create a Seam and end up in the wrong place is basically just teleportation," E Kofi explained, walking back and forth across the front of the stage. "So you're creating the energy for a light window, but not enough for the Seam, so you're just teleporting to somewhere else in Entis. Once you get the prohemium right, the Seam will be right also and you will get to the Alterworld you are aiming for. You cannot teleport to an Alterworld without going through the Seam; basic teleportation does not create enough energy. So keep trying, it's encouraging to see so many of you starting to raise the energy!"

He walked over to Eyre and moved her fingers a fraction. "I think that's where you're going wrong," he said. "Try that."

Eyre performed the prohemium with the required adjustment and a Seam appeared before her. Once again she was pulled through it and she was standing in a very dense, forested area. This time, however, she was not pulled back by E Kofi and she looked around her. The first thing she registered was the violet sky, and then a chat wandered into view from out of the bushes. It was a fluffy, lavender-coloured creature with a long tail. The Ranger had a pet, called Lenny, who was a Hug—a cross between a rabbit and a chat, so she knew what a chat was. Lenny looked a lot like it, but she had longer ears. But the best thing about seeing the creature was that it confirmed where she was, because chats were only found in Terra. She'd done it! She'd done the prohemium accurately and created the right Seam! Obviously that was why she'd been left there; now she had to try and get back. Concentrating hard, she did the hand movements again and a Seam appeared in front of her. With a blur she travelled through and opened her eyes—she was in the Training Shed! E Kofi appeared even more delighted than she was, and he positively grinned at her.

"Oh well done! Another person who will be undertaking the TACI test this year."

Eyre felt happy after her unspectacular practise with the staff—and several students were looking at her a bit enviously. The prohemium was hard, and so important for passing each year.

But as the afternoon went on, more students got the hang of it. Perhaps it was the 'group energy' that E Kofi had spoken of, but as the number of students increased who could perform the prohemium, more joined their ranks exponentially it seemed. By the end of the afternoon about half the students had done it correctly.

"What a difference!" E Kofi said, elated. "Well done, students! I look forward to working some more with you tomorrow."

CHAPTER THIRTY-NINE

EYRE LEFT THE AUDITORIUM with Colton, feeling strangely joyful.

"You did well, Eyre," Colton said, his ice blue eyes crinkling down at her. Always such a kind-hearted person, he well understood her past journey, and Eyre could tell he was happy for her. She'd had such mixed success with so many of the required courses since she'd arrived at the Academy; Colton 'got' that it was nice for her to excel for once.

Eyre smiled back at him gratefully but changed the subject. "I guess I'll see you at the Sector Fair a bit later?"

"Oh yes," Colton laughed. "Dr David has got me rostered on pretty much all evening." Dr Warren David was the head of the Arant Sector, and taught "Design and Invention" to Arant students. A particularly brilliant man, he had created several inventions that had made a difference to the world. Eyre expected that the Arant Sector would have a fairly spectacular display this evening at the Fair.

Eyre headed off briskly to join the Hese students who were working on finishing their stand this afternoon. The last classes of the day had been cancelled to allow students in each Sector to get last-minute things organised for the Fair, which officially started at 6pm. Each Sector had been working all week to finish their displays, in great secrecy. And each stand had been masked by the Head of Sector for quite some time, so no one could see what was going on. It was the topic of much speculation, and everyone was looking forward to finally seeing the exhibition. Parents had been invited to attend, and there were flashes of light already on campus as people arrived. The Jotnar were also busy: scurrying about setting up tables for food and tea and coffee.

The stands were located around the campus and Hese had been allocated the moldavite square for their display. Rigmar had largely led the organisation of the Hese show and Eyre arrived to find Hese students scurrying around to his directions. Some were on ladders hanging banners, others were straightening the display walls, and yet others were stacking piles of information booklets on the ends of tables. Everyone was busy, operating under the Head of Sector's mask so the display was hidden. There was still a lot to do, but Rigmar had it all under control. Like his father, Chairman Essendon, Rigmar was great at organising people and events, and very calm under pressure. He seemed to revel in the whole process, and was cracking jokes even as he sent people in all directions.

"Todd, you haven't encountered another echidna, have you? Wake up my friend! I'm sure you can move faster than that!" he shouted, and everyone chuckled. Rigmar was referring to the TEP exams last year, where Todd had been sent to sleep when he touched a magical echidna. Each of them had their own embarrassing or difficult tale from the TEPs, so Rigmar was being very clever; his humour bonded them all together.

Todd grinned and picked the pace up. No one wanted to be unprepared when the Fair began.

Hese Sector was made up of students who had equal skills in all the Lightworking areas: physical, spiritual and intellectual, but no specific area of distinction. They often ended up in management or leadership because of their balanced talents. The talisman for Hese was a golden quartz, and their Sector colour was bronze, so the Fair stand was decorated in bronze and gold colours. Large golden letters pronouncing "HESE" on a bronze background were printed on a huge banner that was hung across the front of the area. The panels that made up the walls were cut from sheets of golden quartz and they glowed translucent yellow in the afternoon light. A team of Hese students who were good at faceting had worked for a month on the panels to make sure they fit perfectly for the space.

Rigmar had come up with the idea of an "Order from Chaos" theme, which was appropriate, given that Hese Lightworkers often ended up in organisational roles. Rigmar had spoken to the Mimir, and had been loaned a huge pile of gold dust for the event. It sat in an enormous bronze cauldron, slowly melting, but at intervals it erupted upwards, blasting swirling tornadoes of glittering dust into the air. Then the whirlwinds of gold fell like a failed dust storm back into the cauldron, where it melted into a boiling broth, as if something hot and dangerous was brewing there; bubbles of air plopping up from time to time—a golden, primordial soup. Light energy had been bonded to the cauldron to create the whirling twisters of gold, and the whole process of transforming the gold dust into molten gold and then into tornadoes of gold dust had taken three Hese students a fortnight to work out. Eyre loved the entire procedure, even though she'd seen it many times as the Hese team had worked their display out. But that was really only the beginning.

A flat, wide beam of light a metre above the ground formed a perfect circle that ran from the cauldron, around the exhibit area and back to the cauldron. Spokes of light criss-crossed the circle, so it resembled a great wagon wheel turned on its side. The light acted as a gleaming conveyor belt, with gold dust flowing from the cauldron onto each beam of light and diverted to a series of stations around the perimeter of the circle. At each station a bronze Inguz radiated light energy and transformed the gold dust into a smooth, gleaming piece of human anatomy. Then each part was sent to the centre hub of the light wheel, where another Inguz emanated a shining beam and fused the pieces of the anatomy together to form a magnificent statue of Professor Mervyn Chadwick, the founder of the Academy of Light, who had also been a member of the Hese Sector. And a hologram in gold lettering hovered in front of the statue, announcing: "*Order from Chaos*". Once the statue was created, it rotated for a few minutes and then was transported back to the cauldron, where it disintegrated, back into puffing spirals of gold dust. Then the whole process was repeated.

Finally, the students were ready, with only minutes to spare, and Rigmar ordered all the ladders and paraphernalia to be put away. As the bell rang to announce the beginning of the Sector Fair, masks were removed by the Sector Heads, and the exhibits were revealed.

Gasps of surprise and admiration rang from all over the campus. There was a huge number of people attending, as the Academy's Sector Fair was highly regarded, and even people with no children at the school would come, every year, to see the exhibition.

Dean Cecil Fraser walked to a podium, followed by Chairman Essendon. Using telepathy, the Dean addressed the crowd who were spread around and across the campus. "Would you please welcome our esteemed guest, Chairman Andrew Essendon, who will officially open our Sector Fair?" Polite applause travelled across the campus as Rigmar's father, the Chairman of the Echelon, moved forward.

"Every year I am amazed and astonished by the efforts of the talented students at the Academy of Light," Andrew Essendon said, "and I am sure this year will be no different! Please enjoy the evening. I hereby declare the Academy Sector Fair open!"

More applause rang out and the campus bell sounded again; then people began to walk around to view all the exhibits. Eyre was rostered on with a few other students to hand out information booklets on how Hese had put together its display, and to answer any questions. So, for the first session she talked with parents and visitors and explained the display to people. Everyone she talked to was fascinated with the movement and scale of what Hese had done, and many stayed for several rotations of the creation of the statue.

After a couple of hours, the next students arrived to take over the shift, so Eyre was able to walk around and see what the other Sectors had done. The first stand she visited was Virens—the Sector gifted in spiritual and intellectual areas. Virens students had an Inguz that was green in the centre, and their talisman was an emerald, so the whole Virens exhibit was decorated in shades of green. Mistress Leia Entwisle was the Head of Sector for Virens, and she was talking to parents as Eyre arrived, so Eyre walked by her to look at the demonstration. Eyre didn't have many classes in common with Virens students, who often ended up in agricultural jobs, or the plant communication areas, as well as research. They were also gifted in psionics and cognitive forces, subjects Eyre did take, but timetabling through the Sectors meant that they didn't often meet. But Carly spotted Eyre as she arrived and rushed over.

"I loved your stand, Eyre!" she said. "It was *so* brilliant! You all must have worked for hours on that!"

Eyre smiled and thanked Carly. "But I want to see *yours* now Carly! What are you doing?"

Eyre studied the Virens display, a crop of sugarcane which was planted in flawlessly straight rows to form a perfect square. The plants were healthy, two metres tall and deep green, and seemed to be standing to attention like a group of well-behaved students.

Carly laughed. "Well, if you want to see ours, you have to take a seat up there. Watch Phillip, he's so good at this!" Eyre could see that Carly was very proud of their display, and Eyre was keen to see it—but then suddenly Eyre caught a nuance from Carly's tone, that perhaps Carly was proud in another way? Eyre had not had much to do with Carly over the past year, but she noticed how Carly's eyes kept flicking over to Phillip Outray, who stood on the side, ready to begin the demonstration. Eyre was *extremely* curious, but that was a discussion for another day, so she just patted Carly on the shoulder, happy for her friend.

"I've been really keen to see it!" was all she said. It was true though, she was actually very interested to see what Virens had organised. As far as the Sectors went, they were fairly low-key usually. They weren't the dramatic students who amazed the campus with showy accomplishments and triumphs. But they were the Sector who had a great impact on the livelihood of not only the Lightworkers, but the entire people of Entis. Humble, proud and extremely accomplished, if it weren't for them, the world would not survive.

In any case, "Up there" referred to seats hovering in the air above them, circling in rows a few metres above the verdant green crop below.

Curious, Eyre levitated and took a seat. When all seats were filled, Phillip Outray levitated to the centre of the circle, above the green plants, where he stood with eyes closed like a magician about to perform. Everything was quiet, and then a holographic green sign appeared above Phillip's head.

"*Phillip is asking the plants to lean to the left*".

An admiring gasp went up as the whole crop swayed to the left, like a soft wind had blown the plants. Eyre's mouth gaped open. *A magician indeed!* she thought as she leaned forward.

For the next half hour, Phillip instructed the plants to bend, and turn and lean in all directions, which they all did in perfect synchrony. It was a serene and beautiful display. Finally, the performance finished with the sugar cane crop doing a choreographed dance to Tchaikovsky's *"Waltz of the Flowers"*. The whole audience stood to applaud as the demonstration finished and Phillip bowed. Eyre marvelled as she descended to the ground. What an incredible ability!

Carly waited for her and Eyre laughed. "That was amazing! No wonder those plants look so healthy—all that exercise has obviously made them fit and happy!" They both chuckled and Eyre wished Carly luck as she headed for the next display.

Flava had a number of very intellectual students sitting on crystal chairs placed evenly around a two metre high sphere made of clear quartz.

Sappir had decorated their stand all in blue and silver. Sappir Lightworkers had strengths in the spiritual areas, and the best faceters in the world were from the Sappir Sector. It was clear that some of the Academy students were gifted in faceting, because their stand was decorated with the most amazing cut sapphires, the talisman for Sappir. They had constructed several rooms out of silver panels inlaid with gleaming sapphires that formed a beautiful mandala pattern, representing the search for spiritual guidance, and in each room a separate demonstration was going on. The Sappir Sector was known for its artists, healers, psychic skills and cross-species communication. So, in one room they had set up tables with orbuculums, tarot cards and divining instruments. Long lines of students and visitors stretched out of the room, as people queued for a chance to visit with the world-famous Madame Overmantle, the Head of Sector, but also, to see the gifted psychic school students.

Abby was in the next Sappir room, with Lenny on her lap and Eyre stayed to watch, wanting to support her friend. Visitors would ask the soft, lavender coloured Hug on Abby's lap a question and Abby would answer for Lenny.

"What is your favourite food?" an older woman asked.

"Brussel sprouts and chocolate" Abby answered after a moment, and then tilted her head towards Lenny, concentrating. "But only when mixed together."

The line of people gasped with laughter mixed with horror, and the next person stepped up. Eyre groaned. Wyatt Rankins, Ben Perrill's crony. What asinine question was he going to come up with?

Sure enough, Wyatt thought he was being hilarious when he asked. "What is the meaning of life?"

Abby rolled her eyes, but Lenny's green eyes focused on Wyatt as if the gentle creature was about to go rabid on him. Eyre suddenly remembered that Wyatt's parents were the ones who had written to the school to complain about the Ranger. Abby focused on Lenny, as she listened to his response, and then laughed out loud as she communicated.

"Lenny says the meaning of life is to learn to write kind things about one another," she said, and watched in satisfaction as Wyatt flushed a strange beetroot colour. Eyre felt a great satisfaction as she saw Wyatt's discomfort. The rest of the queue did not understand the personal meaning, so they all went, "Ahhh," thinking Lenny was so sweet. Wyatt put his head down and scurried off as the next person in the line, a little girl, stepped up, asking Abby if she could have a hug from the Hug. Eyre smiled and decided to move on.

The next Sappir room was very busy and Eyre had to crane her neck to see what was going on. Zanda was sitting at a table covered in the rainbow ribbons he had shown them at the beginning of the year. The ribbons were now much more vibrant in colour, and danced on the table as if they were alive. Sitting next to Zanda was a guy with long hair that Eyre didn't know. His hair was dark and shining and he had tied many of the ribbons in it. They twirled in the air like magic. Zanda also had rainbow-coloured butterflies made from the same substance, and they fluttered around the room and above his own and his friend's head. Somehow, over the past few months Zanda had worked out how to bond the butterflies to a person's aura, because they stayed above their heads in a kaleidoscope of colour. The ribbons and butterflies were for sale, and Zanda was doing a roaring business. And Eyre noticed that he seemed particularly happy sitting with his Sappir friend. So Zanda too wasn't alone now. Eyre stuck her hand in the air and caught his attention. She gave him a wink and an energetic thumbs-up and he grinned at her. But it was way too busy to get in the room, so she moved on to see what Flava had organised.

Beatrice and Robeson were standing at the front of the Flava exhibit, handing out bracelets made of small citrine crystals with a silver disc attached.

"The discs are Electrum," Beatrice said proudly. "Sourced by Flava students especially for the Fair. It's an energy source."

Robeson nodded and indicated the Sector Head of Flava, who was talking with one of the parents. "Professor Etemad took the senior students to Caelus to find the Electrum. It was sanctioned by the Determinant Dozen."

Eyre took a bracelet and slipped it on. Everyone knew of Professor Felicity Etemad. Dux of any establishment she'd ever been part of, and a world researcher in the properties of Light energy—no doubt this would be an interesting display. Eyre hoped she would actually be able to understand it.

Everyone filed in and took a seat in tiered stands around a central arena. The room was swathed in drapes of bright yellow fabric, as dazzling as the sun. In fact, the entire arena was impressively bright, just like the Flava students themselves, Eyre thought wryly. There was complete silence, finally broken by a shining silver figure walking unevenly from the doorway into the centre of the space.

"Greetings," it began in a metallic voice. "My name is Chiruk. I am a light robot, a prototype made out of Electrum, designed by third-year and graduate Academy of Light students over the past year. My purpose is educational."

Eyre's eyes widened as the robot began to perform Basic Clasis slightly off-balance, but without a misstep. When it had completed all levels of the Clasis, metal Antaraks appeared in its hands and it shifted into Two without a pause. Gasps travelled around the room as it swapped the Antaraks for a Mnae and transitioned effortlessly into Single. It had almost completed all the levels of Ferito when it faltered and stumbled. A sympathetic 'ohhh,' whispered through the crowd. But the robot impassively started at the beginning and this time made it through the whole Clasis without error. Then Chiruk dropped its head and was silent.

As murmurs filled the room, Eyre wondered what the robot was meant to educate people about. Death, maybe?

And then through the doors came a dark, swirling cloud of stinking matter. As several parents instantly raised their hands, Professor Etemad spoke via telepathy.

"Please be still and watch. It is not the Gothak."

Uncertain, but recognising the stench of evil, the crowd moved restlessly in their seats as the foul blackness surrounded Chiruk until the robot was completely obscured. One of its arms moved with difficulty through the miasma until only a shining palm was elevated above the mire.

"I am requesting assistance," Chiruk said in a monotone. "Please raise the hand you have your bracelet on." Its voice was fading as the dark cloud settled and covered the robot in a disturbing, black ooze.

Like obedient students in a classroom, everyone swiftly held up their hands. Even though they knew this was only a robot, and a demonstration, it was unsettling to see its light being dimmed by the vile mass.

As soon as all hands were in the air, a hum arose in the room. A flash of light was followed by a startling thunderclap. Hands wavered at the sound, but remained determinedly in the air as a light zapped from wrist to wrist, reflecting off the Electrum discs on the bracelets until a single beam completely encircled the room. There was a high-pitched *zing* as the light exploded inwards, swirling around Chiruk like a golden whirlwind.

The black ooze was blasted into a fine dust that drifted slowly to the floor, then the dazzling twister swirled upwards and vanished in a radiant explosion. As Chiruk lifted its head with a movement like a sigh, its eyes glowed with a blazing light.

"When we are prepared to put our hand up, when we work as one for the Light, we save each other," it stated in a voice that reverberated around the room.

The audience lowered their arms as Chiruk performed a strange movement and was instantly enveloped in a ball of light. The shining sphere rose from the ground until it hung in the air above the audience, who gasped in astonishment as it transformed into a glowing hologram of Earth. *Entis.*

All eyes watched in dumbstruck silence as a rainbow of colour shot around Entis, almost blinding in its brilliance. Eyre felt tears forming as she understood the meaning of Flava's display: *the reconstruction of the Aura.* The dream that had been in the Lightworking community since 1908. *Educational indeed,* Eyre thought as she looked in awe at the slowly turning Entis with the rainbow glowing luminously around it. This had certainly been a poignant message for all of them.

Professor Etemad's voice came again. "The work by our third-year and graduate students has been ground-breaking and there has been interest from many countries in what they have achieved. Please congratulate them."

About thirty students moved modestly forward, and the room was again filled with noise—feet stomping, applause and several loud '*hurrah*'s.

As Eyre left the room, she gave Beatrice a small salute and her friend beamed. Beatrice hadn't revealed anything about the display, and she was clearly immensely proud of her Sector.

Shaking her head in admiration, Eyre moved on towards the Rufa stand, wondering how any other Sector could compete with such a spectacular presentation.

Rufa had been allocated the Training Shed for their display, and they had used Light energy to cast red lighting, their Sector colour, throughout the area. Their talisman was a ruby, and they had strengths in the physical areas. So they were the pillars of the Defence Force, and also went into specialized areas such as lightsmithing, which was the use of light energy to forge weapons, and they also were strong in areas such as military stores management, which is why they worked so closely with the Mimir. A banner ran from one end of the Shed to the other with *"Walk Lightly and carry a big stick!"*, the motto of the Lightworking Defence Force, written in huge black letters.

Around the Shed there were ferocious displays of Ferito going on. Muscular students fought in mid-air, with and without weapons, in a mighty display of the power of the Lightworkers' martial art. Crowds of people surrounded the students involved in the display, and as each winner was announced, roars of support and applause filled the air. Luke Jordan lost closely to Lindi Jamieson, and they both descended to cheers from the audience. But then Eyre saw that the next person up was Ben Perrill, so she decided to move on to the rest of the Rufa display. Ben was exceedingly good at Ferito, but she had no desire to watch him in action. She'd already seen enough of his aggressive capacity.

In the middle of the Shed, on the sparring arena, students were demonstrating fulminology, and Eyre watched, fascinated as they showed how it *should* be done. Eyre had never had much success with the skill, so she watched with admiration as they pounded, counter-pounded, then skimmed the pound, and created jags of lightning and coronas of lethal energy. Lord Clarembout introduced each student and explained what they were doing as the best Rufa students stepped up to the floor and began their display.

At the other end of the Shed there was an extensive collection of weapons on show, which had been collected for centuries by Rufa and stored fastidiously by the Mimir in the Arms Depot. Ancient weapons from aeons ago lay beside the latest weapons to be created by talented Rufa students. There were articles from all the Alterworlds, strange-looking sabres and swords and daggers, all gleaming under the red light. There was even a Luxoccisor on display, the tall weapon with a curved blade at the top that the Gothak used.

Behind the long tables that displayed the huge collection of weaponry, Jensen was lightsmithing with his hands to produce a Kulbeda from a lump of gold. This was the first level of lightsmithing, but still incredibly difficult. Sparks flew and the heat rose around him as the huge amount of energy needed to perform the skill gradually transformed the misshapen gold into a gleaming, lethal looking dagger. Jensen was obviously gifted at the coveted ability, because the crowd watching him, which included members from the Lightworking Defence Force, were looking incredibly impressed. When he finally held up the dagger, loud applause rang out. Sergeant Tottingham was standing behind Jensen, and Eyre could see she was terribly proud of him as she took the Kulbeda and replaced it with another lump of gold. "Well done," she said. "Who's next then?" Tec Langford stepped up and the Sergeant gave a groan. Once again Eyre decided to leave. She wasn't keen on Tec either, another of Ben's oafish mates. She hoped he produced a toothpick from his effort, and judging by the Sergeant's reaction, he might be lucky with that.

She only had Arant and Tyros left to see, but time was running short, so she hurried along to the Tyros exhibit, which had been constructed next to the Meditation Pools.

The Tyros talisman was amethyst, and Eyre gasped when she saw that they had constructed a huge cave made completely from amethyst crystals. The Tyros Sector was gifted in spiritual and physical areas, and they ended up working in areas of psionics as they were particularly good at telekinesis, pyrokinesis and astral travel. This Sector was proficient at some of the most difficult skills in Lightworking. Immediately on entering the cave, she was overcome with a feeling of well-being. Amethysts were used for spiritual protection and overcoming negativity, so it made sense that she would feel that way as she walked into the crystal showroom, which glowed with a multitude of purple shades. The Tyros students had somehow bonded their special energy to the crystals, so that just walking in there knocked every bad feeling from one's soul. Eyre felt light and joyous, and after the mixed experiences of this year, and her continual worry about just about everything in general, it was a wondrous experience. This alone was unique about this exhibit: it was such a rare phenomenon for her to feel safe and at ease.

But there were additional demonstrations going on. Nick was performing an amazing show of pyrotechnics. He stood at one side of the cave and created a fiery blast with a snap of his fingers, and then shaped it into various images: a horse running, waves breaking against the shore, a bird flying. It was beautiful as well as dramatic, and the crowd oohed and aahed as each image formed in the air.

Warrigal was demonstrating telekinesis at the other side of the cave. He had an array of objects before him on a table, and one by one he moved them around the inner sanctum; in the air, along the ground, tumbling them around together in formations, and then returning them to the table. Telekinesis was a difficult skill that required mind energy working in several directions at the same time, and Warrigal was performing it without even seeming to try. It was an astonishing display of extreme talent, and the audience was silenced by his skill. He was a genius, really, Eyre thought as she too watched in wonder. But she did think, at one point, and knowing the ability of her friend, that Warrigal could perform an even more startling display for the watching people if he had wanted to. However, she knew that the audience wasn't going to see that skill tonight, or maybe ever. He was a Lightworker of such aptitude, with the added purity of being completely altruistic, that he was only focused on the goal of decimating the Gothak. He was decades ahead of the other students on campus, psychologically as well as with his expertise; a wise, courageous warrior already. Warrigal met her eyes for a moment, and it was as if he sensed her thoughts. He sent a statue of a horse spinning in the air towards her. It hovered in front of her face, and then he brought it back to the table.

Jemima Periwinkle, the Head of Tyros, beamed and moved around the room talking to the visiting parents and guests, as if she herself had organised the whole event; it was a triumph as a PR exercise. Self-effacingly, she told them all that it had been a group endeavour, whilst at the same time conveying that she herself had been at the forefront of it all. Quite a talent to manage that nuance, really, Eyre thought as she watched the performance. But in reality, Eyre knew that Ms Periwinkle had been absent from discussions about the Fair. She had left it all to the students, and Nick had told her that Warrigal had arranged most of it. Eyre thought drily that if the Fair had involved floral fabric and handbags, the Head of Sector would have been at every discussion.

As Nick and Warrigal finished and other students took their place, Eyre waved at them and hurried along to the last display of the Fair.

The only exhibit she hadn't seen yet was Arant. Eyre had missed the earlier displays in their program, but she wanted to see their stand. She knew that Arant was situated at the side of the dormitories, but when she got there, she was bewildered. Two students, obviously the welcoming committee, stood holding a small sign saying "Arant" at the end of the allocated area for the Sector, but there was nothing going on. Other people arriving with Eyre were equally confused, until one of the duo waved the attendees over. As she got closer, Eyre could see that it was Anders Johnson, who Eyre had met last year, and who seemed to be enjoying himself immensely. He stood with a slight girl who had a tag saying 'Amanda Lorraine' on her chest and they were both beaming.

"Walk that way," Anders said, indicating an empty space before her. Obviously delighted by her puzzlement, he waved encouragingly. "Go on."

Eyre and the straggling group of latecomers walked forwards and then Eyre felt a sudden dizziness. She shook her head. Her eyes finally cleared and her mouth hung open as she saw that she had been transported into a wild melee of students and people, not an organised group of people, but a ruckus of joyous activity. She was initially confused, and then realised that she'd just walked through a mask, which had been hiding all of this from view. How clever! And what a feat of Lightworking accomplishment! The Arant Sector had decided to keep the mask in place for the Fair, underlining their focus on working outside the borderlines, and their dedication to security. Eyre could see that everyone who followed her was delighted with the unusual beginning to the exhibition. Like magic, everything appeared before them as they walked through the disorientating wall of energy.

Arant were gifted in physical and intellectual areas, and often worked in Intelligence and the Defence Force. Their talisman was a carnelian, coloured like tiger stripes, and it was a perfect creature to describe their role in the Lightworking world. Ferocious, unbeatable, and the apex of their world. The whole area was encircled by wooden walls painted orange, with a tiger's head mosaic made of carnelian in the centre panel. Huge orange ropes criss-crossed the air above the area, with students hanging from them and swinging from one side to the other. Eyre looked up and marvelled. Yep. The physical side was definitely on display. She saw a bird sitting up there too, but then she was distracted as she saw someone she thought was familiar walk by with a slightly-built girl.

"Noah?" she called uncertainly, and the boy looked over at her, initially confused. But then his face cleared, and he walked back to her, beaming, but shaking his head.

"Ah... *err*? Sorry, can't quite remember..." he said hesitantly, and Eyre laughed. "Close! Not *err*, It's *Eyre*, from Water Lodge last year." Noah smacked his head. "Of course! 88!" Eyre laughed. Some people were better with numbers than names, she did understand.

"Are you Arant?" Eyre asked. Then she could have kicked herself when Noah shook his head. "No, I'm with the Unlit." Eyre looked at his bare upper arm and felt embarrassed for him and her; she should have remembered that he'd been the first student to leave the TEPs last year when he hadn't received an Inguz. She had almost gone home too that day, if her very strange-looking Inguz hadn't made an appearance. She rushed in to cover her tracks. "Well, I'm so glad you made it into the Academy!" she blurted, and Noah's eyes twinkled. "Me too," he said. "Unfortunately, you have missed the earlier Unlit displays, but we have a joint demonstration about to begin."

Eyre looked around at all the activity, seeing weapons flying, and people rushing everywhere. "Why are you here?" she asked. "I thought this was the Arant stand."

Noah nodded. "Arant and the Unlit work closely together. So, we usually do a combined stand. Here's one of the exhibits."

He indicated a couple of large tables at the side of the area where some Arant and Unlit students stood talking to people. The tables had an impressive display of locks and puzzles laid out, and visitors were standing trying to crack the codes; it was an interactive exhibit that only the smartest people would find interesting, Eyre thought as she gazed at yet another brainteaser she had no idea how to solve. Where was Beatrice when she needed her?

The attentive and helpful students were explaining what was going on, but, Eyre decided dismally, it didn't necessarily make one feel good about oneself. She looked in confusion at the strange array of hardware on the tables. How would you begin with all that? However, it was indeed a successful exhibit, as those who did choose to participate, including Chairman Essendon, seemed fascinated at the complexity of it all. Eyre, who was fairly impressed with the complexity of a Rubik's cube, decided to move on and leave this display for more worthy people.

The next display was a more physical one. UD1, it seemed, was the head of both Arant and the Unlit, and he stood quietly at the front of huge ranks of impressively straight rows of students, all standing to attention. Some were Arant, obviously, with their orange-centred Inguzes, but others were dressed in plain brown garb, who Eyre now knew must be the Unlit. But all stood equally immobile and focused on UD1. When a hooter went off, the full ranks moved through an impressive array of Basic Ferito, moving in perfect synchronicity, as if choreographed by a master. Not one foot out of place, not one arm in the wrong position. UD1's calm demeanour seemed to keep everyone in complete accord, as if one brain controlled them all.

Then, the students split into two groups: Arant and Unlit. As Eyre watched, they arranged themselves on the manicured grass, which Eyre could now see had been cut into a chequerboard pattern. Arant at one end, set up like draughts on a board, and the Unlit at the other. Arant pulled on orange vests to make the distinction clearer. All the students were grinning: this was obviously something fun for them. Eyre caught someone staring at her from the rear of the board. Jax's green eyes smouldered as he looked at her and she felt a shiver run across her. He might be completely unfathomable, but she couldn't deny the effect he had on her. She looked away deliberately as UD1 moved to the front of the crowd and stepped up on a small podium.

UD1's eyes twinkled as he announced, "I have invited one of our esteemed Heads of Sector to participate in this next exercise."

Heads craned to see who might be arriving for what was obviously going to be an extremely cerebral endeavour. Perhaps Dr Warren David? Eyre wondered. He was one of the most brilliant lecturers ever to be on the Academy's staff.

But then her mouth dropped in confusion as a scarlet-dressed, bouffant-haired force powered through the watching crowd.

"Make way, make way!" a honeyed voice echoed loudly. "Here I come!"

Eyre's round eyes watched as Ms Periwinkle waved a hand with bright red polish in the air, like a conductor commanding the attention of the orchestra.

"Thank you, thank you!" the vermillion-clad lecturer cried, as if the concert was already over. She arrived at the front of the students and walked over to UD1, who watched the whole performance with calm brown eyes. Offering Ms Periwinkle a hand, he helped her up onto the podium.

"Thank you for joining us, Ms Periwinkle," he said softly, and bowed. Jemima Periwinkle preened as if she were a soloist at the Opera House. "A pleasure, my dear," she said, batting startling blue eyes, in a voice that conveyed that UD1 was just *ever* so fortunate to have her turn up.

Once again, Eyre was tempted to walk away, but the fascination of this improbable scene was too mesmerising to leave.

"Let us begin," UD1 said. "Please make the first move, Ms Periwinkle."

Jemima Periwinkle waved an airy hand, but Eyre noticed that there was a sudden feral glint in her eyes, and an unusual alertness to the usually fatuous woman.

Because red—or orange—in this case always went first in a tournament, Jemima Periwinkle was commanding the Arant troops.

"11-15," she called out. The Arant student standing on square 11 jumped to square 15.

"23-18," UD1 countered. The Unlit student leaped over to square 18.

"8-11," Ms Periwinkle shot back at him. As the Arant student jumped across, a twinkle appeared in UD1's eye.

"Ah," he said. "The Cross. Good opening, Ms Periwinkle."

Far from being flattered, a look of annoyance crossed Jemima Periwinkle's face. Obviously she didn't like that her strategy had been identified so early in the game. And Eyre noticed that she especially didn't like it when UD1 didn't play the next move Ms Periwinkle was evidently expecting. Eyre didn't know what it should have been, but as the game progressed, every triumphant placement of Ms Periwinkle's 'piece' was calmly countered by UD1. Then, the worst thing for Ms Periwinkle, UD1 'took' a piece. One of the Unlit responded to his call and leapt over an Arant student, effectively taking him out of the game.

From there, it was a flurry of students moving on the board, jumping over one another and removing each other from the 'board'. Their jumps became more and more elaborate, with the Arant students performing moves using levitation, and the obviously very fit Unlit students tumbling and cartwheeling like Olympic gymnasts over their opponent's pieces. Laughter filled the air as each student tried to outdo the previous one's moves. However, Ms Periwinkle did not seem to be enjoying the game so much. She was looking flustered and irritated, and untidy wisps of her bouffant do had escaped and straggled down her face. She dashed them away and a bead of sweat ran down her face as she studied the dwindling students on her side.

"Ms Periwinkle is the Queensland Champion," Noah whispered. "I daresay she thought this would be a breeze."

After intense scrutiny, Jemima Periwinkle called out her move and Jax leapt sideways, cartwheeling in the air as he did so, to 'bravos' from the crowd. Then a strangled sound came out of the lecturer's throat as she realised her mistake.

UD1 was able to use the space she'd created to not only capture two of her pieces, but to create a king as one of his players reached the end of the board. Jax was one of the players removed, and he left the board in a series of jaw dropping tumbles that brought more cries of 'bravo!' from the crowd. One of the Unlit students who had been previously removed from the board leapt on the back of another to create the 'king', and the game continued. Seeing the king leap over other players was a feat of phenomenal strength and agility, and Eyre found herself caught up in the athleticism of the 'pieces' rather than the strategy of the game.

But in any case, it was a relatively short time until Jemima Periwinkle had to concede defeat. Clearly she was not used to losing, and didn't like it one bit, Eyre noticed with amusement as she studied the dishevelled and infuriated woman. Ms Periwinkle's mood was not improved as a deafening wave of applause filled the air, probably a little louder than was polite. Obviously, others shared Eyre's opinion of the vacuous lecturer, she thought.

UD1 however was a gentleman. He bowed.

"Thank you Ms Periwinkle. You played a very tough match."

Jemima Periwinkle grimaced. "A pleasure," she said tightly, and then stalked off. An awkward silence ensued, but as usual, UD1 was unfazed.

"That was the last game for the evening," he announced. "The Fair will be shutting in ten minutes, so please go and check out the things you haven't seen yet. Thank you for visiting the Arant-Unlit exhibit!"

Another round of applause followed and then the crowd began to disperse, crossing through the mask to rejoin the campus masses. Eyre looked around, but Jax had already disappeared. She felt a strange disappointment, and couldn't understand why really. The last thing she wanted was to come face to face with that complicated guy.

Eyre had pretty much seen everything, so she said farewell to Noah and set off to find her friends so they could head back to the dormitory together. A hot chocolate at the common room and a gossip about the incredible events of the evening was definitely in order!

CHAPTER FORTY

THE NEXT FEW WEEKS flew by in a blur. After the Fair, the students seemed to realise that there was only a short time until the TACI exams began. Their pride at receiving so much praise from the attendees at the Sector Fair seemed to galvanise them all into a lot of intense work and study. And suddenly, the honour of being a Lightworker had resonated with them. It seemed that many of them knew now that *everyone* depended on each other's specific abilities, if the Lightworkers were to succeed in this world, the Overworld and most of all, against the Gothak.

There was so much practising going on, and so much to learn in the lectures, that the time went fast. Most of the students were focusing on making sure their prohemium was perfect, and trying to remember as much as they could about the Alterworld they were about to visit. As well as practising Ferito whenever possible. Their first TACI exam was an unknown factor, and they wanted to be prepared as best they could. No one took it lightly. Usually, students just tumbled into bed at night, then got up the next day to do it all again, without complaint.

So, when the day of the ball dawned, the hum in the Refectory was louder than normal. Sergeant Tottingham tapped her staff for silence.

"You have all been working hard in the past weeks and the staff have been well-pleased with your progress. You have all redeemed yourselves amazingly with your efforts." A slight laugh travelled around the room as they realised she was referring to how dismally they had performed last semester.

The Sergeant continued. "As such, a break for the annual first-year social event tonight has been well-earned by all of you. The dance will take place by the Ponds of Doombee at 4pm, and this year the theme is *'Fire and Ice'*. This is a good opportunity to de-stress before the TACI exams next week and I hope to see you all there. Ranger Chrysanthe will be organising the event as usual and weaving his exceptional magic—I'm sure you won't want to miss it. Classes in the afternoon are cancelled after you undertake your usual morning training at the Shed."

The noise grew louder as students discussed the reprieve, and Eyre felt a great elation—her least favourite afternoon of the week; she was going to miss Genealogy and History of Light. What a bonus!

So she worked hard at the Training Shed all morning, making the hours count as she moved through all her Clasis, practised levitation and telekinesis, and then practised her Staff Forces and her prohemium. She was improving in every area except being able to control the direction of the energy from her staff. *That* was going to take more time, despite the tips the Ranger had given her. Then she gave a wry smile. Actually, not all that good at horsemanship, either.

By the time she finished she was hot and sweating, in spite of the cool air blowing through the doors of the Shed and she dashed back to the dormitory, keen for a shower.

There was an energy in the dormitory that wasn't usually there—and Eyre was amused to see that the dance clearly motivated students more than lectures. Some of them, including Saskia, Ambrosia, and Iris of course, must have been there for quite some time despite the instructions to train at the Shed that morning—they were clean and dressed, hair *curled*—and their faces already expertly made up. Saskia had some of Zanda's rainbow butterflies circling around her head, and Ambrosia had his ribbons twirling through her hair. Some of the dresses the girls were wearing were quite remarkable. Did they always chuck in a ballgown 'just in case'? Eyre wondered. She looked at their spectacular dresses and felt slightly self-conscious. Wasn't she going to look divine in the casual sundress she'd brought? She didn't have anything formal, and she really hadn't realised the ball would be quite this dressy. Then she laughed to herself. What did it matter? She would go and have fun anyway.

She jumped in the shower and savoured the hot water, washing her hair and feeling great by the time she got out. She blew her long red hair dry and decided to leave it out for a change. It hung in russet waves down to the middle of her back and she pinned one side up with a silver clip. She put on her floral dress and flat sandals, and decided it looked nice with the silver chain that was permanently around her neck. Despite not having a formal dress, she was looking forward to the evening. It would be lovely to socialise under the stars, she thought.

Eyre sat on her bed and looked out the window. She could see a bustling form racing back and forwards along by the Ponds and she wondered what

The Ranger was up to. He looked busy but it was too far away to see anything really.

Beatrice and Abby appeared from the bathrooms. They started fussing around, getting ready for the event. Eyre lay on her bed and enjoyed the fact that she wouldn't have to listen to Jemima Periwinkle or Mandig Vela this afternoon; that alone was cause for celebration! She was ready and happy to wait as Beatrice slipped on a sequined red dress that complemented her fair skin, and Abby put on a lovely blue satin sheath. They both looked beautiful, and Eyre was so happy for them.

Just then there was a knock at the door. Eyre jumped up and saw Mrs Abnett there, holding a bag.

"This is for you, Eyre," Mrs Abnett said, holding the bag out. "It's made from gossamer thread from Caelus. I know your mother would have loved to give it to you herself."

Eyre opened the bag curiously and gasped as she pulled the item out. It was a silky dress, made of shining thread, woven together so closely the stitches were seamless. As she moved the fabric in the light it shimmered like silver—it was absolutely beautiful. In delight she stripped off and put the dress on, finding that it fit her perfectly. She turned back and forth, admiring the way the fabric flowed. There was also a pair of shining sandals in the bag, that of course fitted too. Mrs Abnett had done her research.

"Thank you Mrs Abnett," she cried, throwing her arms around the old woman. "It's beautiful!"

Abby clapped her hands and Beatrice grinned as Mrs Abnett left. "Mrs Abnett told Abby about it when she went to the Library last semester. Did you think we'd let you come without a decent dress?"

And Abby just put her hands to her face, ecstatic with the surprise. "Eyre, the silver is so perfect for you! You look amazing!"

It was almost time for the dance to start, so Beatrice and Abby left to find Nick and head over to the Ponds. Eyre felt a bit shy as she walked to the end of the dormitory and waited for Colton to arrive. He wasn't far behind Nick and arrived wearing a light blue shirt patterned with small trees and dark grey long pants. His clear blue eyes looked Eyre up and down and he shook his head slowly.

"You are stunning, Eyre, I feel very lucky you're going with me."

Eyre blushed and they walked down the path towards the Ponds of Doombee. The awkwardness soon passed as they walked. She knew Colton quite well now and they had a lot to talk about as usual.

Finally, they arrived at the Ponds and Eyre stopped dead, looking around in awe at the spectacle before them. Loops of lights ran from one length of the Ponds to other, creating a wondrous fairyland. Shining orbs floated around and sparkles of glittering dust fell at intervals from above—where from, Eyre couldn't see. Sculptures of huge snow-covered trees made of crystal were dotted around, and they were lit up from within by lights in the colours of the seven Sectors. Flames danced around the perimeter, forming shapes of the Inguz that continually formed and reformed. Life-size holograms of animals—a deer walking slowly, a dolphin leaping, a series of birds in flight—were moving on the ground at intervals around the area, so realistic that Eyre had to look twice to check they weren't alive. And a large disco 'ball' in the shape of an Inguz hovered in the air above them, twirling slowly and sending out rainbow-coloured spots in all directions. The Inguz floated above a jukebox which was set in the centre of a large dance floor at the edge of the water. It was playing dance music quite loudly and Eyre had a feeling the dance floor wouldn't be empty for long.

Behind the dance floor, back towards the campus and set up on stable ground, were a series of long tables and chairs, covered in white linen and set with crystal goblets, silver plates and shining silver cutlery. Large candelabras with flaming silver candles were lit and for some strange reason they didn't ever seem to blow out or burn down. A hologram of a flame of fire, with a snowflake rotating slowly around it decorated the middle of each table. As Eyre watched, the hologram changed colours—echoing the Sector colours in the trees. A series of empty tables covered in white linen awaited the arrival of food, and a lone table held a huge crystal punch bowl filled with swirling, rainbow-coloured punch and surrounded by blue crystal martini-style glasses. Above everything, swarms of fireflies danced, swarming in ever-changing formations over their heads.

Ranger Chrysanthe was there, watching happily at the student's amazement, like a conductor directing a masterwork. Eyre and Colton walked over to him. "This is amazing, Ranger Chrysanthe, thank you so much!" Eyre said. The Ranger clicked his fingers and a rose made out of light appeared. He bowed and presented it to her, then clicked again and it turned to fairy dust, flying into the air and sprinkling down in a shining shower, before catching in her hair and lighting it with a myriad of diamond sparkles. Eyre smiled in delight.

"A pleasure, my dear," Ranger Chrysanthe said, "I hope you have a magical night."

Other students came up to talk to Ranger Chrysanthe, so Eyre and Colton headed over to find Beatrice, Nick and Abby. As they moved through the crowd they passed Jax, who was standing with Vaughn Michaelson and Robeson. He was dressed in a khaki buttoned shirt that made his eyes seem even greener, and light tan jeans with black Converse. His dark hair shone in the reflected light, and he looked down at Eyre, an unreadable expression on his face. Colton's eyes were intent as Jax spoke.

"Hi," he said, "Eyre, you look lovely tonight." Just then Pheria pushed through the crowd, tall and gorgeous in an ice-blue gown and strappy silver sandals. Already much taller than Eyre, who was only average in height, the heeled shoes made Pheria tower above her. Pheria held on to Jax's arm and smiled brightly down at Eyre as if talking to a child.

"So nice to see you, Eyre," she said dismissively, "Jax—we really should go and thank Ranger Chrysanthe." She pulled him away past a hologram of a horse galloping.

Eyre rolled her eyes and looked at Colton, and he gave an amused huff. Sometimes people tried a bit too hard to put you in your place, and it had backfired. Pheria's behaviour had looked ridiculous, and from the uncomfortable look on Jax's face as he left, he thought so too.

As Eyre and Colton continued through the crowd, Sergeant Tottingham and the rest of the staff arrived. Oorlock led the way, followed by an unusual-looking Sergeant Tottingham, who was dressed in a shiny floral shirt with bright pink trousers, and was obviously extremely uncomfortable being out of her khaki uniform or track pants. Professor Vela was completely dressed in black, looking remarkably like an undertaker, and he seemed about as pleased as an undertaker to be there. Dr Botolfe, with her white sea-mine hairdo and a long yellow chiffon gown, was floating in behind Lord Clarembout, who had exchanged his red and black outfit for a green suit, and now resembled a rather large leprechaun rather than his usual Santa Claus. Madame Overmantle was in a deep-blue long-sleeved cape, and even E Kofi was there, looking around in amazement. By far the most splendiferous, as might have been expected, was Jemima Periwinkle, in a voluminous white and gold taffeta affair that resembled a badly-made pavlova. Whittaker Ray was the final staff member to walk in and his eyes roamed around until he finally found Eyre and nodded at her.

The staff moved to the head of the tables and sat down. Ranger Chrysanthe handed round blue martini glasses of rainbow punch, and soon the staff were talking animatedly to each other, with plenty of hand gestures that disconcertingly gave off sparks from time to time. Evidently an energetic conversation, Eyre thought.

Colton headed off to find them a drink and she finally reached her own group. Zanda had joined them, and Carly, with a couple of her friends, and Warrigal too, all holding the blue martini glasses of rainbow punch. Everyone was laughing at a comment that Zanda had made about how the

Sergeant had raided her sister's cupboard for the evening. Rigmar and Luke Jordan joined them so that eventually there was quite a crowd. Eventually Colton arrived back and made his way over to stand by Eyre, carrying two martini glasses. Beatrice rolled her eyes meaningfully at Eyre and Eyre had to admit he looked pretty good.

Sipping at the rainbow punch she found it tasted wonderful—a bubbly sweet mixture of various fruits, with a slight tartness from lemon. The swirling rainbow liquid was mesmerising to watch, changing randomly in wild spirals of colour. Eyre gasped as suddenly an image appeared in her drink—a snowflake that rapidly turned into a flame. More of Ranger Chrysanthe's magic she decided, looking at it in wonder.

A noise at the back of the crowd announced the arrival of the Jotnar, carrying great platters of food, which they placed on the empty tables with great ceremony –platter after platter of heaped culinary delights.

Once the Jotnar had left, the students each took a plate off the table, then lined up and filed past the food tables. The food was delicious—cold cuts of meat, piles of mango, pineapple, grapes and all manner of melons, prawns, lobster, oysters, salads and hot vegetables, it was a smorgasbord beyond anything Eyre had ever experienced. She and her friends sat together and ate with gusto until she couldn't eat another mouthful.

The moon had risen by now, casting a silvery glow across the top of the lake—the only decoration not organised by Ranger Chrysanthe, Eyre thought. It was a mystical night, the air here somehow avoiding the humid temperatures that were normal for this time of the year. Just a cool breeze that slipped through the trees and across the water, barely stirring the surface. Stars studded the inky sky, and the fireflies whirred above, forming pictures in the sky of snowflakes, of flowers, of butterflies and fairies. It was completely magical.

Colton stood up and held his hand out.

"Care to join me for Dance Clasis?" he asked and she laughed. She went out to the dance floor with him, feeling a bit awkward to be the first people there. They started to dance, Eyre feeling self-conscious, but enjoying the music. She loved her special dress—it shimmered in the lights like moonbeams and swirled around her ankles. Colton looked down at her; he was a good dancer and he was obviously enjoying it too. Others were encouraged to come up on the dance floor and eventually it was crowded with a dancing rabble. Suddenly a wave of laughter passed round as Rigmar levitated above them and started to cavort in the air. Several students did the same, and Phillip Outray, who had shown an aptitude for levitation, started performing tumble-turns above the crowd.

Eyre stopped in wonder at the sight of Nick, who was performing his specialty—bullio—making light bubbles in his hands and releasing them. They drifted around the crowd, bouncing off the wildly dancing students.

"So clever, Nick," Ranger Chrysanthe said in delight. "Your bullio skills are impressive! You must have the soul of an artist. See if you can do this!" He formed his hands in the air and a bubble shaped like a butterfly drifted above the crowd. Nick concentrated and tried to follow Ranger Chrysanthe's motions. A rather large pig floated up in the air, causing everyone to laugh uproariously. Nick shrugged. "A bit more practise, I guess," he said.

Down on the dance floor Anders and a girl called Jo were performing Ferito moves in time to the music, yelling out "Tollo!" from time to time. The music was fast and it was hard to keep the moves going smoothly, but they were perfectly in time together. A couple more students stood beside them, joining in, and the students levitating came down to be part of it. Soon the whole dance floor was filled with the students in lines, going through Clasis for Basic Ferito, stomping feet and moving arms completely in time with each other. It was a hilarious scene, but Eyre had to admit that it also looked formidable. Two hundred students moving in formation was quite a striking sight.

The staff at their table were watching in amusement and then Sergeant Tottingham stood up suddenly. A few of the students looked a little unsettled as she strode over. Perhaps they shouldn't be doing this? Sergeant Tottingham watched a second longer, then with one smooth move, joined in at Position 14. Ranger Chrysanthe stood down the back and started the Clasis also, then all the staff came to join the students. Except Mandig Vela, of course. At that point he gave a sour look of distaste and disappeared back towards campus. Wonderful to see him go, Eyre thought as the whole group moved sequentially through the positions to music that got faster and faster.

Some of the students levitated again and continued the Ferito three metres in the air as the music blasted on. Eyre was laughing so hard she could hardly keep the moves going, then she suddenly became aware that the Ranger had arrived at the very centre of the crowd performing some intricate dance moves that were hilarious. Everyone was watching him, hooting with laughter, when suddenly Eyre realised that somehow during the process, he had tied the whole student body together with a cord of light. It was unfathomable how he had managed to do that, but when Zanda, who was standing next to him, noticed, he took off in a dancing conga line, with all the students following him.

Even Ben Perrill and his cronies were in the line joining in. No doubt, Eyre thought cynically, Ben's enthusiasm was partly due to the fact he was behind Ambrosia Vollick. Eyre followed Colton around the edge of the lake and Carly was behind her, kicking her legs out wildly as she guffawed loudly. Finally the huge caterpillar of students ended back at the dance floor, laughing, gasping and sweating from the effort. The cord of light disappeared and Abby and Beatrice walked with Eyre as she headed for the table.

Suddenly Jax moved smoothly in front of Eyre, looking down at her with an intense expression. Eyre's hair had come adrift and it framed her face in wild red curls, the sparkling clip had completely failed in its task and her hair fell over her shoulders in long waves, a riotous mass of auburn fire. Jax looked down at Eyre for a long moment, and took a breath.

"Can I talk to you?" he asked. "A dance?" And despite herself, Eyre felt her stomach flip. He was tall and lean and so handsome—part of her wanted to dance with him desperately. However, he had also made quite a fool of her the other day, and suddenly she felt her temper rise. Dance? She felt more like performing Aditus on him as she remembered that morning.

"You know," she said sharply, her sapphire eyes flashing. "I won't dance with you, and I'd prefer it if you leave me alone."

Jax looked shocked (he's probably never been declined before, Eyre thought acerbically) but he raised his hands in surrender.

"Fine with me," he said, his voice flat. "No problem." His face looked at her darkly, like there definitely *was* a problem, but he turned and sauntered away, rejoining Pheria, who put her arm in his and looked up at him adoringly. Eyre looked away in disgust and headed back to her table where Beatrice was watching, vastly amused by the whole thing.

"By the Light, Eyre," she said in admiration. "The two most gorgeous guys in the place *both* asking you to dance! How'd you manage that?"

Eyre looked irritated. "Well one of them can go jump," she said. "He made it clear the other day that I'm not cool enough for his table."

"Still, he's torn," Beatrice chuckled. "The poor guy can't help himself. It's your fault, partially, you know. You look amazing tonight; any of the guys would love to dance with you! No second chances?"

Eyre's look was wounded as she watched Jax dance closely with Pheria. "I'm not into game playing," she said. "I'll give it a miss I think."

Eyre drank some more punch and resolved to enjoy herself and forget about Jax. She danced all night—with Colton, Zanda, Warrigal, Rigmar—so many people. Everyone was just grabbing a partner and enjoying the music, and trying to forget the intense week in front of them. It was wild and light-hearted, and shouts of merriment rang above the treetops.

At around 10.30 the lights started to dim, the swarms of fireflies headed off to the bush; the sparkling disco Inguz stopped turning and the music stopped. Eyre watched in disappointment as the holograms disappeared and the lights in the crystal trees started to turn off, one by one. The fiery Inguzes snuffed out and Sergeant Tottingham clapped her hands for attention.

"Well students, it's been a spectacular night," she said. "And I'm sure you all will want to thank Ranger Chrysanthe for his efforts." Cheers and applause filled the night for some time until the Sergeant raised her hands for quiet.

"Please head back to your dorms—the normal schedule will resume tomorrow, so get a good night's sleep. See you in the morning!"

The Jotnar came in and started clearing dishes, and the staff departed. Regretfully, groups of students started to drift back to the Lodges. Eyre walked with Colton, Beatrice, Abby and Nick, feeling as happy as she could remember for a long time. Nick released light bubbles as they walked, leaving a trail of golden orbs behind them.

"Thanks for tonight," Colton said as they reached the door leading into her dorm. He looked at her so intensely Eyre forgot for a moment they were just friends. Then he leaned down and brushed his lips gently against her cheek.

"You are quite something, Eyre Lightward," he whispered, and walked away.

CHAPTER FORTY-ONE

EYRE BRUSHED ISCHYROS'S COAT until it was shining and smooth, and she combed out the tangles in his mane. Since the incident with the guitar she had continued to visit him in his stall, but she'd not tried to play music to him again. Neither of them had mentioned what had happened, and Eyre had to admit that she was weary of trying to form a connection with the old horse. Ben Perrill was right about that—Ischyros *did* dislike her intensely—and despite all her efforts that year, nothing was changing. But she continued to look after him just to fulfill the requirements to pass the Equestrian Skills course. She had to admit that she liked running out to the stables every morning, and she even liked the routine of brushing and combing his coat and looking after his feet. It would just have been nice if the old horse had shown any indication he might come around to her. But that was obviously not going to happen.

However, it was a good opportunity for her to replay the events of last night through her head. It had been so magical and so much fun, and then that confusing finish to the night with Colton. If she were truly honest with herself, she had definitely felt *something* when Colton had kissed her. But why did she feel unfaithful to Jax? It wasn't as if they were together. She shook her head and decided to forget about it. It was all too complicated.

"Bye, Ischyros," she said softly. "I'll see you when I get back." There was no response so she headed back up the track. The snow was gone now, spring was well underway and the warmer temperatures were welcome after the bone-chilling cold of winter. The International Ferito Competition had been held over the previous two weeks and the whole Academy had watched the exciting event from the auditoriums in the evenings. Except the first-years of course. Despite their hard work in second semester, the Academy's Executive Committee had not relented, and the first-years had been given extra classwork and physical exercises while the rest of the Academy watched the competition. Eyre breathed in the fresh air as she jogged along. At least it had given them extra preparation for the TACI trial, she thought. So it wasn't all bad.

And Eyre's birthday last week had been fun. Her birthday was November 11 and last year no one had known about it. This year they'd made up for it by surprising Eyre with a cake and a picnic by the Ponds of Doombee. Beatrice and Abby had given Eyre some sparkly clips for her hair and Nick had carved her a wooden Inguz for her desk. She'd enjoyed the celebration, but by far the best gift was the friendship the three of them had given her. That was something she would always treasure.

Normally at this time of the morning there was hardly anyone around, but as she headed for the dorm there was activity everywhere, because today was the beginning of the TACI exams. Students from all four years would be leaving for the Alterworlds and everyone on campus was racing around getting prepared for the day.

Students didn't have to pack much. They had been issued a Kulbeda the previous night, which was theirs only for the duration of the TACI test and had to be returned afterwards. The sharp dagger hung in a scabbard on their belts, and they wore a backpack to put the luxes in. The backpack also contained an empty water bottle, and they carried their staffs, but they were supposed to demonstrate that they could survive the environment of the Alterworld without bringing anything else with them. They had learned what to eat and things to avoid over the past months, and how to build a shelter, but a lot of the test would be based around their adaptability and survival skills as their Alterworld guide helped them to locate the gazae. For the first-years the gazae was the luxes; and Eyre knew from the TEPs that the gazae for fourth-years was the Zha'kara diamonds, She'd also learned that for second-year students travelling to Aqua the gazae was an unusual type of sea pearl, and for third-years going to Caelus, it was something called a fulgurite, which had some sort of strange energy.

Eyre and her friends had breakfast together but nobody said too much as they walked over to the Receiving Stone. They were all nervous, and unsure of what was ahead of them. Earlier in the week the Sergeant had allocated the students into groups, and each group had a guide from Terra to go with them. Eyre's group had a young female Nemoris called Gyp O Shuvai who they had met when the groups were allocated. Shuvai (her first name, which she insisted they call her rather than O Gyp, as she told them she was not much older than they were) was quiet but encouraging about the expedition. "I have taken three groups of first-year students on their TACI journey in past years and it has gone very well," she'd told them. Smaller than E Kofi, and with more brightly-coloured scales, she waited with them patiently as the staff got everyone organised.

"Okay, quiet!" The Sergeant called, thumping her staff on the moldavite square. "Let's get everything underway. I would like first-years to line up in their travel groups on the Receiving Stone, as you will be going first. We will be doing this by year levels, so be snappy about it, we have many people to get moving."

The first-years grouped on the moldavite, looking around nervously. The students had been sorted into groups of at least six students, but usually more. Zanda was in a group with Robeson, Luke, Warrigal and Colton and the Sergeant indicated for them to go first. Robeson, Warrigal and Colton disappeared through a Seam instantly, but Zanda and Luke took a couple of goes at the prohemium until they finally got it right, and a few nervous titters could be heard around the square.

Professor Vela was marking off each group as they left, his face wearing its usual sour expression. Carly, Advika and Madeleine's group went smoothly, followed by Pheria, whose group included Georgia and Iris Goff. Eyre had the satisfaction of seeing Tec Langford fumble around for five minutes before he disappeared through the Seam, and one of the Curtis twins had to be brought back from somewhere to try again. Then Jax headed off in a group with Rigmar, Todd and Jensen, the boy who had been attacked by a bunyip and who now had a prosthetic leg. The process wasn't taking long despite the occasional delay, and soon enough Eyre had to step up with Beatrice, Abby and Nick. For some reason their group was smaller than most—it was just the four of them, when other groups were nearly double that size. But Eyre was happy it was just them; it would be a lot easier that way. Shuvai stood beside them as they all performed their prohemiums, and in a flash four Seams appeared before them and they disappeared.

Travelling through the Seam caused a strange tingling sensation, but she was used to it by now and once again Eyre found herself standing near a forest in Terra. There was a moldavite stone in the ground similar to the one at the Academy, which was how the Academy controlled where the Seam would open, so that all the students arrived in the same place. Generally, the return prohemium sent the person to the place of origin, wherever that may have been.

Many students were waiting there, and they stood talking in quiet voices and looking around until all the groups had arrived. E Kofi was there also and he called for attention in his soft rasping voice.

"Congratulations! You have all successfully arrived, so you may now leave the area in your groups. Please remember you are operating as a unit, and no one is to head off on their own. Stay together, and stay with your guide at all times. Good luck; you have one week to source your gazae and return to this location."

The groups started walking off in various directions. It seemed the guides had each been given instructions that took them different ways, and as they headed into the dense foliage it wasn't long before Eyre had lost sight of every group but her own. As soon as they could find the gazae they could head back; staying the week was not required, but as she pushed through the thick undergrowth she realised that they would probably need every bit of that time.

After an hour of solid walking, they emerged into a clearing. A stream coloured bright pink ran through it, but no one made a move towards it. They all knew that to drink from this would cause severe vomiting, and none of them wanted to start the journey that way.

"Rest here," Shuvai said. "We will wait for the Zhuzhus to arrive."

As she sat down, feeling very grateful for the break, Eyre studied the bush around her. The plants were large and thick-leaved, with strange protuberances and seeds growing from them. Her sharp eyes spotted something and she called to Shuvai.

"Isn't that a babar tree?" she asked and Shuvai looked in the direction Eyre was pointing, further into the bush.

"Yes! Well spotted, Eyre. Let's go over."

Eyre knew that a babar tree grew huge berries that were filled with a liquid that could be drunk. She didn't know what it tasted like, but at this point she didn't care, she was so thirsty. So she and her friends pushed their way through to the tall tree and levitated up to the blue berries growing from it. The berries were about the size of a football, so they each took two and dropped back down to the ground. Sitting down, Eyre punched a hole in the top of the berry and took a swig. The juice was delicious, sweet and tasting like a mixture of fruits found back home. She drained the first berry and was starting the second when Abby shrieked as she was violently hauled up into the air.

"Wrap Vine!" Shuvai shouted in alarm. "Quickly!"

Dropping their berries, Eyre, Beatrice and Nick levitated into the air trying to see where Abby had gone. Eyre finally spotted her, way up in the canopy, completely wrapped from head to foot by a thick vine. Shuvai used her taloned hands and feet to scramble up the trunk of the tree as the students levitated upwards, moving fast towards Abby. Abby was choking, unable to take a breath as the vine squeezed tighter, but Eyre was finding her levitation energy was beginning to fail her. She'd never been this high before, and she was starting to wobble. She saw that Beatrice was having the same difficulty, but fortunately Nick was managing to keep going.

"Up, up, UP!" Eyre was thinking furiously to herself, and suddenly Beatrice flew past Nick and landed beside Abby on a branch of the tree the vine was draped around. In a second, Beatrice had her Kulbeda out and had started to hack at the vine as Abby turned a terrible shade of purple. Nick and Shuvai got there next, and while Nick used his Kulbeda too, Shuvai started to tear at the vine with her sharp teeth. Eyre finally arrived and grabbed on to the tree as she used her Kulbeda on the vine. After a long minute they had cut away enough for Abby to draw a breath and she gasped and sobbed as she tried to suck air into her lungs. The vine finally fell the long way to the ground in a coiling whip like a snake.

"Are you okay Abby?" Eyre asked, putting her arm around the shaking girl.

Abby still couldn't speak and they all sat on the branch as she tried to recover. But Shuvai's eyes were darting around.

"We must go," she said urgently. "Where there is one, there are others. Quickly, get back to the clearing."

They jumped off the branch and used levitation skills to go downwards, but Eyre found she didn't have much energy left and descended far more quickly than she wanted to. She landed awkwardly on the ground as the others helped Abby to make it down.

"By the Light, I'm so sorry I couldn't help get you down Abby," she apologized as they ran back to the clearing, out of the danger of the forest. "I seem to have no energy left."

"That's because you shoved me right up onto that branch!" Beatrice said as she helped Abby to sit on the damp rainforest earth. "I've never felt such a force in my life— *The Light save me!* What a ride!"

"Well, I'd like to take the credit for that," Eyre said slowly, "but I really wasn't intending anything at all. I was having enough trouble just getting myself up there."

Their discussion was interrupted by a strange sound in the air. A loud whirring that became almost deafening. Shimmering, beautiful creatures approached, and as they got nearer, Eyre could see that they were Zhuzhu Flutters, five of them circling from high and then heading down to the clearing. The source of their name became apparent as they got closer: the sound of their wings beating was a whirring, a rasping zhu-zhu-zhu sound. The huge creatures finally landed, their iridescent green wings and huge compound eyes shining. A silken cord ran snugly around the middle of their body between the first and second set of wings.

Shuvai stood up and walked to the nearest one, making a sort of singing clucking in her throat. The Zhuzhu rubbed its head against her, its four fluffy antennae bouncing as it did. Obviously, it loved her, and thinking of Ischyros, Eyre felt wistful. And then, also thinking of Ischyros, she started to worry about the ride ahead.

But it seemed these creatures were well trained and had bonded with the Nemoris, and apparently would be quite willing to accept someone on their back. They stood quietly as each of Eyre's friends walked up to them and stroked their bright blue carapace. The arrow-shaped flashes of pink in the skin increased with the stroking; it seemed that the more content the creatures were, the more the pink showed in the shell.

Eyre stroked her Zhuzhu and looked deep into the iridescent eyes.

"Does it have a name?" she asked.

"You name her," Shuvai said. "She has a name, but for this journey, you can call her what you like. Her real name is probably too hard for you to say."

"Then you are Hora," Eyre whispered to the Zhuzhu as she stroked it gently. "Roman goddess of beauty."

She watched Shuvai as she threw a leg over the top of her Zhuzhu and sat between the first and second set of the Zhuzhu's six wings, her feet resting in the cord underneath the Zhuzhu's body.

"Hold your staff in your dominant hand, then hang on with your other hand to the cord and grip the Zhuzhu's abdomen with your knees," Shuvai said. "When you get better at this you won't need to hold on, but for now it is advisable." Eyre copied Shuvai's technique and climbed on, for a moment expecting to be fired up into the tree canopy like Ischyros would have if she'd got on him. Instead, Shuvai gasped and laughed. Hora had turned completely pink and stood quietly as Eyre balanced herself in place.

"She likes you!" Shuvai said. "Most unusual for a Zhuzhu to be completely pink. Ha. Let's see how you fly."

Once everyone was sitting correctly, Shuvai showed them how to nudge the Zhuzhu to take off. Eyre tapped her foot gently against the side of the creature and the wings started to beat, creating that strange whirring sound again. Then it lifted off the ground like a helicopter, going straight up into the air. When they'd cleared the tree canopy, the Zhuzhus flew fast, skimming over the tops of the trees. Shuvai showed them how to use the antennae of the Zhuzhu to direct the creature the way they wanted to go.

To her great relief, Eyre found it was easy, and Hora responded instantly to her touch.

Eyre whooped in joy—this was so much fun, and exhilarating to feel the wind rush over her. She and her friends followed Shuvai and they travelled fast over the dense forest, passing over creeks and waterfalls and huge cliffs. Looking down at it, Eyre was very glad they didn't have to walk through all that, it would take them a year!

Suddenly she noticed something unusual below. People? She stared harder and confirmed that there were indeed straggling forms pushing through the bush. And Lightworkers at that. What were they doing? Didn't they ride Zhuzhus too? She pulled away from her group and circled above, trying to see who it was. Her friends turned back too and joined her as she studied the forms below. Then a sudden realisation dawned on her.

"The Leonid must have started!" she said. "It's the Aethers—looking for the Isar." There were quite a number of them travelling along the ground and Eyre guessed that they *had* to walk it—the message from her parents hadn't given much information on how to find the Isar. It could be hidden under a rock, by a tree, anywhere really, and looking out at the huge expanse of Terra, Eyre was struck by the hopelessness of the Aethers' mission. Terra was huge and somewhere in it was one bar of light, and they only had a short time to find it. And not only that, they had to find an Isar in each of the other Alterworlds too. No wonder Whittaker Ray was sending every Aether in Entis to the Alterworlds; even with so many of them it seemed an impossible task.

They whirled over the Aethers for a while, watching their slow progress through the trees, and one of the Aether looked up and waved. Eyre waved back and then Shuvai led them off again, flying towards a distant expanse of bare red earth.

CHAPTER FORTY-TWO

THE AIR GREW HOTTER as Eyre flew Hora towards the red earth. As they got closer she realised that it was a stretch of land that disappeared out of view both left and right. But ahead of her, across a vast expanse of sand and rock, was a line of hills.

Shuvai waited until they all landed and then indicated the desert.

"This is the Pyre of Va, which you will have learnt about in your classes. You will have heard about the dangers of the desert, and that the Zhuzhus cannot fly above them. So watch out for hazards as we proceed."

Eyre landed with the rest of her group, and led her Zhuzhu into the vast expanse of earth. It was mostly hard underfoot, baked by the sun, although red dust blew across it from time to time. Odd-shaped rocks lay on the ground around her, but they were small and the desert was flat and open—and hot. Barely tolerable despite their boots, the heat was uncomfortable and, head down against the wind, she moved as quickly as she could, anxious to cross this unforgiving terrain.

"Watch out!" Beatrice called and Eyre looked up to see a huge rock the size of a car sliding towards them over the ground.

"Sailing rocks!" Nick yelled as more of them appeared, grinding through the sand at the pace of a speeding car. Just before the rocks smashed into her Eyre managed to levitate, and Hora whirred upwards too. Obviously Hora knew what to do; Eyre hadn't had to encourage her at all. They hovered above the crashing wave of boulders until the moving mass disappeared into the distance.

Coming back down to the ground, Eyre could feel sweat dripping from her, and the heat as she breathed in was painful. The sooner they could get across this the better she thought.

They moved forwards again, but this time Eyre kept her head up. She wanted to be prepared next time if anything was about to happen.

"God," Beatrice moaned when they were halfway across. "This is hard going. If this is Terra, what is Incendium going to be like?"

Abby muttered in agreement and then Eyre saw movement out of the corner of her eye. She turned to see a flock of stork-like birds picking their way across the red sand towards them. They had long sharp beaks and feathers that stuck out like spikes. She remembered seeing the creatures in the video on Terra they'd watched at the beginning of the year, but hadn't learnt about them. She turned anxiously to Shuvai. Venomous? Carnivorous? Lethal?

Shuvai smiled. "Don't worry, Bisi birds, they're okay. Just wait."

The birds walked up to the group and studied them with sharp eyes and then did a strange dance before them. As they hopped up and down, dust and pebbles fell from their feathers onto the ground before Eyre and her friends. Puffs of dirt rose in the air as the big feet of the Bisi birds thudded on the hard-baked earth. Then, the display complete, they strode off again, heading further into the desert.

"Take a pebble," Shuvai said. "You don't often get to see that."

Eyre picked up one of the pebbles that had fallen from the feathers of the Bisi birds, and looked at it curiously. It just looked like any of the other rocks lying around the desert. Shuvai picked one up, and cracking it like a nut, held out the contents. "Rubies," she said. "The Bisi birds pick them up and take them to their nests to decorate them. But they travel so far, the gems get coated by the dirt. First-years always take one home if they're lucky enough to find one."

Eyre cracked open a pebble and found a cloudy, uncut ruby in there the size of a walnut. She carefully put it in her backpack—she knew it would always remind her of this test.

They continued on the hard slog across the burning earth. Finally, after several hours the hills in the distance were getting closer and Shuvai told them to have a rest.

"We are only an hour away and there is water over there, so we will set up camp once we arrive. Catch your breath and we will begin the final trek."

Eyre was so glad to sit down and have a rest, and she patted the head of her Zhuzhu as she sat. Small flashes of pink shot through its carapace at her touch, but the creature was obviously stressed, because it stayed mainly a deep blue colour.

"The Zhuzhus do not like the Pyre of Va. It is a measure of how much they trust us that they follow us through. It will be good to finish this part of the journey," Shuvai said, looking over to the hills.

Suddenly Nick looked behind him with a surprised sound. "We've got company."

Eyre leapt to her feet, but was completely nonplussed when she saw what was heading towards her. A group of about ten students, led by a Nemoris were not far from them, heading across the desert with Zhuzhus in tow. But they weren't from the Academy, these students were dressed in a black uniform. Must be hot for them, Eyre thought.

The Nemoris walked up to Shuvai and they began talking in a soft, clucking tongue as the students eyed each other up. One of them stepped forward. "We're from Finland," she said in accented English. "How about you?"

"Academy of Light, Australia," Nick replied. "Are you doing a TACI exam too?"

"Yes," the student said. "I'm Ditte and we are doing a makeup exam. The northern hemisphere schools normally do their exams in June, but we all had the flu then and couldn't go, so we're doing it now." Seeing that they were surprised by this, she carried on, "You'll probably see schools from the southern hemisphere around the place—South Africans, the Philippines, you're all here somewhere. What's your gazae?"

Eyre was startled. "We have different gazae?"

Ditte, obviously the Finnish equivalent of Beatrice, was happy to fill them in. "All schools source the Zha'kara diamonds in their fourth year, but the gazae for other years varies from school to school. We're after Eeb nuts, which apparently are found in those hills. We use them for our staffs." Eyre nodded, remembering she'd used the oil to polish the branch from the Rainbow Eucalyptus.

"Luxes for us," she said.

Ditte smiled. "Well, good luck—hope it goes well!" The other Nemoris did a strange hand movement to Shuvai and the Finnish group started to head off. But as they moved away, an ominous clattering could be heard rising from the distance and a strong wind started to gust across the sand. Shuvai and the other Nemoris shouted in alarm and the Zhuzhus folded their wings flat to their body and curled up in a ball.

"Flying sticks!" Shuvai cried. "Make your shield!"

Eyre hadn't known about the Bisi birds, but she did know about this, and all the students moved quickly, sending out a shield with bright light energy. Eyre concentrated hard and sent her shield slamming over her and Hora as the storm of flying sticks clattered closer. When it hit it was like a violent tornado, with roaring winds and whirling sticks hammering against the shield. It was terrifying, but Eyre forced herself to keep her focus and maintain the shield against the onslaught. Finally the storm moved on, the sound of snapping sticks and the dark cloud of dust circling away down the desert. Eyre dropped her shield and lay on the ground, exhausted. The Zhuzhus unwrapped themselves and stood quietly, every one of them a deep blue. Eyre could hear someone moaning, so she stood up slowly, feeling so tired her bones ached. She'd never maintained a shield of that strength for so long before. One of the Finnish boys was sitting on the ground with a stick embedded in his thigh. Obviously he had been unable to maintain his shield, because his Zhuzhu was covered in red dirt and it cowered on the ground. Their Nemoris guide was comforting the boy as he performed a prohemium and disappeared into the Seam, then she walked over and stroked the Zhuzhu until it stood up again.

Shuvai was grim. "An unusually intense storm and that poor boy has been badly injured. A shame for their group."

The Finns headed off one way and Shuvai led Eyre's group another, but both groups were heading towards the hills. Abby rolled her eyes at Eyre, the red marks from the Wrap Vine still clear around her neck. Eyre nodded in understanding. They knew it was going to be dangerous, but the reality of it was still confronting. She was looking forward to making camp and resting for a while.

By the time they got to the other side it was dark. They stayed by the perimeter of the desert as they had been taught, only venturing into the bush to cut rushes and branches for their shelter. As the foliage piled up, Shuvai took their water bottles from them.

"Tonight I will get the water; there is a stream nearby. It is too dangerous in the dark for you all to go, you will make too much noise. You begin the shelter while I go." She disappeared into the dark and Eyre and her friends began to try and weave the green cuttings together. Learning about it was one thing; doing it was another, and it was irritating trying to get the branches and leaves to stay together. They were all tired and Beatrice was being bossy, trying to instruct them all, and Eyre gritted her teeth when her woven plait undid itself yet again. By the time Shuvai arrived back they had constructed a very strange looking hut that was leaning drunkenly to the right. The branches showed gaping holes between them, and as they looked at it, it suddenly fell completely apart, firing leaves and branches everywhere.

"Well that's just great," the usually sunny Abby said in exasperation and Nick lost it. Peals of laughter rang through the night and everyone sat on the ground, chortling until tears ran down their faces. Shuvai looked on in bemusement.

"That is a very strange reaction to having something fail so badly," she said, looking confused. "Perhaps you are feverish?" She cocked her head but obviously was unable to solve this Entis puzzle. Then she waved her hands to silence them. "Quiet! Too much noise will bring the attention of things we would rather avoid. Here."

She gave the water bottles to each of them and they drank deeply. The water was cold and delicious and it felt wonderful on their parched throats. When they'd had enough, Shuvai indicated the pile of leaves and branches.

"Come, let us try again. I will help you."

CHAPTER FORTY-THREE

THE NEXT MORNING EYRE awoke and didn't know where she was for a moment. Then her eyes took in the tightly-woven ceiling of the shelter and everything came rushing back. She sat up and took a deep breath of the cool air that drifted in from the flap of the hut. Although they were close to the desert, the effect of the air flowing from the hills was keeping it comfortable and Eyre laughed as she looked at Nick. Overnight a chat had wandered in and he was sleeping with it tucked beneath his arm, its head on his chest. Eyre looked out the door where the Zhuzhus were bunched together, heads inwards, tails outwards and was relieved to see that they were all okay. Pink had made its way back into their carapaces, so that was a good sign.

Shuvai was crouched in the corner, which was apparently the way that Nemoris slept, but she was awake already. Seeing Eyre had also woken, she roused the rest of the sleepy group.

"I hope you feel rested after our first day. It was not as easy as it's been in previous years, but you have done very well. We will leave the shelter here for our return journey and continue on."

Nick yawned and sat up and Abby giggled as the chat bounded out of the hut, not keen on hanging around. "I'd rather take that home than the lux I think," she said.

It didn't take long to get organised. Eyre shrugged her backpack on and grabbed her staff. Shuvai had refilled their water bottles, so she slid hers in the top of the backpack, and made sure her Kulbeda hung straight. Then they all headed out the door of the shelter and into the hills.

There were rockfaces around them, but at this point the terrain was relatively open and easy to push through—the bush was not as dense as the jungle they'd passed through yesterday. It was easy to find a track through the huge flowers and plants that grew in amongst the rocks and the coolness after the searing desert was wonderful. It was more like a giant garden, really, with scented flowers, brightly coloured berries and shining leaves on oversized plants. Unusual insects flew by, and Eyre noticed one that looked like a purple and yellow striped bee, the size of a sheep, sucking nectar from a flower just near her. Not one to be stung by, she thought uneasily, edging away from the rotund creature as it hovered just above her shoulder. But the bee, and indeed all the insects, were ignored by Shuvai: they were clearly no cause for concern. As the group walked up the leafy path, they passed the source of the water Shuvai had filled the bottles with —gushing out of a hole in the side of a rock on the side of the track. The water fell like a miniature waterfall and wound its way downhill through the green plants.

The slope headed gently upwards but it wasn't difficult, and Eyre found herself enjoying this far more than the previous day's slog through the tangled jungle. The Zhuzhus followed behind, their green wings tucked against their side.

"Zhuzhus aren't keen on walking," Shuvai said. "But we don't have far to go. We are nearly there."

Indeed, it was only five minutes later that they arrived at the top of the hill and Eyre gasped. They were teetering on the edge of a massive crater, with towering cliffs falling far below. The hills they'd seen from the desert rose craggily from the other side of the chasm into the violet sky, and a purple mist hung around its edges.

"That's where we go," Shuvai said, pointing downwards. She was obviously enjoying the looks on their faces. "It's why we need the Zhuzhu." The Zhuzhu knew what was next and they were unfolding their wings and stretching, the fluffy antennae swaying as the creatures groomed their legs and wings. Shuvai waited patiently and when the Zhuzhu finally stopped, she stepped forward and stroked her Flutter gently.

"Here we go boy," she said. "Best part of the journey. Up you get," she instructed Eyre and her friends.

When everyone was securely seated, Shuvai tapped the side of her Zhuzhu with her heel and he flew off the side of the cliff. Eyre didn't need a second to think about it—she *loved* flying and she patted Hora and nudged her into flight. Hora loved it too, apparently, because she shot off the edge and spiralled high into the sky. Then she zoomed downwards, following Shuvai as she led the way. Beatrice, Nick and Abby were hooting with glee when suddenly from above a dark, taloned form streaked towards them. Eyre didn't hesitate, and blasted a light beam from her hand that roasted the creature in a second.

"Garman," she said to Nick and he nodded. They'd been warned about them.

"Shame you weren't able to do that to Perrill," he commented, and swerved off in a huge arc, zooming up and down in the air, doing 360-degree loops. The Zhuzhu loved it and heaved its wings up and down hard as it performed the aerobatics, responding to his touch.

"He rides really well in class," Abby explained to Eyre as she caught up. "The Kikkuli Master loves him." Eyre laughed. She would have no idea how anyone was doing in riding class, it had been so long since she'd been. But she was doing well at *this* and she whooped with joy.

The flight down took quite some time; it was a long way. As they whirred downwards she could see what was at the base of the cliffs: a clear blue grotto like they'd seen in the film E Kofi had shown them in class. Manoeuvring carefully, Eyre nudged Hora to land on one of the huge quartz rocks by the side of the pool.

The water was crystal clear, and massive flowers of all colours rose from the pond, their perfume strong in the air around them. A pale blue mist wove its way through the flowers and as it wafted past Eyre she realised this was the source of the scent in the grotto. Small birds the size of her palm darted in and out of the huge petals of some of the flowers, dipping their beaks into the nectar pooled in their centres. But they avoided one type of plant, a large vermillion-coloured flower that looked like a chrysanthemum. From time to time, orbs were released from a hole in the centre of the flower and they floated upwards, almost like bullio, until they disappeared into the atmosphere. As Eyre watched, one hapless bird ventured too close to the brightly-coloured flower and was sucked into the hole in its centre.

She raised her eyebrows and Shuvai shrugged. "As you were taught, another carnivorous plant. Don't go too near it."

Eyre didn't need to be told that; she was not keen to have another close encounter with a ravenous plant. So she levitated carefully out of reach of the red flower and waited until an orb was released. It floated up towards her and she tried to grab it, but she moved too quickly and the air from her hands pushed it away. She ended up chasing the orb upwards like an escaping balloon until eventually her energy bonded with it and the lux stopped, bobbing above her head. Her friends had been watching on the side laughing hysterically, and she landed beside them, putting the lux in her bag.

"Yeah, yeah, yeah," she said. "You have a go. It's not that easy!"

Eyre took some satisfaction in watching them careering around trying to grab one of the bright orbs; they found it as hard as she had. But before too long they all had a lux in their backpack and gave each other a high five.

"Gazae snared!" Beatrice hooted, "time to go back and *party*!" They put their backpacks on and prepared to remount the Zhuzhus.

CHAPTER FORTY-FOUR

EYRE HAD JUST SLUNG her leg over Hora's back, when a terrible pain blossomed in her head and a blackness blinded her. She could hear horrifying cries, and shouts for help, and the sounds of beasts roaring. For a moment she could not move at all, and then the vision passed, but a horrible knowledge seized her.

"Did you see that?" she cried and her friends looked at her curiously. "*By St Illuminado*," Eyre gasped, terrified, "something *terrible* is happening. We have to help them!"

"What are you talking about?" Beatrice said. "I didn't see anything!" Suddenly Abby's face went pale and she looked at her friends. "No, Eyre's right. I can feel it too. But I don't know what."

Eyre's head pounded and she was filled with a desperation, a feeling that she had to *be* somewhere, fast.

"Please, please, just come with me," she pleaded. "There's no time." She nudged Hora into the air, streaking straight up as her eyes searched the horizon. A gut-wrenching fear had filled her, the worse for not understanding what it meant.

Shuvai had waited uncertainly for a moment, but then followed Eyre upwards—she was after all, responsible for her. And Beatrice, Nick and Abby followed quickly after. Whatever was going on, they would be there.

As Eyre's desperate eyes looked along the rim of the hills, she saw a beam of light, shining brightly and heading straight up to the sky.

"That's got to be it!" she cried, pointing at the light.

"What? What's it?" Beatrice said, looking in the direction Eyre was indicating, but unable to see anything.

"The light, over there in the hills, I can feel that's where something awful is happening, just follow me, please. We've got to help them!"

Eyre's head was filled with the screams of people dying, and the terrifying roars of creatures and she flew towards the beam of light with a desperation she didn't understand. Her friends flew beside her in silence, knowing on some level that there was something horribly wrong. They held their staffs ready as they raced forwards, filled with a terrible foreboding.

As she neared the beam of light, Eyre saw smoke rising from the hills and trees burning. A black stench hung in the air, and there was the odd muffled boom as something blew up. And then she saw the bodies—lying everywhere, and she held back a sob as she saw it was the Aether. A terrible battle had gone on here, and it was obvious who had won. The pure beam of light in the centre of the smoking, blackened ground and the bodies of the dead was almost an atrocity in itself. How could something so beautiful be rising amongst this devastation? Eyre jumped off Hora, using her staff to steady herself as she landed.

Whatever had happened, it was over now, and they were far too late. All of the Aether were dead, and the battleground was a sight she never wanted to see again in her life. Bodies lay unmoving as far as her eyes could see, draped over slaughtered Strigis. Some of the Aether were only her age; some were ancient, but all of them had died horribly. It had been a violent and bloody battle. Beatrice was weeping, kneeling on the ground beside one of the Aether, who looked upwards with sightless eyes. There was blood and gore, and limbs of the dead everywhere. Broken staffs lay on the field, and dropped Antaraks were shining amongst the blackness. Shuvai walked around silently, her face a mask. "Gothak," was all she said.

Eyre walked to the beam of light that rose silently in the air, and saw it emanated from a shining bar of silver that lay on the ground, about 30 centimetres long and a centimetre thick.

"What is this?" she called to her friends, and they looked over at her blankly. She realised with a start that they could not see anything.

"You can't see it?" she asked them, puzzled, and picked up the silver bar. Instantly it warmed in her hand and the beam of light shot down from the sky and zapped back into the bar. As she turned around she could see from the shocked looks on her friends faces that they could now see it too. She held the object in her hand and Beatrice walked over in awe, her legs black from kneeling in the scorched earth.

"By the Light," she breathed. "Eyre, you've found the Isar!" Eyre looked in amazement at the smooth silver bar and then around her.

"Well, we have to get back quickly, before the Gothak realise," she said. "Can we do the prohemium here?" she asked Shuvai desperately.

A voice from behind her, a rasping voice she had heard before, made the hair rise on her neck and she turned slowly around.

"But the Gothak *do* realise, my dear. I'm so sorry about that. I've been waiting to make sure we got all of you. How very nice to see you again."

Standing before her was Kaar, the hated Gothak who had killed her parents. His pallid skin contrasted with the weird metallic suit he wore, his long limbs cracking with an unnerving sound as he walked towards her. Mesmerised by his flat, shark-like eyes, Eyre could only raise her staff and point it at him, taking a step backwards. "Come and get it," she said in a low voice.

Fast, faster than Eyre had ever seen a creature move before, Shuvai whipped her hands and a Seam appeared. Kaar was so focused on Eyre, Shuvai had shot Beatrice, Nick and Abby through it before he could even move. Eyre felt herself pulled towards the Seam too, but Kaar was concentrating on the silver bar in her hand, and he grasped her arm as soon as she began to move. With his other hand he fired a blast of atra at Shuvai and she burnt to a crisp in a second, her body falling to the ground. The Seam closed and a void of silence ensued.

Eyre sobbed as she saw all that remained of Shuvai fall to the ground. But she was filled with a wild, raging fury, more than she had ever felt before. The power rose within her with a force that caused her body to shudder violently, and using her mind, she blew Kaar's hand away from her arm. Stepping backwards, she aimed her staff at him and shot a beam of light out the top. But of course, it flew sideways uselessly and Kaar gave a small, hollow laugh.

But before he could say anything, Eyre had sent a massive light beam of Viq right at his chest, and if he hadn't deflected it with his hand, it would have cut him in half. His eyes narrowed as he realised that something more than a frightened student stood before him, and with an imperceptible movement, he sent a black ball of atra at her. It streaked through the air, the black soot emanating waves of heat. She was ready for him though, and had already levitated out of the way before it crashed into the ground behind her. As she hovered in the air, she felt the power within her growing, a force so strong she felt she herself was going to blow apart. Kaar shot up and hung in the air before her.

"I've sent for more," he rasped. "They'll be here soon. Be smart and give it to me."

Eyre's shoulders slumped and she drew a shuddering breath, lowering to the ground. "Okay," she said softly as she landed.

Kaar's eyes were watchful, but his greed and ego overcame his caution and he descended to the ground as well.

Eyre threw the silver bar in the air, and as Kaar reached up to grab it, she blasted his legs off with a hot beam of energy. He thudded to the ground, his eyes wide in disbelief as he screamed. Eyre flipped in the air and caught the bar before it hit the ground and landed next to Kaar, who was writhing on the ground in agony, black blood gushing from the stumps of his legs.

"I gave it to you Kaar alright," she whispered. "And this is for my parents."

Taking her Kulbeda from her belt she aimed and threw it hard, some energy not entirely of her own doing seeming to help her to pierce his heart dead centre. He screeched, the call echoing all around the battlefield, and then he dissolved into a black pool of oil in front of her.

Tears running down her face, Eyre sucked in huge gasps of air as she looked at the black puddle that used to be Kaar. Ferociously she kicked dirt over it, covering it over until nothing was left; there was no sign he had ever been there. Then she fell by the remains of Shuvai and held her tight, weeping.

A nudging nose brought her back to her senses and she jumped up in fright. But it was just Shuvai's Zhuzhu, quivering beside her with his wings dragging on the ground. He had turned completely black, and he jumped nervously as Eyre stroked his side. The other four Zhuzhus were rolled up tightly into balls.

Eyre walked up to Hora and softly patted her head until she uncurled herself. Watching the skies anxiously, Eyre urged the Zhuzhus into flight. "Go, go, *go*, head back home as fast as you can, dark times are coming. Quickly!" She gave Hora a last hug and watched as they all finally uncurled and stood up.

The Zhuzhus took off and streaked away fast, leaving Eyre in the middle of the huge blackened plain, alone except for the bodies of the valiant Aether. A wretchedness took hold of her at the terrible sight. It was too big to comprehend.

She started to do a prohemium, holding her staff and the Isar tightly, when suddenly the ground beneath her heaved and something monstrous broke through the rock, setting her off balance and ruining the prohemium. One great black claw appeared first, then another, and then the skeletal shape of a huge scorpion the size of a bus dragged itself upwards from the ground. A Tuus! One of the Strigis, Eyre knew, and then swarms of Zyx began to appear above her. When Gothak wielding Luxoccisors filled the skies on Interfector Hornets, she knew she was about to die. Not without a fight though, she said to herself, tears streaming down her blackened face. She would take as many of them with her as she could. She sent waves of Viq at the huge Tuus, and it backed away, screeching. Its massive stinger smashed into the ground beside her and she put her hand up and fired a bolt of energy so intense she fell to the ground. It burned right through the chest of the Tuus and the horrible creature toppled slowly on to the black dirt, the earth shuddering as it hit. But then the Gothak landed on the ground, and dozens of them surrounded her in a malign circle as the swarms of Zyx increased.

Eyre lay on the ground, spent, covering the Isar with her body. Perhaps if they burnt her they would also burn the Isar, which would be better than the Gothak getting it. The massive energy she had expended during the fight with Kaar and the Tuus had drained her so much that she couldn't move at all. She closed her eyes and waited for the inevitable.

A harsh, dry voice addressed her as she lay there. "You are a Lightward, I believe," it said, and she opened her eyes. "The ones we dispatched last year?"

The creature was huge and misshapen, one of the Gothak but much larger, with green pustules covering its pale white skin. He had a heavy jaw and slitted eyes, and there was such a miasma of evil about him that Eyre nearly passed out just looking at him.

"This Lightward has gotten rid of Kaar," she hissed. "And give me a moment and I'll do you too." An empty threat, since she was utterly paralysed, but the anger poured out of her like molten lava.

The gross creature looked slightly surprised and looked over at the Tuus. "Well, the Tuus didn't do so well either," he said in a contemplative voice. "Who would have thought?"

Eyre knew he was just toying with her and didn't answer. A peace descended on her as she accepted the inevitable. But then a Seam suddenly appeared before her eyes, literally centimetres from her nose, and a large hand reached out and grabbed her, dragging her through before the creature could react. She could hear its enraged screams as she zapped through the Seam and ended up on the moldavite square in front of the Academy.

The Sergeant picked her up and a second later she was in the Infirmary, and a second after that she had completely passed out.

CHAPTER FORTY-FIVE

EYRE OPENED HER EYES slowly and registered that she was lying in a bed in the Infirmary. And then she realised how much she hurt: it felt like a mountain had landed on her, and she was still unable to move. Abby was sitting by her bed and she called out to Beatrice and Nick, who were hovering in the hall.

"She's awake!"

Eyre's friends grouped around her and hugged her, and Beatrice sobbed.

"Are you okay? We thought you were going to die!"

Eyre's eyes brimmed as she regarded them. "Shuvai died," she said. "Kaar got her."

"We know," Abby said, and a tear ran down her face. "The Sergeant told us. But at least you made it. You've been asleep for hours and we've taken turns watching you. I'll get Whittaker Ray, he wants to talk to you." But she didn't leave; she merely closed her eyes and a second later Whittaker Ray appeared in the room. Apparently Abby's telepathic skills were strengthening.

"We'll go," Beatrice said, hugging Eyre again. "See you soon."

Whittaker Ray pulled a chair to the side of Eyre's bed and regarded her silently for a moment.

"You still can't move?" he asked finally. Eyre shook her head. Apart from her head, the rest of her body felt as immobile as when the Kikkuli Master had dropped her from the air to the stable floor.

Whittaker Ray looked down. "You've had a terrible experience," he said. "And so have many of the other students—the Gothak were in every Alterworld, looking for the Aether."

A tear ran from Eyre's eye and Whittaker Ray looked desolate. His voice was despairing as he shook his head. "All the Aether are dead, Eyre, every single one of them. We had three students at the Academy who were Aether, and they're gone too."

Eyre moaned and shut her eyes. The thought of the same devastation occurring in all the Alterworlds was almost more than she could bear. But Whittaker Ray continued.

"I'm sorry Eyre, but I have to talk to you now. I made a big mistake in not listening properly to you and the message your parents passed on. I listened to the content, but not the to the most crucial part of it—the need for secrecy. So many people knew about the Aether travelling to look for the Isars, and someone from our own people has betrayed us. In one terrible day the Gothak have been able to eliminate every Aether in Entis."

His eyes focused on Eyre. "Well, that is, every grown Aether—we have young children and babies, and we will have to wait years for them to grow up and get their Viq so they can search for the Isars. But you somehow have brought one Isar back from Terra for us, and that is an unbelievable feat. The Mimir have it hidden away securely, and if we manage to find any others, they will guard them too."

He hesitated for a moment, taking in Eyre's strained face, then continued. "I need you to tell me where the Isar was, or if you have any information that might help us locate the other Isars when these children are old enough to go and search for them."

Eyre was exhausted already, but she knew it was important that she help Whittaker Ray.

"There was a beam of light," she said, "going up vertically from the Isar into the sky. That's how we found it. We followed the light beam—or I guess I did, because the others couldn't see it. The vertical beam is a marker to find the Isar. When I picked up the Isar the others could see it too."

Whittaker Ray's face showed confusion, and then he looked at Eyre as realisation dawned. "*You* could see the Isar?" he choked. Eyre nodded, and Whittaker Ray shook his head. "But you can't be an Aether—never an Aether after an Aether, not in Lightworking history. How has this happened? Are you sure? The others couldn't see it?"

Eyre shook her head. "Not until I picked it up," she said. Whittaker Ray eyed Eyre and then looked at her odd Inguz thoughtfully "Well, whatever the reason, it could be wonderful news Eyre—if you are an Aether, perhaps *you* can find the other Isars. And we now know exactly how to look for them."

"I'm happy to look," Eyre said. "If I can ever move again." She jutted her jaw and looked at Whittaker Ray. "I killed Kaar," she said fiercely and the old man looked astonished. Then he patted her arm gently. "Then you have the heart of an Aether. You have been incredibly brave," he said. "And we can discuss the details of it all later. I'll leave you to rest now. But you mustn't tell anyone you are an Aether—not anyone at all. I have learnt my lesson from this atrocious situation, and from now on I will talk to you alone about this. Secrecy is of the utmost importance. You might be our last hope."

With that he left the room and Eyre fell into a deep, dark slumber.

CHAPTER FORTY-SIX

AS THE DAYS WENT on, Eyre was finally able to get up and move around. But her healing powers didn't work this time, and she was covered in scrapes and bruises that were taking a long time to go away. The Academy had decided to finish out the school year, despite the terrible occurrences, and students had automatically been given a pass in their TACI exam whether they had sourced the gazae or not.

The news of all the Aether being wiped out was reported across the world, throughout the Alterworlds in fact, and an air of desolation pervaded the campus. That the Gothak could reach in and cause such devastation on one day was a terrible omen for the future. The whole Overworld was reeling with the shock of what had happened.

Classes were finished, and each year of students went through the prescribed graduation ceremony in the Auditorium, but the mood was bleak and depressed. Eyre felt disinclined to do her normal morning run, and she didn't visit Ischyros in his stall. She was suffering from a black depression that just wouldn't lift.

Her mood wasn't helped by the fact that she seemed to have completely lost her Viq. Her weird Inguz was still on her arm, but she could no longer do any light skills at all; despite resting and meditating and soaking in the Therapeutic pools, her power was completely gone.

When she'd talked to Whittaker Ray about what had happened with Kaar and the Tuus, he'd tried to comfort her by saying that she'd expended an incredible amount of Viq and that sometimes light energy could take a while to come back after a shock or a huge event like that. But his eyes were uncertain as he said it, and she felt that it was a bit like describing her Inguz as a 'form of Hese' last year—a euphemism that was designed to just cheer her up. She felt dismal as she contemplated the possibility that she'd used up a lifetime supply of light energy in one go. But Whittaker Ray had regarded her with a pragmatic look.

"You know, it might be a good thing," he said to her. "It is a good excuse for you to join the Unlit, which is where traditionally the Aether have been placed. You will be protected and anonymous there, and we will send you to look for the Isar when the next Leonid comes. If you are still able to see the Isar, what an amazing piece of fortune that will be for the whole Overworld."

Eyre had nodded and smiled, but as she left, a horrible rage was simmering within her. Never mind saving the Overworld, she didn't want to be Unlit and she wanted her powers back. To have been progressing so far with them, and then have them taken away was like a punishment that was too hard to bear. Beatrice and Abby were understanding and didn't try to pretend it would be wonderful to go to the Unlit—they wouldn't want to go there either, not least of all as a second-year student, struggling to catch up. They understood how horrible it would be to suddenly lose your light power, and had been very sympathetic about it, which had helped a bit.

Eyre hadn't told them that she might be an Aether, deciding that she might not be an Aether now anyway, and in any case, she was sworn to secrecy by Whittaker Ray. And fortunately, in the fear and confusion, none of her friends had worked out that she must have been an Aether to see the Isar. They hadn't seen clearly what was going on, and thought Eyre and Abby had helped to find the battlefield telepathically, and that was how Eyre had located the Isar. The long history of no Aether ever being born to an Aether was so ingrained in Lightworker lore that it never crossed their minds that she could be an Aether. And as Eyre headed down the dormitory hall, she gloomily contemplated the fact that it was highly unlikely she was an Aether now. She wasn't even an Elevated Lightworker any more.

But there was a comforting encounter the last morning of school when Colton came over to sit with Eyre and her friends at breakfast. Although he was part of their greater friendship circle, he didn't normally sit with them, so everyone looked slightly surprised as he pulled up a chair.

"How are you doing, Eyre?" he asked, as after a moment everyone continued to eat.

"Yeah, I'm fine now, thanks," Eyre said. Then after a pause she gave a rueful smile. "But I still don't have my Viq back. Can't even produce a zap of static electricity any more." Everyone laughed, but there were sympathetic looks from many of them.

Colton took Eyre's hands in his and Eyre could see Beatrice nearly fall off her chair in shock.

"You were incredibly brave," Colton said softly. "My young brother Iwan was an Aether. He drowned in Blue Lake because of the Gothak. They dragged him in, and when I tried to get him out, they blew me out of the water. By the time I came to, it was too late, I couldn't find him. I am going to do whatever it takes to destroy their dark, evil souls." Eyre recalled the story Colton had told her at the TEPs, and the grief she had seen in his memories. But he hadn't told her the full story then, and she now understood the barely contained rage in his voice. It hadn't been a tragic accident; it was murder.

A powerful energy force seemed to emanate from Colton as he spoke, and even though Eyre had no Viq, she and everyone else could see the bright, white light that surrounded him as he vowed to avenge his brother. Finally, after a pause he added, "your sacrifice will not be for nothing. You helped to save the Isar from those gross creatures, and your courage is an example to us all." Eyre flushed with the compliment, and felt slightly better for the first time since she'd realised her Viq had disappeared.

It was still hard to adjust to the new situation though, and she felt the familiar gloom dog her as she opened her cupboard to start packing for home. But it took her a moment to actually register what she was seeing inside. Her *guitar* was leaning in there, up against her staff, and she pulled it out, turning it around in shock. The neck had been completely rebuilt out of a spectacular piece of wood that Eyre recognized—one that could only have come from the Rainbow Eucalyptus. Hands had carefully carved, whittled and polished the wood into a thing of great beauty, and as she ran her fingers experimentally over the strings, the sounds that came from the guitar were exquisite. The strings seemed to sing as she pressed them against the colourful wood; somehow there was magic in this instrument now.

There was only one person who was capable of manipulating wood like that and she shook her head in wonder. Jax must have sourced the wood and been working on it all these months. How he'd managed to obtain the magnificent wood from that grand old soul of the forest was beyond her. But after all the terrible things that had happened lately she cradled the guitar in her arms and wept.

After a while she picked it up again, and noticed a small square of paper looped around one of the tuning knobs. It was blank, but when she touched it, it started to heat up like fire and silvery words appeared on the paper. A peragro! "I can't be with you," the words messaged, "but have faith in me. There are reasons. Have a great Christmas." Then the paper disappeared in a flare of light. Another request for faith that she would try to understand and respect. Whatever that message might mean, the despair she'd felt since Terra suddenly left her, as quickly as the silvery words had disappeared from the peragro.

Eyre strummed the guitar, tuning it carefully, and then lay it on the bed as she started to pack her clothes. Life hadn't gone as planned this year, and terrible events were afoot, but she was lucky to be alive. She needed to pick herself up and get on with it. Looking at the shining instrument on her bed, Eyre understood that hope comes in many forms, and this one was shaped like a guitar. Jax's gift suddenly lifted the awful weight from her shoulders and she felt a lightening of the gloom that had dogged her like a black lux over the past few weeks. And with a rush, joy came flooding back through her, and a clarity of purpose. She would go to the Unlit if that was what she had to do, and she would work at learning everything she could there, in case her light skills never came back. UD1 was a mysterious and brilliant man, and it might just be a great year next year.

Beatrice and Abby interrupted her thoughts when they burst through the door to start packing.

"Be quick Abby, Eyre's ready. Let's get out of here!" Then Beatrice gasped as she saw what was on the bed and she turned to Eyre in surprise. "Your guitar?"

Abby picked it up, turning it over. "Wow, it's so beautiful," she said. "I don't need my psychic powers to know who did this."

"I know," Eyre said. "It's a wonderful gift."

"Dad's coming in an hour," Abby said, with a hint of pride. "I checked with him telepathically." Then her face fell. "Oh, sorry, Eyre, I forgot..."

Eyre smiled. "No, it's fine," she said, and realised it was the truth. "I'm okay with going to the Unlit. You will just have to do my telepathy—and any other Lightworking skills—for me!"

"I am not levitating with you," Beatrice said sombrely, and they burst out laughing.

"Well, I reckon it might be interesting going to the Unlit," Eyre said. "They do all sorts of things there that we don't know about. It will be okay."

She stood up from her bed. "And I had another thought about the Unlit," she said, a mischievous tone in her voice. As Beatrice and Abby looked enquiringly at her, Eyre continued. "I don't think they have Lighthorses!" Abby giggled and Beatrice slapped the wall, causing a rainbow of riotous colours to cascade around the room.

Eyre put her bag on her bed next to the guitar and leaned her staff beside them.

"I'll let you finish packing—but first I'm going to say farewell to that cantankerous old nag."

And she flew out the door to go and make the difficult old horse in question as shining and beautiful as she could.

Her gifts gone. An ancient adversary closing in. Have her warnings of catastrophe fallen on deaf ears?

Eyre Lightward is devastated to realize she could be thrown out of the Academy. With her light-powers extinguished, she's resigned to joining the Unlit and leaving the friendships she worked so hard to forge. Though instead of enduring new limitations, Eyre's eyes are opened when she's forced to care for strange creatures and undergo rigorous physical training.

But when her old school is attacked again, Eyre discovers a traitor leaking the secret location of a powerful shard of Earth's protective shield to their bitter enemy. Alerting those in power, her actions backfire when she angers her close friends and brings the entire cohort under threat.

Can the young outcast reclaim her skills and save Earth's future defenders from disaster?

Aqua is the third book in the captivating Quest for the Aura YA fantasy series. If you like intricate magical systems, high-school angst, and age-old battles, then you'll love R.S. O'Neal's action-packed tale.

Buy *Aqua* to dive in and protect the planet today!

Follow the link or the QR code below to grab your copy.

https://thequestfortheaura.com/aqua

About the Quest for the Aura

Discover more exciting facts about the Quest for the Aura and download a free glossary from R.S. O'Neal's website here:

https://thequestfortheaura.com/

www.ingramcontent.com/pod-product-compliance
Lightning Source LLC
Chambersburg PA
CBHW022356110726
47902CB00002BA/309